TALES OF THE OUTLAW MAGES
Book Two

AMY CAMPBELL

Publisher's Cataloging-in-Publication data

Names: Campbell, Amy D., author.

Title: Effigest : tales of the outlaw mages , book two / Amy Campbell.

Series: Tales of the Outlaw Mages

Description: Houston, TX: Amy Campbell, 2021.

Identifiers: LCCN: 2021912821 | ISBN: 978-1-7361418-2-3 (print) | 978-1-7361418-3-0 (ebook)

Subjects: LCSH Magic--Fiction. | Animals, Mythical--Fiction. | Pegasus (Greek mythology)--Fiction. | Alchemy--Fiction. | Asexual people--Fiction. | Outlaws--Fiction. | Fantasy fiction. | BISAC FICTION / Fantasy / Action & Adventure | FICTION / Fantasy / Dragons & Mythical Creatures | FICTION / Fantasy / Historical | FICTION / LGBTQ+ / General

Classification: LCC PS3603.A4685 E44 2021 | DDC 813.6--dc23

Cover design by Anna Spies, Eerilyfair Design

Edited by Vicky Brewster

Author photograph by Kim Routon Photography

Map by Amy Campbell, designed in Wonderdraft

Pegasus chapter heading art © Depositphotos.com.

ISBN-13: 978-1-7361418-2-3 (paperback), 978-1-7361418-3-0 (ebook)

First edition: November 2021

10 9 8 7 6 5 4 3 2 1

www.amycampbell.info

For Kirk. We've come a long way since Molten Core, but you're always the warrior I want at my side. Love you!

Previously...

In *Breaker,* we meet Blaise Hawthorne, a young man with dangerous magic—he has an uncontrollable penchant for breaking anything he touches. He would love nothing more than to realize his dream of opening a bakery, but instead he's an outcast, stuck at home with his family, the only ones who accept him.

Blaise has a chance to prove his competence by completing a monthly delivery to the elusive Black Market. His exchange with the proprietor is overall a success, though his luck changes on the way home during a run-in with the outlaw mage Wildfire Jack Dewitt. The accidental destruction of Jack's sixgun wrought by Blaise's Breaker magic pits the pair against each other, and Blaise escapes only through the intervention of the outlaw's pegasus, Zepheus.

When Blaise returns home, he discovers that his encounter with the outlaw isn't the only problem. The Salt-Iron Confederation has sent soldiers to Blaise's home country of Desina, searching for mages. His mother, Marian, insists that he must hide, and that if the soldiers come for him, he must run. She dreads the Confederation turning her son into a weapon.

Their fears are realized when soldiers arrive in the dark of night. Blaise flees, but in doing so, he invokes his magic and uses a tree to crush his pursuers. He runs as far as he can into the Gutter, a territory where the Confederation soldiers cannot easily follow.

Blaise encounters a trapped pegasus and frees him. He's astonished to discover that pegasi can speak telepathically, and becomes fast friends with the stallion, Emrys. The pegasus, feeling duty-bound to return the favor, takes Blaise to the outlaw town of Itude.

They're greeted by a teenage girl, who ushers them into the town. When Blaise arrives at the saloon, he's so overwhelmed he doesn't notice Wildfire Jack's presence. But the outlaw sees *him*, and he punches Blaise because the girl is his daughter, Emmaline, and he's taken offense at the Breaker being anywhere near her. The town Healer patches Blaise up and Clover, the Knossan bartender, offers him work at the Broken Horn Saloon.

Blaise slowly becomes a part of the town, accepted by everyone except for Jack. Vixen, another outlaw mage, agrees to work with Blaise to help him learn to control his magic. When they learn of Blaise's talent for baking, Vixen, Clover, and Emmaline hatch a plot for Blaise to lease the bakery. They succeed, and Blaise discovers his dream is finally attainable.

Meanwhile, Jack is not only distracted by the dangerous Breaker's presence in his town, but he has continued his decade-long search for his missing wife. He hears a rumor of maverick mages in Desina, and wants to go after them, hoping one of them is Kittie. The other Ringleaders allow him to go—but only if he takes Blaise with him.

The pair grudgingly set out, and they discover it was an ambush. Jack is grievously wounded and Lamar Gaitwood, the outlaw's bitter enemy, captures the pair. Blaise uses his magic to free them, and they make a harrowing escape. On their way back to Itude, Jack tells Blaise more of his past, revealing the old wounds behind his angry visage—including the fact that he's a mage without magic.

Jack has a long road to recovery once they reach town. His

outlook toward Blaise has changed for the better, though, and he's less hostile. But Jack's demeanor becomes stormy again when he receives word of a rich entrepreneur from Ganland hoping to visit their town.

Jefferson Cole arrives in Itude and finds himself intrigued by Blaise from the start. But no one trusts the stranger, and Blaise remains aloof, too. Jack has his suspicions about the entrepreneur after he offers a ridiculous sum to buy the bakery. The outlaw does some digging and uncovers that the stranger is actually Malcolm Wells, a political player from Ganland.

But all thoughts of the newcomer vanish when a mysterious attacker wounds Blaise during a training exercise. Jack tries to uncover his assailant but fails. Blaise wonders who's trying to kill him—and is it because of his magic?

The outlaws celebrate the Feast of Flight, and despite some awkwardness, Blaise feels like he might fit in again. Jefferson Cole even asks about working with him as a business partner. Things are looking up for Blaise until the town's wind pump falls...and he's a suspect.

Unable to cope with the heartbreak of having his new friends turn their backs on him, Blaise flees to Jefferson Cole in Rainbow Flat. This plays into the hands of Jack's old enemy Lamar Gaitwood, who had hoped to separate the Breaker from the outlaws. Gaitwood attacks the town, killing many of the citizens, kidnapping the surviving mages, and leaving Jack trapped in agony, knowing that he failed his town.

In Rainbow Flat, Blaise and Jefferson learn more about one another, and the entrepreneur expresses his romantic interest. Blaise has never considered a relationship before—with anyone— and he's flustered by the news. Flora Strop, Jefferson's aide, arrives with dire information about the attack on Itude. Blaise resolves to go back, and Jefferson supports his decision. Before leaving Rainbow Flat, Jefferson asks Blaise to destroy the airship that attacked Itude.

Blaise returns to Itude, horrified by the destruction he finds.

He uses his magic to break Jack free of Lamar's vile trap, and the survivors make plans to get their own back from Fort Courage— all while Blaise discovers the truth of Jefferson's duplicitous nature. Along with Flora, Blaise and Jack go to Fort Courage to free the kidnapped mages, including Emmaline.

While there, Blaise diverts from the group to destroy the airship. Distracted as he pits his magic against the salt-iron reinforced ship, Lamar traps him aboard the failing vessel, making escape impossible. Jack attempts to kill Lamar, but Zepheus whisks him away lest the airship crush him. The airship crashes, taking Blaise with it.

Blaise awakes weeks later, surprised that he's not dead. But he may as well be. The Confederation has him and they've taken him to far-away Izhadell. His only ally is Jefferson Cole, and he's not sure he can even trust the man anymore.

Meanwhile in Itude, Jack and Emmaline have a glimmer of hope that Blaise survived when the younger Effigest feels the hum of life in the Breaker's poppet. And Jack discovers, to his great surprise, that the Breaker may have somehow restored the magic that had been stripped from him so long ago.

Pronunciation Guide

Everyone who's ever learned a word by reading it has, on occasion, come across the problem of thinking, "Wait, how do I pronounce that out loud?" I hope this will help with that! However, this is just a guide so if you enjoy pronouncing one of these differently, there's no harm in that!

Argor – ARR-gor
Blaise – BLAY-z
Canen – KAY-nun
Chupacabra – CHOO-puh-cah-bruh
Desina – Dess-EE-nuh
Effigest – Eff-IH-jest
Emmaline – Em-uh-LINE
Emrys – Em-RISS
Faedra – FAY-druh
Faedran – FAY-drun
Ganland – Gan-LUND
Garus – Gair-USS
Geasa – GESH-uh
Hugh Fasig – Hyoo Fah-sig
Itude – Ih-TOOD

Izhadell – Iz-UH-dell
Knossan – NOSS-uhn
Knossas – NOSS-us
Kur Agur – Kur Ah-GRR
Leander – LEE-ann-dur
Leonora – LEE-oh-nor-uh
Lucienne – Loo-SEE-ann
Marian – Mayr-EE-uhn
Marta – Mahr-tuh
Mella – Mell-UH
Nadine – Nay-DEEN
Nera – NEER-uh
Nexarae – Nex-UH-ray
Oberidon – Oh-BEAR-uh-don (alternate: Oby – Oh-BEE)
Oscen – Oss-KIN
Petria – Pet-RIA
Phinora – Fin-OR-uh
Ravance – Ruh-VAN-s
Reuben – Roo-ben
Seledora – Sel-uh-DOR-uh
Seward – SOO-urd
Tabris – Tab-RISS
Theilia – Thee-LEE-uh
Theilian – Thee-LEE-uhn
Theurgist – THEE-ur-jest
Vollie – Voh-LEE
Zepheus – Zeff-EE-us

IPHYRIA

SEA OF HERMEIA

PHINORA

⊛ *Izhadell*

Duskgarde
⊛

OSCEN

UMBER

ARGOR

UNTAMED TERRITORY

Greylight ⊛

Salt-Iron Lake

• *Asylum*

THE GUTTER

• *Fortitude*

Rainbow Flat

PETRIA

Ironrun •

Fort Courage ◇

• *Bristle*

MELLA

• *Morton*

DESINA

Ondin ⊛

Sable Point •

GANLAND

Seaside •

⊛ *Etla*

GULF OF STARS

Nera
⊛

CHAPTER ONE
Biggest Toad in the Puddle

Jack

Outnumbered again. Jack wasn't about to let a little detail like that stop him, though, as he peered through the spyglass at the distant campsite.

It was a jumble of tents and canvas huts arrayed like discarded toys, men and women outfitted for hard labor in a mine, trundling back and forth like worker ants. They were burdened with tools, laughing and calling to one another. He wondered how many of them were there of their own free will and how many were criminals or wrongfully accused, working off indentures.

He scowled, shifting his view to observe the guards along the mining camp's perimeter. Guards to keep the laborers in line and to protect them from the threats of the Gutter. *Threats like me.*

A year ago, Jack would have had little trouble running off squatters like the feckless son-of-a-guns that had staked a claim on the northern ridge of the Gutter. He had a posse of outlaw mages ready to scare them off. But that was before the devastating attack on the town of Itude. Before their world changed forever.

But what he lacked in manpower, he made up for with magic. Jack limbered up his fingers in anticipation. He had been without it for so long, he was still becoming reacquainted with that long-lost part of himself. It was a strange thing, having to retrain himself to pull out his old bag of tricks. It was insignificant when he reflected on all that had been lost.

"Don't think about that," the outlaw grumbled to himself. The more he thought about the avalanche of events that had led to the destruction of his town, almost losing his daughter, and losing... well, it was an outright lie to call Blaise Hawthorne anything less than a *friend*...the angrier at the world he became. There was a time for anger, but this wasn't it. *Later.*

A warm breath huffed against the back of his neck as Zepheus peered behind him. <There are so many. Will this work?>

Jack glanced back at the pegasus stallion. Would it? He didn't know, but he wasn't about to admit it. Jack survived on the notion that if he believed something was true, it would simply be so. "'Course it's going to work."

The palomino tilted his head so that his long, silvery forelock fell over one eye. <Is this the sort of working where if the spell fails, it rebounds on the caster?>

Jack snorted. "Do I look like a wet behind the ears greenhorn to you?"

<You're out of practice and this is a large spell.> Sometimes Zepheus was too damned practical.

The stallion was right, of course. Even in his days as a theurgist, Jack would have approached a spell of this magnitude with caution. It was the sort of working that a coven of Ritualists would cast together, each adding their own specialty. But Jack didn't know any other Ritualists in the area, and even if he did, he wouldn't want to work with them. Too much room for error, the way he saw it.

"It'll be slick as a whistle," Jack said, terse. Anyway, it wasn't as if he were unfurling the working willy-nilly. The moment he caught wind of the incursion in the Gutter, he had begun designing the spell. It annoyed him that his previous run-ins with Confederation filth had done nothing to deter others from playing the same game.

Jack laid the blame for that at the Confederation's feet because of the decimation of Itude. Before the attack, they would have thought twice about setting foot on this land, as the outlaws of Itude had a reputation for running off Salt-Iron Confederation intruders. As word of the town's assault spread, the emboldened vultures of the Confederation decided the time was ripe to swoop down on the Gutter as if it were a bloated carcass to be squabbled over.

He and Zepheus waited in their position until the sun sank low on the horizon. It gave him time to study the canvas tents dotting the ridge, nestled beside more permanent fixtures. Someone had hauled in fresh lumber to assemble a rudimentary stable yard for horses, mules, and donkeys. Skeletal frames for future buildings dotted the area, though they didn't have enough sturdy coverage to be called habitable. If Jack had his way, the place would never *be* habitable.

Once nightfall claimed the last gold-tinged rays of sunlight, Jack and Zepheus made their way down to the mining camp. The pegasus magicked his wings away in case they were spotted. Much easier to explain a man arriving on horseback. But Jack's goal was to remain undetected. The moon was a crescent slash on the horizon, and it wasn't long before he had to rely on Zepheus's superior night vision and the distant lanterns of the camp to orient him.

The stallion stopped a half-mile away from the nearest sentry, and Jack slipped down from the saddle. He unbuckled the saddle-bags and drew out a canvas sack, pulling a single feather and bit of leather thong out before tying it to his gun belt. Aside from his belt, he had dressed as simply as he could, donning a cotton button-down shirt and heavy trousers just in case of discovery. At a glance, he would fit in. But his sixguns would give him away, and there was no chance he was leaving those behind, magic or not.

The outlaw drew a tiny figure from his front pocket, a doll wrapped with a lock of his own hair. He used the bit of leather thong to secure the feather to the poppet's midsection. He cupped it in his hand, his flesh prickling as he awoke his power. Every mage worked a little differently. Some had to speak for their spells to work, some needed specific reagents, and others had to draw symbols or work with a coven. And then there were those like Jack, who exerted his will through sympathetic magic to invoke a spell.

An invisible spark of magic danced over the poppet as he activated his first spell, Owlsight, to allow him to navigate more easily in the dark. But he needed more than to *see* in the inky darkness. The next one was an old favorite, and he was so adept at it he didn't need a reagent: Obfuscation. It was the closest he got to invisibility. People could see him, but if their eyes drifted over him, they wouldn't be inclined to challenge his presence or remember that he was there after the fact. Proper spell warding would disrupt it, as could certain other magics, but Jack didn't think either of those scenarios were likely in this situation. If the camp ahead of him boasted any mages, they were more likely to be indentured workers than anything more treacherous. He had seen no signs of theurgists among the guards.

<Be careful,> Zepheus advised.

"Stop fussing at me like a mother hen," Jack grumbled, patting the stallion's neck. He took a calming breath to focus on the job ahead. "You'll keep tabs on me?"

<Of course. Someone has to be ready to pull your tail from the fire.>

"My fat's not in the fire yet," Jack said dryly. Zepheus gave a soft nicker of amusement.

Jack ambled into the camp unchallenged, striding right past the closest sentry as a preliminary test for his Obfuscation. The man on duty stared at him for a moment in confusion, scratching his forehead before scanning the area. Jack smirked. *I'm the biggest toad in this puddle.*

He took his time once inside the perimeter, getting his bearings as he studied the camp proper. He listened in on sleepy conversations and heated dice games, hoping to glean bits of useful intelligence. One such conversation confirmed that the mining company's purpose was to prospect for gold and, to Jack's disgust, salt-iron. He bared his teeth, revolted by the mention of salt-iron. *Not if I can help it.*

Jack discovered that the mining company boasted a small contingent of indentured mages. That gave him an idea. He started with their section of tents first.

He tugged the canvas bag from his belt, opening it and pulling out an effigy. It differed from his standard poppets, which were humanoid in design. Constructed of supple willow sticks woven together with a leather thong and beads, it looked like a square decoration that might hang over a hearth. Jack had prepared his spell on the effigies beforehand but hadn't accounted for the presence of mages. He pursed his lips. *This'll require a few modifications.* When he was done, he hung it atop the framing at the back of the tent before moving through the camp and stringing up his other effigies throughout.

Once he completed his round, Jack slipped to the outskirts of the camp, mindful of range to activate the working. He was rather proud of this spell, something he had developed himself. The effigies were linked to one another like a daisy chain, and once triggered, his magic would pulse down the line. It reminded him of the new-fangled electric circuits he had read about in Confederation dispatches.

Jack pulled the keystone effigy from his pouch, the one used to trigger the others. He settled down on the ground, legs crossed and hoping that no blasted scorpions or rattlesnakes were in the area. Wouldn't do to get stung or bit in the middle of this. He'd never tested his Obfuscation spell against critters, but he hoped it made him uninteresting to them, too.

He cradled the effigy in his hand, bringing out his own poppet and settling it in the middle of the square. Then he sent his magic spiraling from the poppet to the effigy, a soft pop punctuating the air as the spell began.

Effigest spells weren't flashy. That was the way Jack liked it. It was inconvenient in times like this, however, when he wanted a quick indication if it had been effective or not. But instead, he had to bide his time, his ears straining against the chorus of cicadas as he listened for human voices.

And then it began. Jack grinned, cracking his knuckles as he waited. Before long, the shadows of men and women became visible, running away from the camp, some of them jumping onto the backs of confused donkeys or mules in their haste to leave the area. Maybe casting Rising Dread on a large area wasn't sporting, but it was certainly entertaining.

<You're going to go to Perdition for that,> Zepheus commented.

Jack shrugged. *Yeah, going to Perdition for a lot of things.*

But he hadn't yet seen any sign that his spell on the mage tent had succeeded. He crossed his arms, having no choice but to wait it out a little longer.

Silhouettes stormed from the camp, making a beeline in his direction. Jack rose, standing lightly on the balls of his feet as the indentured mages closed in on him. Five in all—far fewer than he had hoped for—approached with a mix of wariness and outright hostility.

Weak sparks danced on the fingertips of one man while a tornado of sand blew around the legs of a woman in the lead. The sight of the fire piqued Jack's interest, though it quickly cooled. *Not Kittie.* He shelved his disappointment, cocking his head as they drew to a stop, some of them holding weapons that glinted in the moonlight. Jack approved of their precautions.

"Howdy," the outlaw drawled, dispelling his Obfuscation spell as he spoke. His tweak to Rising Dread had rendered them resistant to the fear portion, instead drawing them to the keystone.

The indentured mages startled as they noticed his presence. Guns clicked, an ominous warning. Jack was ready to draw if needed, figuring he was quicker than any of their lot. He hoped it wouldn't be necessary.

"Who are you?" the Pyromancer asked.

"A concerned citizen," Jack replied.

"*Outlaw*," a woman murmured.

"Outlaw *mage*," another corrected.

Jack shifted his weight from foot to foot. "You're not wrong. You can thank me for rescuing you later—"

"Rescuing us?" the Pyromancer spat, the sparks on his fingers spiking higher before settling. "You've ruined us! We'll never be free now."

Rather beef-headed, aren't you? Jack raised a brow. "You're free of your captors now, the way I see it." He gestured to the expansive darkness behind him. "You're in the *Gutter*. The Confederation has no claim to any mage here."

An Earthshaper shook her head, kicking grit toward Jack. "They'll come for us. They always do." Her voice rose with dismay.

Jack ground his teeth. He had forgotten the blinding terror that was ingrained into indentured mages. For so many of them, utter obedience was a way of life. It was how they survived from day to day. "We can protect you from that." *But can we?* He kept the doubt from creeping into his words.

"We know what happened here," another of the mages whispered. "It's not safe."

The outlaw scowled. "You don't have to come back to Fortitude with me. Not if you don't want." He jutted his chin toward the camp. "But it'll be a cold day in Perdition before I let an operation like that stay here." He pocketed his poppet. "Seems to me you have three choices: either come to Fortitude with me, set out for another town in the Untamed Territory where you can live free and clear, or go crawling back to your Saltie masters." He spat on the ground for emphasis.

<Someone's coming.>

A mage opened his mouth to speak, but Jack lifted a hand to command silence, focused on the sharp clatter of hooves arriving from the south. A moment later, Zepheus trotted in Clover's wake as she bolted toward Jack.

Clover was a Knossan, a race that looked like the result of an amorous pairing between human and bovine. She towered over him, a formidable seven feet tall and faster on two legs than an unspelled human. She slowed as she approached, ignoring the cluster of indentured mages who backed away at the sight of her. They hadn't planned on coming face-to-face with a Knossan, much less an agitated one.

"Clover?" Jack cocked his head as she came to a stiff-legged stop, her sides heaving. He didn't know if he wanted to find out what disaster had forced her to seek him out at this time of night.

"She's gone," Clover gasped, her eyes white-rimmed.

He blinked, slow to digest Clover's meaning. "Who?"

Clover gave him a forlorn look. "Emmaline. She's *gone.*"

"Don't you come in here and threaten my son, Jack," Nadine growled as he stalked up and down the aisle of the clinic, hemmed in by empty cots.

Upon Clover's announcement, he'd left the fate of the indentured mages in the Knossan's hands so he could high-tail it back to town. He had almost torn apart his own home in the search for clues but found no helpful letters left behind. Oberidon, Emmaline's pegasus, was missing from the stables, and none of the remaining good-for-nothing stallions had a clue where he'd gone except that the spotted stallion and his rider headed out sometime the previous afternoon.

That left Jack with only one other source for questioning: Reuben Collins. Nadine's son had worked with Emmaline extensively at the bakery, and over time, the two became close enough to earn Jack's disapproval. Reuben seemed to have a good head on his shoulders and recognized that Jack was a threat to his exis-tence if he got too *friendly* with Emmaline, so the kid behaved. *So far*. But now, he wasn't telling Jack anything helpful. *Curse him to Perdition.*

"And *you're* not the one with the missing *child*," Jack spat in response. Tension crackled through the air as Nadine squared her shoulders, pulling on her own formidable magic. Jack usually had the common sense to not bait a life-sucking Healer, but at the moment, he didn't give a damn.

Reuben cleared his throat, ducking his head. He was about as magically inclined as a loaf of bread, but even without power, he knew how close the two outlaws were to violence. "Sir, she's *not* a child."

Jack's eyes narrowed, and he prepared a scathing retort, but Nadine beat him to it. She prowled over, poking him in the chest. "Before you nay-say that you *think* about it and you think *good*. That daughter of yours has been through trauma, and what have *you* done about it?"

The outlaw's jaw worked open in surprise, then snapped shut. Nadine's words were like a punch in the gut. After Emmaline's capture and imprisonment at Fort Courage, their relationship ran into a snarl. They'd had their share of troubles as she grew into her teenage years, and things had only gotten worse. After Courage, she'd grown more distant and refused to speak of what happened. And Jack hadn't known what to do to bridge the gap between them, thus had done nothing. Not a damned thing, because he was too afraid that he would sever whatever small connection they still shared.

But rather than say all that aloud, he crossed his arms. "That's neither here nor there. I need to find her. Before..." *Before I lose her like I lost her mother.* His heart squeezed in his chest. He swung his bleak gaze to Reuben. "What did she talk about with you? I need to know if she's put herself in danger." He failed to conceal the raw *need* in his voice.

Reuben swallowed, fidgeting with the buttons on his shirt as he debated his response. Jack tried not to glower but suspected he failed. "She's been talking about leaving Fortitude for a while now." He paused, looking up as if expecting Jack to have an irrational response. The outlaw almost did, but he mastered himself and motioned for the kid to continue. "Em's been upset about a lot of things. Blaise's capture. Whatever they did to her at Fort Courage..." He made a helpless gesture. "She's, um, mad at you, too." He whispered the last bit, cringing.

Jack sucked in a breath, stung. But that was fair. It was likely true. Emmaline had argued that they needed to get Blaise back— because he was her friend and had sacrificed everything. But the Breaker was far behind enemy lines, all the way in Izhadell from what Jack had gleaned. And he wasn't a starry-eyed greenhorn like Blaise. He was a wanted man, and going that deep into Confederation lands was a dangerous and foolhardy prospect. *Oh.* Emmaline wasn't a wanted outlaw, though. At least not the same way he was. *Blame it all, but it makes sense.*

"Has she gone to free Blaise?" Jack asked.

Reuben shrugged. "I...I don't know. Maybe she's just gone out to think? Clear her head?" He licked his lips, full of cautious hope. But the pegasi had seen Oberidon leave with full saddlebags (and *why* had none of those sugar-addled studs thought to ask about that?), which meant they weren't going out for an overnight jaunt.

Jack raked a hand through his hair. Reuben knew nothing. Emmaline hadn't told Clover, and she usually confided in the Knossan bartender. Which meant his daughter knew Clover wouldn't allow her to do whatever balderdash she had come up with. He blew out a frustrated breath. *If I were Emmaline, what would I do? Where would I go? I'd want information first...*

"I'm a bally fool," Jack growled.

Nadine frowned. "What?"

He waved a hand at her. "I'll tell you if I'm right." Without another word, he spun and stomped out the door of Nadine's clinic, jogging down the steps of the porch as he made a beeline across the ruins of the town to his home.

The door slammed in his wake as he stormed into his bedroom. *I'm a fiddlehead. I should have thought to check here earlier.* Jack studied the wood floor, noting that the dresser was an inch out of place, judging by a disturbed layer of dust. He shouldered it out of the way, revealing the hidden panel on the wall. *Not so secret anymore.*

He removed the box of letters contained within, flipping through them. He cursed, realizing that the most recent acquisitions were missing. Letters from Jefferson Cole, also known as Doyen Malcolm Wells of Ganland.

"You're as dead as a can of corned beef if she goes running to you, Cole," Jack snarled softly.

CHAPTER TWO

Magelover

Jefferson

"*Y*ou *lied* to me."

Blaise Hawthorne, the Breaker of Fort Courage and one of the greatest current threats against the might of the Salt-Iron Confederation, stared across the weathered expanse of the table, chewing on his lower lip. Unwashed tendrils of hair fell over his haunted blue eyes, the young man's gaze flitting to the cell door every few seconds as if expecting an attack.

Jefferson bit back his excuses because they came up short as far as Blaise was concerned. He owed the Breaker nothing less than the full truth, but that wasn't something to reveal here. Not in the prison wing of the Golden Citadel. It was far too dangerous. "I'm sorry," Jefferson murmured, painfully aware that it wouldn't be enough. "I never misrepresented who I am, though. There were matters I couldn't divulge to you." *Please don't ask me to say more than that. My position is delicate as it is.*

Blaise bowed his head, studying his hands. He seemed to withdraw from the conversation for a moment, as if willing himself to another place and time, his eyes unfocused. It worried Jefferson to see him like that, but all he could do was wait and hope that Blaise would return to the conversation.

The silence stretched on, and he longed to reach out and touch Blaise's arm. But that, too, would be unwelcome. "I never wanted to hurt you."

Those words stirred the Breaker from whatever thoughts he'd banished himself to. He lifted his head, his lower lip trembling. Fury rose in Jefferson, and he reined in the inclination to storm out and demand answers. What cruelty put Blaise in such a state? There was a time for that later, when he could play the game from a position of power. For now, he had to do his best for the man who sat before him, shattered.

"I thought..." Blaise started, then gave a shake of his head like a dog drying water from itself, leaving Jefferson to wonder what he had been about to say. He started on a different path. "You didn't come to see me for so long once they brought me here. I thought..."

Jefferson pursed his lips, able to fill in the rest of the unspoken words. *I thought you hated me. I thought you had used me after telling me you wouldn't. Maybe you think I'm less than a person.* "No," he said sharply. "It's nothing you may think. It's the rules of your predicament." *Predicament.* Yes, that was an apt word. It made it sound like something they could over-come. Jefferson hoped so, at any rate. He gave Blaise an earnest look, rewarded when the other man met his eyes, which he hadn't done until that moment. "They make it exceptionally difficult for someone like you to have visitors. My lawyers had to dig up some rather obscure legal precedents."

"War criminals like me," Blaise whispered, correcting him.

You did what needed to be done. Jefferson wanted to say the words aloud, but to do so here would be treason and he was on rocky footing as it was, being connected to Blaise. His lawyers, truth be told, were going through creative legal contortions just to keep him from facing a similar fate, which would prove quite inconvenient, all things considered.

"That's not who you are," Jefferson responded, insistent. He knew better. He knew the *real* Blaise, the person trapped behind this current troubled visage.

Blaise flinched, an echo of old pain crossing his face. "Funny you say that when I don't really know who *you* are." And then the spark of defiance receded as Blaise averted his eyes once again. "You told me you would explain."

Blast it all. Jefferson gave a gentle shake of his head. "I can't. Not here." The disappointment that flashed across Blaise's face spoke volumes, and Jefferson regretted it. Any trust Blaise had in him was eroding fast, and he was the only one within these walls on the young man's side.

"Why did you come?" Blaise asked, his voice little more than a rough whisper.

It stung that he had to ask. "I needed to make sure you were okay." But it was clear that he wasn't, not at all. Jefferson wished he could pull Blaise into an embrace and take him from this place, but that was outside the realm of his power. There were some things money couldn't buy.

"I'm not." The Breaker swallowed, staring hard at the table. He idly ran his thumbnail over the woodgrain, his hand shaking. "What's going to happen to me?"

"I don't know," Jefferson replied, spreading his hands. "It's in discussion among the Council."

"Oh." Blaise scrubbed at the side of his gaunt face, his beard shaggy and unkempt. Jefferson made a mental note to ensure that the prisoners had proper hygiene items. Blaise opened his mouth as if to say something else, then clamped it closed.

"We're going to get through this," Jefferson murmured, tapping his fingers atop the table. "I promise you."

Blaise shook his head. "Don't make promises you can't keep."

Gods, whatever they had done had stripped Blaise of the optimism he'd possessed. The young man had never been bold, but he had been persistent. And that was gone, wiped out by whatever the Confederation did to crush the will of a mage. Jefferson leaned over the table, fierce. "I told you once before I would fight the entire Confederation for you. *That*, I assure you, was no lie."

If the mage was about to say something else, a reverberating knock on the door to the visitation room squashed it. "Time's up!" the guard hollered, his brassy voice making Blaise tremble.

Three muscular guards strode into the room, two bearing salt-iron shackles for Blaise, and the third to escort Jefferson from the premises. It cut Jefferson to the core, watching Blaise offer his swollen, welt-covered wrists for the guards. They slapped the shackles on and dragged him from his seat before he even had a chance to stand.

"Mind yourself with him!" Jefferson snapped, bolting up from his chair and slamming a palm onto the table.

The closest guard sneered at him. "You're not the boss of us, *magelover*. Get a move on before we find a reason to keep *you* here."

I may not be the boss of you, but I know how things work. Jefferson composed himself, straightening his greatcoat as he rose, offering a disgruntled glare to the guard escorting him to the exit. He hoped he had more luck with the situation as his alter ego, Malcolm Wells.

Malcolm

UNDER THE BEST CIRCUMSTANCES, SALT-IRON COUNCIL SESSIONS were exercises in patience and maintaining one's composure. Under the guise of his true-born self, Malcolm Wells discovered he was stretched to the brink when the topic up for debate was Blaise Hawthorne. He fiddled with the lapel pin that marked him as a Doyen to give his fractious hands something to do.

Doyens from each of the eight Confederation nations sat on

the Council, accounting for twenty representatives in all. The older nations had three representatives, while the newer nations only held two positions. Malcolm was the youngest among the Council, one of its rising stars.

As with any gathering of opposing groups, the Council boasted factions who shared ideologies. Among them, he was one of the most outspoken for those on the Faedran faction who supported the idea of mage equality. Malcolm wasn't alone in that regard, but the Mossbacks, who preferred to keep the mages firmly under their thumb, outnumbered his faction. His best hope was that they could play on the sensibilities of the Moderates.

"There is no reason this man should draw another breath," Doyen Hollis Burrows of Canen said in response to something Malcolm had missed. Regardless, his words set Malcolm's teeth on edge. As if Blaise were a mad dog to be put down.

Predictably, Burrows's words caused an outburst among the group. Hollis enjoyed stirring the pot. But to Malcolm's surprise, Gregor Gaitwood of Phinora was the first to command the floor. "Let's not be hasty," Gregor cautioned, lifting his hands in a placating gesture. His gaze slid around the room, reminding Malcolm of a snake hunting for mice. "While I understand we have disposed of threatening mages in the past, we should explore *all* of our options."

Roberta Thayer of Argor consulted her notes, lifting a finger to get Gaitwood's attention. "According to the report, more than a hundred men and women died at Fort Courage. Is that not true?" She was the sort of Moderate who loved her facts and figures, using numbers to guide her vote.

Not all by Blaise's hand. Malcolm bit back the retort. He cleared his throat to draw their attention. At the time of the attack, Argor was so new to the Confederation it didn't have a Doyen sitting on the Council, so she wasn't privy to all the details. And the report, of course, neglected certain points. "If I may, Doyen Thayer, it's important to note that Breaker Hawthorne was *not* the only outlaw mage at Fort Courage that day."

"But he's the only one we have at hand," Burrows replied sourly. He pounded his desk with a fist. "I say we use this one as an example. The outlaws need a reminder not to cross the Confederation. Garus watch over us if they grow bolder."

"My dear colleague, may I remind you of the circumstances?" Doyen Leonora Peppers, also of Canen, asked as she rounded on her countryman. She held up a sheaf of papers. "If you like, I can read the first-hand accounts of our own soldiers who were present at the attack on the Gutter town, Itude. Confederation forces were the original aggressors." Leonora followed her words with a tepid smile.

"The Gutter isn't a recognized nation, and as such, has no protections," Burrows argued.

"All the same, it violates the Oscen Agreement." Malcolm looked up, eyes narrowed as the burr of an idea hooked into his mind. He would think more about that later.

Irving Dempcy, Gaitwood's crony from Phinora, snorted. "The OA doesn't cover mages."

Leonora shot a look at Malcolm. "Would you like to respond, or shall I?" Malcolm offered her a small *go ahead* bow, and she smiled like a hunter going in for the kill. Malcolm had always liked Leonora, and not only for their common ground regarding mage freedoms. She was as keen as a razor's edge and enjoyed using her words to eviscerate those who disagreed with her. "You are correct, Doyen Dempcy, regarding the lack of coverage for mages. However, it covers *human* civilians. Human civilians died at Itude. Quite a few of them."

Doyen Selma Dahen of Phinora, who usually counted among the Moderates, frowned. "I would say that's a consequence of associating with outlaws." She gave an elegant shrug. "Lay down with dogs and get fleas."

Malcolm couldn't allow that to stand. He shook his head, vehement. "Listen to yourselves. I know how most of you feel regarding the mages. You're *better* than they are." He hated every word that spilled from his mouth, but he had to play to the crowd.

"That is the tenet most of you subscribe to: that the taint of magic makes them unstable and unreliable. Undeserving of trust. Incapable of being a true member of society, like a normal human." The heads of the Mossbacks nodded in agreement. His fellow Faedrans frowned as they waited to see what point he would make. *Wait for it.* "If we don't allow the OA to cover the human civilians of Itude and don't allow that to factor into the reason they attacked Fort Courage in the first place, it makes us no better than the mages."

Murmured conversation followed his revelation. Leonora gave him a small nod of agreement as she connected the dots. "As Doyen Wells has shown, Breaker Hawthorne and his group had justifiable cause to attack Fort Courage that day."

Gregor Gaitwood rose from his seat, seizing the floor. "Doyen Peppers speaks the truth. The Commander who led the misguided attack on the outlaw town has been disciplined."

Malcolm curled his lip at that. Leave it to Gregor to throw his own brother to the wolves, though it was true that Lamar Gaitwood had been the aggressor.

"And Doyens Cole and Peppers are correct: the fault lies with us." Gregor spread his hands, plaintive, as he continued. "Our forces failed to bring in the Breaker for proper *training* when the opportunity arose in Desina. This is our chance to amend this oversight."

You had better not suggest what I think you are. Malcolm narrowed his eyes, tension settling into his shoulders.

Leonora had the same thought, judging by the sudden tilt of her head. "Doyen Gaitwood, are you suggesting we apply the geasa to the Breaker? Assign a handler to him?"

"I am."

Her frown deepened. Knowledge of theurgists wasn't one of her strengths, however, and she deferred to one of the other Faedrans with more background on the topic. "Doyen Jennings, is there any record of a bound Breaker?"

Seward Jennings of Mella startled when she called his name.

He coughed, fumbling through papers and scrambling to grab his pen. "Ahem. I would need to consult the archives." Round wireframe glasses slipped down his nose, and he pushed them back into place. "Doyen Peppers, you are correct in noting that if we vote to apply the geasa to the Breaker, we must do so with caution."

"Why is that?" Doyen Vollie Musselman of Desina, one of the newest representatives, asked.

Jennings was an academic on mages and their history, taking great pride in that knowledge. He straightened, reminding Malcolm of a molting owl preening its feathers. "Certain strains of mages do not cooperate when bound to a handler. That is to say, effects can range from killing both parties to issues such as mental instability in one or both." He gained confidence as he spoke. "Interesting fact: did you know that binding to a Necromancer will instantly kill the handler?"

Vollie paled at that, cupping a hand over her mouth.

"Yes, thank you for that *interesting fact*, Doyen Jennings," Malcolm said quickly.

Gregor Gaitwood tilted his head, thoughtful. "Doyen Jennings, will you look into the matter so that we can hold a vote on this issue when we revisit the topic?"

Jennings's eyes went wide. It wasn't often they called on him for such duties. "It would be an honor, Doyen Gaitwood."

Settle down. You're on our side, Seward. Malcolm gritted his teeth. He bided his time as the discussion ended with an agreement to continue the topic in the next session. Malcolm was the last to leave the Council chamber, tussling with the problem at hand. He would have to keep close tabs on Seward to see if he discovered anything about Breakers before the vote.

Malcolm sighed. He hoped Blaise wasn't right to advise him against making promises he couldn't keep. Because he desperately wanted to keep this one.

CHAPTER THREE

Selfish Piss Goblin

Jack

"There must be another way." Clover snuffled with worry as she paced up and down the short hall outside Jack's bedroom. She paused, hooves scuffing the hardwood floor. "We'll think of something."

Jack's back was to her as he methodically folded clothing on the bed and snugged them into a water-resistant bag. "There's no other way. No one else *can* go after her."

The Knossan sighed. Jack glanced over his shoulder when he heard the groan of wood. Clover leaned her bulk against the door-frame. "It's too dangerous."

At that, the outlaw grunted. "I'm no delicate flower."

She stomped, her hoof thundering against the floorboards. "You know very well that's not what I mean." She tossed her horns toward a wanted poster hanging on Jack's wall. Most people thought he kept the damned thing there as a bit of vanity, assuming he enjoyed the notoriety. And while that held a grain of truth, there was more to it. It also served as a reminder, a cautionary tale of what awaited if he dared too far into Confederation lands. "If you're caught, they'll *hang* you, and then it will all be for naught."

Jack frowned. "I'm aware." He had his own share of fears about going after Emmaline. Clover was right. If the Salties captured him, he was a dead man walking. Death was always an option when Jack did just about anything, but he worked to skew the odds in his favor. Dying didn't scare him. But it would be extremely inconvenient to die before getting his daughter to safety.

"Perhaps Hank can take a letter to Mr. Cole—" Clover started, but abruptly halted when Jack's lips peeled back over his teeth in rage.

"He's done *quite* enough," Jack growled.

She shook her horned head, confused. "You either need to explain yourself, or I will see to it you do not leave town."

He froze at the genuine threat in her voice. Jack narrowed his eyes. "Don't tangle with me. I don't have the patience for that."

Clover lashed her tail, crossing her arms. "I would not dare go up against your magic. But Nadine could."

Jack hissed out an irritated breath. He was being an unfair cuss, but the stress of Emmaline's disappearance had his patience stretched to the limits. And Clover was right. If anyone could put him in his place, it was the town Healer. Nadine didn't look like much, but she had sucked the life out of soldiers at the Battle of Itude to keep herself on this side of Perdition.

"What are you not telling me?" she asked.

He sealed the bag after slipping a final pair of socks inside, keeping his focus on the simple actions of preparing to leave the town he had built up and ultimately failed. "Cole's been sending me letters."

"About?"

Jack wrinkled his nose. "Guess."

"Blaise?"

"Yeah." Jack licked his lips, wishing he didn't have to discuss it. The first letter from the duplicitous entrepreneur had piqued his curiosity, but that interest transformed into anger when he realized Cole was asking for *help*. Help freeing Blaise. Emmaline had discovered the letter and demanded to know what they could do to free the Breaker.

Nothing. There was absolutely nothing to be done because Blaise was in Izhadell. It would be easier to set foot on the dusty path that led to Perdition and meet Nexarae, the goddess of life and death, for a whiskey than free Blaise from the Golden Citadel.

Predictably, Emmaline hadn't liked her father's answer. Not that Jack could blame her after Blaise had given up *everything* for them. And Jack repaid the debt by letting him rot in the Confederation's clutches.

No one knew how much Jack stewed over the conundrum. Rumor had it he still didn't like Blaise and was happy to see him gone. Yeah, the Breaker could be whiny, irritating, and priggish. But underneath that veneer of anxiety and flour, he had a lot of gumption Jack had come to admire.

"So you believe Emmaline has gone to help Cole free Blaise?" Clover asked.

"She went through my cache of letters," Jack said, spreading his hands. "Em didn't leave a note or anything else for me to go on, so that's all I can assume." Teenagers were damned frustrating. No wonder his instructors at the Golden Citadel had always been so angry with him.

Clover sighed. "You'll go to Jefferson Cole, then?"

"That's the plan." *And if he even so much as looks at me wrong or thinks to betray me, he dies.*

The Knossan rubbed her muzzle. "Will you send a coded letter when you arrive?"

At the worry in her voice, Jack hesitated. Blame it all, he had forgotten that he and Emmaline were the closest thing Clover had to family, too. Their situation terrified the Knossan just as much as it did Jack. "It's come to my attention that Hank knows how to contact Cole. So yes."

A hint of the tension left her frame, though Jack knew she wouldn't truly relax until the people she cared about were safe. "Thank you."

Jack shoved the bag of clothing into his saddlebag, buckling it closed. "Got something I need you to do for me until I get back."

At his change of topic, Clover made an interested noise. "What's that?"

Good. Maybe giving her a task would keep her occupied. "Help those new mages settle in. And work with Kur Agur to keep an eye on the Gutter for any new incursions."

Clover *hmm*-ed with thought. "We can't run them off as you can. Even with the new mages, I am uncertain about our chances. And we should not risk Nadine."

That was accurate enough. Among their original mages, the Confederation had stripped Raven, Vixen, and Butch of their magic at Fort Courage. Jack wasn't sure how long any of them would stick it out in the town. Raven and Vixen had telegraphed signs of being ready to move on with their lives and skip town for weeks now, and Jack didn't blame them. As for their other mages, they had either died in the attack or left Fortitude in the ensuing weeks.

Jack waved a hand, dismissive. "No need to do all that. Just watch them. I'll handle the rest when I'm back." Because he *would* be back.

His words offered the reassurance she needed, and Clover nodded. "We can do that." She tilted her head as he dropped his saddlebag on the floor by the door. "When do you intend to leave?"

"At first light."

"Mornin', Jack!"

Jack grunted at the chipper voice, squinting into the early morning sunlight. "You're up awful early for you, Vixen." He pulled the brim of his hat up, so he had a better view of the flame-haired outlaw standing outside the stables. The tap of boots on the hard-packed dirt announced Raven's arrival. He slipped up beside Vixen and put an arm around her. It hadn't escaped Jack's attention that since Fort Courage, the pair had become close, bound by the shared anguish of losing their magic.

"Word is you're going to Phinora after your daughter." Raven studied him with flinty eyes. "We want to go with you."

What in Perdition are you thinking, pup? You'll get eaten alive. Jack didn't say it aloud, though. It stung to be reminded that you didn't have a lick of magic. It was about the worst violation for a mage, having a part of yourself stripped away like that. "Nah."

Vixen blinked. "What do you mean, *nah?*"

Jack wheeled on her. "It means no. You're not going with me." Raven opened his mouth to speak, and Jack held up a hand to silence him. "I'll make better time alone. Be easier to lay low. Less risky."

Raven tensed, and Jack caught the glint of a knife in his hand. "You know why we want to go." His voice crackled with emotion.

Yeah, he did. "And that's why I can't let you go." Jack said it with more gentleness than he wanted, catching himself too late. Fortunately for him, the pair had their hackles up over his denial. He raised his hands to show he wasn't done speaking, not yet. "I've been in your boots. Don't you forget it. Why in Perdition do you think I stuck to the Gutter and Untamed Territory?"

They exchanged glances, and Jack realized that had never occurred to them. But then again, until his shameful secret had come out after the assault on the town, everyone assumed he'd had magic all along. None of them had realized it was all bluster and bad attitude until after the fact.

"Maybe we thought you had a lick of common sense," Vixen said at last, crossing her arms.

Jack couldn't help it. He laughed. "Here I thought you knew me better'n that." He shook his head. "Your mugs are still on wanted posters all across the Confederation. We go together, some Saltie is gonna figure us out. Magic or not, they'll be happy to hang you either way."

"We're not defenseless babes." Raven's knife winked, a dangerous reminder.

Jack cocked his head. Truth be told, he had a lot of respect for Raven and Vixen, with or without their magic. He wouldn't want to be in a dark alley with Raven getting the drop on him. Time to pull out the big guns. "You're not. But Fortitude is. The Gutter is." He gestured around, encompassing the buildings that had been gutted by fire. "And if I do say so myself, her best protector is about to be gone, so *y'all* might have to do." Jack crooked his index finger at the pair. He hoped they took it for the compliment he intended.

Vixen blew out a frustrated breath. "We love this place as much as you, but sitting here ain't gonna get our *magic* back." She rubbed her arms and added, "Or our friend."

Jack heard the guilt she failed to hide in her words. He knew a thing or three about guilt, having lumped the Breaker's situation squarely on himself. "You don't owe him a thing."

She gave him a sour look. "You're such a selfish piss goblin, Jack. And you think you're tougher than a chupacabra covered in salt-iron, but everybody knows we'd have been lost to the Salties at Fort Courage if not for him. We owe him. And I'm the one who helped him learn his magic."

Jack snorted. *Mentor's guilt.* That was a new one. He was damn sure the woman who taught him how to use his magic never suffered a day of guilt in her life for all his atrocities. The brief thought of his mentor was a shock to his system, and he curled his lips like he had just bit into a lemon. "Y'all are good, but there's no way you're getting into the Cit without magic. Especially if you're not familiar with the place."

"But *you* are," Raven pointed out.

"I am," Jack agreed.

"Did Em go to free him, do you reckon?" Vixen asked, her eyes glittering with hope.

The outlaw shrugged. "Don't know." And he fervently hoped Emmaline didn't get anywhere near the Golden Citadel. His gut clenched at the very idea. If things went well, he'd catch up to her before she even arrived in Phinora.

Vixen stepped up to him, staring him down. Jack wondered if it was an old habit from when she had magic. If she still had her Persuader abilities, then he would have had cause to worry. "You need to get him out."

He wanted to snarl back that he didn't *need* to do anything; that she wasn't the boss of him. But she was right. Instead, he ducked his head, his jaw tight. "Once I find Em and get her somewhere safe, I'll see what I can do about the Breaker."

His words almost surprised him, as much as they did Raven and Vixen. They stared at him. No doubt they expected him to rant and rage that he would do no such thing. But then Vixen's lips spread into a crimson grin. "And you'll bring him back here?"

Jack shrugged. "If I can get him out, that'll be up to him." He had little hope for the state Blaise might be in if he escaped the Cit. None of the other Ringleaders had been on the inside. And the Confederation did a bloody effective job of dispelling rumors about the conditions within. But Jack knew. The Blaise that walked out of the Cit might very well be a shadow of the man he had been.

"That's fair," Raven said after a moment. He rubbed the back of his head. "Fine. You go to Phinora and find your daughter and free Blaise. We'll do our best to keep things in line here."

"No more damned mining companies." Jack shook a finger at them. "You see any more, figure out a way to make the new mages earn their keep and run 'em off."

"They're not outlaws. Not yet," Vixen said with a shake of her head.

Jack pivoted on his heel, heading into the depths of the stables. "They're living in the Gutter. You better learn 'em, then." He waved a hand over his shoulder. "Now, if you'll excuse me, I need to be sure my good-for-nothin' pegasus has eaten and then be on our way."

CHAPTER FOUR

The Secret Appeal of Tragedies

Malcolm

*M*alcolm idly swirled the wine in his crystal goblet, studying the revelers dancing below the veranda. He was off his game. Flirting, wheeling, and dealing were his usual pastimes for such an occasion. He had spent much of the evening chatting up the Moderate Doyens in attendance, taking their figurative pulse on the issue of Blaise Hawthorne.

Nothing encouraging so far. Even those among Malcolm's own Faedran party, who were normally receptive to the idea of mage equality, *feared* the Breaker and had questions surrounding his powerful magic. Malcolm couldn't very well tell them that Blaise would be happier baking cookies than tearing apart a town. How could he explain away such intimate knowledge?

He didn't have nearly enough time before the vote. Malcolm and his fellow Faedrans were in an uphill battle. Already, one of his cohorts had suggested they cede Blaise to the geasa and refocus their attention on securing more rights for the mages who *hadn't* committed atrocities. The cold logic infuriated Malcolm.

But he knew that for the goals he had been striving toward for years, it was the best path.

But he wasn't ready to give up on Blaise. Not now. *Not ever.*

"Can I tempt you with a nibble, sir?" A serving girl interrupted his thoughts, offering a silver tray with an assortment of tasty finger foods. She nestled it close to her ample bosom, tilting her head coquettishly. She smiled, making it clear that she was serving up more than the goods on the tray.

"Thank you. This will do." He nodded to the girl, selecting a finger sandwich. She made a frustrated sound before striding off to either do the job they hired her for or to snag another high-profile bedfellow. Malcolm returned his attention to the task at hand, circulating through the crowd until he found his target. Doyen Seward Jennings completed a rousing dance with his wife, who was a stunning and talented actress Malcolm had seen grace many a prominent stage. At first glance, Malcolm thought it might be a marriage of convenience, but the intense heat between the pair made him reconsider that idea. *Lucky man, Seward.*

"Doyen Jennings, you and your lovely wife cut quite a figure on the dance floor," Malcolm commented, amiable as he approached them, raising his goblet in appreciation.

Seward blushed at the compliment. "I normally don't like to dance, but Lizzie insisted."

Lizzie patted his arm. "You *do* like to dance, just not in front of people."

Malcolm chuckled. *They're a cute couple. Something to aspire to.* "Then it stands to reason you may need a break from such social demands. Can I beg a moment of your time?"

Seward cocked his head. "Did you come to the gala with the express purpose of furthering your agenda?"

"Is there any other reason to attend?" Malcolm replied. Though truth be told, yes, there were plenty of reasons. He quite enjoyed them, for one. It was pleasing to be fawned over and admired. To be propositioned and coveted. But he knew Seward had only come out of a sense of duty (and probably at the behest of his wife).

"True enough," Seward agreed, blowing out a breath. He glanced at his wife. "Lizzie, will it bother you if we speak?"

She waved a hand. "Do what you must. Wait." She paused, her coils of dark hair bouncing as she turned to study Malcolm. "Ah! You're the one my Cuddle Bear told me about! You know the Breaker?"

Seward's eyes widened at the nickname, and Malcolm managed not to quirk a smile. Truth be told, he was more focused on Lizzie's question. "My cousin is well-acquainted with him."

Lizzie stepped forward, conspiratorial. "Have you seen this *dashing* rogue in person? I've heard he's as powerful as a hurricane and twice as scary." She shivered in delight.

A muscle in Malcolm's jaw twitched. Gods, he longed to correct whatever gossip she had gotten about Blaise, but for his purposes, Malcolm Wells had never met him. Only Jefferson Cole had. "I have had little chance to speak with my cousin, madam. But from what we've been told, the Breaker is no different from any other mage."

She deflated with disappointment at his words. "That's unfortunate."

That caught Malcolm by surprise. "I beg your pardon?"

Lizzie shrugged. "It would make a better story if he were. His story has me inspired to write a play, and an *unusual* character always makes for a better tragedy."

This will be no tragedy. He met her gaze. "As much as I enjoy the theater, I don't believe that would be a good fit."

Lizzie waved a hand. "No, no, it absolutely would! Do you know the secret appeal of tragedies?"

Malcolm frowned. He hadn't expected to debate theater with anyone tonight, but here he was. "And that is?"

She offered a demure smile. "A masterfully presented tragedy is an elegy for someone who *matters*. Whose story is worth telling, even if they never achieve a happy ending or lose it all along the way. Even if they fail, they *mattered* to someone."

He blinked at her provocative description, heart squeezing. Yes, Blaise mattered, but if Malcolm had a say, there would be no tragedy. He dipped into a shallow bow. "I'll admit I've never thought of it that way. Best of luck with your endeavor."

Lizzie slipped over to chat with a cluster of other ladies, and once she had moved away Seward grimaced. "I apologize if her question came across as crass. She wants to help bring visibility to the issues we support but is figuring out the best way to go about it."

Malcolm shook his head. "It's not a problem. We need all the allies we can get." And Lizzie's excitement planted another seed of an idea. Something else for later, if ever there was a later. "I wanted to ask what you had discovered in the archives."

Seward blinked for a moment, then a smile broadened his face. "Ah! Yes, I was there earlier. Are you aware it's been over fifty years since the last record of a Breaker?"

"I wasn't aware," Malcolm replied truthfully. He paused, thoughtful. "But isn't magic hereditary?"

The other Doyen waggled his fingers. "It can be, but magic isn't a dominant trait passed down from parent to child." At Malcolm's raised brows, Seward ducked his head. "I have my own thoughts on how magic crops up in a family line, but it's quite difficult to prove." He cleared his throat. "As I was saying, we haven't seen a Breaker in a long time. I could not locate any references to any of them being bound to a handler via the geasa."

That was interesting. Malcolm took a sip of wine. "Why do you think that is?"

Seward glanced around, as if making sure no one was listening in. "I suspect it's because of what the magic can do. In an untrained Breaker, it's as dangerous to friend as it is to foe."

Malcolm swallowed, recalling what Blaise had told him of his past. But that was no longer the case. Blaise had mastered his magic. "Seward, in your opinion, what is the best course of action regarding Breaker Hawthorne?"

The other Doyen sighed. "Personally, I would love to see research done. However, that's unlikely to happen." And Malcolm was glad for that, at least. But Seward was right—the natural philosophers were eager to crack Blaise open like a walnut to see what made him tick. "I disagree with execution, so the next best option is the geasa."

Malcolm frowned. "Are you viewing it from the lens of a criminal case, then? Would you consider it differently if not for Fort Courage?"

Seward nodded. "It's hard to argue against the lives lost, Malcolm. I think the Breaker should face the consequences of his actions. If we do anything else, we risk looking like we favor mages regardless of their crimes, and that will damage our credibility."

Disappointing, but that made sense in a depressing way. "I see. I admit, I know very little of this business about the geasa and how it's done. Can you enlighten me?"

Seward's face became animated, and it was clear this was a topic he had taken pains to research. "Absolutely! It's really very interesting. It's the intersection of alchemy and magic. They use the mage's own blood as a base to create the Ink. It's a brilliant process."

Malcolm was proud that somehow, he maintained a neutral but interested expression. Inwardly, he seethed at the idea, suspecting there would be nothing kind about the process.

"The blood is delivered to the alchemists at the Arboretum, where it's mixed with reagents to create the Ink for the geasa. The mage in question already has a tattoo, applied when they were first registered. But if they don't, they're assigned a sigil and issued the tattoo. The person selected as their handler receives a matching tattoo, made from the mage-blood Ink." Seward beamed. "Isn't that interesting?"

"Quite," Malcolm lied. Awful was more like it. "Matching

tattoos, hmm? What's the design look like?" Seward blinked, the question catching him off guard. Malcolm cleared his throat as he sought to cover his unusual question, lest Seward become suspicious of his prodding. "I've heard they're quite artistic." He'd heard no such thing, so hoped it was plausible.

Seward relaxed, taking on the posture of a man who enjoyed a good lecture. "Oh, each one is unique. That's the thing. Geasa tattoos cannot be repeated. The sigil is made of runes—specialized alphabet, you see. As unique as a fingerprint. One sigil, one mage, one handler."

That bit was interesting. Malcolm tipped his head. "What happens if two handlers bind to the same mage?"

Seward shrugged. "Intriguing question, but I've never come across mention of that. I would presume the first binding may block the second. There have been cases where a theurgist or handler was bound to a new partner in events where one or the other died, but that's the extent."

Malcolm nodded. That was good to know. He was about to speak again, but Lizzie trotted over, grabbing Seward's arm. "So sorry to interrupt! But Cuddle Bear, there's someone I must absolutely introduce you to." Her eyes were wide as she offered Malcolm an apologetic smile. "It's the one and only Edward Monroe. You know, star of *Angry Rainbows* and *Honor of the Eclipse?*"

Seward blinked, startled. Malcolm chuckled. He had to admit, he liked Lizzie and her enthusiasm. "I appreciate the time you gave me, Seward. Mrs. Jennings, I won't steal you away from your husband and the heart-throb that is Edward Monroe any longer." He gave her a good-natured wink.

HE REMAINED AT THE GALA UNTIL THE GREY HOURS BEFORE DAWN. To keep up appearances, once he finished his discussion with Seward, he entertained the company of anyone who caught his fancy. It involved dancing and conversation, though he had his share of amorous invitations. Had he been Jefferson, he might have taken them up on the offer because that was a very Jefferson thing to do. Malcolm was a little more restrained, though not by much. But thoughts of Blaise distracted him, keeping him from temptation.

With a contented sigh, he retired to his bedroom in the estate house. Malcolm drew open the drawer of the bedside table, opening a small velvet box and plucking out his cabochon ring. His mind was abuzz with everything he had learned at the gala, and he had discovered he slept better as Jefferson. But even though his body was tired, his mind clung to the information provided by Seward like a dog with a bone. By the time the pastel rays of sunlight painted the eastern sky, Jefferson was certain that the best course of action was to keep Blaise out of play. As far as the geasa went, he had an idea of how to circumvent it. But he needed help. It wasn't something he could do alone.

He rose from the bed and removed his ring, tucking it into the bedside drawer. Malcolm dressed, and after his breakfast, he sought Flora, his half-knocker acquaintance. It was early afternoon by the time he called her into his private study.

Flora narrowed her eyes, as if she detected he was up to something as soon as she settled into the armchair opposite him. "I see that look in your eye, boss. What are we doing?"

He grunted at her use of *boss*. It was a tease, since Malcolm much preferred to consider her a friend rather than an employee (though she was that, too). "I need you to steal something for me."

Flora hopped out of her chair, pushed a footstool in front of him, and climbed onto it, laying her hand across his forehead.

"What are you doing?" Malcolm asked.

She leaned over to peer into his eyes. "Checking your vitals because something is wrong with you. *I'm* supposed to be the one with that sort of idea." She jumped off the stool and climbed back into her seat. "What am I going after?"

He steeled himself because this would be audacious even by

her standards. "A specific vial of Ink from the Arboretum."

Flora tilted her head, studying him as if expecting he might laugh and call it all off as a joke. When he didn't, she put her hands on her hips, giving him her best glare. Between her short stature and pink hair, she looked adorable—not that Malcolm would tell her that. "Mal, *no*. You can't be serious!"

Malcolm sighed, scrubbing at his face with one hand. "I don't know how else to help him. I can't break him out of the Cit." Tabris knew he and Flora had discussed it, but without more willing helpers, that was a non-starter.

Flora pulled out a butterfly knife and flipped it around. Anyone else might have found it an intimidating move, but Malcolm knew her too well. "I'm not great at being the voice of reason, so this is awkward, and I'm kinda mad you're putting me in this position." She scowled at him for good measure. "But have you thought this through? I mean *really* thought beyond this first step."

Malcolm managed a small smile. "I have. The Ink isn't the only thing I need you to get. I also need you to find out the sigil assigned to Blaise Hawthorne."

At that, she closed her knife and tucked it away. "That's not what I meant. Why are you so infatuated with him? It's not like you."

He winced at her question. It took him back to the time Blaise had asked the same. Malcolm wasn't sure if Flora would understand. "The only thing he ever wanted from me was a chance to be himself. And I…" He trailed off, swallowing as he struggled for the words to explain.

"And you want the same thing," Flora supplied.

Malcolm lifted his eyes, filled with gratitude that she understood. Flora had been his close friend for years, but even so, he had feared she wouldn't understand this. But maybe that had been short-sighted since Flora knew something about that, too. "Yes, and I think we could have that."

"Hmm." Flora pulled the knife back out, fidgeting with it.

"Back to your scheme, then. There's only one reason you'd need that sigil. Are you sure about this?" She scrutinized him. "I can get away with shenanigans. I'm a *nobody*."

At that, Malcolm straightened. He loved Flora and thought the world of her. "You're *not* a nobody."

She shrugged. "My point is, I'm not *you*. Not a Doyen. You have responsibilities and all these wonderful plans. You want to change the world."

Malcolm sighed. "I can still do that."

Flora offered a sad smile. "I like your mettle, but I'm not so sure. Look, Mal, you've already got your hands full with your masquerade. Do you really want to add more to the load?"

As annoying as it was, she had a valid point. Maintenance of his two personas was exhausting. But this was *Blaise* they were talking about. "He doesn't deserve this."

"No," she agreed softly. "But you can't save everyone."

Malcolm swallowed, meeting her eyes. "No. Sometimes it's enough to save one."

Flora put her hands on her hips, staring back at him. "Saving him? Are you sure *this* is saving him and not *using* him?"

Malcolm dropped his gaze to the floor. In his mind, it seemed like such a good idea. The only one that might even work since nothing else had come to fruition. "They're going to use him. *You* threw your lot in with me. I don't use *you*."

Flora was quiet for a few minutes, no doubt reflecting on their own history. She pursed her lips. "I had a choice." And to that, he had no adequate response, so he continued to stare at floor. Finally, she sighed. "Right. Far be it from me to be a hypocrite. But I still don't know how you'll ever make things work out if you get him free. Especially if you're planning what I think you're planning. Not and still do what you want to do."

Malcolm glanced away, guilty. That was another cog in his plan he hadn't worked out yet. He hoped that by the time he got there, an answer would present itself. And that was funny because that wasn't usually the way he operated. Malcolm had the long game in mind. He hadn't expected Blaise Hawthorne's appearance on the board, however.

"I've been juggling things for years. Just one more ball in the air."

She snorted. "More like juggling a flaming chupacabra. This is going to make your masquerade seem boring by comparison."

He shrugged, rueful. "Never a dull moment with me, you know."

Flora laughed. "And I'm here for it." She took a deep breath, as if reaching a decision. "Okay. I'll do a little breaking and entering. Once I have the goods, what do you want me to do?" She raised her brows. "Because I should definitely not bring them back here."

Right. Malcolm massaged his forehead. He already had a good idea of where to go once he had the necessary items. "Do you have any dead drops around Faedra's Garden?"

Flora nodded. "I do. Two streets over." She rubbed her hands together. "Around the back of the Sour Eel Bar, there's a loose brick in the wall that I've used a few times. Do you know the place?"

Malcolm didn't, but he waved away the concern. "I'll figure it out. Can you get it by tonight?"

Flora glanced at the clock on the wall. It was almost two in the afternoon, and Malcolm knew she preferred to sneak around in darkness. Not ideal.

She shrugged, unbothered by the implications. "It's doable. I'll have it at the dead drop by seven."

Malcolm breathed a sigh of relief. He had suspected Flora might put up more of a fight. He was glad to see she was on board. "Thank you."

Flora leveled a finger at him. "You know I'm only doing this because if I don't, you'll find someone else who will."

Was he that obvious? He chuckled. "You're right."

She rose from her chair, stretching. "What are you going to be doing in the meantime?"

Malcolm smiled. "Paying someone a visit."

CHAPTER FIVE

Trust Issues

Jefferson

*B*laise looked up for an instant before bowing his head again as Jefferson eased into the visitation cell. The younger man stayed in his seat as the guards ushered the entrepreneur inside. Jefferson pulled out the chair opposite Blaise and sat. The Breaker's hands were in his lap, but spatters of dried blood staining his sleeve didn't escape Jefferson's notice.

Jefferson half-rose in his chair as soon as the guards left them to their sham of privacy, hands braced against the table as he peered over to get a better look at Blaise's arm. "What is that? What happened?"

Blaise shook his head, silent.

Tabris grant me grace. Jefferson reined in his anger. Blaise experienced enough of that without him adding to it. "You can tell me."

For a moment, Jefferson thought Blaise had shut himself down again, refusing to speak or acknowledge him. But then the young mage shifted his left arm, resting it on the tabletop. A bandage made from dirty strips of cloth was wrapped around his forearm between his elbow and wrist, though blood had seeped through that, too. Blaise moved it with care, as if it bothered him. Malcolm imagined it did. "They took blood. That's how they do it."

"Oh," he murmured, heart squeezing at the sight. Curse them. They hadn't even sent for a Healer to attend to it. A simple matter. Even basic wound care and clean bandages from a physician would have been a good start. Gods, were they *trying* to kill Blaise from lack of effort or pure sloth? "One moment, please."

Blaise withdrew his arm back into his lap as Jefferson rose from the table, keeping his anger coiled within. He knocked on the door, and a guard opened it, allowing him to slip out.

"Done so soon?" The guard had the audacity to smirk.

Jefferson summoned up all the haughtiness he possessed. "I need to speak to your superior."

The guard blinked slowly. "What? Why?"

"*That* is not your concern." Every ounce of contempt he possessed oozed into his voice. *Magelover* he may be, but the power that wealth and affluence brought were in his corner. He was a genuine danger to this man's status as a guard if he didn't act, and soon. The guard realized this and scrambled away.

Jefferson hated to keep Blaise waiting and wondering, but he would not tolerate this any longer. After a brief wait, an older man ambled up the corridor to him, a perplexed look on his face.

"Mr. Cole, Grand Warden Kerney. I heard you had *concerns?*"

Jefferson heaved back his shoulders. "I do. Why has this man not had proper medical treatment?" He jerked a thumb toward the visitation cell where Blaise waited.

Kerney stared at him, uncomprehending. "What?" Then he realized who Jefferson meant, and he chuckled. "Oh. *Oh,* I follow. He's treated as is his due."

Jefferson clenched his fists. "I disagree. And I believe there are several accords being violated with this." He narrowed his eyes. "I have the ear of a Doyen."

The Grand Warden flinched at that, though he didn't let it cow him. "We're doing nothing wrong here." He frowned, lips curling with disdain. "If he wanted to be treated better, he should have thought about that before he did what he did." With that revelation, Kerney turned, waving him off as he trudged away.

Jefferson ground his teeth. He wished he could say aloud that it wasn't Blaise's fault. He motioned for the remaining guard to allow him back in, frustrated that the net gain had been absolutely nothing.

Blaise was stiff and aloof as Jefferson crossed the short distance and took his seat. "I told them it hurts. They won't help me."

Jefferson sighed. "You're right, they won't. But I want to."

The Breaker kept his blue eyes on Jefferson, his shoulders loosening. "They let you come visit me again." His tone was neutral, giving no indication of how he felt about it.

Jefferson nodded, relieved that Blaise had spoken at last. "You're allowed three visitors a week, per regulations." No doubt that would change if a handler was assigned to Blaise. So much would change in that case. No sense in dancing around the subject. "I've brought an update you deserve to hear."

Blaise swallowed, the muscles in his cheeks tightening. "What did you find out?"

"The Council plans to bind you to a handler."

As soon as the words left Jefferson's lips, outrage flared in Blaise's eyes. But as quickly as the anger appeared, it fled, and his demeanor changed. His gaze fell back to his lap as the news hit home. "Oh."

What have they done to you? Jefferson reached across and placed a hand over Blaise's. It was a gamble—he was very aware the other man was averse to unwelcome touch and might shrink away. Blaise's skin was icy, as if his gaunt frame could no longer hold its own heat. But he didn't withdraw his hand. "We'll figure something out, I promise."

The younger man's chin dipped against his chest. "You know how I feel about being used."

Jefferson leaned forward, heart pounding. "I know." And he

had an idea for how to skate around this, but what would Blaise think of it? He warred with the idea of telling him. A large part of Jefferson wanted to. He wanted to be open and honest with Blaise because he deserved nothing less. But caution won out. He was sure they were being observed, and if anyone suspected Jefferson's plan, he was certain to be stopped. "I'm not done fighting for you."

Blaise shook his head. "Is it even worth it? If you continue, I'll only drag you down with me."

Jefferson narrowed his eyes. "You're worth it. And don't let anyone tell you otherwise."

At that, Blaise looked up at him again, quivering as if he were about to break. Gods, Jefferson wanted to know what they were doing to him in the Golden Citadel. Blaise's fingers twitched beneath his.

"I...I mean it." Blaise's hesitation showed the lie for what it was. "Now that they have me, they'll never let me be free. Never let me just...be me." He bowed his head again, and it cut Jefferson to the core.

Jefferson tightened his fingers around Blaise's wrist. "Do you trust me?"

The younger man blinked, surprised. He lifted his head, and it gratified Jefferson when Blaise met his eyes. "Yes."

"Then trust me when I tell you this is not the end. You will get to do what you love again." Jefferson prayed he wasn't lying to Blaise. "I'm doing everything I can to make it so."

Blaise sighed. "I want to believe you."

Sometimes, a spark of belief was all that was needed to ignite hope. Jefferson rubbed Blaise's hand. "Then *do*. I'm fighting for you." Blaise rewarded him with a small nod.

They spoke for a few more minutes before Jefferson was escorted out. He hated these brief visits, these glimpses of the way the young mage's spirit was cracking, the pain reflected in his eyes. And it was all Jefferson's fault.

He strode to the exit, absorbed in thoughts of his plan. There was a very real chance Blaise would hate him for it, but Jefferson believed it was the least of all the evils. Blaise was correct on the point that now that the Confederation had him, they were loath to let him go. Jefferson was still searching for a way to free him, but until he could make any headway on that, this was the only way he knew to stop Blaise from being bound.

They couldn't bind Blaise to someone else if Jefferson did it first.

Flora

FLORA COULDN'T LOSE THE FEELING THAT SHE WAS BEING WATCHED. Over the years, she'd developed keen instincts. She had to, or she wouldn't have made it this far. It was a simple thing to gain access to the Arboretum, the lovely parcel of land that had, in a former incarnation, once been a sprawling public park. But, as was typical, the Confederation claimed it as a place for the alchemists, with imposing walls constructed around it and buildings added to the complex. Flora supposed it was because of the variety of plants imported from all over Iphyria that grew across the grounds in neat, maintained beds. *Need a rare, plant-based reagent? We've got you covered.*

Getting into the Arboretum was simple for Flora, though she was thorough and made a full reconnaissance of the land. She liked to know all the entrances and where any sentries might be posted. Security was overall lax, with most of it concentrated at the main gate. It made sense, as none of the alchemists were mages or had a straightforward way up and over the walls without help. Barbed wire lined the top to dissuade anyone who might try to scale them.

Interesting. Were they trying to keep the alchemists in, the public out, or a combination of both?

Flora set that puzzle aside to think about more when she had the time. The sun was still high overhead, and she had to make her way around the grounds with care. She preferred nocturnal escapades—not only was it easier to stay hidden, but darkness improved her vision, too. Humans didn't realize that under normal daylight conditions, knockers were nearsighted. Thanks to Jefferson, Flora had glasses that corrected her problem. All the same, she preferred the night.

It took some doing, but she located the Ink storage area in a supply room. Even better, it was unattended because no one expected their supplies to up and run off. Flora slipped into the storage room, not bothering to turn on the mage-light. Her eyes quickly adjusted to the darkness, and she read the labels on the bottles one by one. She didn't like the idea of mages being bound any more than Malcolm did. She entertained the idea of fouling the whole lot out of spite. But Malcolm's instructions were clear. The Ink for Blaise Hawthorne *only*.

She picked up the vial with the Breaker's name on it. Flora frowned at it. "You had better be worth all this fuss."

Flora was certain she heard something behind her, perhaps the door opening. She spun, knife in hand. But the storage room was still dark. Flora scowled, scanning the area for signs of anything amiss. Nothing seemed unusual. She opened the pouch at her side and drew out some gauzy linen, wrapping it neatly around the precious bottle before depositing it back in the pouch and closing it securely.

She set her jaw. *Right.* Now time to figure out where they kept the list of sigils.

CHAPTER SIX
Something Off the Menu

Jefferson

lora's dead drop was easy to find, thanks to Jefferson's many years of acquaintance with the half-knocker and figuring out how she worked. The loose brick was low to the ground, and it was a simple matter to tug it away when no one was around to see.

A thrill of victory surged through him as he pulled out a small leather sack containing a vial swathed in cloth and a folded square of paper. Jefferson tucked the vial into a pocket and opened the paper. Flora had scratched the sigil onto the slip with a charcoal pencil, nothing more. Jefferson hoped the Inker would understand what it meant.

Sometimes living two lives was a nuisance. There were so many intricacies to keep track of, and when he had settled on the idea at first, he hadn't realized how involved it would turn out to be. It was one of those things that seemed like a good idea, but over the years had lost some of its luster. This, however, was one of the times it was exceedingly helpful.

After all, it would have been odd for Doyen Malcolm Wells to be seen going to one of the seedier parts of Izhadell. Not unheard of for politicians to go there—oh, no, far from it—but he curated a certain persona for Malcolm that differed from Jefferson. Malcolm wasn't as adventurous and would turn up his nose at going to the red-light district. Jefferson, on the other hand, kept an open mind and would go just about anywhere if either a profit or a good time were sure to follow. Preference given to profit, of course.

As far as houses of ill repute went, Faedra's Garden was one of the more specialized among them. It catered to those with a certain taste—specifically, those who sought the thrill of rolling in the sheets with a mage.

If Malcolm had such inclinations, he would never have considered going to such a place since it warred with his beliefs. The mages who worked there were all serving out indentures, and from what he understood, they had a chance of paying them off, thanks in part to their affluent clientele. In his guise as Jefferson, he had gone to Faedra's Garden with associates a few times. It was an upscale club, offering dinner and a show besides the more carnal pleasures that resided within. All in all, a fun place, though Jefferson had never been one who hurt for willing partners.

Jefferson joined the loose line of men and women entering Faedra's Garden for the evening show. A buxom hostess approached to seat him, but he shook his head and pulled out a bronze chit, handing it to her. Jefferson had paid an exorbitant amount for the token that would grant him what was usually an amorous encounter with a mage. "I'm looking for a more *intimate* experience."

The hostess nodded at this part of their standard dealings. "Follow me." She turned and passed through a curtain of beads. "Itching for anything in particular?"

"An Inker."

The hostess paused. "You understand what you're getting into?"

"Absolutely."

She muttered something that sounded very much like, "Some men just get off on the pain."

She was right about that. But he had other plans.

The hostess led him down a long hallway, placards on each door listing the name of the occupants and their status. Many of them were otherwise engaged, and Jefferson was thankful that the resident Inker was unclaimed.

The hostess drew to a stop before a crimson door at the end of the hall, knocking crisply three times before holding it open to allow Jefferson to enter. "Lindsay, you've got a customer. Good luck." The last bit she addressed to Jefferson. And then she strode out, heels tapping as she receded.

A woman sat before a mirror, adding a trio of combs as the finishing touches to her flaxen hair. The Inker was dressed in a black and gold dress that was all lace and left her arms bare, displaying a colorful tapestry of tattoos. She aimed a coy glance over her shoulder, then back at her reflection as she added the final comb into place. "What do we have here? You want a new tattoo, a good time, or a little of both?"

Jefferson glanced around the room. "Something off the menu. I intend to pay you well for the effort."

The Inker pivoted on her chair, tilting her head so that her hair cascaded over one shoulder like a waterfall. "What are you interested in? I get asked to do lots of freaky things." She shrugged as if it were just another day on the job. Which it was.

Jefferson pushed aside the distaste he had for mages forced to serve out indentures. "I'm looking for a tattoo. It must be applied with specific Ink."

She crossed her arms, a smile playing on her lips. "I see. We have ourselves here someone who fancies dabbling in the mystical world of an Inker." She winked and laughed. "Leave it to the professionals, Mister..."

"Chisolm," Jefferson supplied, knowing very well that only

fools offered their actual names in situations like this. Even if he weren't dabbling in something seditious, she could still use information about him as leverage or to earn favors of her own from others. Potentially pay off her indenture faster. Information was dangerous, and he had no illusions that even the amount of money he was about to offer her would help.

She narrowed her eyes. "Right. Chisolm, then. As I said, you're better off telling me what you're after and letting me apply the proper Inks." Her gaze flicked over him. "You're handsome enough, so I doubt you're looking for a tat to attract a lover. Hmm. Something to keep you virile, perhaps? I'd be happy to try that out with you." Lindsay rose from her chair and sashayed closer.

Malcolm snorted. "Lindsay—may I call you Lindsay? I know what I'm after and I don't need help in that area." He pulled out a promissory note and passed it to her.

Lindsay took it from him, puzzled as she read the terms. She raised her brows. "Is this real?"

"Every bit of it," Jefferson said.

She gave him a dubious look. "This would..." The Inker shook her head. "This can't be right. You must have written it wrong. This would pay off my indenture." She stared at him, the note quivering in her grasp.

Jefferson cocked his head, unable to hide the twitch of his mouth into a smile. "Oh, would it?"

Was it his imagination, or did she almost seem afraid at the prospect of her indenture being paid off? Her gaze shifted to the floor. "I can't accept that. I don't have anywhere to go."

Blast. He hadn't thought of that simple thing. Indentures were notoriously hard to pay off, and when they were, the mage in question was still something of a social outcast, excluded from basic rights like owning land, a residence, or a business. They relied on family members who were themselves non-mages. Otherwise, they entered service to someone who would pay them a wage and offer room and board—someone like Jefferson himself. He had a few such mages in his employ.

But another thought occurred to him. "Do you need to stay in Phinora?"

She shook her head.

There it was. "Pay off your indenture and go to the Gutter or the Untamed Territory."

Lindsay stared at him like he had lost his mind. "Are you kidding me? That's wild country. Outlaw lands. I wouldn't survive a day there. I'm better off staying here."

Jefferson smiled. This was an area of expertise. "To the contrary. I'll sweeten the deal. After you pay your indenture, I'll make sure you have safe passage on a steamer to Rainbow Flat, if you so desire. I think you'll find it more pleasant than Izhadell."

She blinked. "You're serious about this."

In reply, he inclined his head.

Lindsay took a shaky breath. "Right. What do you want from me, then?"

Jefferson slipped his hand into his front coat pocket and pulled out the tiny vial, carefully unwrapping it from its linen protections. "Are you familiar with the designs used for the geasa?"

The Inker froze, startled by the question. "You want a geasa tattoo? Why?"

"I have my reasons." He held up the vial. "This is the Ink you need to use."

Lindsay took the Ink from him, turning the vial over in her hands. "This is the real shit." She hissed out a breath. "What sort of mage does this belong to? Do you know what this would sell for in the shadows? This would pay the indenture of every single man and woman working in Faedra's Garden."

Jefferson's lips tightened. "I'm not at liberty to speak about the mage." He resisted the urge to snatch the vial back from her. He hadn't known how valuable the geasa Ink was, though he had assumed it was difficult to come by.

She shook her head. "My suggestion is forget whatever you

were planning and sell this." Her tone turned urgent. "How did you even get it?"

He waved a hand. "You don't need to know how I got it. Will you do the tattoo or not?" Frustration tugged at Jefferson with each passing minute. He didn't know what he would do if Lindsay refused the task. One thing was certain: he couldn't allow her to stay in Izhadell with knowledge of what he possessed.

Lindsay's eyes flicked from the Ink to him. "Do I have a choice?"

As far as questions went, Jefferson despised that one. "Everyone has a choice."

The Inker laughed bitterly. "Spoken like someone with a drag-onshit load of privilege." She took a deep breath, thinking. At last, she said, "I'll do it, but know that this is dangerous. There's a reason they only apply these at the Golden Citadel." Lindsay opened a drawer and pulled out a spool of thread and a needle.

Jefferson blinked. "I thought you were an Inker."

She placed the spool and needle on a silver tray, alongside a pair of shears and a handkerchief. "I am, but like other mages, each Inker works their craft differently. I'm a skin stitcher." She lifted her chin, a challenge. "Having second thoughts?"

"No," Jefferson replied, full of determination. "How does this work?"

Lindsay settled him in a sumptuous armchair, setting the tray down on a decorative table and pulling a stool over. She threaded the needle, then held it up between her thumb and index finger. "I dip the thread in the Ink and pull it through your skin with the needle. Simple."

Jefferson licked his lips. "I'm a human embroidery hoop, then?"

"Something like that," Lindsay agreed with a laugh as sharp as her needle.

He pursed his lips, glancing between the young woman and the Ink. Jefferson's gut clenched at the idea of the needle dancing in and out of his skin. But all he had to do was summon up a mental image of Blaise and his haunted gaze at the Cit. The

Breaker was going through far worse. Jefferson could handle a little discomfort. "Fine. How long will it take?"

The Inker's eyes flicked to the vial of Ink. "Hmm. A couple of hours."

Lovely. Jefferson nodded, and she scooted closer. He watched as she dribbled a tiny amount of the precious Ink into a shallow bowl, leaving her thread to soak in it. Lindsay turned her attention to her human canvas, gripping his upper arm and frowning.

"You have a glamor." The Inker said it matter-of-factly, as if it weren't an unusual occurrence in her line of work. Perhaps it wasn't. "You'll have to remove it for this."

Damn. He hadn't been counting on that. "Why?"

"I have to see what I'm doing. Whatever you have going on there will obfuscate my view." She waved a hand in a broad gesture to encompass his entire body.

He stilled. "How do you know it's a glamor?"

She snorted with disdain. "Oh, please. You're not the first person to come here with some cheap glamor to hide your true identity, Mr. Chisolm. Whatever it is, drop it, or this won't work."

Jefferson gritted his teeth. He hadn't planned on that problem in all of this. And cheap glamor? It was most certainly not, though he knew what she was talking about. If one had the coin and the contacts, glamors of dubious quality were available for purchase. Though they were nowhere near as thorough as his ring. With a grimace, he pulled his ring off and pocketed it for safe keeping. The magic sluiced off him, his features melting into those of Malcolm Wells.

Lindsay nodded, cocking her head. "There we go. Hmm, not bad looking without the glamor either if I do say so myself. You certainly weren't trying to make yourself more handsome, that's for certain." She blew him a kiss. "Are you sure you don't want to do anything else before I get to work?"

"Only the tattoo," Malcolm answered, uncomfortable at his sudden vulnerability. But he was in a room with the shades drawn. No one would know.

"Right." The Inker nodded. "Do you have the sigil?" He withdrew the slip of paper from his pocket, unfolding it and handing it to her. She raised a perfectly arched eyebrow. "Huh. Okay, let's get to it." She rose and brought over a blank sheet of paper and a charcoal pencil, making room for them on a small side table. She tapped the pencil against the paper for a moment and then began to sketch.

"Is something amiss with the sigil?" Malcolm asked, worried that Flora had copied it incorrectly or nabbed the wrong one.

"No," Lindsay said as she drew. "It's more elaborate than the geasa tattoos I used to apply back in the days of my early training." She slanted her eyes at him. "The more elaborate the flourishes, the stronger the mage." An unspoken question hung in the air between them. Malcolm's blood chilled. He opened his mouth to spin a defense, but the Inker continued her musings. "Although I may be a humble worker at Faedra's Garden, my mama didn't raise a fool. No, she didn't. I know when my silence is being bought."

Malcolm clenched his jaw, frustrated at her insight. While that hadn't been his intent—not fully, at any rate—he understood why she perceived it in such a way. Any denials at this point would be fruitless and only make her more suspicious. "You'll honor it? Keep your silence?"

She nodded, brushing a lock of her hair back into place. "That's what we do at Faedra's Garden, Mr. Chisolm. We keep the secrets of our clients." A tight smile touched her lips, but no matching warmth filled her eyes. Her earlier flirtations had vanished, replaced by the professional veneer of someone wanting to complete a task and be done with it. Without a doubt, Malcolm had lost whatever esteem she may have had for him. As Lindsay had said, she wasn't a fool, and she realized the intent of the tattoo. She didn't approve.

"I appreciate your candor," Malcolm murmured, glancing at the silver needle. The thread gleamed wetly within the basin, and he had to tamp down the momentary squeamishness that rose when he thought about it being laced under his skin.

"I'm satisfied that the design is ready. We can begin if you like." Lindsay placed the finished drawing beside the bowl.

Malcolm nodded. "Please."

He fervently hoped he was making the right choice.

***

"OH, MY APOLOGIES," MALCOLM MURMURED AS HE BUMPED INTO A dark-clad man outside Faedra's Garden. The stranger turned, and Malcolm squinted his bleary eyes into the gaslamp-lit gloom, startling because he *recognized* the face. A Gaitwood. The tattoo had taken hours to apply, and his tired brain stalled as he tried to recall the name. *He only has one arm. Lamar.* He staggered back and away as Lamar stared at him, and Malcolm quickened his step to hail a hackney cab to take him home.

As he settled onto the plush bench seat, Malcolm was frustrated with himself. He was off his game and had been sloppy with his failure to resume the façade of Jefferson before leaving Lindsay's room. But he had as much right as anyone else to carouse at Faedra's Garden. *It will be fine.*

Before allowing him to leave, the Inker covered the fresh tattoo with ointment and a bandage with strict instructions to keep it on for at least twenty-four hours. That was fine with Malcolm. It meant no one would see what he had done for at least a day. He rubbed idly at the bandage as the hackney arrived at his home.

His head felt like he had been kicked by a horse. Malcolm supposed it was maybe due to a lack of food. Lindsay had offered him refreshments, but he had declined. Perhaps he should have taken her up on them. He pushed his way inside, stopping by the dark kitchen to grab a snack and a drink before finding his bed. Aside from two security staff patrolling the outside, his estate was blessedly quiet. Malcolm enjoyed the peace the early hour offered, though the food and drink did nothing to relieve his headache.

Rest. Rest would set him right. It had been a very long day. With a yawn, he started up the steps to the master bedroom, his eyelids heavy with the need for sleep. Malcolm was barely undressed before collapsing in the welcoming comfort of his bed. Yes, sleep would solve everything.

CHAPTER SEVEN

Arboreal Annoyance

Jack

"Huh. Forgot it was that time of year already," Jack muttered at the sight of the gallows standing beside the road they were traveling down. A corpse hung from the gallows, the unfortunate man's body spiraling like a grotesque marionette at the end of a string. The stench of decay tinged the light breeze.

Zepheus tossed his head, ears flicking this way and that. He sashayed to the side as if he were a skittish yearling and not a battle-hardened warrior. But then, he hadn't expected such a sight to greet them at the limits of Izhadell. <Time of year for *what?*>

"Luminary Festival." Jack's lips were tight, his blue eyes hard. It was a stark reminder of what he was risking by coming here.

The palomino pranced down the road, tail swishing with his unease. <They celebrate with death? Why would they do such a thing?>

Jack chuckled without humor; his voice low so anyone who saw him speaking to his mount might assume he was keeping a fractious animal calm. "The highlight of the Luminary Festival is the execution of mages that they've declared criminals. *Outlaws.*" Gods, not for the first time he hoped Emmaline was safe. "Though half the time, the poor sods you see like that don't have a lick of magic."

Zepheus snorted. <And they think mages are the monsters.>

Jack grunted. Yeah, Zepheus had the right of it. The outlaw was quiet as they continued onward, wondering how his life would have differed if he hadn't been brought into the fold as a theurgist so young. But that was a consideration for another time. "Let's get the lay of the land first."

Izhadell was every bit the eyesore Jack remembered. As far as he was concerned, Phinora as a whole was one big cesspit, with the capital city the worst of it. Izhadell sprawled for miles outside of the walls that had originally contained the city. Inns, saloons, homes, warehouses, factories, and every other sort of building imaginable cropped up wherever land was available, pushing farms out to the farthest reaches.

A group of children ran through the streets, playing chase and yelling at one another. One boy stopped, staring at the golden stallion with wide, wondering eyes. The others skidded to a stop, their clothing matted with grime and their hair unkempt. Orphans, by the looks of them. They probably survived by begging and stealing, and no doubt pegged Jack as a likely target, since he had taken to dressing as a merchant to better fit in. The outlaw tugged gently at the reins, asking Zepheus to stop so that he could dismount as the urchins gathered in a goggling clump.

<I'll keep an eye out for cut-purses.> The stallion relaxed nearby.

Jack kept his eyes on the children. He reached into the pouch at his waist, drawing out coins for each child. They watched with sharp-edged avarice, and as soon as a little girl received her coin, she ran off like a squirrel. Jack held up a finger to caution the remaining three from fleeing. "Got more for you. It's not much, but it's something."

He moved to Zepheus's saddlebags, pulling out dried corn husks, string, and bits of colorful rags. The children watched as he expertly crafted a trio of tiny dolls. For half a second, Jack considered spelling them, giving them a simple little working to grant the kids luck filling their bellies or protection. He had done that before, once upon a time. But he knew more now than he did back then, and doing so would put him in jeopardy. He figured the waifs would enjoy a toy even if it didn't have magic attached.

"For you," he said, crouching down and offering the dolls to them, along with a shiny coin. A hesitant girl crept forward first, claiming the largest of the poppets, before running off with a mad giggle. The remaining children, both boys, snagged the last pair and bolted.

<Good thing no one you know is around to see that. Might ruin your reputation,> Zepheus teased, though he sounded pleased by his rider's actions.

"You know I like kids," Jack muttered as he climbed back into the saddle. "It's everyone else that raises my dander."

The stallion bobbed his head and continued onward into the city. Zepheus blew out a snotty snort at the filth surrounding them, flicking his ears this way and that. A film of mud and dung lined the cobblestone streets, and a haze of persistent smoke veiled the air. <This place stinks. I don't like it here.>

Yeah, me either. Jack patted the stallion's neck in silent agreement. It didn't escape his notice that he received many a covetous look, due in part to Zepheus's golden coat. Most Phinoran steeds favored earth tones, so the palomino stood out more than Jack liked. But he knew better than to leave Zepheus behind. Not that the stallion would allow such nonsense.

While Zepheus stood out, Jack had gone to great pains to make sure that he himself did not. He wore brown trousers, a plain button-down shirt, and a frock coat that gave the illusion of a merchant and used a henna dye to darken his blond hair. He grudgingly traded his slouch hat for a checked tweed hat, though it did make him look more respectable, and that was ultimately what he required.

Zepheus threaded his way through the afternoon crowd. Jack didn't have a firm destination in mind, not yet. He had been away from Izhadell for so long he wanted to get the lay of the land. In his previous occupation as a theurgist, and during his time as an outlaw, he had discovered the value of familiarity with an area. And in a place like Izhadell, it often meant the difference between life and death.

It took the better part of the day for them to transcribe a circle around the city. By the time they finished, Jack had a better sense of the layout. They found an unassuming inn to spend the night, and after he settled Zepheus in the stable, Jack headed inside to claim a table in the common room and eat.

The outlaw was halfway through his meal when the first sign came that the respite would be short-lived. <There's a unicorn sniffing around here,> Zepheus advised, his voice distant.

Outwardly, Jack didn't so much as twitch at the news. He took a sip of whiskey, setting it down as he surveyed the room. As far as he could tell, there were no Trackers in the inn yet, but it might only be a matter of time. Jack weighed his options. Going to ground in the inn would cause problems—too many witnesses, too many potential things to go wrong. Not enough clear routes of escape. He rose from the table, pulling a handful of coins from his pouch and dropping them to cover his expenses.

He slipped out of the inn, debating his options. Jack considered using a spell, but the whole point of the unicorn was to sniff out a mage, and that would draw the beast to him like a pegasus to apple pie. No, his best bet was to confuse his trail.

<You can ride me bareback from the stables,> Zepheus offered.

Jack gave a mental headshake. That wouldn't do. It would make his need to escape too obvious, and then someone would call the guard on him simply for behaving suspiciously. Best to play it as if nothing were amiss.

He strode past the stables, heading to the unclaimed land

beyond the inn. Whatever idiot had founded Izhadell had started the city beside a giant swamp. As Izhadell grew, the outer bounds of the city grew to encompass the muck. Architects and indentured mages had worked to raise much of the occupied areas up out of the wetlands, but that only meant bayous and soggy marshes existed beyond those bounds. Jack leaped down from the road onto the grassy bank lining the swamp.

The swamp had two things going for it: first, Jack knew the further he got into it, the more it would reek because of the Phinoran habit of dumping their refuse there. Unicorns sought magic users by scent, and the pungent aroma would interfere with that. And second, the unicorn would be less inclined to hunt him on the spongy ground. Unicorns were native to flatlands, not swamps.

He was out of range from Zepheus's telepathy, so could no longer rely on the pegasus for help. Jack strode through the grasses, listening to the croaking frogs and the occasional splash of an alligator slicing through the water. As far as critters went, he wasn't too concerned about gators. He'd tangled with worse. He'd take a gator over a chupacabra any day. A single shot from his sixgun would warn off the reptile. That just pissed off a chup.

Jack paused after slogging through the swamp for an estimated five minutes. A bird called a warning, and a sleepy heron swooped overhead, making Jack duck in surprise. He heard the telltale slop-sucking sound of hooves moving through the bog and the frustrated snort of a unicorn. Jack brushed his fingers against his holstered sixgun, hurrying onward.

Then he realized he could hear multiple sets of hooves. Damn, the Tracker and unicorn weren't working alone. This complicated things but didn't make them impossible. It meant he needed to shoot and kill the unicorn, which was a shame. The pegasi harbored a grudge against the unicorns for working for the Confederation. But Jack knew they were pawns as much as he had been. He would rather set the unicorn free if given half a chance.

Sometimes, Jack reasoned in his cold way, death was a sort of freedom. He pulled out his sixgun and sidled up against a cypress, waiting.

Dusk had fallen over the swamp, casting long shadows. His pursuers didn't follow him with mage-lights, which was a pity. It would have made them easy pickings. Jack bided his time, listening to the sucking movement of the unicorn and horses getting ever closer to his position. He hazarded a glance and spotted the shining unicorn's horn.

"May Faedra guide you to Perdition," Jack murmured, then sighted on the unicorn and fired.

The equine made a terrified scream as the bullet struck, the beast's rider lurching off in surprise. Jack couldn't see where he had hit, but he already knew it hadn't been a clean kill shot. Cursing to himself, he aimed again as men and women shouted in confusion. This time he was rewarded as his bullet carved a path squarely through the unicorn's head. It sank to the swamp, twitching as the life fled it.

"Mage!" The scream went up as they realized who was responsible.

Jack turned and bolted. Yeah, maybe he had only pissed them off further by killing the unicorn. But now, he could use his magic unfettered, and that gave him an advantage. Even with...he paused, making a quick mental count of the number of pursuers he had seen when he aimed at the unicorn. Counting the fallen rider, four. Even outnumbered, his magic gave him the upper hand. And no doubt they didn't realize they were on the trail of Wildfire Jack, Scourge of the Untamed Territory.

Oh, but they would regret that.

Jack holstered his sixgun and pulled out his personal poppet as he slogged through the swamp, sending frogs scattering in a hopping frenzy before him. He flipped through the mental catalog of spells he could try. Some of them he hadn't used in so long, they were a risk in this situation. Others required reagents— something he despised carrying around with him. Jack much preferred to get creative with his magic and improvise as needed.

Water breathing was the simplest, but Jack would rather not immerse himself in the swamp and get up close and personal with any inquisitive gators. He could try a speed spell, but it was likely to be fouled because of the terrain. Speed was only good if he didn't lose his boots to the sucking mud. No, maybe the best way was *up*.

Jack shimmied against another cypress, peeling off a strip of bark and touching it against the poppet. The effigy glowed for an instant as his spell charged it, and he hoped he wasn't about to suffer from a serious rebound. The Climber's Grace working required a nut of some sort to symbolize a squirrel or a hair from a cat, but Jack had neither. He chose the bark as a stand-in and reconfigured the spell accordingly.

And damn it, his improvisation failed. As soon as he pocketed the poppet and touched his hand to the tree, intending to scale it, instead the tree *grabbed* him. Jack yelped as he sank into the cypress, panic seizing him.

He couldn't move, and it was the scariest sensation he'd felt since Lamar Gaitwood had trapped him. But this time, it was his own fool doing. Jack forced himself to calm down and focus. He'd gotten himself into this mess, and he for damn sure could get out of it. None of his magic was permanent (unless it was something lethal). As long as he didn't continue to fuel the spell, it would fade in time. Jack could dispel it if only he could get his hands on the poppet, but that was an impossibility in his current state.

Once he was calm, he realized he wasn't trapped. The cypress was a living thing, and his spell had temporarily incorporated him into it. Jack could observe everything outside of it once he steadied enough to know he would (probably) be okay.

The Tracker limped through the swamp, accompanied by three others. With a start of surprise, Jack realized that one of them was none other than Lamar Gaitwood. Two thoughts rushed into the outlaw's mind. First, what in Perdition was Lamar doing searching for him in a swamp? And second, where was

Blaise when he needed the Breaker around to drop a Jack-eating tree on top of Lamar?

Lamar turned in a slow circle, a scowl on his handsome face. As he moved, Jack noticed that his old friend was missing an arm. Leave it to Blaise to only wing someone with an entire airship. Jack wished he could grab his sixgun and send Lamar to Perdition. Sadly, cypress trees were piss-poor with sixguns, so instead, he watched in arboreal annoyance.

"He was just here, Commander," the Tracker said, shaking his head. "How does a maverick just disappear in this swamp?"

"This is no *maverick*," Lamar corrected him. The Commander's gaze scanned the area, but it had grown darker still, and Jack was certain Lamar was more likely to be half-jackass than half-cat, thus unable to see in the fading light. "I only know one person who would shoot a unicorn out from under you like that." As he spoke, he stared at the cypress tree.

C'mon, tree, fall on him. You can do it, Jack encouraged his current host. The cypress remained in place, unimpressed.

Lamar and his group cast around for what seemed like an interminable time before giving up and calling it a night. Jack remained within the tree until the first blushing rays of dawn touched the horizon, at which point, the tree expelled him out beside a startled young alligator that launched into the water as soon as he appeared.

Jack winced, slowly rising to his feet. Every muscle in his body felt wooden, and little wonder, since he had been motionless for so many hours. With a soft groan, he took a moment to stretch and limber himself, glad to be in command of his own body again. It wasn't often his spells went wrong, and that had been a humbling experience.

He made his way back to the inn, stopping by the stables first since Zepheus peppered him with questions as soon as he was close enough. The mother hen of a stallion hadn't slept all night, worried for his rider.

<Where were you? You were out of my range.> The pegasus shoved his soft nose into Jack's chest, nearly bowling him over.

Jack stroked the broad, white blaze down Zepheus's face. "Talk is for later. I just spent the night as a tree, and I need a few hours of shut-eye."

<You can't tell me you spent the night as a tree and expect to leave it at that,> Zepheus retorted, lipping at him.

"I can and I will," Jack rumbled. He needed to get some rest for the day before they did anything else. While Jack had discovered the cypress tree *slept* at night (who knew?), he hadn't had the same luxury. But the stallion's concern warmed him, and he left Zepheus contentedly chomping on a bucket of sweet feed. Jack groaned, stretching his arms as he plodded back to the inn. He was looking forward to peeling off his muck-encrusted boots and getting some much-needed sleep.

<What's it like being a tree?> Zepheus asked, glancing over his shoulder at his rider.

Jack grunted. He should never have breathed a word about his predicament last night, but he hadn't been thinking straight. "Trees know better than to ask stupid questions."

<So prickly. You sure you weren't a cactus?>

"I hate you." Jack tapped the stallion with his heels. He ignored Zepheus's amused snort. Truth be told, he was only mildly irritated. He felt better after several hours of sleep, secure in the knowledge he'd successfully evaded Lamar and his crew. Though Lamar sniffing around was bothersome.

After Jack tucked into some grub, they made their way through Izhadell to Doyen Malcolm Wells's residence. As far as things went, this was the straightforward part. In his doe-eyed madness, Jefferson Cole had sent Jack his address since the outlaw was aware of his two-faced ploy. That was helpful, since he had no desire to make inquiries around town that could draw suspicion.

Getting into the residence and securing an audience with him might be another issue, but Jack figured he'd tackle that once they arrived. After all, he was riding a pegasus, if it came down to it. Though Jack was a firm believer in leaving his ace in the hole.

By late afternoon, they found the Wells residence. A towering stone wall and thorny hedge stretching for the sky protected it from curious eyes. Sharply dressed security with rifles manned a shack at the front entry, which made sense as it was the home of a Doyen. Jack rode past, scanning the scene.

<How are we going to get in?> Zepheus asked.

Jack tilted his head, considering. After all the letters, he was certain if he approached the gate and identified himself, he would be allowed entry. But he would rather not have more people aware that Wildfire Jack Dewitt was in Izhadell. "Give me a minute. I'm thinking."

Zepheus started on a lap around the estate, but Jack pulled him up short, eyes narrowed. Something about the ground ahead didn't sit well with him, though he wasn't sure what. He slid out of the saddle, taking a few steps forward and then kneeling. A soft hiss and a pop served as Jack's only warning as a tiny knife shot through the air, grazing his shoulder. Another followed, though Jack had the sense to duck, and it claimed his derby, sending it whirling into the nearby hedge.

Zepheus shrilled a cry, and Jack cursed, spinning to search for attackers. Sixgun in one hand and poppet in the other, he was primed and ready for action.

"Trap," Jack growled, glancing down at the stripe of red across his shoulder. It stung, but it wasn't very deep and could wait. As long as the knife wasn't poisoned.

<Who puts traps around a place like this?>

Someone with secrets to hide. It made a heap of sense to Jack, based on his knowledge of the Doyen. "Someone smart."

<Someone who has people after them,> Zepheus added,

nostrils distended as he sucked in stories from the air. <There's a body up ahead.>

"And if you're smart, you'll turn tail and get out of here," a familiar, high-pitched voice rang out.

Jack knew the speaker, and despite the threat, was glad to hear her. "Hello, Flora." He and Zepheus slowly turned until they were facing the short, fierce woman.

She had her pistol in one hand and a knife in the other, as if she hadn't quite decided which form of violence to choose. The half-knocker squinted at him through her glasses, gaze moving from Zepheus's unusual color to Jack. "Do I know you?"

"You do," Jack confirmed. "Can I show you?"

"Nope," Flora denied him with a quick shake of her head. "I'd rather you leave and not come back."

She was touchy about something, and that had Jack's interest piqued. But Flora looked ready to shoot him with little provocation, which normally he could understand, but right now, it would prove inconvenient. <I'll handle it,> Zepheus advised him, arching his neck.

What...? Jack didn't have time to ask. The palomino shook his mane, and with the movement, his wings unfurled into existence. He ruffled them before settling them at his sides like a bird going to roost in a tree. *Gods, I ride such a damn prissy peacock.*

Flora blinked, then holstered her pistol and shoved her knife back into some hidden sheath on her person. "Well, why didn't you just come out and say so?"

"Think I tried that, and you said no," Jack retorted.

"You're different." Flora walked closer, peering up at him. "I mean, you still look like someone I'd have a good time with, if you know what I mean, but you used to be blond, right?"

Jack shrugged. "Still am, under the dye."

Flora winked at him. "Oh yeah, that's smart." Then her countenance shifted, aloof. "What in Perdition are you doing here?"

"I'm here to see Cole."

Flora looked them over. "If you weren't a damned outlaw, I'd send you off and tell you to come back another day, but you can't exactly do that, can you?" Before Jack could speak, she answered herself. "No. Guess we'll have you as a guest, then. C'mon." She turned and waved for them to follow, as if moments earlier she hadn't thought about putting a bullet in Jack's skull or burying a knife in his back.

Zepheus concealed his wings again and plodded after her. Jack pulled a bandanna out and dabbed at the weeping gash on his shoulder. "What's the story with the traps around the perimeter?" he asked, as Flora guided them around various tripwires and pressure pads.

"Everybody needs a hobby," she replied, poking at a bit of soggy ground with a stick. A giant steel trap leaped out, crushing the stick between rusting teeth. "Go forward about ten feet and stop while I reset this."

"This seems a little extreme for a hobby. Even by my standards," Jack remarked, watching as Flora expertly wrestled the steel trap back into position. "But then I imagine politicians aren't popular."

"There are those who would be happy to see Malcolm dead, yes," Flora agreed, her voice shrill with annoyance. "And I do everything in my power to prevent that."

Flora looked like a brisk wind might blow her over, but she had a tenacity that Jack admired. He might not like or approve of her boss, but he could get behind her brand of grit. She finished resetting the trap and ushered them through a side gate. Flora showed them to the stables first.

<Jack,> Zepheus said, tossing his head and flaring his nostrils. <Emrys is here.>

The outlaw looked past the palomino, and sure enough, in a nearby paddock, a familiar black stallion napped beneath a shade tree. Zepheus whinnied, a command and a query. Emrys awoke, rolling to his feet with a snort and shaking his massive body, raising a cloud of dust. The ebony stallion paused at the sight of the palomino, though he whinnied when he caught Zepheus's scent.

"Oh yeah," Flora said, following their interaction. "Blaise's pegasus is here."

"How long?" Jack asked, his voice rasping.

The half-knocker shrugged. "Couple months."

<You should go talk to him,> Zepheus admonished Jack, shoving him with his nose.

Jack grumbled. There was no love lost between him and Emrys. The stallion held a deep grudge about the way Jack had treated Blaise when they had first met. And for reasons beyond that. With resignation, Jack climbed the fence and dropped to the other side, though Emrys laid his ears back when the outlaw approached.

"Emrys, what are you doing here?" Jack asked.

<I came to find someone who would help Blaise. What are *you* doing here?> Emrys snapped his teeth to emphasize his annoyance. <Did you decide to care about someone other than yourself? >

Jack clenched his jaw. There it was. Like Emmaline, after Blaise's capture, the black stallion had also told Jack to go after the Breaker—and he had refused. And what was Jack supposed to say to that? He hadn't come here expressly for Blaise, even though he harbored guilt about the situation.

When he didn't answer, Emrys swished his tail and turned away. <As I thought.>

Jack shook his head. "Yeah, I'm lower than a snake's belly, and I didn't come just for Blaise. I think Em ran off to Phinora and I have to find her."

That made the stallion hesitate. He swung his head around, one dark eye focused on Jack. <And Oby was with her?>

Jack nodded. "Yeah. You haven't seen them, have you?"

Emrys snorted. Before he had vanished from Fortitude, Emrys and Oberidon had been companions. <No, I have not. But I don't leave this place much.>

Just as well. The pegasus needed to keep a low profile for his own safety. Jack understood that. "Thanks anyway."

Emrys bobbed his head, walking over to a tree and leaning his rump against it, wiggling his hindquarters to scratch an itch. <I like Emmaline. I hope you find her.>

Jack turned away, heading to the enormous manor house behind Flora. He was accustomed to the disgustingly elaborate homes of the wealthy from his time as a theurgist and had no need to gawk at the sights. Flora called for a housekeeper to prepare a guest room, then took him into a parlor where a young woman brought in refreshments.

Jack eyed Flora. "I thought you worked for Cole, but this is Wells's home. Doesn't that cause problems?"

"Jefferson doesn't have a residence in Izhadell, so he stays with his *cousin* Malcolm," Flora clarified, testy. "It's perfectly reasonable for me to be here."

They enjoyed some refreshments in silence, waiting for Jefferson Cole or Malcolm Wells or whoever to make an appearance. Jack figured that had to be damned annoying, not knowing who to expect. At least the food was excellent.

A short time later, a staffer slipped into the parlor and murmured something in Flora's ear. The half-knocker looked alarmed, hopping out of her chair in a rush to the door. Before Jack could ask what the matter was, the door opened, and Malcolm Wells staggered in.

The first thing Jack noticed was the eerie brightness in his eyes —not the keen look he would have expected, but the glassy expression that often accompanied fever. His hair was damp and matted, too. Malcolm looked around the room, as if he was having a hard time focusing.

"Malcolm!" Flora snapped at him, grabbing his arm. "You don't look well. You need—"

"I need to talk to Jack." Malcolm's unfocused gaze finally found him. "Emrys told me he had come at last." His voice quivered, proof that he was unwell, but it held an edge of manic hope.

"Talk when you feel better." Flora's tone had a veneer of desperation. Jack narrowed his eyes. She was hiding something. What was it with this cursed politician and his penchant for concealing things?

Malcolm glanced in her direction, shaking his head. "My chair, Flora." He lurched over to an armchair, shivering all the while. He sank into it, his breath shallow. Flora stood nearby, furious, but apparently unwilling to go against his wishes. The Doyen opened his mouth to speak, but no words came. Instead, his head lolled to the side, and he went limp.

"Mal!" Flora cried, shaking his arm.

Jack sighed. It would be just his luck that Wells was going to die in front of him from a pox or something, before the man could be useful. "What in Faedra's name is wrong with him?"

Flora gritted her teeth. "That's not for me to say." She rubbed the side of her face, looking much older than she was, though Jack didn't rightly know how old that was. "When he's up to taking visitors, you can speak to him. But not until then."

Jack narrowed his eyes. He needed to get on Emmaline's trail. And figure out how to get Blaise out of that cursed Cit. "I don't have time to waste."

"And I'm out of patience for arguing with outlaws," Flora snarled. "You're a guest here for now, but not if you press your luck."

Jack crossed his arms, though she had a point. He aimed a finger at her. "I want to speak to him as soon as he's awake."

"You'll speak to him when I say you can." Flora turned her back on him, and that was that.

CHAPTER EIGHT

Dodgeball

Blaise

*T*he stone wall of the cell was cool against Blaise's cheek. He sat on the rough stone bench, leaning against the wall with his eyes half-lidded. He was always tired, always hungry. His captors in the Golden Citadel did the bare minimum to ensure his continued existence, and little beyond that.

A tear trailed down his cheek, forging a path through the grime on his face. Blaise couldn't remember the last time he had felt clean. It probably aligned with the last time he hadn't been scared. Or hadn't felt hopeless. He scrubbed away the tear with the back of his hand, wincing as the movement aggravated the blisters on his wrist. His only solace was that within the cell, his captors removed the salt-iron shackles. There was no need when the walls surrounding him were reinforced with the metal. His proximity to the salt-iron caused a chronic throbbing at the base of his skull and soured his stomach so that even the limited food they offered him didn't sit well.

He missed his life. He missed Emrys and would have given

anything in that moment to fly away on the stallion's back. Blaise missed his friends in Itude. He missed his family. And, gods help him, because it was such a *complicated* thing, but he missed Jefferson, even though he had visited recently. Magic rose as his anguish grew, and Blaise curled his fists at his side.

The harsh scrape of metal and wood announced he wasn't going to be alone much longer. He jerked upright, pulse racing. A silhouette darkened the doorway, and a deep laugh greeted him.

Oh no. Blaise had no love for this guard. None of the men and women who staffed the Cit were kind to him, but Heathcliff took it to another level. He fancied himself a mage-trainer, coaxing his charges to learn new tricks with their power. His practices were anything but gentle.

"Breaker, time to put you through your paces."

Blaise huffed out an unhappy breath, his eyes flicking to the damaged walls of his cell. Between a strange potion the guards plied him with and his constant state of unease, his control had become erratic, and cracks lined the walls, proof that he was just as dangerous as everyone said. He didn't want to go with this man, but by the same token it wasn't something he could avoid.

Slowly, his muscles complaining at the effort, he rose from the bench. He shuffled into the corridor, wincing at the bright mage-lights that lined its length. Heathcliff led him to the recreation yard, a salt-iron enclosed dirt lot that other imprisoned mages were allowed to use to stretch their legs and take in fresh air, enjoying a few moments of relief. Blaise wasn't afforded such liberties.

"Stand in the middle," Heathcliff directed.

Blaise licked his lips nervously, noticing the guard stood beside a ramshackle pile of stones and broken bricks. He moved to obey, his empty stomach lurching as Heathcliff picked up one of the stones, tossing it from one hand to the other.

"You familiar with dodgeball, Breaker?"

Blaise's mouth went dry, panic rising. He knew the childhood game. Had even played it a few times before he had been shunned for his magic. It was a game he'd never been good at, much too graceless and clumsy.

Heathcliff leered. "I see you are." He glanced at the smooth stone in his hand. "We're going to do something similar, except if this rock hits you, you'd better break it." He narrowed his eyes. "Or it's going to *hurt*."

And then without so much as a warning, Heathcliff began to hurl the stones and chunks of brick at him. Blaise avoided the first few, but then one struck his leg, forcing him to his knees. He couldn't rise, not with the guard throwing more at him, all the while screaming at him to get up.

I'm going to die here. Hopelessness warred with panic for a few heartbeats but was quickly replaced by growing fury. Anger because he didn't deserve this. No one deserved this, no matter what they had done. *This is not going to be my end.*

A nub of brick grazed his cheek. Blaise yelped, raising a hand to probe the fresh wound. Blood slicked his fingers, but Heathcliff didn't offer him even a moment of peace to recover. Another brick flew, this one striking his shoulder.

His magic boiled, as angry as a disturbed hive of bees, demanding to be used. Blaise didn't understand what Heathcliff expected of him. He missed Vixen's lessons and the way she had always helped him figure out what to do. This...this was brutality disguised as education.

A flat, grey stone whistled toward him. Blaise saw it coming, and time seemed to slow, his world narrowing to only him and impending injury. It was going to hit his face, and it was going to *hurt*.

Blaise threw up a hand as a shield, preferring to break his fingers than lose an eye. He felt the itch of his magic swarming across his palm, coating his skin. His mind jogged backwards, to a time when he had been surrounded by people who had believed in him. Vixen, and her unrelenting assurance that he could do anything with his magic. Emrys, with his steady faith in his rider. And Jefferson, so certain that Blaise was all that had stood between the Confederation and the lives of thousands in the Untamed Territory.

Sweat beaded his brow. A prisoner he may be, but he didn't have to be a *victim*. Blaise gathered his magic, concentrating it in his raised hand. He didn't stop there, pushing it out. Other mages could build constructs with their magic—after all, that was what the cage of a Trapper was. Within the confines of the Cit, he'd had ample time to think about that. Blaise grunted with the exertion of forcing his magic out into a brief, shimmering shield reminiscent of a soap bubble. Then he closed his eyes, fearing the worst.

The stone never struck his flesh. He heard something that reminded him of the sound of gravel being smashed beneath strong hooves. He flinched, still expecting imminent impact.

Heathcliff whistled, followed by a colorful curse. Blaise uncurled from his defensive position, breathing a sigh of relief that the guard had eased his assault. Heathcliff's dark eyes gleamed with malevolent pride. "You did it, Breaker. I didn't think you would, but you *actually* did it. I might be able to forge you into a weapon after all."

Blaise swallowed, following the guard's gaze. A fine spray of gravel littered the ground nearby. No, not gravel, he realized. It was all that remained of the stone Heathcliff had hurled at him. His magical shield had worked.

CHAPTER NINE
Honor, of a Sort

Malcolm

$\mathcal{M}$alcolm huddled in a chair by the fire, a thick blanket covering his lap and a cup of warm tea with honey close at hand. Marta, his cook, checked on him frequently, a frown creasing her face. Flora came and went, and once Malcolm tried to ask her about the dream where a man with Wildfire Jack's voice stood in the parlor. She told him to go to sleep.

He didn't know what illness gripped him, but he awoke with a fever and chills. Marta insisted on going for a skilled Healer, but Malcolm put his foot down. He feared a Healer would discover the tattoo, and then it would all have been for nothing. He didn't even allow his own staff Healer, Agnes, to check on him because out of all his staff, only Flora knew what he'd done. He couldn't trust anyone else with the dangerous choice he'd made.

So he sat in his chair, shivering and going through the mail that he hadn't attended to yet. He hoped Flora would return soon so he could ask what she knew about the effects of the tattoo.

Perhaps a mild illness was normal. He had entertained the idea of sending a query to Seward, but that would have been a little too bold.

Malcolm heard a commotion outside the door. It had to be Flora. He set aside the correspondence he had been reading, so tired it was hard to keep his eyes open. He had thought the tattoo would hurt after it was applied, but the sudden illness outweighed whatever discomfort he'd expected. *Stay awake.* Malcolm took a sip of tea, wishing Flora would hurry.

The door to his study opened, and Flora traipsed in, followed by someone taller. Malcolm blinked as the stranger took off their hat, revealing a vaguely familiar face.

"Wells," the stranger's deep voice growled. The hair color didn't match, but he would recognize Wildfire Jack's sixgun-serious tone anywhere.

"Jack?" Malcolm asked, blinking in confusion. "You look different."

"You're not the only one in this room who can change their looks," the outlaw pointed out.

"He demanded to see you," Flora said with a sigh.

"Been waiting two days to talk to you. You sleep more than a bear in winter."

Malcolm shivered. Two days? He was now certain that Jack had tried to speak to him before he had gone to sleep—no, not sleep. He looked to Flora. "What happened to me? Oh no. I missed the vote." Malcolm raised a trembling hand to scrub at his face, mindful of Blaise's fate.

She crossed her arms. "I don't think the vote matters worth a hill of beans right now."

Jack glanced between the pair of them, suspicious. "What did I walk into?"

Flora huffed, jerking a thumb at Malcolm. "I'll tell you to save him some breath. He got a geasa tattoo to bind him to Blaise."

Malcolm's eyes widened as she spoke the words. He was too slow and weak to ask her to call them back. Jack's expression frosted over, and he turned to Malcolm with cold, calculating eyes. As if he were deciding exactly how he wanted to kill the man before him.

"Now, why would you go and do a thing like that?" Jack's voice was as dangerous as the promise of distant thunder.

Flora realized her tactical error and had her knives in hand. "Don't you *dare* threaten him."

Their threats were exhausting. Malcolm wished he had just stayed asleep. But it was important that Jack understand why he had done it—because even with Flora's protection, Malcolm didn't think he stood much chance against Wildfire Jack if he were truly angry. "Let me explain. *Please.* Flora, put your blades away."

"I'll only put them away if he agrees to not murder you."

Jack and Flora glared at one another.

Malcolm sighed. "I did it out of love, Jack."

Those words shook the outlaw, and he broke the staring contest to round on Malcolm instead. "Don't make excuses about *love* when you chose the route that bends someone to *your* will. To manipulate them."

Malcolm glanced down at his hands, fumbling with them beneath the blanket. "What else could I do? You wouldn't come or answer my letters. And I…" He bit his bottom lip, uncertain how to explain the sickening conclusion he had reached. Maybe it *was* greedy and manipulative to bind Blaise to him so no one else could have him. "I didn't see another way."

"There has to be another way." Jack's voice dripped with loathing. Of those in the room, Jack knew the most about the subject.

"That ship has sailed," Flora said. "Can't undo what he's done."

The outlaw looked Malcolm up and down. "I know exactly how to undo it."

If Malcolm hadn't already been chilled, Jack's brutal assessment would have done it. He was too tired for this. "Did you come all this way to kill me? That seems out of character, even for you."

Jack tilted his head, eyes flinty. "No, but I'm not one to take options off the table."

He talked big, but Malcolm suspected Jack had come for a purpose. Other than Blaise, at that. Even though the outlaw owed the young man so much. He set that frustrating thought aside for the time being. "Why are you here?"

Jack's blue eyes settled on him, cold as ice. "I'm looking for my daughter."

That caught Flora's attention, too. "What? Was she taken?"

The outlaw shook his head. "No. She ran off."

Ran away, more like. Malcolm had only been around Emmaline a few times in the bakery, but he knew Blaise thought well of her. They had become friends, so much so that Blaise was determined to get her back when Lamar's force kidnapped her and the other mages. Despite that, something didn't add up...

"And why did you come to me?"

Jack's jaw tightened. "Because she found the letters you sent me, asking for help."

Ah. That made more sense. "I'm sorry, but we haven't seen her." Though, just to be sure, Malcolm glanced at Flora. It was something she would be aware of.

She shook her head. "I'll keep an ear out."

That took some of the wind out of Jack's sails. He seemed to deflate, as if he had been hoping they had concealed his daughter somewhere on the estate. "I'd appreciate that."

Well, at least he was back to being decent to Flora. *Progress.* "Yes, we'll do anything we can to help you find her."

That earned him a suspicious look. "Would you?"

Malcolm rubbed his cheek. "Whatever you may think of me, I don't wish you or your child ill."

Jack crossed his arms, a mixture of relief and annoyance washing across his face. Malcolm assumed the outlaw had bridled against coming to ask for help at the doorstep of a Doyen of the Salt-Iron Confederation. Jack shifted his weight from one foot to the other, but only offered a slight nod in response.

Malcolm picked up his tea and sipped it, appreciative of the relief it brought. "I doubt I can do much in my current state, but we will help you."

"Yeah, about your current state," the outlaw said, his sharp gaze assessing Malcolm as if he were a practice target. "I'd check into it fast, if I were you."

"Why is that?" Malcolm asked.

Jack gestured to him. "I'm no Healer nor doctor, but just from what I know of history, seems to me like you have the symptoms of Manifestation Illness."

What? "That can't be right." Malcolm traded looks with Flora. Manifestation Illness was the disease that had spawned the first mages two hundred years prior. *How would I have contracted that?*

She patted his hand. "I'll look into it, Mal. You're going to be fine."

Jack snorted, as if he didn't quite believe that. Malcolm opened his mouth to say something, but darkness swam before his eyes and claimed him.

Jack

FLORA CURSED AS WELLS LOST CONSCIOUSNESS, MOVING TO SHIFT him so he didn't fall out of the chair. She brushed the back of her hand against his forehead. "What makes you think it's Manifestation Illness?"

Jack glanced away. "Stories from when I was a theurgist."

The half-knocker gave him a cutting look. "Got any info you can give me? It's kind of important."

The outlaw shook his head. "I have no love for that man, but I won't feed you some old wives' tales. No, if I were you, I'd snoop around the source." When she made a *go on* gesture, he suggested, "Ask an alchemist."

Flora considered it, then nodded. "Not a bad idea. I'll do that tonight."

She halted their conversation, taking it upon herself to get the ill Doyen to his bed. Jack was rather impressed that she was ready to carry Wells there all by herself. It was a bit like watching an ant carry something ten times its size. The outlaw helped her with the burden once she got Malcolm into the hallway, figuring it would reflect rather poorly on him if he followed in the wake of the tiny woman carrying around a grown man.

Flora got Malcolm settled on his bed and then turned back to Jack. "And what are you gonna do?"

"Search for my daughter."

Flora frowned. "So, I know you have the whole disguise thing going on, but you're still a wanted man."

"Don't care. I can't stay here sitting on my thumbs. I have to *do* something." Truth be told, he cared. Jack was aware that he wasn't invulnerable, and his magic and savvy wouldn't always save him. But this was his *child*, and she was all that he had left in the world to prove he was worth a damn.

Flora glanced at her boss tucked beneath the covers. "Why didn't you answer his letters?"

Jack frowned at her swift change of topic. "What does that have to do with—?"

"Answer the question." Her voice was as sharp and commanding as the crack of a whip.

Few people could get away with talking to Jack like that. Flora was one of them. He had seen what she was capable of firsthand. And she was stressed and upset about someone she cared about. Jack could relate. "Coming to Izhadell is an invitation to the gallows for someone like me."

"You should have given him the courtesy of a reply," Flora retorted. "And to be frank, your answer is dragonshit. You're here *now*."

Jack snorted. "I'm the first to admit I'm a damn hypocrite. But I have good reason."

The half-knocker pointed an index finger up at him. "Blaise gave up everything for you. And then you didn't lift a finger to help him."

Jack bristled at that. He wanted to snarl at Flora that she didn't understand. How dare she judge him? But he couldn't because he felt exactly the same. His shoulders rose in agitation, and his eyes narrowed. "Again, what does *that* have to do with *this*?" He waved a hand at Malcolm's prone form.

"Mal thought he was the only one who cared about Blaise. And he's probably right." Flora leaned against the foot of the bed. "The Council has been debating what they're going to do to your *friend*."

"I know that," Jack growled. He had heard that much through his intelligence channels. Not a blamed thing he could do about it.

"*They* decided to bind him. It wasn't all Mal coming up with the idea on his own."

Jack stilled at that. He had tried not to think about what was happening to Blaise behind the walls of the Golden Citadel. The Breaker was at the tail-end of the age where they could—and would—bend a young mage to the will of the Confederation. He hissed out a breath, staving off old memories of the screams he had heard from the corridor that led to the cells of the older mages. Jack had been one of the lucky ones. He had been young when the Confederation molded him into a theurgist.

"So don't hold it against him. He really saw no other choice. It was this or allow Blaise to bow to a new master in a few days." Flora turned away, scrubbing a hand over her face. She offered Jack a sympathetic look as she changed the subject again. "I meant what I said. If I hear anything about your daughter, I'll let you know. Come back here tonight. I'm sure he'd want you to be welcome." She nodded her head toward Malcolm.

Jack wanted to snarl and deny the hospitality just because he liked to be contrary most of the time, and he didn't like Malcolm Wells and whatever game he was playing with Blaise. But by the same token, he couldn't afford to be choosy. Wells had as much to hide as he did, so perhaps it was an ideal place to go to ground. "Much obliged. There a good angle for a pegasus to come in from after dark? Some way that the griffin riders won't see?"

Flora pursed her lips, thoughtful. "The griffin riders have been out of Phinora for a couple months now. Ever since Fort Courage, they've been deployed to the borders."

"That so?" Jack murmured. It sounded right. They had seen griffin riders when they had gone through Argor but couldn't recall spotting any since. That was odd. "They change protocol on that?"

Flora shrugged. "I don't know. I heard there was trouble around the Gutter, so they might send more to keep tabs. Don't suppose you'd know anything about that?"

Ah-ha. Jack had seen no griffin riders around the mine, but the eastern Confederation border was massive, and the few pegasi sentries left in Fortitude had reported seeing them occasionally. It pleased him to know that the trouble he had caused the mining companies bore fruit.

"I wouldn't know a thing," he said with a wink.

Flora laughed because she liked to cause trouble as much as he did. "If you approach from the north and fly over the fence, you should be able to come in unseen. I'll even do you a favor and disarm the traps I have there."

Jack touched the brim of his hat. "Kind of you." Then he paused, his gaze back on the Doyen's prone form. "You believe him? About his reason for doin' it?"

Flora ran a hand through one side of her pink hair. "Yeah. I don't understand it, but he has a good heart."

The outlaw scrunched his nose. He wouldn't go that far, but if the gritty half-knocker thought the story had a grain of truth, it probably did. Jack crossed his arms, considering. "I could stick around a couple hours before I head out on my search. If you need someone to play nanny."

"He's a very sick man, not an infant."

"I said what I said. And you're gonna be gone, too, so the way I see it you won't mind him having some extra protection."

Flora frowned. "A few minutes ago, you were threatening to kill him. That doesn't scream *trustworthy* to me."

Jack shrugged. "Got a better option?"

She didn't, and they both knew it. "We just can't let word get out about what Mal did."

Jack smirked. As much as he'd love for word to get out to see the politician squirm, he knew it meant things would go south for Blaise, fast. "On my honor as an outlaw mage."

She quirked a brow. "You have honor?"

"Of a sort."

CHAPTER TEN

Bone to Bone, Flesh to Flesh

Jack

*J*ack hadn't been forthright about his reasoning to stay behind and watch over the sick man. Once Flora left, he made it his business to go through the contents of the bedroom—books atop the short bookcase near the door, a notebook temptingly left on the dresser, and all the drawers. To his disappointment, nothing of interest presented itself.

"You're no blasted choir boy," Jack muttered to Malcolm. The Doyen didn't so much as twitch an eyelid at his comment. If not for the gentle rise and fall of his chest, the outlaw would have thought him dead. His skin was as pale as porcelain, his face glistening with sweat.

It was going to be damned problematic if the two-faced Doyen up and died before he could use his resources to help Jack free Blaise. Because even though he had been careful not to mention it in the earlier conversation, that remained one of his goals. Jack was skilled, but this was the Golden Citadel he was going up against. He needed any advantage he could get.

He drummed his fingers against the wood of the dresser. "Hmm." Jack was no Healer, but his magic was more flexible than most. He thought back to the time Emmaline had kept him from Perdition's gates with her magic, a plan coming to mind. It was a modification to another spell he had cast before—a working to keep infection of a wound at bay until a Healer tended to it. The more Jack thought about it, the more it seemed worthwhile.

Jack left to grab the items he needed, sneaking back into the master bedroom with no one any the wiser since his guest room was down the hall. He twisted a rudimentary poppet together— not his best work, but an effigy didn't have to be pretty to be effective. Strands of hair clung to a brush on the dresser, but since Jack had no way to confirm it belonged to the Doyen, he went straight to the source and plucked three hairs from Malcolm's head. He enjoyed pulling the frustrating peacock's hair out. He was disappointed Wells didn't so much as stir.

After securing the hairs to the poppet, Jack tightened his hand around the tiny form and called on his magic to activate it. He felt the soft pulse of power as the connection formed between Wells and the doll. Jack pulled a chair up beside the bed and plopped down. His mentor at the Cit had excelled at using magic to impact the human body, though mostly for ill. But she had ingrained in him the law of opposites—just as a working could rot a man's gut, so too could it cleanse. Or at the very least, hold off the rot.

Too bad Emmaline wasn't here. She was a natural at it. Jack shook away the thought. He focused on crafting the words for the charm. The outlaw preferred spells that didn't require chanting or reagents, but sometimes it was necessary. For a charm like this, the words held as much power as his intention. He was no poet or bard, but at least no one was around to judge his performance.

Jack cradled the figure in his hands. "Bone to bone, flesh to flesh. Blood to blood, marrow to marrow. Faedra, walk this one away from Perdition's gate."

The poppet looked the same as it had, though Jack's magical sense assured him that something was happening. If someone had asked him to explain, he wouldn't be able to. It was like the pressure in the air before a rainstorm, a rising tide of power. Jack tucked the poppet into his coat. Flora would probably lose her mind with rage if she found out he could hex her boss. Jack figured it was solid insurance to have on his side.

With the spell complete, the outlaw was restless. Since the manipulative peacock seemed stable, he decided the best recipe was to walk around the grounds, so Jack headed out to the barn. Zepheus grazed beside Emrys in the paddock. They raised their heads at his approach, and Emrys broke away first, approaching him with ground-eating strides. He pulled up short, just in front of the outlaw, tossing his head.

<What's wrong with Jefferson? Something is wrong.> The stallion's mental tone was ripe with worry, his eyes white-rimmed.

The stallion's use of the alter ego's name made Jack blink. It was odd for a pegasus to be concerned for anyone besides their rider. Zepheus had a soft spot for Emmaline, and that itself was unusual. "He's sick."

Emrys pranced in place, unsettled. <I've seen sick humans. I have brushed against their minds. Something is *wrong*.>

Jack squinted at the black pegasus, then turned to look at Zepheus as the palomino plodded over. "Zeph?"

<I don't know the man's mind enough to weigh in. But Emrys has been here for several weeks, and while Wells is not his rider, they have formed an alliance.> Zepheus said all of this privately to Jack, so that Emrys wouldn't catch his mental advice.

An alliance. Jack bet Emrys didn't know about the stunt the politician had pulled. And as Blaise's pegasus, he had a right to know. He laid a hand on Emrys's neck, which might invite snapping teeth if he wasn't careful. But the stallion was out of sorts, seeking comfort, and didn't fight it. "There's something you need to know." Jack explained the politician's ploy.

When he finished, Emrys flicked his ears, as if processing the information. Finally, he bobbed his great head, reaching a conclusion. <I approve.>

Of all the things Jack thought the stallion would say or do, that wasn't it. "*What?*"

<I understand what he's doing and why.>

Jack scratched his head because he sure didn't. All he saw was greed and abuse of power. "How do you see it?"

Zepheus traded a knowing look with Emrys, bobbing his head as if he had drawn the same conclusion.

<You see it as something like the relationship between a spirit-broken nag and an unkind master. But it is not that. No, he is approaching it like a pegasus and rider. A partnership.> Emrys sounded certain.

Jack frowned, not agreeing with any of that. "But Blaise is being exploited. He doesn't have a say."

Emrys shook his ample mane. <You're wrong. He already made a choice in his heart.>

For the Breaker's sake, Jack hoped Emrys was right. But that wasn't something to worry about, not now. He had done his due diligence. The outlaw turned to Zepheus. "Be ready. As soon as Flora gets back, we're going to start the search for Em."

CHAPTER ELEVEN

Just a Dream

Jefferson

efferson was no stranger to this dream.

The sun warmed his back as he stood on the outskirts of Fortitude. Or perhaps it was Itude, before the assault. The small town that stretched before him looked as empty as a ghost town, but curiously, the buildings appeared whole, which shouldn't have been the case. He strolled up the street, enjoying the brisk air.

Every building was just as he remembered it from his last visit, their façades unscarred by fire and battle. The Broken Horn Saloon stood on one side of the town square, welcoming anyone in need of a drink. The Jitterbug Diner sat beside the cheerful yellow bakery. Jefferson's breath caught at the sight of the bakery.

He walked up the street to the building, his strides long and purposeful. The bakery drew him like a magnet, his first connection to Blaise. Jefferson knew that if he walked into the bakery, he would find the young mage, and at least in his dreams, everything in their world would be *right*.

Jefferson trotted up the steps and tugged open the door. The hinges creaked, announcing his arrival. As expected, Blaise stood in the middle of the bakery, but something was off. Legs braced, arms curled into a protective stance as he glanced around with uncertainty. Blaise was never uncertain in the bakery. It was his domain, one of the few places he seemed sure of himself. This wasn't how Jefferson's dream went at all. "Blaise?"

The Breaker turned at his voice, but otherwise seemed rooted in place. "I was in a nightmare..." He swallowed as his words trailed off, and the fear in his eyes made Jefferson want to rush over, but he knew that would be the wrong move. As hard as it was, he waited at the threshold while Blaise gathered his thoughts. "I can't sleep. And when I *do* sleep, it's always the same nightmare. It's never..." He shook his head and sank down to his knees, as if the effort to finish the sentence was overwhelming.

Jefferson stared at him. This Blaise before him wasn't the one who usually existed in his dreams. This one had the hard edge of panic so prevalent in Jefferson's recent visits with the younger man. Had that bled into Jefferson's subconscious and become a part of his dreams? Or was something else going on here?

Blaise had never spoken to him about a lack of sleep—or anything else about the treatment he received. Jefferson leaned against the door-frame, thinking. What had he been doing before he fell asleep? Wait. He hadn't gone to sleep. He'd been talking to Jack and Flora.

What is going on? Jefferson swallowed. He recalled he had been ill but determined to speak with the outlaw. And then he remembered darkness overtaking him.

"Jefferson?" Blaise's voice was little more than a whisper.

"Sorry," Jefferson murmured. "I'm here."

"You're never in my nightmares." Blaise looked up at him, trembling.

But you're always in my dreams. Jefferson nodded. "This isn't a nightmare." At least he hoped it wasn't. He didn't know what it was or what was going on. "Mind if I come in?"

"I can't stop you."

Jefferson's stomach sank at Blaise's words. It seemed impossible, but he was becoming more certain by the moment that the real Blaise had bled into his dream. He took a step closer. "I'm not like that. I won't ever force anything with you." *Liar. You're bound to him with a*—oh no, *is that what's doing this?*

Ignorant of Jefferson's thoughts, Blaise blinked at him. "You can come in." He rose from the floor, reaching up to grab the counter to get to his feet, as if he didn't have the strength to do it otherwise.

As the Breaker rose, Jefferson got a better look at his condition. He was almost skeletal, arms spindly and cheeks sunken. Jefferson came closer and saw a crescent-shaped gash on the mage's cheek, surrounded by bruising. "Who did this to you?"

Blaise seemed to shrink into himself. "You can't do anything about it."

"I *am* doing something about it," Jefferson retorted with such ferocity that Blaise took a step back. He swallowed, lowering his voice. "I am."

The mage narrowed his eyes, suspicious. "Wait." Blaise closed the distance between them, surprising Jefferson by putting a hand on his arm, just below the fresh tattoo. The Breaker's fingers were like ice, just as they had been at their last visit. Jefferson felt the too-real tingle of magic against his skin. "What is this?"

"It's me."

Blaise stared at him, tears welling in the corners of his blue eyes. "I don't understand."

"I don't either. Not yet," Jefferson admitted. He would have to tell Blaise about the tattoo later. But not until he had figured out what was going on with this. "But it's *me*. Really."

"And we're in Itude?" Blaise glanced out the window, brow crinkling in confusion. "But the town…"

He didn't finish, but Jefferson knew. The last time Blaise had seen it, the town had been in ruins. "Fortitude. Your friends renamed it Fortitude after the battle." Jefferson licked his lips, uncertain. "I think it's just a dream, though."

Blaise's shoulders drooped. "Is it sad that I wish it were real?"

"No, not at all," Jefferson said. "You were happy here." Maybe it was the first place Blaise had been truly happy before everything had gone wrong.

Blaise nodded. "I was." Then his expression hardened.

"What's wrong?"

"I don't get to be that anymore. Happy."

Jefferson shook his head. "That's untrue. It may be a dream, but we're in *your* bakery. You can be happy here."

Blaise worried at his bottom lip. "It's just a dream. It doesn't help anything."

"I disagree. You spoke of nightmares. I think a pleasant dream is what you need." Jefferson gestured around them. "Tell me, if you could do anything right now in this dream, what would you do?"

The Breaker stared at him, then the corners of his mouth curled into the slightest of smiles. "You know what I would do."

Yes, Jefferson did. It was a relief to see any cheer on Blaise's face. Although it wouldn't have been Jefferson's choice of activities, he knew exactly what would bring Blaise the happiness he deserved. "I suppose I'm in the mood for dessert. So, tell me, cake or cookies?"

Blaise pulled out a set of mixing bowls, and the joy that replaced his earlier fear was all the reward Jefferson needed. "Why not both?"

"Both is good," Jefferson agreed. "I'll get the flour and you can tell me how to help."

As far as fever dreams went, it wasn't what Jefferson had expected. But he didn't mind it. Not one bit. And for the record, Blaise's dream cookies were every bit as good as the real thing.

Flora

MALCOLM WAS A ONE-TRACK-MINDED IDIOT SOMETIMES. FLORA sighed as she skulked to the perimeter of the Arboretum. She considered the barbed wire lining the fence again. The half-knocker had never given much thought to the alchemists before and hadn't cared to learn about them. She knew they brewed some wicked potions besides those she found helpful in her line of work.

But now, she realized their plight was the same as the theurgists. If Malcolm found out, he would be furious and would no doubt plot ways to improve their conditions, as well.

She snorted at that. He had a good heart but was always busy thinking of things from a political angle. The problem was, he hadn't learned yet that he *couldn't* save the world. But he sure was going to try. Flora decided to keep the knowledge of the alchemists to herself, at least for now.

While they had designed the perimeter to keep the curious out, Flora wasn't most people. She had enough knocker blood in her to make it a non-issue. Flora sidled up against the wall, then closed her eyes as she concentrated on finding her attuned metal. Like full-blooded knockers who had an affinity for specific metals or precious stones, Flora could always locate hers. Then it was simply a matter of locking on and using her magic to pull herself to it. Malcolm was aware of her ability, but he didn't know what her metal was. No one did, and that was how Flora liked it.

If anyone learned salt-iron was her metal, she would be eyeball-deep in trouble. The Confederation would want to use her, as surely as they used the mages. Her fellow knockers would hate her because like all magical creatures, they despised the stuff. Flora didn't understand why she not only tolerated it but could *locate* it. Probably thanks to her human mother. But it was a dangerous ability to be graced with.

The Arboretum had little salt-iron, unlike the Golden Citadel. She got in and out of there easily and had done so many times.

Hadn't told Malcolm about that either, but she liked Blaise and had checked on him. She felt sorry for the Breaker. No one deserved what he was going through. Flora thought Malcolm was out of his mind to be so obsessed with the younger man, but she would go along with his insane plans because Blaise deserved happiness and freedom. Not abuse.

There. It took some concentration, but she finally homed in on the bit of salt-iron within the Arboretum. Flora focused on it and hopped into the air, her magic activating with the movement. There was a moment of disorientation as the world grew dark and then brightened, and then Flora found herself by her target. And she wasn't alone this time.

The other person in the room threw something at Flora, a glass vial that smashed to bits at her feet. The contents hissed against the floor, rising in a thin veil of orange mist. Flora held her breath, something that she could do for a very long time thanks to her knocker heritage. But whatever the potion was didn't need to be inhaled. She felt her motions slowing even as she tried to go for her blades. *Oh schist!*

"Who are *you?*" the woman demanded, her voice equal parts afraid and angry. Maybe closer to angry, Flora reflected.

Actions spoke louder than words, though. The half-knocker dropped into a crouch—*slowly*, painfully slowly. Under the sway of whatever that concoction was, her natural speed had been banished. A herd of turtles could probably move faster than her now.

Flora didn't like losing the upper hand. At long last, her fingers tightened around the hilt of her knives, and she brought them out, though the woman didn't seem the least bit impressed. With the speed Flora was moving, all she had to do was take a step to the left to easily avoid any threat.

This is the worst. Flora glowered at the woman.

"Let me ask you again," the alchemist hissed. "Who are you?"

Flora cocked her head, assessing the situation. If not for that annoying bit of alchemy, she would have found a way to remove the woman from the equation. But that wasn't a possibility until the potion wore off or she was given a counter. She was in one dill of a pickle.

Sometimes she had to cut her losses. Fighting wasn't going to do her any favors here. "Name's Flora. I'd offer you my hand, but it would take five minutes to shake." She was glad the potion didn't seem to have an impact on her mouth, aside from a strange dryness that attacked her tongue. "And you are?"

"Wondering what you're doing in the Arboretum," the woman replied, hands on her hips. "Especially here." She gestured to the charred interior of the building where they stood.

To be fair, Flora had the same questions for the alchemist. Or at least, why was she in the burned-out building? Flora had thought it might be a safe place to appear, but clearly, that wasn't the case. "I'm here on business." It wasn't a lie. Not fully, anyway.

The woman raised her brows, skeptical. "I'm sure the gate guards appreciate you popping on by them."

Maybe it was a threat, but the flippant way the alchemist said the words made Flora think otherwise. "Oh, you know, I'm just making life easier on them."

"I'll bet you are," the alchemist replied. She reached into a hip bag, pulling out a blue vial. "I have the antidote for that potion, so long as you don't intend to gut me."

"I'll behave," Flora promised. "You can't blame me for taking offense when you throw a potion at me."

"I stand by what I did," the woman said, uncorking the blue vial and sprinkling the contents over Flora. Whatever it was, it dried almost the instant it touched her rough skin. But it did the job, breaking her free from the effects of the first potion. Flora wiggled her fingers with greater appreciation as the alchemist asked, "Something I can help you with?"

"Actually, yes." Flora wasn't one to look a gift horse in the mouth—or gift alchemist. "You know anything about the Ink used for the geasa?"

The alchemist went still. "What about it?" Then she narrowed

EFFIGEST 93

her eyes, suspicious. "Wait. One of our Inkwells is missing. A very specific one." Something dangerous flickered in her eyes. "Would you know anything about that?"

So they had discovered Flora's theft. Not surprising. Flora widened her eyes, affecting a look of innocence. "Oh, that's awful. Who would do something like that?"

"Who, indeed?" the alchemist murmured. She paced the length of the room, pausing by one of the charred stone walls. "I'll answer your question if you do something for me."

Lovely. Flora didn't want it to come down to barter, but sometimes that was how life worked. "I won't kill anyone." No, she only did that for Malcolm. And even he didn't know about it most of the time.

The alchemist shook her head. "Nothing like that, I hope." Her expression turned hungry. "It's my family. They've kept me apart from them. I haven't heard..." She swallowed. "I need to know if they're okay. And you seem to be uniquely skilled to discover that."

Well, she was right about that. "I'll try. Who am I looking for?"

The woman hesitated, walking to the door and peering out. When she was satisfied, she turned back to Flora. "Daniel Hawthorne and my children, Lucienne and Brody."

Flora blinked. Hawthorne? It couldn't be a coincidence. She knew for a fact Blaise's mother was an alchemist... "Wait. Are you Marian Hawthorne?"

The alchemist tensed. "And if I am?"

Flora wasn't sure if she should squeal with glee at her good fortune or curse. Marian hadn't mentioned a thing about Blaise, and Flora wasn't sure what that meant for the situation. "I know your son."

Marian's face registered confusion. "Brody?"

"Blaise."

The alchemist took a step forward, her hands balled into fists. "Are *you* among those responsible for what's happened to him?"

Flora's eyes flicked as a new vial appeared in the alchemist's palm, lifting her hands in a gesture of placation. "*No*. No, I'm a friend."

Marian's chin jutted upward, the muscles in her neck taut. "How can I trust that?"

Well, it was now or never. "Because I work for someone who wants to free him."

The other woman crossed her arms. "That's imposs—wait, is this why you're asking about the Ink? *You* took it, didn't you?"

"I will neither confirm nor deny that accusation," Flora replied. "But the reason I'm asking is because of Blaise."

Marian licked her lips. "Ask."

"If someone were to hypothetically find themselves tattooed with an untested Ink, what are the side effects? What sort of reaction would you expect? Hypothetical reactions, of course." Flora cleared her throat, glancing away.

Marian almost dropped the vial in surprise. She tucked it back into the hip bag. "Side effects depend on the person and the mage. As far as reactions, since it's made from the blood of the mage being bound, it has trace amounts of the original Manifestation virus. In most cases, it's so small it has no impact on the handler. But *this* is not like most cases." Her face hardened.

Flora crossed her arms. "And why is that?"

The alchemist shut her eyes briefly, as if staving off a bad memory. "I told them they shouldn't try to bind him, but no one would listen to me. Because I'm only an *alchemist*." She nearly snarled the last word in her frustration. Flora understood—as far as she was concerned, alchemists were brilliant creatives. But alchemists were similar to mages in that those higher in the Confederation government didn't heed them. "I told them it was dangerous, but they're more focused on turning him into a weapon."

Flora nodded, trying to appear sympathetic despite not understanding. And she very much wanted to understand so that she could help Malcolm. "What makes it so dangerous?"

Marian's eyes settled on her; the corners crinkled with regret.

"I shouldn't tell you. I need to share this information directly with whoever was misguided enough to bind to my son."

The half-knocker narrowed her eyes. "Wait. You can leave this place?"

The alchemist raised her brows. "You seem like the resourceful sort who could get me out."

Flora sighed. *Humans.* Sometimes they really were so annoying, but Marian's faith was also flattering. "I probably could. Would you be able to help, though? He's very sick."

Marian's mouth puckered with thought. "There's a potion I can make. I used it once before when...well, I'll get into that later. I'll trade the potion for my family's safety."

"Hey," Flora protested, "I'm already helping Blaise *and* getting you information about your family!"

"You're helping *your* friend, which, in turn, helps Blaise," Marian corrected.

Flora made a face. "Fine. Yes. I'll bring back information about your family tomorrow. And figure out a way to get them somewhere safe."

Marian smiled. "Then we have a deal."

CHAPTER TWELVE

Shut Your Piehole and Accept the Praise

Jack

Once Flora came back from her errand, Jack and Zepheus made a foray into Izhadell but came across no fruitful leads, forcing them to retire to the Wells estate again for the night. When Jack returned, he discovered the Doyen had awoken and was asking for him.

That was a good sign, and Jack pushed his way into the master bedroom at the insistence of a staffer. Malcolm was still abed, but he was more upright with a bevy of pillows at his back. He sipped something from a mug—soup, judging by the salty tang that filled the air.

"You're still this side of Perdition," Jack rumbled, leaning against the threshold.

Malcolm nodded, and he set the mug down on the bedside table. "Fortunately, yes."

The outlaw studied him. The man's skin was still too pale, and he shivered, but at least he was conscious. "What do you want?"

The Doyen chuckled. "Getting to the heart of the matter, I see."

"I'm a straight shooter," Jack agreed with a smirk. *In more ways than one.*

Malcolm nodded, and his normally handsome visage seemed more haggard than before. "You, ah...have more knowledge of theurgists and handlers than anyone else I can speak to right now. Would you mind if I asked you about that?"

Jack tensed. As a matter of fact, he minded. It was something he didn't like to think or talk about. And it still pissed him off that this man had the gall to do that to Blaise. Even if it was a way to help him, there was no way the Breaker would have agreed to it. But Jack knew the way to free a mage from a handler. All he needed was for Wells to help him get Blaise out...and how unfortunate if something happened to the Doyen after that. He patted a hand against his pocket to assure himself the poppet was still there.

"Please. I think it's important," Wells added in a whisper.

"I do enjoy hearing you beg," Jack drawled. "What's your question?"

"When you had a handler, what was the connection like?"

Jack frowned. Damn this man. He really was going to scratch Jack's old wounds like that. Maybe this would help him understand why what he had done was a violation, though. "You ever seen the way they break a unicorn?"

Malcolm looked puzzled but shook his head. "No. What does that have to do with this?"

"Everything," Jack snapped. "They force a salt-iron bit in its mouth, which blisters and burns their tender gums. The beast has no choice but to submit to ease the pain. That's their version of *this.*" He shoved up his sleeve to display his old, dead tattoo. "A handler is like the unicorn's Tracker, imposing their will onto someone who can't do a damn thing against it."

Malcolm swallowed. "But it doesn't have to be like that."

"Doesn't it?" Jack asked. That ran counter to his experience.

"I'm asking because..." The Doyen sighed, seeming at a loss for how to explain himself. "Did you ever have dreams about your handler?"

Jack brayed a laugh. "That's the most gods-damned ridiculous thing I've ever heard. Sleep was my *escape* from that—" He cut himself off. For one thing, Reynolds had never come down with any illness when they were first bound. And for another, Wells regarded Blaise differently. There was a very real, if slim, possibility that something was afoot. "What are you saying? And this better not just be about you being hornier than a dragon."

The Doyen felt well enough to raise an eyebrow but didn't comment. "What I'm saying is that when I was asleep or unconscious—I honestly don't know which—I had a dream and Blaise was in it."

Jack shrugged. "So?" After all, it was no secret Wells was obsessed.

"That's not the unusual bit. I've dreamed about Blaise before, and he behaves a certain way in those dreams." He glanced away, leaving the gist of such dreams to Jack's imagination. The outlaw curled his lip. "This was more like the *real* Blaise. I mean, the one I've visited in the Cit." Malcolm rubbed his face. "Scared and damaged."

Jack narrowed his eyes. Yeah, he knew Blaise wouldn't get on well in the Golden Citadel. No one would, but especially not someone as fragile as him. "Let me make sure I follow. You think you had a dream, or perhaps a hallucination, with the *real* Blaise in it?"

"I would argue it can't be a hallucination if Blaise was real."

Jack waved a hand. "Whatever." He frowned. "Human minds are blamed good at fooling us, Wells. And you've been sicker than a three-legged dog."

"So, you don't think it's…"

"What?" Jack gave him a sharp-eyed look.

"Magic?"

The outlaw snorted. "Never have I ever heard of any sort of magic with dreams. Nah. Fever's been addling your brain. Probably just means you need more rest." He pointed a finger at him. "Which you should get now."

Jack headed to the door, shutting it behind him. He'd seen a lot of mages in his day, but this? Dream magic? He snorted. *Yeah, and a chupacabra's my uncle.*

THE NEXT AFTERNOON, JACK AND ZEPHEUS PROWLED THE STREETS around the Golden Citadel once again. The number of buildings that had sprouted up outside the Cit's walls was surprising. During Jack's time as a theurgist, the area surrounding the extensive complex had been open land. Time changed all things, he mused.

The first spot of luck happened when Zepheus caught a brief whiff of a familiar scent. According to the palomino, pegasi had a different scent bouquet than the average horse, though human senses weren't refined enough to process it. The stallion turned off the busy street and down a quieter avenue, finally drawing to a stop outside a saloon.

<Oby's around here somewhere,> Zepheus said, flicking his ears. <You want to go put your ear to the ground while I stay out here and see what I can discover?>

"May as well," Jack murmured to the pegasus, patting his shoulder. He made a show of loosely tying Zepheus to the hitching post outside the saloon. Jack always made certain that, if necessary, the stallion could free himself. It had benefited him countless times before.

The outlaw sauntered inside, listening to the familiar sounds of a saloon busy with the evening rush. A group in one corner sang bawdy songs off-key, much to the chagrin of the pianist. Billiard balls clacked against each other, though raucous laughter from a nearby table quickly drowned out the sound. Jack took it all in as he claimed a stool at the bar. This place, he understood. The rest of Izhadell, not so much.

The bartender took his drink order, and while Jack drank, he listened in to the surrounding conversations. He monitored the door, and before long, he saw a familiar face slip in and snag a table in the corner.

Jack fought the impulse to stalk over to Emmaline, grab her by the arm, and haul her out of there. She was his daughter—she would fight him if he did that. And he didn't want to draw undue attention to himself. Instead, he stayed where he was and watched her, wondering what she was up to. Was she meeting someone? That's what he would be doing in her shoes.

But time passed, and no one came. She nursed a drink and half-heartedly ate. Jack paid his tab and slowly rose from his stool, turning and ambling over to her table. Emmaline saw him coming and her eyes widened, but that lasted only a heartbeat as a sullen expression crossed her face, and she hunched over as he took a seat opposite her.

"You shouldn't be here," she said after a moment, her voice tight.

"No place else I should be," Jack replied, doing his best to keep his tone even. "Why'd you run off?"

Emmaline lifted her head, eyes alight with challenge. "You wouldn't understand."

Jack leaned forward. "Try me."

"You just want to drag me back to the Gutter. You want..." Emmaline shook her head as she trailed off.

Heavy footsteps clopped nearby. Jack glanced over his shoulder and saw the bartender looming close. "This man bothering you?"

Jack bristled, his right palm brushing against the holster at his side. Emmaline lifted a hand, and whether it was to quell him or her prospective rescuer, he couldn't say. "I'm fine." She shot a look from Jack to the bartender, and after a moment, the bartender drifted off, though he gave the outlaw a menacing glare for his trouble.

"How do you know what I want?" Jack asked once they were

alone. "You've hardly said two words to me for the past few months."

"Your actions say plenty," Emmaline fired back. "Always watching me. Not wanting me to do this or that."

He frowned. "Of course I'm going to protect you after…" After he had failed her. He had failed his entire town.

"I can take care of myself, thank you very much." Emmaline said it with all the bravado of a sixteen-year-old. And maybe, just maybe, she was right. She was the product of an outlaw town. She had survived things that the townies of Izhadell could only imagine. But here she sat, in the middle of Izhadell, a maverick mage. And that was dangerous.

"You may think so, but you know shit about the pisspot of scumbaggery you're in right now," Jack retorted. "We should leave."

<Jack?> Zepheus tried to interrupt.

"*You* should leave, yes," Emmaline corrected, crossing her arms. "It's not safe for you here."

<Jack, I *really* need you to stop talking and listen.>

Jack narrowed his eyes. "You're coming with me. You came here to free Blaise—"

"What?" she snapped, scowling. "That's not the only reason I came."

<You need to *get out* of there. Lamar is coming!>

That got Jack's attention. "What?" The question came out as a growl, and Emmaline no doubt thought he was addressing her. He turned to glance at the door, and he and his daughter cursed in unison as tow-headed Lamar Gaitwood stepped inside.

Half of the lanterns in the saloon's interior were out, which meant that his nemesis wouldn't spot him immediately. Jack weighed his options. As much as he'd like to see Lamar dead, this wasn't the ideal place. Too many witnesses. And too deep in hostile territory. And Emmaline in the line of fire, though Jack had faith she could handle herself. But he didn't want to take the risk, and any ballsy move he made would endanger her, too.

"Lamar," Jack hissed at her. "I'm not here."

Her eyebrows rose in question at his statement, but he didn't have time to explain. Jack already had his poppet out, preparing his spell. Obfuscation was a tricky working. Anyone who knew where he started from would still see him. But anyone who didn't —for example, a Saltie asshole like Lamar—would have to physically run into Jack to find him. Unless he had a unicorn with him, in which case all bets were off. But Zepheus had made no mention of unicorns.

He felt the frisson of magic as it fell into place over him like a mantle. That done, he rose from the table. He had no desire to be caught in close quarters. Jack edged along the perimeter, careful to keep clear of anyone who might inadvertently run into him as Lamar stalked into the bar.

Emmaline was no fool. Her eyes followed her father's progress for the briefest of moments before she changed tactics. She pulled a small book out and flipped through it, pretending to pay studious attention to it. Jack found a good vantage point near the end of the bar that led to the kitchen. Lamar scanned the saloon, intent as only a man on the hunt would be. Jack had the unsettling feeling that Lamar truly was after him.

Jack didn't like being quarry. He much preferred the roles to be reversed. It was a shame that he didn't think his Obfuscation spell would stand against taking a shot at Lamar. *Too obvious.*

Lamar's gaze settled on Emmaline, and Jack reconsidered his stance on shooting his old friend then and there. The Commander strode over to her with quick, purposeful steps, moving to occupy the chair Jack had claimed only moments before.

Jack bit back the urge to walk over and plant a fist in Lamar's handsome mug. Or a bullet. Instead, he stayed where he was as his enemy leaned close to his daughter and said something. Emmaline offered him a baleful glare in response. *That's my girl. Now gut him under the table.*

Emmaline said something to Lamar, and Jack would have paid a mountain of gold to hear. Lamar's head jerked back, and he tightened his hand into a fist. He glanced around the bar again, and Jack wondered briefly if she had mentioned his presence.

Nearby, the same bartender who had approached Jack earlier studied the situation, a scowl on his face. He put down the pitcher he had been wiping dry, moving around the bar to head back to Emmaline's defense. Normally Jack had little love for the heroic ranger type, but since he couldn't intervene in this situation himself, he approved.

The bartender loomed over Lamar, all muscle and attitude, his eyes on Emmaline. His voice was a rumble that carried to Jack's position. "You need a hand?"

"This man is bothering me." Emmaline lifted her chin, eyes bright.

Lamar glared at the bartender. "This doesn't concern you."

"My bar, my property." The bartender cracked his knuckles for emphasis. "Get out and leave the girl alone."

Lamar straightened, annoyance etched on his face. He tapped one of the gaudy medals decorating the front of his uniform. "You're speaking to a Commander of the Salt-Iron Confederation."

"Don't care. You're harassing a paying customer. Get out."

Yeah, aside from the kerfuffle earlier, Jack liked this bartender. Now, if only he would follow that up with a punch to Lamar's face. That would be perfection.

Meanwhile, Lamar seemed to debate his next steps. But mage or not, it wouldn't be good for the Commander's image to haul off a young girl who was minding her own business. From what Jack had discovered, his old pal had been in hot water after the mess of Fort Courage, so he had to take it easy or risk more blow-back. Lamar frowned, lowering his voice to offer parting words to Emmaline before he rose and headed for the door.

Jack watched Lamar go, debating all the while which path to take. On the one hand, it was tempting to trail after his nemesis and end him at last. But on the other, he had found Emmaline, and he wasn't eager to let her slip away again. Because he knew she would. His daughter had lost track of him, courtesy of his spell, and he saw by the way she tensed her muscles she was preparing to make her own escape as soon as possible.

She bided her time, though, as if wanting to make sure that Gaitwood was gone. Jack supposed Oberidon might be in the vicinity and apprising her of the situation, as Zepheus had done for him. Not for the first time, Jack wished he could communicate directly with his pegasus. It would be handy at times like this.

After a half-hour had passed, she finally rose and slipped out of the bar. Jack followed in her wake, keeping his spell active so no one realized she had a tail. She made her way up the street to a grungy inn, where she let herself into a room on the third floor. No sign of Oberidon, but that didn't mean much of anything.

Jack put his boot into the door before she could close it. The solid wood hitting his foot shattered his Obfuscation spell, and Emmaline jumped in surprise as he shimmered into view on the other side of the door. She had a pistol in her hand quick as a rattlesnake, though thankfully, she didn't fire.

"Daddy!" she hissed, eyes narrowed.

"I wasn't going to give up that easy," Jack murmured, shouldering his way inside and shutting the door behind him.

Emmaline turned the bolt on the lock, slipping her pistol back into its holster and crossing her arms. "Your pig-headedness is going to get you killed one of these days."

"I'm only here because you ran off," he countered.

She threw up her hands. "You should be happy to hear I'm fine. Go back home. Go back to the Gutter and be the heartless outlaw I know you are."

He bristled at that. Was that all she thought he was now? When had he become that and stopped being her father? Jack tried to rally and think of something wise to say, but her words stung. Emmaline meant the world to him. And he meant so little to her?

It took Jack a moment to realize she was giving him a strange look. He hadn't given a hot-tempered reply, as was his usual mode of conversation. No, instead his mouth opened and closed, like a fish out of water, as he tried and failed to figure out how to repair things with her.

"Daddy?" Emmaline asked. Her voice was soft, having lost some of its righteous fury at his inability to respond.

Jack wasn't one to let his emotions show. And maybe, he realized, that was wrong in this case. He recalled, so many years ago, when their little family had first been torn asunder, there had been many a night when he and Emmaline would curl up and cry until they fell asleep, missing Kittie like she were a physical part of them that had been torn away. Over time, the place where Kittie had been scabbed over, and Jack tried to always keep a brave face on for his daughter as she grew. Tried to be the tough one. And now that was all she saw: the stone-faced, icy bastard of an outlaw.

"Do you know why I came looking for you?" Jack's voice trembled with uncharacteristic softness.

Emmaline pursed her lips. "Because you don't think I can take care of myself."

He shook his head. No, he had faith that she could do that. "The same reason I would fight a fort full of soldiers for you. You're my child. You're a piece of my heart walking around outside my body. I *love* you."

She gave him a mistrustful look. "Something's wrong with you. Are you drunk?"

"Am I—?" Jack sputtered, then snorted. "Gods, girl. I can't tell you I love you without you having to ask that?"

Emmaline glanced away. "It's not something I hear from you."

And that's my fault. "I know." He had thought that being there for her and showing her was enough, but it wasn't. Jack pulled her into an embrace, relieved when he felt her relax against him. "I *know* you can take care of yourself. You're my girl, so I'm pretty sure there ain't nothing you can't do if you put your mind to it."

"Really thinking you're not my father," she muttered into his shoulder.

"Shut your piehole and accept the praise."

Emmaline lifted her chin. "Okay, so maybe it is you." After a moment, she pulled away again. "Do you know why I came here?"

Jack allowed her to step away from him. "I assume you were hoping to free Blaise."

At that, she glanced away, as if shamed. "I...I thought about it. I came around here to see if I had a chance, but I don't think so." Emmaline worried at her bottom lip, and Jack knew she was regretting that she couldn't save her friend. "But really, this is why I came." She dug a hand into a pouch at her waist, carefully pulling out a doll.

Jack stared at it, swallowing. "Explain."

"I'm looking for Mom."

Her words shocked him to the core. How many years had he done the very same, and with nothing to show for it but more heartbreak? Jack shivered because with Emmaline's magic, she had a genuine chance of success. He exhaled softly, not even daring to hope. "And?"

"She's alive. Hiding." Emmaline's voice was soft, breathy, and victorious. "Made herself purposely hard to find. But *I can do it.*"

Jack's pulse raced. Then he paused, frowning. "Wait. Did you take hair from your mother's poppet without asking?"

"Um. Maybe?" She shot him a pleading look. "It's easier to beg forgiveness than ask permission."

He snorted. "Yeah." Another thing she'd learned from him. "For future reference, it's rude to steal a reagent from another mage."

Emmaline blinked. "But we're outlaws."

"Outlaw doesn't mean we're uncultured trash goblins, though." He crossed his arms, though he couldn't keep up the stern front for long. Not with knowledge of what she could do. "You're going to find her?"

His daughter gave a determined nod. "Yeah." Emmaline glanced away, as if suddenly embarrassed. "I was mad at you. I thought if I figured out where she was, I could live with her."

That almost ripped his heart right out. Gods, he was such a

terrible father, to drive her to such thoughts. She cringed, as if expecting him to rail at her. And a part of him wanted to. But then he would fall into the same trap that was driving her away. He prided himself on being able to adapt and learn new tricks. This was no different.

Swallowing, he met her eyes. "I want you to know I hope you find her."

Emmaline stared at him, and he was sure she was going to make another retort that he couldn't possibly be her father. But maybe she saw he was desperately trying to make things work. She nodded. "Thanks. You can come along."

Oh, how he wanted to. But he shook his head, surprising her. "Nah. I have something else to take care of that you thought I should do. I'll catch up after."

Her face crinkled in confusion. "What?" Then after a beat, her eyes widened. "Oh. Daddy, are you going to get Blaise out?"

"I am," Jack whispered, the words a pledge. He gasped in surprise as she flung her arms around him again. He stroked her hair, breathing in her scent, content. For the moment, his daughter was safe, and things were a little better in his world. He might have to confront some of his old demons at the Golden Citadel, but for the moment, he allowed himself to just *be*.

CHAPTER THIRTEEN

Dream On

Jefferson

etal and wood shrieked as they fractured under strain, clamorous and ghastly. A haze of smoke cloaked his view of the world as the floor he stood on bucked beneath his feet. No, not a floor—a *deck*, Jefferson realized as he absorbed the surrounding scene. He *knew* where he was. And at the same time, he wasn't certain how he knew that.

He was on board what had once been *his* airship before the Confederation had commandeered it and turned it into the warbird *Retribution*. Screams rose from the ground below as the ship bobbled again. Someone crouched on the deck ahead, back arched as his hands braced against the wood. Even with the young man's back to him, Jefferson knew who he was looking at.

"Blaise!" he called out above the bedlam. The Breaker didn't seem to hear him at first and remained where he was, trembling with effort. Jefferson strode closer. "Blaise!"

The mage jerked to attention at the new voice, glancing over his shoulder at Jefferson with an incredulous expression that swiftly shifted to one of horror. "*No*. You shouldn't be here."

The deck shuddered beneath them, so real and heart-stopping that Jefferson dropped into a crouch as well. "*I* asked you to do this." Jefferson glanced around, stomach lurching as he realized the scope of what he had urged Blaise to do so many months ago. "What happened to you is my fault. There's no place else I should be."

The warbird listed to one side. Blaise yelped as he lost his balance and stumbled. Jefferson dove to him, wrapping his arms around the younger man. There was a soft pop, and the warbird shimmered out of existence, replaced by the floor of the bakery. Jefferson pulled himself away from Blaise, watching as the Breaker curled up, hugging his knees against his chest as he stared at the change of scenery, bewildered.

"You're safe now." Jefferson raised his hands in a calming gesture.

Blaise quivered. "What's happening? That's never happened in my nightmare before."

Your nightmare? Oh, Blaise. Jefferson got to his feet, leaning against a counter. The wood felt solid and so *real*, just as real as the airship had been. "You're not there anymore. You're safe."

Blaise rubbed his arms as if he were cold. "I'm not safe."

Jefferson cocked his head, trying to decide if it was better to stay put or move closer. *Nothing ventured, nothing gained.* He stepped over to Blaise again, slowly sitting on the floor opposite him. "May I talk to you about something?"

The question seemed to jar Blaise from whatever bleak thoughts had gripped him. He blinked. "What?"

"Do you remember the last time we were together?"

Blaise glanced away, his expression unreadable. "Rainbow Flat."

"No," Jefferson corrected, voice gentle. "*Here*. Your bakery. We made cookies."

Blaise shook his head. "That was just a dream."

"No. I mean, yes, it was, but…" Jefferson paused as Blaise looked at him with confusion. "I think this is *us*, Blaise. The real you. The real me. But in a…dream world." He felt silly even saying the words, but they somehow seemed right.

The Breaker pressed his lips together in thought. "How?"

Jefferson chuckled nervously, rubbing his chin. "I only want to help you. You know that, yes?"

Blaise stared at him. "What did you do?"

Jefferson flicked his gaze to the floor, guilty. Heart drumming so loud he fancied Blaise could hear it, he struggled to find the words. Why was it a simple matter to go toe to toe with the other Doyens, but so difficult to tell Blaise this one thing? *Because I care about him, that's why.* "I couldn't come up with any other way to save you. I'm sorry."

"What did you do?"

In answer, Jefferson rolled up his sleeve. His tattoo wasn't there at first, but he brushed his hand over the skin, and the ink swirled into existence like thin, living serpents. Blaise hiked up his own sleeve and watched as his geasa tattoo rose to visibility in response. His face falling, Blaise yanked the sleeve back down and turned away, his expression crumpling.

"It was the only way," Jefferson whispered, at a loss for how else to explain it.

Blaise's mouth shifted into a thin line and a muscle in his cheek twitched. "You *know* how I feel about being used."

Yes, he did. Jefferson sighed. He wanted to argue that he wouldn't allow anyone else to have Blaise, but he knew the mage would misunderstand. He didn't want to be seen as a possession. And he *wasn't.* Jefferson wanted his love and trust, nothing more. "I won't allow anyone else to use you. To be bound to you and…" Jefferson faltered, wilting beneath the spark of anger in the other man's eyes.

"I wish you hadn't." Blaise's voice was tight. "You didn't…gods, Jefferson. You didn't even *ask* me." He shook his head in frustration and levered to his feet, stalking the short distance to the other side of the bakery before whirling, his back against the counter. "Why didn't you ask?"

"I *couldn't.*" Jefferson realized this wasn't one of those cases where it was better to beg forgiveness than ask permission. He knew Blaise would be angry, but he had been so confident that the result justified the terrible cost. "It's a poor defense, but the visitation room at the Cit isn't exactly a safe place for such a conversation."

Blaise turned, staring out the small window. The angle of his shoulders radiated his resentment. "You're smarter than that. You could have figured something out."

Jefferson rubbed his forehead. "Nothing else was working, and we were running out of time."

Blaise shook his head. "I *still* can't believe you didn't ask." He shifted to face Jefferson again, crossing his arms. Blaise was no longer the wild-eyed prisoner, righteous fury suffusing him. "I thought you *cared* about me."

Oof. That one hurt. Jefferson clenched his teeth. He could make fancy arguments with the other Doyens all day, but this...*this* was painful. He *did* care. Jefferson swallowed, tucking his chin against his chest. "I...made a mistake."

"Yeah, you did," Blaise agreed. When Jefferson looked up, the young man was running a hand through his hair. "But what's done is done, and I assume this is something we can't change?" At the slight shake of Jefferson's head, Blaise sighed. "I'm going to be mad at you for a while."

"You can. That's fair," Jefferson said. Anger could ebb, worn down by apologies and the healing of time. Hatred was not as easy a thing to die.

Blaise sucked in a deep breath, as if he were steadying himself. "Is that how *this* is possible?" He waved a hand to encompass the bakery.

Jefferson waggled his fingers in an indecisive gesture. "Maybe? I'm still figuring things out, so I can't answer that." He cleared his throat. "There were some unforeseen consequences brought about by being bound to you."

Blaise's brow furrowed. "What do you mean?"

"The tattoo made me quite ill," Jefferson murmured, rubbing absently at his bicep. "Manifestation Illness, if you can believe that."

Blaise stared at him, gaping.

Jefferson gave a rueful smile. "I probably had the same expression when I found out."

Head tilted, Blaise studied him. "Manifestation...wait, that's not good. It could kill you." His earlier anger fled, replaced by a rush of worry.

"I think I'm past that," Jefferson said. "Though I will admit, I've never been sicker in my life."

Blaise studied him, frowning as he thought. Jefferson wished he knew what was going on in that head of his. The younger man said nothing for several minutes as he digested the information. "Does that mean you're like me? A mage?"

"Something like that," Jefferson agreed. "But not a Breaker. I suspect I have some sort of magic that allows me to manipulate dreams. Do you know anything about magic like that?"

Shaking his head, Blaise sighed. "I'm not the person to ask. I didn't know a thing before getting to Itude." He rubbed his hands together, as if the mention of magic agitated his own. "What does this mean for you? You're a *Doyen*."

Jefferson coughed into his fist. That was something he would rather not think about, but it was a valid question. "It means I have to keep this new ability quiet."

Blaise frowned, his eyes frosting. "More secrets."

"But not from you," Jefferson replied, adamant. At the Breaker's raised eyebrows, he blew out a flustered breath. "Right, very well. You think I misled you, but that was *not* my intent."

Blaise crossed his arms, and strangely, it pleased Jefferson to see how focused the other man was on him. Jefferson was a source of frustration, which meant he distracted Blaise from

other concerns—like his predicament in the Cit. *Minor victories.*
"You didn't tell me who you *really* were, and you had the chance to
do so in Rainbow Flat." Blaise held up a finger, ticking it off. "And
then you do that." He gestured to his bicep, raising another finger
for the tally.

Jefferson licked his lips. "May I tell you who I am, then?"

The Breaker nodded. "I've been waiting on this explanation for
a while."

"WE WOULDN'T HAVE GOTTEN ALONG WELL AT ALL WHEN I WAS
younger," Jefferson began, watching as the bakery melted away
from around them, replaced by the parlor of his childhood home.
Blaise rose and moved to stand beside him, glancing at the
opulent brocade drapes, the gilded portraits hanging on the walls,
and the grandiose carved furniture. Every facet of the room
resonated with wealth and power.

"Some things seem to be the same, though," Blaise murmured
at the splendor.

Jefferson gave an unapologetic shrug. "You can see why I'm
accustomed to the finer things in life." He sobered, crossing the
room to the door. Blaise remained where he was, so Jefferson
beckoned him over. "Come on. This is your chance to learn more
about who I am. Who I *really* am."

At that, Blaise followed. Jefferson headed down a hallway until
they reached a door that led outside. The weather was fair, the
temperature pleasant. The fragrance of jasmine clung heavily in
the air from the nearby gardens. Jefferson paused, the ambiance
taking him back. He didn't care much for that particular scent, not
anymore. It reminded him of who he had been and where he came
from.

Blaise noticed and glanced at him. "What?"

Jefferson rubbed the back of his neck. "I'm not a good person,
Blaise. I'm trying to make up for things, but..."

The Breaker studied him. "I know a little about that."

Jefferson paused, shaking his head with regret. "I don't think you do, actually. You don't have an unkind bone in your body." He sighed, rallying himself. Blaise deserved to hear the truth. "In that respect, we're nothing alike."

The surrounding estate was pristine, kept that way by a legion of servants, some of them indentured mages. He led Blaise through the landscaped garden, the hedges so high they shrouded his family's dirty secret. Jefferson remembered a time when he hadn't thought twice about that. How many young women and men had he dallied with beneath the fragrant rose arches? He had lost count. His wandering subconscious made ghosts of his past romances appear, and by the way Blaise flinched, he saw them, too.

"They're all Malcolm," Blaise murmured, studying a frozen tableau where the man in question cradled an amorous redhead in his arms.

"We're on the Wells Estate, so yes," Jefferson agreed. He tilted his head, trying to remember the woman's name. She was the daughter of a dignitary. Rosalind? Raquel? Something like that. Didn't matter. She had been an amusement, nothing more. "You, ah, should know that I have a bit of a lascivious past."

Blaise raised his brows, shooting him an amused look. "Do you see my surprised face?"

Yes, well...Jefferson found himself embarrassed about confronting it with Blaise. He didn't want him to get the wrong idea. Blaise was *nothing* like the others. Jefferson had no intention of tossing him to the wayside. "Right. Well, this isn't even the worst thing about me. Rather tame, honestly. Come on."

He led Blaise deeper into the garden, examining his own sudden discomfiture over his past. Jefferson had never been embarrassed about his romantic exploits before, but now he found himself in the odd position of not wanting to scare Blaise away. His relationship with the Breaker was as delicate as the scales on a butterfly's wings, and Jefferson feared damaging it further than he already had.

They reached the massive stone fountain that occupied the center of the garden. Jefferson walked over to a nearby bench, tapping a rhythm into the bricks beneath it. Blaise watched him, perplexed, but then jumped as the flagstones around the fountain shifted with a grinding clatter, a wooden hatch concealing stairs that led down to a subterranean passage.

"What's this?" Blaise asked.

Jefferson pressed his lips together. "The actual way my family amassed our *shipping* fortune." He started down the steps. "Not *me*, mind you. I told you the truth about that. So please remember that."

Blaise followed him down, glancing up as the daylight vanished, replaced by the lambent glow of lanterns. Jefferson's pulse quickened at the cries and moans echoing against the stone walls. He heard Blaise's quick intake of breath when the sound carried to him. Jefferson pressed onward until they were in the holding area, surrounded by cells filled with humans and people of mystical races.

It was a dream, so Jefferson made the inhabitants ignore him and Blaise, but that didn't stop how real it was. The Breaker stared around him, face pale in the light. "What am I looking at?"

Jefferson rubbed his forehead. "My family invests in flesh. The Wells family is part of a thriving trafficking network that spans the entire Confederation." He cast a furtive look at Blaise, half expecting to see outrage reflected in his eyes. The Breaker's mouth twisted into a deep frown, and his blue eyes appeared more troubled than angry. Jefferson continued, "We—I mean *they*, I don't do this anymore—sell to a variety of clientele. Brothels. Menageries. Ritualists. Apothecaries. Alchemists." He ticked them off on his fingers one by one.

Blaise walked down the middle of the long, narrow room, studying the prisoners. He trailed his fingers along the dark metal bars. They were salt-iron, but in the dream world they were harmless. The metal crumbled at Blaise's touch, tumbling down like a satisfying rain. "I assume there's a lot of money to be had here."

"You have no idea," Jefferson murmured. Oh, and if his family knew he had access to a Breaker...gods, he didn't even want to think about that. He had burned his bridges thoroughly, but greed could pave over them.

"So what happened?" Blaise asked.

At the question, Jefferson licked his lips. "I have a sister. Younger than me—a little older than you." He sighed, and not for the first time, wondered if fate had put Blaise in his path as a reminder. "When she was ten, her magic manifested."

Blaise stared at him. "You have a mage in your family?"

"*Had.*" Malcolm failed to keep his bitterness from bleeding through to his voice. "Our father prided himself on coming from a line without the taint of magic—his description, not mine. He blamed our mother." And looking back, Malcolm pinpointed that as the moment his mother went over the cliff of her addictions and never turned back. "Father sold my sister to the highest bidder."

Blaise hissed out a breath. "What became of her?"

"I should clarify: he sold her off as a bride, which I suppose isn't any better." Malcolm shook his head. "And I...I knew it was wrong, but the girl I grew up with went from being my sibling to something *other.*" He winced. "I was raised to look down on mages."

"What changed?" Blaise asked, tentative. As if he were worried Malcolm had somehow misled him.

"Flora. I came across her, and she...showed me the error of my ways." He ran a hand through his hair, roughing it backward. "That's a long story for another time. But I wanted you to understand that once upon a time, I *would* have used someone like you."

Blaise glanced at him. "How can I be sure you won't now?"

The question made Jefferson's heart ache. He didn't know how he could make his intentions for Blaise any clearer without scaring him off. "I won't. And if I even think about it, I assume Flora will shank me."

"I could see that," Blaise agreed. He turned in a tight circle, thoughtful. "What will your family think of this?" He gestured from himself to Jefferson.

Jefferson sighed. That was something he didn't want to consider. "We're not on speaking terms. I ended up being disinherited when I became a magelover. Had my engagement broken off and everything."

"Engagement?" Blaise squeaked.

Oh, are you jealous? Jefferson very much wanted to ask but decided to hold on to that question for another time. "Yes, to an heiress. If you care to take a gander, Cinna is the one I'm fadoodling by the unicorn topiary." He made a face. "That was a rather fortunate side effect of being disowned. Ending that engagement was a gift from the gods."

"*Fadoodling?*" Blaise shook his head, then pursed his lips. "Didn't she love you?"

Jefferson chuckled. Blaise was adorably naïve about the workings of elite society, and that was a blessing. "Few unions are based on love in the higher social echelons of the Confederation. But you're kind to think that."

Blaise quirked an eyebrow at him. "And you still haven't explained how *Jefferson* figures into all this. Flora told me it was so you could travel through the Untamed Territory without problems."

"Ah, that's true to a degree," Jefferson agreed. "That's my favorite use, yes." And he didn't know how to explain to Blaise that he just felt more at home in this skin. Less like the filth he associated with the Wells name. Maybe someday, he would figure out a way to explain it. "I purchased the ring before I met Flora but hadn't used it much. But then to do what needed to be done required Jefferson and not Malcolm."

"To do what?" Blaise asked.

Jefferson chuckled. "That's part of the story for another time.

Flora taught me the important lesson that you can be magical and still a person."

"You don't say?" Blaise asked wryly.

"It was a very radical idea after my upbringing." Jefferson shook his head. "And after dealing with Flora, I wondered why mages and magical beasts were treated one way in the Confederation, but differently in places like Ravance or the Untamed Territory. That was something Jefferson could investigate more easily, as an unknown."

Blaise frowned. "Were you a Doyen then?"

Jefferson shook his head. "No, but I was a Wells, which made life difficult. I was reviled among my former cohorts for my inclinations, and elsewhere I was viewed as the enemy." He smiled. "Jefferson's goal was to travel, gather information, and make money. I discovered I enjoyed that. Jefferson was the person I decided I'd like to be if I had a choice. Nor did he have the legacy of a family built up on the suffering of others."

Blaise worried at his lower lip, and for a moment, Jefferson wondered if he had said something wrong. But the younger man shook his head. "You said you were a bad person. Bad people don't care about becoming better."

Those words warmed Jefferson's heart, and he thought perhaps Blaise understood him, at least a bit more. "I'm not perfect."

"No. You're spoiled and entitled," Blaise agreed.

"Devilishly handsome."

"Egotistical." Blaise nodded.

Jefferson chuckled. "Forgive me for the deception?"

"I forgive you for the Malcolm and Jefferson thing. Still mad at you about the geasa." Blaise crossed his arms.

"But maybe a little less mad since I pulled you out of a nightmare?" Jefferson held his thumb and index finger a tiny bit apart.

That won a small smile from Blaise. "A little. I just wish I didn't have to go back."

Yes. Jefferson desperately wished the same.

CHAPTER FOURTEEN

Monsters

Malcolm

*H*e awoke to the jarring sensation of someone forcing his mouth open to pour a concoction down his throat. His gag reflex took over, and Flora cursed, her strong hands forcing his head up.

"Oh, no, you don't," she growled.

He swallowed the potion, eyes snapping open at the bitter taste and oily feel of it sliding down his throat. To his surprise, Flora wasn't the only one in the room with him. A woman with curly brown hair stood on one side of the bed, arms crossed as she watched him.

"Ugh. What *is* that?" Malcolm moaned, casting a covetous look at the glass of water nearby. Flora handed it to him, and he drank, feeling slightly less vile as the water cleansed his palate.

"Something to help you survive," the unfamiliar woman replied. "So *you're* the one misguided enough to bind himself to my son."

"Yep, that's the blowhard you're looking for." Malcolm hadn't noticed Jack sitting in the corner.

He ignored the judgmental outlaw, focusing on the woman's harsh and confusing words. Malcolm thought that was rather unfair since he still wasn't feeling well enough to figure out what she meant. *Bind myself to...wait.* "You're Blaise's mother? Marian Hawthorne?" He was rather proud that her name came to mind, considering how disconnected he felt. "And before you rail at me for poor decisions, I was running out of options to help him."

Marian cocked her head. "I won't be the one to judge what you did." Apparently, she understood how Blaise would react, too. Her eyes were steely. "But you're a *Doyen*. Surely *you* could do more."

Oh, if only. "It's not that simple, and it's an uphill battle as far as mages are concerned." Especially Blaise, after the disaster at Fort Courage. He pursed his lips. "The Council was determined to bind him, and our side wouldn't have the votes to stop it."

She nodded, expression cool. "And so you took it upon yourself. Thinking that you were giving him a mercy." Jack snickered from his corner.

And here he thought she wasn't going to judge what he had done. He grimaced. "Better me than someone else. Someone who doesn't love him."

His words brought her up short. Marian raised her eyebrows, casting a quick glance at Flora, who nodded. "I see." Her tone softened. "Doyen Wells, I don't know if you can fully appreciate what you've sacrificed for Blaise."

Malcolm had some idea, but he wondered if he'd misunderstood the full scope. "And that is?" He didn't miss the way Jack stayed quiet the entire time, absorbing their conversation.

The alchemist paced the length of the room, as if debating her words. "The Ink used for the geasa originates from the blood of the mage being bound. It has trace amounts of the Manifestation virus. In most cases, it's so small it has no impact on the handler. But this is not like most cases." Her face hardened.

"And why is that?" Jack rumbled, leaning forward in a manner that reminded Malcolm of a hunting hound at the end of its leash.

Marian angled to address him. By the slash of her brow, Malcolm suspected she didn't know what to make of the outlaw. He presumed they had been introduced while he was knocked out. "Because there are too many unknowns surrounding my son, which makes it dangerous." Marian fidgeted with something in her hands, and Malcolm realized she was spinning a silver ring around one of her fingers. Whatever information she had, the alchemist was nervous about sharing it.

"We'll keep anything you have to say in our confidence," Malcolm said. He hoped Jack would, though he knew it was a gamble. The outlaw gave no indication one way or the other.

Marian nodded, the corners of her eyes crinkling with emotion. "Blaise wasn't born a mage. He was *made* into a mage."

Jack shot out of his seat, hands fisted at his side. "*Dragonshit.* That's not possible."

Malcolm was inclined to agree with the outlaw, but he didn't have much information on the topic. A glance at Flora proved she wanted to hear more before jumping to conclusions.

The alchemist fixed an impassive look at Jack. "The whole *point* of alchemy is to achieve the impossible. Transmute base metals into precious metals. Mix a panacea to cure any disease—"

"Bind one man's will to another. Block out all magical ability. Yeah, I know *all* about alchemy," Jack retorted, his entire body taut.

Blaise's mother was as placid as a lake, though Malcolm suspected she held back more information beneath the surface. "I won't argue with you, as it's the truth. One such pursuit years ago was an experiment to transmute our own mages."

Jack's mouth pressed into an angry line. Malcolm's gut lurched at her words. He suspected she spoke the truth because it was very much something the Confederation would do. But how could a mother do that to her child? Malcolm fought off a shiver, afraid that perhaps Blaise had grown up with his share of monsters, too.

The outlaw must have come to the same realization. His blue eyes glinted with a menacing chill, and Malcolm wondered if the alchemist knew the peril she was in.

Marian didn't quail at the heightening danger in the room. And perhaps she didn't need to—alchemists didn't look like much, but they were formidable. "Before you judge me, know this: I love Blaise with every bit of my being."

Jack's eyes smoldered like banked coals. He unfolded from the chair, rising slowly like a dragon on the prowl. Even though he hadn't crossed the room to be closer to the alchemist, he still seemed to loom over her. "How could a *parent* do that to a *child?*" The outlaw's voice was a low rumble, outrage and menace lacing every syllable.

To her credit, Marian averted her gaze under the storm of his words. "Even parents make mistakes."

Jack growled something unintelligible, crossing his arms and turning away in disgust. Malcolm's gut clenched as he realized Blaise had a history of people using him. And this...there was no way the young man knew this. Surely, he would have told Malcolm as much.

"What happened?" Malcolm asked.

Marian pressed her lips together, shaking her head. "That's not for me to tell you. Not when Blaise doesn't know." She took a tremulous breath.

Malcolm's brow knit, thoughtful. He wondered if the Council at the time was aware of this. But the Doyens of the past had a history of destroying records they didn't want discovered by others, so it would be hard to uncover. *To do this to a child, though...*

Jack uttered a raspy laugh. "And y'all think the *outlaw mages* are the monsters."

Marian lifted her chin. "I'm not proud of the things I did. Are you?" She met the outlaw's eyes, as if she were taking his measure.

He bared his teeth. "Not denying I'm a monster. Are *you?*"

She flinched and made the wise choice not to reply. "Blaise almost died from the process. I developed a potion that helped him pull through." Her lower lip quivered, her eyes glistening with unshed tears. Malcolm thought she might say more, but she released a shuddering sigh and wiped at one of her eyes.

"Why work for the Confederation?" Flora asked, her eyes owlish behind her glasses.

Marian glanced at Jack. "You assume I had a choice." The outlaw twitched at her words, and for an instant, understanding sparked between the pair. "When you're treated well, as the alchemists are, you don't question it. Don't misunderstand me—we're commodities as much as the theurgists are—but our egos are so coddled that it doesn't *matter*." She combed her fingers through her curly hair. "At least, it didn't matter to me until Blaise. I took him, and I ran." Marian glanced away, clamming up. If there was more to the tale, they wouldn't hear it from her today.

"You ran," Jack repeated, grudging admiration in his voice.

Marian smiled, bitter. "I did. The first and only alchemist to do so. That's why the Arboretum is locked up tight now." She shook her head. "But it was all for nothing. The Confederation has Blaise. All I did was delay it."

"Not if I have a say in it," Malcolm replied. He ran his tongue over his teeth, which were still greasy from the potion. "So that potion..."

She glanced at the empty bottle on the bedside table. "The same one that helped Blaise pull through when he was sick."

That explained that. "Going back to the start of the discussion...you mentioned that binding to Blaise might be dangerous."

She nodded. "The Confederation has a brief memory. For the most part, they only know what Blaise *is* and not how he came about. And it's important it stays that way, or they'll uncover the true danger behind him."

"You mean beyond the whole *breaking things with a touch* magic he has going on?" Flora asked, eyebrows so high they brushed against the fringe of her bright hair.

Marian leveled a finger at Malcolm. "We had his blood at the Arboretum. I stole samples and studied it myself." She was quiet for a moment, though her heels tapped as she paced the floor again. "A mage's power is a biological part of them—it's literally in their blood. Blaise's magic tried to attack the virus, but that's the one thing it can't destroy." She sighed, pushing dark hair out of her eyes.

Malcolm cocked his head. He wasn't sure if he was following her train of thought very well in his present condition. "What happens, then?"

She gave him a wry look. "It ends up twisting the virus since it can't break it. My theory is that it spawns new types of magic."

"*Oh.*" Malcolm blinked, his mouth going dry. He gestured for the water, and Flora handed it to him.

Jack muttered a curse that no one else quite heard. Flora glanced between the two of them. "Something you're not sharing with the group?"

Malcolm rubbed his chin, recalling how he had grabbed Blaise and pulled him from the nightmare, and how his previous flings had appeared at a thought. "Maybe." He explained his experiences as best he could, though he suspected he sounded like he was raving.

Marian nodded and made a soft humming sound. "The fact that you actively manipulated the dream points to potential magic," she said. "Most people are at the mercy of their subconscious."

"Really?" Jack snorted, incredulous. "You think that's what this is? *Dream* magic?"

"Says the man who plays with dolls," Flora pointed out sweetly. Jack bristled.

The alchemist held up a hand to halt the brewing argument. "The point stands that Doyen Wells likely has a new type of magic if my theory holds true."

"I'm a mage," Malcolm murmured, though the words sounded strange to his ears. He had bandied around the idea with Blaise, but it struck him differently now that he was awake.

"And in typical *you* fashion, you have to be special." Flora crossed her arms. "But then you always were a dreamer."

Marian raised her eyebrows. "Dreamer. Yes, that fits. *Dreamer* is what you are." She studied Malcolm again. "We should be glad it's not a flashy magic."

"Just what we need. An untrained mage," Jack grumbled.

Malcolm swallowed. The outlaw was right—untrained mages were unpredictable and dangerous. And factoring in that he had a new type of magic, it was a recipe for disaster.

"If only there were a freeloading mage around who could earn his keep," Flora taunted, earning a glare from Jack. "Oh wait, *there is*." She waggled a finger in the air. "Though I suppose maybe you'd rather not, since from what I heard you didn't have the balls to train Blaise, either."

Malcolm groaned. Flora had just thrown down the gauntlet, and he didn't think this would end well.

Jack strode over to the half-knocker, glowering as he towered over her. "I had a *damned* good reason for not training him. First and foremost, I would have likely killed him if we were in the same room for too long." Then he froze, glancing at Marian with an air of chagrin. "No offense to present company. Just speakin' the truth."

Marian raised her brows and didn't comment on that, at least. "It's right that a new mage needs training. Especially since it's vital we keep this quiet. We can't let it get out that Blaise's blood can spawn new mages. Much less new strains of magic."

A range of emotions flickered over Jack's face. Finally, he crossed his arms. "Fine. I'll see what I can do."

Why did Malcolm think that sounded like a veiled threat to punch him in the face?

A FEW HOURS LATER, MALCOLM FOUND HIMSELF IN THE DUBIOUS position of being Jack's student. Flora had taken Marian

Hawthorne back to the Arboretum, which left the outlaw alone with him.

"No time like the present," Jack commented as he swept into the room where Malcolm sat up in bed, going through correspondences he had missed.

"Oh." Malcolm shuffled the envelopes to the bedside table. "I thought you might need to search for your daughter."

The outlaw gave him a sideways look. "Don't need to. Found her."

Malcolm blinked at that. "Oh. That's good?" He wondered why Jack was still here if that was the case.

Jack frowned, assessing the room. "Now I have to focus on my promise to free Blaise. Which means you need to know a thing or three about magic, so you don't hinder us."

His words gave Malcolm pause. "You want to free Blaise?"

The outlaw stared at him as if he were daft.

Malcolm waved a hand. "Right. That's fine. Magic, yes. I'm listening."

Jack grabbed the wingback chair and dragged it closer. He settled down into it. "Good. 'Cause I'm not one to repeat myself." He put his booted feet up on the cushioned stool, which made Malcolm cringe, but he said nothing. "And we're gonna start with the basics since I figure you can't tell skunks from house cats as far as magic goes."

Malcolm clamped his mouth shut. The outlaw wasn't wrong. While he supported the mages, he was aware there were mechanics of their power he might not fully grasp. And he wanted to.

"First, gotta start off with resources. Magic exists everywhere, in anything that lives, whether it's plant or animal. It's a form of energy that we can tap." Jack held up a leather pouch that Malcolm hadn't previously noticed. He displayed a handful of items: feathers, a beeswax candle, a fang as long as his index finger. "It's even in the reagents some of us use. And most importantly, every mage has a reservoir of magic we tap into to manipulate the world around us."

Malcolm nodded. That was the longest non-threatening discussion he'd heard from Jack so far. "So magic is a part of every living thing? Even non-mages?"

"Harder to make magic sound frightening if it's so ingrained in the world around you, ain't it?" Jack mused. "But yeah, that's why my magic works on people without power. Sympathetic magic." He shrugged. "That's a more advanced topic."

Malcolm shook his head, bemused. *It seems magic has as many nuances as politics.*

"Next thing to know," the Effigest continued, "is magic is neutral. It's like this." He uncurled his left hand to reveal a bullet nestled in his palm.

Malcolm frowned in confusion. Leave it to the outlaw to compare magic to his preferred form of mayhem, which didn't seem very neutral at all. "Bullets aren't neutral."

"Aren't they?" Jack asked, tossing it into the air and catching it. "By itself, it does nothing. Give it to me, and I can take a life. Give it to a wrangler defending his herd from a murder of chupacabras, and it offers protection."

Now Malcolm saw what he meant. "Give it to a hunter with a starving family, and he can feed them."

Jack aimed a finger at him, and the outlaw looked almost pleased. "The goal is to turn you into that hunter. Just gotta learn how to wield your magic to make it serve you."

"But I *have* been wielding it," Malcolm said, then paused. Or he *thought* he had.

The Effigest rolled the bullet between his thumb and index finger. "Every greenhorn mage says that until they learn better." He gave Malcolm a long, considering look. "Without training, a maverick mage is likely to draw attention, through misuse or accident. Nothing brings a Tracker 'round faster than that."

Malcolm winced. "I see." The last thing he needed was a Tracker and unicorn on his tail. Affluence and position would only shield him from so much. "How are you able to help me learn, if our magics are so different?"

"Back in the day, it was easier to lose a Tracker. The Confederation didn't have unicorns and there were entire hidden villages of mavericks," Jack said. Malcolm pursed his lips, wondering how this was going to answer his question. The outlaw smirked at his expression. "Sometimes magic is inherited in families, like to like. But not always. There's ways to figure out basic magic theory, and to apply it to other types." He tapped his temple with meaning.

Malcolm nodded, interested. "And how do we do that?"

Jack narrowed his eyes, studying him. He removed his boots from the stool and leaned forward, vaguely predatory. "That's what we need to figure out, you and I, *Dreamer.*"

CHAPTER FIFTEEN

Light in the Darkness

Blaise

*E*ach morning, when Blaise awoke from whatever paltry sleep his nightmares allowed, he did his best to forget everything from the day before. Maybe it wasn't the best strategy for dealing with the trauma of his current situation, but he had few options. Banishing the memories to a far corner of his mind and pretending they had happened to someone else was the only way he had come up with to get through this.

And then Jefferson had appeared in his dreams, and as crazy as it was, he didn't want to forget that. Even if he was mad at the man. *Is it real?* Out of reflex, he rubbed at the tattoo on his upper arm. He didn't think they could be real—probably just a figment of his shattering mind, desperate to hold on to something, *anything,* that might offer hope. And above all, that was what he needed. Hope, and to know that he wasn't alone. That there was a light in the darkness.

A key scraped against the lock, and he tensed before scooting away from the door. Blaise hated when the guards came in. It never ended well for him—or for the guards. But that wasn't his fault, not really. The pair of guards threw the door open and stepped inside, the woman on the left training her revolver on Blaise as her counterpart moved closer—and gods, he realized it was his tormenter, Heathcliff, bearing salt-iron shackles.

The pair moved cautiously around him, as if he were a rabid animal that might strike out at any moment. Obedient as ever, he held up his arms so that they could clap the shackles around his wrists. He was almost tempted to make a snarky comment about the futility of the restraints, but he didn't know what they had in mind for him today and didn't want another beating.

"Get up," Heathcliff barked, as the female guard motioned toward the open door with the muzzle of her revolver.

Easier said than done. Blaise rose slowly, his muscles complaining for a variety of reasons—lack of exercise and use, inadequate nutrition, abuse. When he finally got to his feet, it took him a moment to keep his balance and get them to cooperate. Blaise took a shaky breath. He hated the Confederation for what they had done to him.

Once he got moving, it was a little easier to walk. He kept his head down, staring at his feet as the guards guided him through the halls. He had stopped trying to speak to them weeks ago. They considered him little more than an animal. It wasn't worth the expended energy to engage with them.

Heathcliff led him to a room he had been in several times before. Blaise swallowed, planting his feet firmly. *No. I don't want to go in there.* Old memories reared up like monsters, and he banished them with a shake of his head as his pulse raced.

"C'mon," Heathcliff growled, grabbing his arm. "Move it."

Blaise's magic swelled, boiling up like a thunderhead on a sultry summer afternoon. Panic seized him as he heard the other guard readying her weapon. His magic sizzled against the salt-iron fetters, the sound reminding him of grease in a too-hot frying pan. Both guards escorting him knew that somehow, over the course of his time in the Cit, his magic had grown resistant to

salt-iron. Blaise didn't know if it was the potion he was adminis-
tered or the fact that he had gone up against the metal before. The
shackles irritated his skin but did *nothing* to his well of power.

The female guard jigged aside as Heathcliff cursed. Blaise's
power assaulted him, and with a howl he sank to his knees as
magic broke the small bones in his wrist. Blaise squeezed his eyes
closed, frantic to pull back the reflexive surge of magic. His heart
pounded and he cringed, expecting the next sound to be the roar
of the revolver ending his life.

There was a click, but the blast never came. Instead, he heard a
frustrated sigh. "Get that man to a Healer. Garus grant us wisdom,
is everyone around here *incompetent?*"

Blaise bit his lower lip, opening his eyes to look at the speaker.
An older man stood in the doorway, scowling at Heathcliff as a
guard arrived to help him away. Another guard slipped up to
replace him, offering a crisp salute. Whoever the man was, he
wore authority as easily as the charcoal-colored, tailored greatcoat on his shoulders.

"Bring him in," the man said, jerking his head to indicate the
room.

Blaise balked at the command. He didn't want to go in there.
Nothing good ever happened in that room. He quivered but
allowed them to lead him inside and sat down in the chair in its
center, watching as they fastened leather straps to hold him in
place. It wouldn't take much for him to break out of those bonds,
as he had proven on multiple occasions.

He closed his eyes, focusing on keeping his magic under wraps
as he listened to the authoritative man consulting with someone
Blaise knew to be an Inker. No one bothered to introduce him to
anyone because why would they? He was nothing to them, even
though they were honing him into something that could tear
down the very building around them. It would be very much like
talking to a revolver the way they saw it.

"We applied the geasa to the handler yesterday. Why is it not
taking?" the older man demanded of the Inker.

At that, the Inker sighed and walked over to Blaise, tugging up his sleeve without asking. Blaise's eyes flew open in alarm. The Inker brushed his thumb over Blaise's tattoo, eying the design with a critical eye. "I'm unsure, Doyen Gaitwood. Any other mage would be compliant by now, but there are so many factors with this one."

Gaitwood? Blaise blinked at that, studying the man. Come to think of it, his voice had a similar ring to it, like Lamar's. This was the man who had wanted him all along. *Why?*

Gregor Gaitwood's eyes flicked to Blaise before going back to the Inker. "You need to make it work."

The Inker stared at him, mouth dropping open with disbelief. "Ah, with all due respect, we're trying but no one on record has bound a Breaker." He hesitated. "And one of our alchemists strongly suggested we not do this."

"Alchemists work for *us*, not the other way around," Gregor retorted. "Find a way to make it happen. I want this mage." He pointed a finger at Blaise, as if it weren't obvious who he meant.

Blaise narrowed his eyes. What if his dreams with Jefferson were real, and he really *was* bound to the other man? What if that was what was fouling their attempt to bind him to someone else? Those thoughts rallied his spirit, and he lifted his chin. "I don't belong to you."

Gregor spun, glaring at him for daring to speak up. "You'll be mine, or you'll *die*, Breaker. Precious little is keeping you from the second option right now."

But he wasn't dead, not yet. Gregor wanted him for something, and no doubt, that was one of the few things keeping Blaise alive at the moment. He fantasized about unleashing his magic and watching the carnage of the Golden Citadel falling to pieces around them. Nothing about that scenario was survivable for him, but that didn't stop him from considering it. But the idea made him heartsick because that wasn't who he was.

"I want to try binding him again this afternoon," Gaitwood declared.

The Inker winced. "That won't be possible, sir. The alchemists need more time to prepare a fresh batch of Ink."

Gregor froze. "What happened to the rest of the first batch?"

"It...ah...went missing."

Went missing. Blaise's thrill at the news was short-lived. Gregor's face twisted in rage, and he swept an arm across the Inker's table. Glass vials and other implements Blaise was unfamiliar with crashed to the stone floor. The Doyen whirled on the Inker. "Inexcusable. Make another batch."

Blaise's heart raced. There was still a chance the dreams were just figments of his tortured mind. But there was also a chance they weren't. And if that was so, maybe Jefferson, in his misguided, selfish way, really *had* bound himself to Blaise. In which case, he was *still* going to be mad at Jefferson. But why else would the Ink have gone missing?

"Sir, we'll be starting over from scratch," the Inker clarified, hesitant. "We'll need more blood."

Gregor's gaze settled on Blaise. "Drain as much as you need. Call in a Healer if his condition becomes too precarious."

Blaise swallowed, and he thought about breaking the restraints and fighting back. But he knew that wouldn't end well. Instead, he focused on the one thought that gave him hope: he had an ally.

CHAPTER SIXTEEN

Unlikely Alliance

Lamar

The most insulting thing about the aftermath of Fort Courage was Lamar's requirement to report to his brother on a regular basis. Perhaps he should have been grateful since the agreement allowed him to keep his title of Commander, even though many of his direct reports were shuffled to others.

He paused outside the door to Gregor's office, gathering his thoughts before lifting his fist to knock on the door. Lamar waited, pounding again when several minutes passed and no one answered.

"I know you're in there, you addled snollygoster," Lamar muttered, digging out a key. Gregor had been adamant that he had to be invited in, but at this point his brother was just being rude. He shoved the door open, striding into the empty reception area and through the open door that led to the office where Gregor sat, frowning at him. "You seemed to not hear me knock."

"That's because I didn't want to be disturbed." Gregor turned away. "I'm busy."

"It's my assigned day to report to you, *dear* brother, so here I am." Lamar made an ironic bow, flourishing his single arm knowing the sight would disturb his sibling. Gregor made no effort to mask his disgust at his brother's disfigurement. "And I have news."

That, at least, piqued Gregor's interest. He set aside the papers he was reviewing. "Then tell me your news and leave."

"Wildfire Jack is in Izhadell. His daughter, too."

Gregor blinked, his mouth screwing up with thought. No doubt trying to recall just who Wildfire Jack was and why he mattered. "And?"

Lamar clenched his jaw. "He's the outlaw traitor who worked with the Breaker."

Recognition flared in Gregor's eyes. "Is he, now?" His voice held an edge of annoyance. "Did you capture him?"

Lamar's gaze slid to the floor in humiliation. He had been so close. He knew he had been close in that swamp, and still didn't understand how the blasted outlaw had escaped him. "I lost the trail. But he's *here*. One of my informants told me as much." Recruiting the urchins to keep an eye on the city borders had been one of his brilliant ideas. He had been more than happy to pay the lad who had brought news of the man riding the palomino stallion. Jack had even been fool enough to give the child a handmade doll. Lamar had recognized his style immediately.

Gregor scowled. "Can't let him get anywhere near that Breaker. For whatever reason, that causes no end of trouble for you. Find him."

"That's the goal," Lamar replied, keeping his voice even.

Gregor picked up a pen, tapping it against a blank sheet of paper. "He can't be skulking around Izhadell without help. Didn't you tell me you took his magic?"

"I did." Lamar narrowed his eyes because that bothered him. The only way Jack could have evaded him was with magic. He couldn't possibly have it back. "And I received a report from another operative of a sighting."

Gregor nodded. "Where did they see him?"

"Near Doyen Wells's property."

At mention of his adversary, Gregor's teeth ground together. Lamar didn't mind dropping that name one bit. He knew Wells got under his brother's skin. Not only did the men have opposing views, but they vied for the same donors. "What news is there from his property?"

Lamar shook his head. "Not much. It's a hard place for spies to get into. A deathtrap."

Gregor made a dismissive sound.

Lamar quirked a smile. "When I say *deathtrap*, I'm not exaggerating. I believe he's hired Jefferson Cole's vile little woman to place traps around it."

Gregor crossed his arms. "She's another to kill when the chance presents itself. Dirty half-breed."

Lamar curled his upper lip. "Yes, well, if you can help me do that without creating an international incident, I'd be appreciative." He had no love for Flora Strop, either.

Gregor doodled on the paper before him, contemplative. "They're all connected. They must be. Wells. Cole. Your outlaw. The Breaker."

Lamar wondered what his brother was getting at. The Breaker was held in the Golden Citadel. And while he knew a thing or two about Wells and Cole, he wasn't ready to enlighten Gregor. "He won't matter once he's bound."

Judging by the twitch of Gregor's eyelid, that was the wrong thing to say. "And therein lies my problem." Gregor pursed his lips. "What could prevent a mage from being bound?"

Lamar blinked. That was a question he hadn't expected. He frowned, dredging his thoughts, but couldn't come up with an answer. There were types of mages that were unwise to bind, but it was still possible (although fatal). "Nothing, as far as I know. That's...unprecedented."

"*Frustrating*, that's what it is." The Doyen rose from his chair to stalk the length of the room. "All my work for nothing. The annoyance of a tattoo for *nothing*."

Lamar swung his head around at that, eyes narrowed. "Tattoo?"

"He was to be *mine*," Gregor muttered, and it would have reminded Lamar of a petulant child if the words weren't so chilling. "*Mine* to reshape the Confederation with, as I like. *Mine* to remove the obstructions of the other Doyens and leaders."

The Commander stood very still, analyzing that sentence with great care. *Dangerous* words. *Treasonous* words. Heart pounding in his chest, he considered what he would say next with caution. "I wasn't aware of these aspirations." Lamar kept his voice neutral, feigning mild interest and nothing more.

Gregor made a contemptuous snort. "It wasn't something I'd make known to *you*."

"Why do you do so now?"

Gregor smiled at him. "When you were an esteemed, decorated Commander, it would have been dangerous to tell you my plans. I know how you think. You would have gone running with the information and been my ruin." His brother prowled around him, transcribing a broad circle. "But now you're in *my* debt—I'm the reason *you're* not ruined—and you will keep my secret. For that matter, you'll *help* me."

Lamar swallowed. He wanted to deny it, but Gregor was right. His brother the Doyen had been the only thing standing between him and a career in shambles after Fort Courage. While his situation wasn't the rosiest, he wasn't a beggar on a street corner or behind salt-iron bars like he might have been otherwise. What else could he do? He nodded.

"Excellent." Gregor chuckled. "Stick with me, and you'll be justly rewarded. If we find that outlaw of yours, I'll even let you kill him."

"You're too kind," Lamar rumbled, though his mind was already whirring. He had no wife or children—he had dedicated himself to the ideals of the Confederation. It was a way of life for him. Gregor was his brother in blood and name, but his loyalty to the Confederation overshadowed their tumultuous relationship. And Lamar wouldn't see it brought down by anyone. Even his own brother.

Gregor was right. He was shamed, and no one with any clout would listen to him. But he knew someone *without* clout who might.

Flora

FLORA HOPED THAT JEFFERSON APPRECIATED THE LENGTHS SHE WAS going to for him and his mancrush. She had no problems with snooping around on his behalf for political or financial reasons, but this was uncharted territory. Throw in a guilt-ridden alchemist and an unstable outlaw, and it was a powder keg.

She did like Marian Hawthorne, though. The woman had a keen mind and a healthy mistrust of anyone she didn't know. Flora had earned a small measure of her trust once she brought back news of her family. Turned out the Confederation was treating them better than anyone else in the Hawthorne family, housing them on a secured estate but allowing them more freedom than the alchemist or Breaker.

Flora had just escorted Marian back to the Arboretum after another visit to check on Malcolm's condition. Security had been brought up a notch, though the alchemist made no mention to Flora if it was because they had discovered her jaunts outside the walls. Whatever the reason, Flora found a way around it.

Some of Flora's knocker brethren could take passengers when they transported to their metal of choice, but that was beyond her capabilities. However, she was accustomed to coming up with new and creative ways to circumvent problems. Elaborate distractions at the main gate made getting Marian in and out through a service entrance a snap.

She was resecuring the door when she heard the heavy crunch of boots behind her. Flora considered using her magic to vanish and be done with it, but she wanted to know what sort of threat she might have to deal with. She turned and frowned when she recognized the one-armed man walking up to her.

"Look who's here to single-handedly ruin my day," Flora commented, nonchalant.

Lamar Gaitwood froze at the cut of her words, his face scrunching in irritation. Was it nice? No, but Flora didn't care. Gaitwoods were trouble, and she was happy to make him feel unwelcome. Maybe it wasn't wise to bait the man, but Flora had a deep and abiding dislike for him. Lamar was aware she worked for Jefferson and had ties to Malcolm.

The Commander paused, and she had the sense that he was counting to ten to keep himself calm. Nice that he had some anger control mechanisms. He might need them if he continued talking to her. "I came to speak with you," he said when he regained his composure.

"Congratulations, you just did. And now we're done."

"Why are you at the Arboretum?" Gaitwood asked.

She narrowed her eyes. "Can't a girl take a walk around a pretty garden without being all suspicious?"

Lamar stared at her. "The Arboretum isn't open to the public."

"I know. I'm not the public." Flora dimpled at him. "I'm not *human,* so I didn't think it applied to me." Yeah, she was half-human, so she was fudging a bit. But she let enough vitriol leak into her tone to lend it credence.

Something about her words struck him, and for once Lamar seemed to falter. But he had magic, so maybe he understood not being considered human by others. Though *she* definitely considered him human. A big, especially dumb human. Magic or not, if it looked like a duck and quacked like a duck, it was a duck. Or a human, in this case.

Lamar shifted in place, glancing up at the rising moon overhead as he gathered his thoughts. Flora hoped he hurried it up. She had places to be and things to do. "I can't believe I'm telling you this," Gaitwood muttered with a shake of his head, which piqued her interest.

If he was fishing, it was a fine hook. "Telling me what?"

The Commander shuffled in a nervous circle, and Flora wondered if it was an act or if he was really this agitated. If he had two hands, she was certain he would have wrung them together in distress. As it was, he had his sole fist clenched by his side. "My brother is trying to bind the Breaker to *himself*."

Flora almost gaped at the announcement, but she kept her jaw locked and played it cool. As far as declarations went, this was right up there with Malcolm's preposterous idea to bind Blaise first. She made a *so what* gesture. "Okay?"

Lamar stared at her. "You can't allow him to do that."

She laughed. "Oh, I can't, can I?" Flora made a grand flourish to encompass herself. "So you came to the mighty Flora Strop, hero for hire, to solve the problems of a big, strapping man?"

Gaitwood clenched his jaw. "No, I came to Flora Strop, minion of Jefferson Cole, dandy with more money than sense."

He probably thought she'd take offense at being called a minion, but there were worse disparagements out there. "Yeah, well, this may come as a surprise to you, but his line of credit isn't good for buying war criminals on the free market." She shrugged. "Nothing we can do about it."

He watched her, eyes glittering. It was several heartbeats before he spoke, and when he did, his voice was low and soft. "That's not true. I know about the tattoo on Malcolm Wells's arm. In fact, I know he and Jeffer—"

Flora was on him *fastfastfast*, knife out as she leaped at him like a poxed squirrel scaling a tree. She scrambled up his chest and held the knife at his throat, keeping purchase on him by grasping his collar with her other hand. "Give me one good reason not to end you right now and dump your corpse into the swamp for the gators."

Lamar's eyes bugged out, which was gratifying. The tip of the knife nuzzled against his neck. "I didn't come here to get into a fight with you, Strop."

"This is no *fight*. For it to be a fight, you'd have to stand a chance," Flora scoffed.

He swallowed, the movement scraping his skin against the blade. A bead of blood appeared. "I came because I don't want my brother to have his way."

Now that was interesting. Flora cocked her head but didn't withdraw her knife. "No? Why's that?"

"Would you put away your weapon so we can speak like normal people?"

"I'm not a *normal people*, so I decline." Flora stared at him. "Keep talking."

Lamar sighed, a rivulet of sweat streaking down his forehead. "My position in the Confederation—"

"Yeah, rather strained after Fort Courage, so I hear."

He made a frustrated sound at her interruption. "As I was saying, I serve the *Confederation*. My brother seeks to destabilize it and take control of the whole thing."

Okay, maybe she needed to let him keep talking. She wished she had popcorn because this was getting *good*. Truth rang in his words, and as much as she hated him, she had to grant him that. In one smooth movement, she sheathed her knife and released her grip, dropping to the ground. "I'm listening."

Lamar's shoulders drooped with relief. He rubbed at the scrape on his throat. "Just because I'm privy to the secrets I mentioned, doesn't mean I'll divulge them. In return for my silence, I request an alliance."

Flora raised her eyebrows. She didn't like that Lamar knew some of Malcolm's secrets, not one bit. But it cost nothing to hear him out. "Yeah? What do you want?"

The Salt-Iron Commander straightened. "I want the Breaker out of the Cit and as far from Confederation lands as possible. Do that, and the secret will remain safe with me."

Yeah, that was about as safe as using a chupacabra as a sheepdog. But the way she saw it, she or Jack could take care of that later. She definitely liked the first part, though. "That won't be easy."

He smiled. "No, it's not. But it will be much easier with the help of a Commander, don't you think?"

"Well, when you put it that way..." Flora nodded. Then a thought occurred to her. Two birds, one stone. "I'll work with you if you do one thing for me."

Gaitwood's face blanked. "But I'm getting your friend out and keeping those secrets—"

Flora waved a hand. "Nuh-uh. That's all stuff to benefit my employer. This is a little something for *me*. You can help my hero for hire service that you seem to think I have going on. You agree to this, or I don't pass on any information to my boss."

His brows knit at that. "You would betray him like that?" His voice was a sneer, as if he could think of nothing lower.

Flora shrugged. Lamar didn't know her, didn't know that she would do just about anything for Jefferson and that this was all a bluff. "He's just a payday."

The Commander studied her, as if searching for the lie and not finding it. "What is it?"

Flora glanced at the Arboretum. "I need you to use your position to get Alchemist Hawthorne's family out of Phinora."

Lamar's eyes hardened. "Why?"

"'Cause I made someone a promise, and now you have me haring off to save a Breaker with you." She gave a dramatic sigh to demonstrate how inconvenienced she was by this. After a beat, he nodded agreement, and she offered her hand. He took it awkwardly, and Flora crushed his hand a little in hers, just because she could. "It's a deal."

Lamar nodded. "Oh, and Strop?" She glanced up at him. "I

meant what I said about the secret. I'm a man of my word, and I will keep it. But in the event I have an untimely demise, it's included in sealed letters to my lieutenants with instructions to open after my death. And at that point, all the world will find out."

She swallowed but nodded. *Keep the rattlesnake alive, got it.*

CHAPTER SEVENTEEN
Bitter End

Emmaline

*E*mmaline's back was ramrod straight in the saddle. She knew she was being watched. It was a sense she'd developed early. It didn't worry her, though—not really. To all appearances she might look like an easy mark: a young woman riding alone. But she prided herself on being more than met the eye. *Pegasus, sixgun, magic.* Yeah, she wasn't her father, and she wasn't sure she'd ever be in his league of sheer menace, but she could hold her own.

At least, that was what she told herself. It was a struggle to have such confidence after Fort Courage.

<Someone at three o'clock. Keeping their distance,> Oberidon informed her, flicking a speckled ear to the side in question.

Emmaline patted his shoulder in thanks. She held the reins loosely with her left hand, only doing so for show. A tiny poppet rested in the curl of her palm, the leather of the reins rubbing against it with each step Oberidon took. If someone asked how her magic worked to find someone, there was no way to describe it. When Emmaline held her mother's poppet, she felt a tug in her belly that told her if she was going in the right direction or not. If she went the wrong way, her stomach soured as if she had eaten something bad. Whatever this magic was, it was ingrained in her and likely not something she could teach another Effigest.

Oberidon kept to the trail that wound to the northwest, though as they continued through the area known as the Uplands, the forest surrounding them became dense, sometimes blocking the path. Every time he diverted from the trail, her gut twisted and didn't settle until they headed the right way again.

<Are we close?> Oberidon asked, turning his head to look back at her.

This spell worried her pegasus. It cost her a lot to maintain the working, but she wasn't about to let it falter. "Not much farther." And the words felt right to say, although she couldn't put a finger on the *why*.

The pegasus bobbed his head, continuing onward. Emmaline used her free hand to take a swig from her canteen and was mid-sip when a peculiar sensation shoved against her. She screwed the lid on the canteen and dropped it back into place, alarmed. "Oby?"

<I felt it, too. Magic of some sort.> He stopped in his tracks, pinning his ears and taking a few strides backward. <We shouldn't go this way.>

Emmaline's stomach roiled as her pegasus moved counter to the demands of her magic. She clenched her teeth, clamping her right hand over her stomach as her back arched in pain. "No. Keep going. *Please.*"

Oberidon froze beneath her, quivering. <I can't.>

Son of a bat-eared harpy. Emmaline sucked in a breath to quell the pain. Gods, she would have thought it was her monthlies if she didn't know better. But they no longer came—not after what had been done to her at Fort Courage. Gingerly, she dismounted, standing beside the spotted stallion as she considered their options. "Why can't you go forward?" There was no physical barrier stopping them.

Oberidon fluttered his nostrils. <Because I *can't.*>

Emmaline frowned. Sometimes Oberidon was a goof, like the time he submerged himself up to his eyes in a pond and swam around, munching on lily pads. But he knew how important this mission was to her. Oberidon wouldn't fool around, not for this. Pegasi were intelligent—smarter than a lot of humans, in fact. But sometimes, people—or pegasi—could be misled into believing something was true, even when it wasn't. The magic continued its insistent push against her, but the beckoning of the effigy over-rode it.

"You stay put," Emmaline murmured, rubbing his velvety nose.

Oberidon's ears flopped sideways, miserable that he was letting her down. She turned away from him, but before soldiering onward, she had an idea. Emmaline turned back and snagged his reins. Oberidon couldn't take *her* forward, but perhaps *she* could lead *him.* He snorted and doggedly trailed after her.

It took ten steps before reaching whatever was pushing magic against them. It was a sort of invisible barrier, pulsing before her with the looming command to run in the opposite direction. Emmaline gritted her teeth as it assaulted them.

"I didn't come this far to turn back now." Head down and trembling with exertion, she powered through the magical bulwark. Oberidon followed in her wake, snorting and skittish.

Emmaline hadn't realized the cost of breaking through. She stumbled to her hands and knees, the poppet falling away from her. But her stomach didn't sour, and she knew she was still going the right way. Distantly, she was aware of the sounds of feet slapping against the ground as people made their way toward her. It alarmed the outlaw part of her, the part that was always on edge and alert. But she had other priorities. She scrabbled a hand through the grass, searching for the poppet. She *needed* it.

<Em! We're outnumbered!> Oberidon's panic bled into her mind, and Emmaline lifted her head to stare at the semi-circle of

men and women a dozen paces ahead of them, many with rifles and revolvers out and ready.

"*How* did you break through those wards?" an older man with a shiny bald head demanded from the crowd.

"I was tailing her! She just walked on through," a young man piped up, pushing his way through the underbrush to join the group.

Emmaline licked her lips, surveying the group. *Defenders. Maybe sentries. I think we stumbled onto some sort of hidden settlement.* Yeah, that sounded right. Like Fortitude before the battle. Except this place had some sort of fancy ward, which was a marvelous idea. She blinked as she realized she hadn't answered them yet. Gods, she hadn't realized how bad the fatigue from magic drain could be. "Um, magic?"

Someone shoved past the man who had posed the question, booted feet carrying them to Emmaline's side. Oberidon made a querying nicker, uncertain. The stranger knelt in front of Emmaline, helping her into a sitting position. Emmaline quivered at the odd flutter in her stomach. She looked up and into a face that could have been her own in a decade or two.

"Katherine, who *is* this? Who broke through our wards?" another of the gathered mages demanded.

"My daughter," the strange woman whispered, her voice afire with emotion. "My *daughter* broke the wards."

Emmaline blinked as the words registered. She shook her head, vision clearing with the effort. "*Mom.*" That accounted for the flutter. She had found her target. Completed her mission.

Her mother pulled her close, and Emmaline was so tired her mind drifted to the last time she had been curled against this woman when she was three years old. The stale scent of alcohol wafted off her mother's clothes and breath, but all Emmaline focused on was the *rightness* and security of their embrace. Something scratchy bit into the palm of her hand—*oh, the poppet.* Magic coursed through it, still draining her.

Her mother tensed, as if she felt the power, too. She angled to peer at the poppet, though she wobbled with the movement. She placed her hand over the tiny doll in Emmaline's grasp. "Cancel your spell, baby. I don't know how you did it, but you're done."

Emmaline tightened her fist around the poppet and ended the spell, relief settling over her as the ongoing draw on her limited magic ended. "I found you. I can't believe I found you."

"She broke our wards," the older man from earlier complained again.

"Shut your stupid mouth, Basil," her mother snapped, unsteadily getting to her feet. She offered a hand to Emmaline, who declined because, as tired as she was, she didn't want to topple her mother. "You act like you don't know the first thing about repairing it."

"But if she did it then—"

Emmaline blinked as a ball of flame appeared in her mother's upturned palm. *"Not. Another. Word."*

Basil's mouth was wide and gasping, like a fish out of water. "Katherine, you're drunk. You wouldn't—"

"Don't tell me what I wouldn't do," she retorted. She closed her hand, quenching the flame so the smoke wisped away to nothing. She put an arm around her daughter. "Come on. We'll speak more after we get grub in you and some rest." Her mother tottered a few steps. "And maybe I need to sober up a little more."

Emmaline glanced back at Oberidon, who followed along, obedient. The other defenders parted to allow them to pass, and a short distance later, signs of civilization appeared. Small homes and even what looked like businesses clustered in a clearing. "What is this place?"

Kittie smiled. "Welcome to Bitter End."

Kittie

Kittie brushed back an errant lock of her daughter's golden hair, the simple motion taking her back more than a decade. She swallowed, fighting back the tears that threatened to spring from her eyes unbidden. Not now. She needed to be strong, even if all she wanted to do was curl around her exhausted child and protect her from the world.

Effigest. Emmaline was an Effigest like her father. Kittie set aside that information for later—she had so many questions, but they would wait. She had her own battles to fight first. Starting with her allies.

She steeled herself, head high, as she opened the door of the small cottage she shared with her husband, who was away. As expected, a small throng awaited her. Leander Benton, sentry chief for Bitter End, led the group with his arms crossed. "You've got some explaining to do, Katherine."

Kittie studied him. Leander was taller and bulkier than her—than anyone else in town, in fact. He liked to think that his sheer size gave him an advantage, and maybe against others, it did. But she'd gone toe to toe with better men.

Stanley Cavin, who fancied himself the mayor of their idyllic little band of misfits, stepped around Leander, putting an arm in front of him. "What he means, of course, is that we're curious how that slip of a girl breached the wards like a hot knife through butter."

Kittie glanced at the closed door behind her, debating how much to tell them. None of them knew anything about her life before her arrival at Bitter End. "I already told you: she's my daughter."

Stanley frowned, shifting his weight from foot to foot as if her explanation bothered him. It probably did, in the grand scheme of things. He glanced at her hands like they were coiled rattlesnakes. "What else haven't you told us, Katherine? Does Hugh know?"

She scoffed at that. As if she would have told her husband anything of who she was. Of who she had been. Of the life she believed lost to her forever. No, she wasn't willing to bare those wounds to anyone here. "He doesn't know. I'll tell him when he returns." Even though he would be furious. But she could take the heat.

Stanley and Leander traded glances. "She's a mage?" Stanley asked.

Kittie nodded. She hadn't been able to speak to Emmaline much since she burst through the barrier, her daughter had been so worn out. But there was no doubt she had magic.

"What is she?" Leander asked.

Kittie smiled. "A maverick. That's all I can tell you right now."

Leander scowled. Stanley licked his lips. "We need to know if anyone followed her. That's all we ask."

"And all you need to know is that if she was followed, I'll turn anyone on her trail to ash." Kittie turned on her heel and strode back into her house.

CHAPTER EIGHTEEN

Unconventional Teaching Methods

Malcolm

"Up and at 'em," Jack declared as he threw open the door to Malcolm's room.

Malcolm blinked from where he reclined on the bed, supported by a flock of goose-down pillows. He had been going through the notes of the recent Council sessions he had missed, staying up-to-date with political events. "What?"

The outlaw jerked a thumb at the open hallway behind him. "We're going to practice. And you're not gonna laze around here all day to do it."

Malcolm frowned. *That's unfair.* "I'm not lazing around. And I'm in the middle of something, thank you very much."

Too late, he realized that was the wrong tack to take with Jack. The outlaw crossed his arms. "That so? Guess you got all your sleepwalking magic figured out then." His eyes glinted. "And if I came at you now, you could stop me, is that right?"

"Wait, what?" Malcolm asked with growing alarm. Surely he had misheard the volatile mage. "*Stop* you?"

Jack grinned. "If I were to attack you, could you stop me in my tracks?" At Malcolm's blank look, he added, "Using your magic."

Brow scrunching in confusion, Malcolm shook his head. "But my magic isn't offensive. Or defensive, for that matter." At least, he didn't think so. The disapproving crinkles in the skin around Jack's eyes told a different tale, however.

"Thinking like that is gonna get you in trouble," the Effigest rebuked him, leaning against the door-frame like a languid cat.

With a frustrated sigh, Malcolm folded up the meeting minutes and shoved them into a folder, which he set aside. "Fine, but you already know the answer. Why even ask?"

"Because," the outlaw rumbled, studying him, "you're gonna learn."

Defend himself with magic? Dream magic, at that. Malcolm rubbed his chin, thoughtful. Jack worked with him a few times a day. Jefferson had made a little progress and could now call up the dreamscape without falling asleep. He had a better idea about how to manipulate his power, but it still felt like rowing in a rain-swollen river: he was more likely to go with the flow than direct the current. He wanted to respond that he couldn't do it, but the outlaw would be sure to argue against it. Which meant that Jack had devised tactics he could use already.

Malcolm shifted upright and tossed the sheets back, freeing himself to swing his legs out of bed. "If you were me, what would you do?"

Jack jabbed an index finger at him. "By the grace of the gods, I'm *not* you because that would be damned annoying. And that's for you to figure out. C'mon."

"But I'm not even dressed—"

The outlaw aimed a contemptuous look at him. "You're dressed enough. We're not going to a gods-forsaken gala."

That was true. Malcolm winced as he took in his disheveled state. His current shirt was rumpled and unkempt, and the trousers he had on were a comfortable pair from five seasons previous. But the outlaw had little patience, so Malcolm gingerly pulled out a pair of shoes and crammed his feet into them, following Jack out.

The Effigest headed out to the stables. Malcolm cocked his head, curious, but didn't ask. Square hay bales crouched outside the two stalls used by the pegasi, though someone had draped saddle blankets over them to serve as cushions. Emrys and Zepheus peered over their stall doors, curious.

"What are we doing?" Malcolm asked.

The outlaw sat on one of the covered bales, elbows on his knees. "We're taking the training up a notch. You been in your fancy dreamscape every night?"

Malcolm swallowed, the mention of the dreamscape turning his mind to Blaise. "Yes."

Maybe Jack detected the twinge of emotion in his voice. He narrowed his eyes but didn't comment. "Good. Means you're using your magic regularly, so you may know more about it than you think. Long as you're not terrified of your magic, it's possible to learn how to wrangle it naturally."

Malcolm nodded, knowing Jack was referring to Blaise before he had wrestled his power under control. Little wonder the young man's dangerous magic had intimidated him.

Jack glanced back at the pegasi, then to Malcolm. "I want you to make Emrys sleep."

"Excuse me?" Malcolm was sure he'd misheard.

The outlaw smirked. "You heard me."

The black stallion bobbed his head. <I volunteered. It is fine.>

Malcolm pursed his lips, uncertain. "I've never—"

Jack held up a hand. "Stop your caterwauling and do it."

Right. It was clear the outlaw wouldn't relent until he tried. And *succeeded*. Malcolm winced, glad Jack hadn't been the one to train Blaise. That would have ended poorly for everyone involved. Malcolm took a deep breath to center himself. His magic was easiest to manipulate when he was asleep, but Jack was training him to use it while he was awake, too. He wasn't very good at it, though. It was an uncomfortable feeling, being so clumsy at something like this.

He imagined the magic was within him like a lump of clay, ready to be formed. *No, I don't like that analogy.* Perhaps it was more like the words of a script, to be acted upon. *Yes, I like that.* He was no playwright, but at the theater he knew what to expect. He was the director. Malcolm smiled, enjoying the idea.

"Stop fooling around," Jack reminded him.

Malcolm wrinkled his nose at the interruption, then imagined he was directing the script—his magic—to his actor, Emrys. He held the stallion's proximity in his mind, and there was a sensation like static when his power found its target. *Sleep.*

Jack's sharp intake of breath was all the proof of success he needed. But just to be sure, Malcolm opened his eyes and turned to the stall behind him. Emrys was still upright, but his head was low, eyes closed. One hoof was cocked in a relaxed posture.

"Don't stop now. Give 'im a dream," Jack ordered.

Give him a dream? Malcolm frowned. "I don't—" He stopped himself before Jack could interrupt. "Wait, I think I can." It couldn't be that much different from what he had done on instinct with Blaise. Except now he had to do it while he was awake and Emrys was asleep.

Malcolm closed his eyes, concentrating. He focused on the stallion's presence, finding him. There was no way he could tell if the pegasus was still asleep, but he hoped that was the case. Malcolm imagined the dreamscape unwinding before him. It was a vast, grey space, ready to be formed. Itude was easiest, so he called the town up. But this was Emrys, and he deserved something special. Malcolm recalled the broad tables that had covered the town square at the Feast of Flight, and they appeared before him.

"Hmm, yes," he murmured, another idea coming to him. Every imaginable sort of dessert popped into existence on the tables.

Pleased, he sought Emrys and pulled the stallion into the dreamscape. The pegasus trotted along as if all were normal, though he came to a stiff-legged halt at the sight of the heavily-laden tables. His ears pricked forward with interest.

<Is that what I think it is?> Emrys quivered with delight.

Malcolm grinned. "Every sort of treat Blaise ever made? Yes."

<For me?> The stallion arched his neck, nostrils flared.

"And only you."

Emrys bolted over to the tables, thrusting his muzzle into a decadent cake, nearly toppling it onto a nearby pie. He took a chomping bite from each one, going down the line as if he hadn't eaten in weeks. Malcolm was glad it was a dream because he would have felt terrible if he colicked Blaise's pegasus.

Something—no, someone—grabbed Malcolm by the shirt collar, hoisting him up. With a gasp, he opened his eyes and found Jack glaring at him. The outlaw levered back an arm, and Malcolm was certain he was about to take a punch. *Not my face.* He tried to writhe away, but the outlaw was stronger and better prepared. Jack snaked a foot behind Malcolm's ankle, jerking his leg out from under him so he stumbled to the ground with frantic, pinwheeling arms.

The outlaw stood over him, a foreboding shadow. Panic gripped Malcolm. After all this, Jack had become untethered and was going to kill him. *No.*

Malcolm pulled at his dream magic, hurling it at the outlaw. *Sleep, you bastard!*

Jack slumped to the ground, landing on a saddle pad that had been moved to cushion his fall.

"What?" Malcolm gasped, pushing into a sitting position as he panted for breath. He glanced back at Zepheus. Jack's palomino was the only other witness who was awake. "What is *wrong* with him?"

<It was a test,> the pegasus answered, chewing thoughtfully on a wisp of hay.

A test. Malcolm made a face. "Why didn't he—oh." Jack had, in fact, given him ample warning. He leaned back against the prickly hay bale, his heart pounding like a runaway horse. Gods, that had been terrifying. To think Jack had only been *play-acting*. Malcolm didn't want to ever fight him in earnest.

He sat there for another half hour until the outlaw stirred with a yawn. Jack rubbed at his face, sitting up slowly. "You did it, huh?"

Malcolm crossed his arms. "You really need to work on your teaching methods."

The outlaw grinned. "My methods may be unconventional, but I'm a very effective teacher, I'll have you know." He clambered to his feet, stretching as if he'd had a nice cat nap. "It worked?"

Malcolm massaged his forehead. "Yes."

"Then why are you mad?"

"I *thought* you were going to kill me!"

Jack laughed. "If I wanted to kill you, you'd be gettin' dressed for the bone orchard already." He turned and headed for the stable door, waving a hand over his shoulder. "Keep practicing, Sleepwalker."

CHAPTER NINETEEN
Breaker Unleashed

Blaise

Sleep didn't come easily to Blaise, not in his current circumstances, but he was exhausted and weak from the day, his body bruised and tender. Previously he had been afraid to sleep because nightmares greeted him as soon as he drifted off. But now he welcomed the dreams that he knew would rescue him from the darkness.

He was back in Itude, his body hale and clean. Blaise glanced down, self-conscious. He didn't think Jefferson would care what he looked like, but all the same, he worried about being a disappointment.

Jefferson was nowhere to be seen. Blaise walked through the empty town, reveling in the simple joy of his body working as it should. No aches and pains. No cuts or bruises. He shaded his eyes as he caught a strange shimmer of movement. Blaise glanced down and noticed a gleaming thread of magic stretching from himself to the distant horizon. He'd never seen that before—but then again, he'd been distracted. Gently, he touched it with a finger, mindful of his magic. Something about the thread was comforting. It reminded him of Jefferson.

"Is this the geasa?" Blaise murmured, studying it. Such a fragile thing, easily sheared apart by his magic. If the Confederation bound anyone else to him, he was confident he could break free.

"You can do it if you want," a familiar voice said. Jefferson strode up, resplendent in a tan frock coat. Blaise couldn't remember ever seeing him in such a light color before, and it brought out the gold in Jefferson's hair. "Break it, I mean. I wouldn't blame you."

Blaise looked over his shoulder. "Are you reading my mind?"

Jefferson chuckled. "I don't think so. But I know how you feel about this." He tilted his head, shoving his hands in his pockets. "May I ask you something?"

Curiosity tempered Jefferson's tone. Blaise nodded. "Sure."

"Why haven't you tried to escape?" Concern lined Jefferson's green eyes.

Blaise dropped his gaze, recalling that Jefferson hadn't seen him recently. Didn't know that each day he was weaker than the previous. "It's not as easy as breaking down a door or a wall and walking out of here." He rubbed the back of his neck. "I could probably do that, yeah. But after that? There's all the guards I would face. They have guns, and we already know what a bullet can do to me." As if summoned by the memory, the old wound in his arm twinged. At the same time, Blaise recalled the short-lived shield of magic he had created. He shook his head, dismissing it. "Magic doesn't solve everything."

"No, I suppose it doesn't," Jefferson agreed. Then a smile curled his lips, and he took a step closer. "What if I told you we're going to get you out?"

The words came as such a surprise that Blaise was certain he'd misheard. "What?"

"We're going to get you out. Soon. Within a few days, I hope," Jefferson said, the words coming in a rush of excitement. He flapped his hands around as if he couldn't control them. "You'll be free."

Blaise stared at him. Freedom. That seemed like such an elusive concept right now. His mouth went dry. "How? Where will I go?" He looked down, eyes welling with tears. "You haven't seen me...the *real* me...for a while. I'll have a hard time getting out. I'm too weak."

Jefferson studied him. The corners of his eyes crinkled with worry. "All the more reason to get you out."

Blaise swallowed, overcome with emotion. He couldn't help it; the idea was so overwhelming all he could do was sit down where he was, which was in the middle of one of the dusty streets. He put his face in his hands.

He heard the scuff of Jefferson crouching down beside him. "What's wrong?"

How could he explain? Blaise shook his head. He didn't know how to express the mixed sense of relief and renewed hope, but also the anxiety that he had forgotten how to fit in. Or worse, that no one would want him. That they would free him and see him for the broken thing that he was. And he didn't want to say any of those things because then Jefferson might decide to leave him behind.

An arm slung around his shoulders, warm and comforting. The spearmint scent of Jefferson's aftershave wafted to Blaise. "Hey. Come back to me."

The words were almost a plea, and they were what Blaise needed to hear in that moment. "I'm here."

Jefferson gave him a sideways glance, as if he feared Blaise would spook away from beneath his arm like a skittish horse. But Blaise didn't—it was kinder than any touch he'd experienced recently. "This is our time. What do you want to do?"

"Talk," Blaise said softly. "No one talks to me like I'm..." He shook his head. "Like I'm a person."

Jefferson's eyebrows slashed together before relaxing. "We can talk. Whatever you like."

Blaise nodded, thankful, and got back to his feet with care. They walked together through the town, passing by the bakery. He glanced at it for a moment, reconsidering. *Another time,* he promised himself. Right now, he needed to be heard.

"I'm going to tell you some things because I don't think I'll be brave enough to tell you outside of a dream," Blaise whispered. "It's just too much."

Jefferson took his hand. "I understand. I'm listening."

Blaise bowed his head, and with the wind of the dreamscape whistling overhead, he told Jefferson of the things he had endured. The beatings and the experimentation. How they sometimes bled him until he was too weak to move. The way the guards and staff treated him as if he were nothing.

Jefferson listened, intent, never interrupting, his expression open as he nodded, somehow knowing that all Blaise needed was to be listened to. Blaise felt like he was talking about someone else —it was difficult to recognize that all those things had happened to *him.* It was good to tell someone, to have someone listen and simply be there.

He finished, tears streaming down his face and his shoulders sagging with exhaustion, and he didn't fight it when Jefferson pulled him into an embrace that offered comfort, strength, and love. "I'm sorry. Gods, I'm *so* sorry," Jefferson said after a few minutes, his voice taut with suppressed anger.

Blaise swiped at his runny nose. "Why is my nose snotty when I cry in a dream?"

"So I can do this," Jefferson said, pulling out a handkerchief and offering it to him. "But I don't know. I guess we expect it, and it happens."

Blaise nodded, dabbing at his nose with the handkerchief. "I'm sorry I'm a mess."

Jefferson shook his head. "You're not a mess, and there's no need to apologize. I just wish I could do more."

Blaise glanced away, rubbing at the tattoo on his bicep. He felt a little better for having told someone what he had endured. It was cleansing to have validation, even if he was still in the situation. But that wasn't the only thing weighing heavily on his mind. "I'm not like the others."

Jefferson drew away, blinking at him in bewilderment. "What? Not like who?"

With chagrin, Blaise realized there was no way the other man could have followed the wild path his thoughts went down. "The people you were with in the dream garden."

"*Oh.*" A cringe flashed across Jefferson's face. Then he clasped his hands, shaking his head. "I don't expect you to be." He shifted until he was shoulder to shoulder with Blaise again.

"Doesn't that bother you?"

Jefferson raised a brow. "Why would that bother me?"

Blaise pursed his lips, uncertain if this was a conversation he even wanted to have. But they had dabbled with the topic previously in Rainbow Flat—and gods, that felt like a thousand years ago. "I don't know if that's something we would ever do."

He expected to see hurt or anger on Jefferson's face. Instead, he merely nodded his head. "There's more to love than sex."

Blaise rubbed the back of his neck. Unschooled as he was in that topic, he was quickly becoming out of his depth. "Is there?"

"Of course." Jefferson's voice turned soft. "Intimacy is amazing, but if that's all that exists, then it's purely lust." His gaze flicked to Blaise, green eyes assessing. "It's also being accepted by someone else for *who* you are."

Odd as it was, Blaise realized Jefferson was speaking about himself, not Blaise. How strange, since Blaise had never stopped to think the other man sought acceptance, too. Jefferson had given Blaise a glimpse of his past life, one that had been bereft of caring. He'd been a commodity, something to be bartered and used.

"And it's being there for someone you care about, come what may," Jefferson continued, unaware of Blaise's thoughts. He ran a hand along the ridge of his jaw. "Granted, if we had this conversation ten years ago, I would give you a very different answer. And that's what you saw in the garden." Jefferson ended the statement with a self-deprecating shrug.

Blaise nodded. He appreciated Jefferson's words, though he was uncertain if the other man truly understood him. "And if I never...want to be like the people in the garden?" Blaise inwardly winced. Why was it so hard, so uncomfortable, to talk about sex? It was a part of life, but one that he didn't want to think about.

Jefferson cocked his head, lips pursed as if he were trying to figure out why Blaise was so adamant about this discussion. "I won't mislead you. I was hoping for that with you. But if you listened to anything I just said, that's not what I *need*." And then, as if he wanted to make certain that Blaise didn't misunderstand, he added, "You. *You* are all I need in whatever way you're willing to grant me that."

"You realize I have boundaries. Things I may never be comfortable doing." Blaise wanted nothing less than certainty.

Jefferson chuckled. "I'm aware. Sort of like your preference for switchel over wine." He gave an exaggerated sigh, then grew serious again. "I know that. And believe it or not after the garden, I *respect* that."

Blaise swallowed, shaken by the intensity in Jefferson's voice. *He understands. And he doesn't mind.* That could change with time, Blaise feared. But that was something to worry about if it came down to it. He released a heavy breath, then put an arm around Jefferson, resting his head against the other man's shoulder.

They talked for as long as they could, until the wakefulness of early morning tugged Blaise away, returning him to his stark reality. The ragged blanket he laid on was a far cry from the safety of Jefferson's bulk, and the cell was foreign after the sun on his skin in the dreamscape. But he felt more hopeful than he had in the past. The memory of Jefferson's face bathed in the sun's glow, watching him with compassion and affection, was a balm for his soul. He felt wanted. He felt human.

And that was all he needed to hold on until rescue came.

GREGOR PACED BEFORE BLAISE LIKE AN AGITATED GRASSCAT, peppering the Inker with questions on why yet another attempt to bind him had failed. Blaise tuned out most of the Doyen's rant. At this point, it wasn't anything he hadn't heard before. He allowed his mind to wander from the hopelessness of his situation. There was nothing he could do at this point to change his predicament.

He often thought of Jefferson and his sandy brown hair. Jefferson, who came to him each night, lighting the darkness with stars and dreams that Blaise knew were real.

"*Look at me when I speak to you!*" a voice raged in front of him, sharp as the crack of a whip. Gregor Gaitwood was inches from his face.

Blaise jumped, though he was fastened tightly to his customary seat, and he didn't move far. But his magic reacted, rising to the surface and breaking free like a stampede. He didn't care to call it back, but let it loose. It snapped the binds that held him in place, the leather flaking and falling to the floor in chunks. The salt-iron shackles on his wrists groaned and grated under the magical assault. Metal shavings drifted down as his power slowly, inexorably did the unthinkable.

The Inker shrank back. "He's breaking the *salt-iron.*"

"Of course he is. He's unlike anything we've seen before," Gregor said, his focus still on Blaise. "*Why can't we break you, boy?*"

Blaise met his eyes, something he rarely did anymore, and smiled. Days ago, he wouldn't have dared to do it. But Jefferson had renewed his sense of self and his shattered confidence. They could do everything in their power to beat him and keep him down, but they weren't going to win. Not while he had people fighting for him.

"Because *I'm* the Breaker, and that's what *I* do," Blaise answered, his voice little more than a raw whisper as his power chewed through the shackles. They fell to the floor with a clatter.

Guards rushed in and swarmed him. Maybe he would regret

his words later, but in this moment, he didn't. His words had sown doubt in Gregor Gaitwood, and that was all Blaise needed to feel empowered at last.

But Gaitwood wasn't about to let him have the upper hand. The guards crushed Blaise's face against the stone floor as the Doyen announced, "Give him the potion. I'll make use of him before it's too late."

CHAPTER TWENTY

How To Save a Life

Flora

No one thought anything amiss when a courier brought Flora a coded letter. It was a frequent occurrence, and not a single one of Malcolm's staffers so much as batted an eye as she withdrew, tucking it beneath her arm. Just as well. It would have been awkward to explain away a letter from Lamar Gaitwood.

Maybe she should have told Malcolm and Jack that the Commander was throwing in his lot with them. Flora didn't know Jack well, but she knew enough to understand that he was capricious and bore a grudge against Lamar. In fact, a crashing airship had almost smashed the fool to a pulp because of that grudge. She couldn't fault him since Lamar was the walking equivalent to skunk stank. Flora wasn't above using every tool at hand. And Lamar may disagree, but he was definitely a tool.

Flora considered passing the information to Malcolm, but he had enough on his plate. And besides, this wouldn't be the first time she quietly took care of something on his behalf. That was her job. The information that Lamar had on her employer concerned her—*how did he find out?*—but she would figure out how to scrub that dangerous information out of existence. It was delicate and would take longer, but if Lamar kept his end of the bargain, she would fix it.

She found a quiet room and tore the correspondence open. Flora hissed out a frustrated sigh at the simple code the Commander had used. *Amateur.* Her Uncle Jasper could've figured it out, and he didn't have a mind for such things.

The precious cargo you requested for transfer is headed to Rainbow Flat. Other target must move tomorrow. Meet me tonight at the Sour Eel. 22:00. Alone.

Flora frowned at the note. On the one hand, if he could be believed, then Marian's family was on their way to safety, and that was promising. But on the other...they weren't quite ready to free Blaise. They were close, but this was too soon. She wondered if this was some sort of double-cross. If Jack got wind of it, he would think so. But it wouldn't hurt to meet the good Commander tonight to see what he had to say and feel things out.

Jack

JACK SHOT A GLANCE AT FLORA. THE HALF-KNOCKER SEEMED jumpier than usual, which maybe was to be expected when planning a jailbreak from a place like the Cit. But he'd witnessed the casual carnage she wrought at Fort Courage, and that seemed more in line with what he knew of her. Something was up, and he didn't like it.

But all the same, he was glad for the change of pace. He had spent the last several days lurking around Wells's fancy-pants estate, his training sessions with the pretty boy his only entertainment. It was high time for action.

Now, they clustered in the broad center aisle of the stables so that the pegasi could plot along with them. Flora had produced a map of the Golden Citadel and the surrounding area, spreading it out on a crate in the middle of their huddle. When asked how she acquired it, she simply replied that she had connections. *Strop's blowing a bunch of corral dust at us, but why?*

"Getting in is going to be the challenge," Jack murmured, running his fingers over the entrance on the map. "Won't be able to use my magic."

"What, you can't use your hexing to look like someone else?" Flora asked.

A muscle in Jack's cheek twitched in annoyance. "*First of all,* hexing is harmful; charming is helpful. I go both ways."

"You do, huh?" Flora's brows rose.

"Shut your piehole before I hex *you,*" the outlaw growled. "I'm an *Effigest,* not a Hexxer or a Charmer. And besides, you're thinking of an Illusionist. My workings can't change how someone looks." He shrugged. "And even if I could, it wouldn't help me get in."

Malcolm frowned. "Why not?"

"Because," Jack said, tracing the perimeter of the Cit on the map, "there's a ward in place all the way around that detects magic."

The Doyen blinked in surprise. "But I'm able to enter as Jefferson with no fuss."

Yeah, and Jack wondered how that was. "And no one's ever questioned you?"

Malcolm shrugged. "I mean, not yet..."

"How *do* you keep that two-faced guise of yours?" Jack asked, leaning forward. He didn't care if the question was insensitive. In fact, he kinda liked the way the other man winced at the words.

Malcolm traded a glance with Flora, appearing to debate the wisdom of divulging his secret. She crossed her arms, then gave a small nod. Malcolm pulled a gaudy ring into view. "This ring is spelled with a glamor."

An item. That was sort of what Jack expected. He tapped his fingers against the map, considering. "A glamor from an enchanted item is different. Remember our little chat about magic?" Jack lifted a hand to gesture to the world around them.

"About it being everywhere?" Jefferson asked.

"In anything that *lives*," Jack corrected. He jerked his chin to indicate the ring. "Not alive."

Flora canted her head, thoughtful. "Kinda major oversight by whoever designed the ward."

"Not all theurgists care to be thorough," Jack said with a shrug. He had known the designer. The mage was long dead, but the magic remained intact. The odds of the Confederation upgrading it were slim. Why change something that worked?

"If I had another enchanted item, we could get you in easily!" Jefferson said as he caught on to the intricacies of the ward. Then he scratched his chin, deflating. "But there's no time. So how do we get Jack in? Disguised as a guard, perhaps?"

Jack snorted. "That's not gonna work. You can bet the gate guards can identify everyone who works the grounds by sight." Absently, he rubbed at his shoulder as old memories stirred. "Too bad we can't wait 'til nightfall."

Flora snagged Malcolm's watch from his breast pocket, flipping it open to check the time. It was after midnight, and none of them were under any illusions to go haring off without a solid plan. "We'll miss our window if we wait. And Mal still has to contact Blaise."

The outlaw blew out a frustrated breath. "Well, not sure how far y'all would get inside the Cit without me."

"No, we need you," Malcolm agreed.

Flora shifted, scratching at her stone-colored forehead as she reached a conclusion. "I have an idea, but Jack won't like it."

Jack tilted his head. "Try me."

The half-knocker gave a nervous laugh. "Full disclosure, I got the map we're looking at from Lamar Gaitwood." Malcolm's jaw dropped, and Jack stilled. "Also, he's the one that told me about Gregor's plan to move Blaise tomorrow."

At Lamar's name, fury flooded through Jack's veins. Flora Strop was a damned traitor. He launched at her, but she expected his move and dodged out of the way with unnatural alacrity. Jack twisted, pulling on the magic of his own poppet to grant him speed as he went after the half-knocker. He was so pissed off he forgot Malcolm was there. And that he had magic of his own.

Jack awoke an hour later, flat on his back. Zepheus's muzzle hovered over him, blowing equine breath into his face. <You should let people explain things first before you try to murder them,> the pegasus advised.

The outlaw grunted, sitting up. Something scratched against his head, and he reached up and plucked straw from his hair. He glared at Flora and Malcolm. The Doyen was watching him like he was a dangerous beast. Flora didn't so much as glance his way, poring over the map.

He leveled a finger at Malcolm. "Don't you *ever* do that to me again."

Curse him to Perdition, but Malcolm *smirked* at him. "I was just making sure I could stop you in your tracks."

Jack grunted, getting to his feet. "There better be a damned good reason Strop's thrown in her lot with Lamar."

"We discussed it while you napped." Malcolm nodded. "Long story short, Gregor is betraying the Confederation, and Lamar doesn't like it."

"Hmm." Jack rubbed his chin. From his history with Lamar, that was likely. "Explain."

He listened as Malcolm recounted Flora's information. Gregor wanted to take out the other members of the Salt-Iron Council? As far as goals went, Jack thought that was a pretty good one. But it would leave Gregor the sole surviving member, and it sounded like he was keen to make a power grab. Yeah, that checked out for Lamar's motivation. Didn't mean Jack liked it, though.

"My idea is that Lamar can take you into the Cit," Flora said once Malcolm finished. She held up a hand before Jack protested. "Don't tell me he's going to betray us. He's on our side for the time being. He wants Blaise as far from Izhadell as we can take him so Gregor can't use him."

Jack pursed his lips, glancing at Malcolm. "You trust this?"

The Doyen sighed. "I don't know what other choice we have. Either we assume the information is good and act on it, or we mistrust it and don't. If we don't..." He looked away, shaking his head.

It would be the end of the line for Blaise, and maybe for all the mages in Phinora if Gregor succeeded at killing the Council. Jack bared his teeth. Yeah, Gregor would start a war. There would be a genocide of anyone with magic.

Dread tickled his spine. Emmaline was still in Phinora, going after Kittie. He closed his eyes briefly. They would be at risk, too. "Fine. We'll do it, but if Lamar betrays us, I'm killing him."

"Yeah, I know how you operate," Flora said with a roll of her eyes. "So we're doing this?"

Jack didn't want to. Every instinct screamed *wrong, wrong, wrong.* But if he was honest with himself, it was more than Lamar's presence setting him off. It was the Cit itself.

<I will be outside the walls. It will not be like the last time you were there,> Zepheus assured him, bumping him gently with his muzzle.

The outlaw nodded. "Yeah, we're doing this." He yawned. "Time to get some shut-eye for real while I can. Sleepwalker, tell Blaise we're coming for him."

"It's *Dreamer,*" Malcolm muttered with a shake of his head. "And I would love to."

CHAPTER TWENTY-ONE

Hurricane

Jefferson

*T*he dreamscape was a discordant nightmare.

Falling asleep after finalizing their plans to free Blaise hadn't been easy. It was the second glass of wine that eased him into slumber. At first Jefferson thought it was the wine that had forced the dream into a confusing jumble.

It was difficult to make heads or tails of what he was looking at—warped skeletons of buildings existed and then faded away, the landscape shifting from the Gutter to a forest and then to a prison cell. An unnatural wind whipped against Jefferson, screaming with unrelenting fury, making it impossible to walk forward.

It had never been like this before, and he didn't understand what was happening. He was supposed to be the master of his magic. Jefferson froze, tapping into his power. It rose to his summons, and he sent it out against the nightmare dreamscape, struggling to bend it to his will. In the distance, something shattered with the brittle tinkling of broken glass.

Jefferson gritted his teeth and glanced down at his feet. With a start, he realized that the dreaming world around him was fracturing. The ground beneath him grew into a crack that yawned wider and wider, threatening to swallow him whole. He dodged aside, breaking into a clumsy jog against the biting wind.

"Blaise!" Jefferson called, stumbling as he suffered an annoying moment of not being able to run in his dream. It took everything he had to break free and bolt onward. "Where are you?"

He knew Blaise was there. Jefferson sensed his presence through their bond. But it was as if he were everywhere, all around him. And with a shock, he realized Blaise *was* all around him, in a way. Breaker magic was assaulting the dreamscape, ripping it asunder. But that made little sense. This was a safe place for Blaise, a haven. *Something has changed.*

Metal crunched, and Jefferson had the sickening suspicion that it was a memory of the destroyed airship. Screams sounded in the distance. The pressure inside the dreamscape built until Jefferson feared that he, too, might end up cracked like an egg. He needed to *do* something, but what? The wrath reminded him of the hurricanes that swept ashore in Ganland. The magic swirled around him, inexorably tearing at everything in his dreamscape, destroying it bit by bit.

Blaise was doing this. The power was like a building flood, wild and lethal. Jefferson had the uncomfortable thought that it might be possible for Blaise to kill him here. But no, he wouldn't intend this destruction. Blaise's magic might be a hurricane, but Jefferson could find the eye of the storm.

He focused on the bond through the geasa. Surely Blaise wouldn't fault him for using it, not right now. *There.* Jefferson found him, and he truly *was* everywhere. It was like he was coming apart at the seams. A profound sense of despair coursed through the link.

"Oh, Blaise," Jefferson murmured. Gods, he needed to plan a strategy, but there wasn't time. Breaker magic battered all around him, though Jefferson pushed back with his own to keep it at bay.

Think. The geasa means I can exert my influence on Blaise. He had promised never to do that. But this was an extreme circumstance. "I'm sorry. You have my permission to be mad at me about this later."

Gritting his teeth, Jefferson fumbled with the geasa, searching for the thread that connected them. *There. Got it.* It reminded him of reins attached to a bridle, though he had kept them slack all this time. He reached out with his mind and imagined himself giving them a light tug—nothing harsh, just enough to draw attention. And mercy of mercies, it worked. The magical onslaught around him abated.

"Good, I have your attention. I know you don't want to do this, so let's see if I can figure out how to curb that magic of yours." Jefferson was uncertain if Blaise could hear him, but speaking didn't hurt anything. It made *him* feel better about the situation, at any rate. He kept a firm grasp on the geasa, assessing the howling storm of Breaker power that whipped around him but which blessedly had stopped tearing at him.

Where had all this unleashed magic come from? Jefferson wished he could shove it back where it originated from. He didn't see any way to do that, though.

Take some. Please.

The voice in his head surprised Jefferson. It wasn't his own. It was weak and desperate. *Blaise.* Jefferson swallowed. Take some of his magic? Was that even possible? He had never heard about anything like that between a theurgist and a handler, but—oh, he wasn't just a handler. He was a mage, too.

"All right, if you insist," Jefferson murmured.

Blaise must have been waiting for his assent. As soon as he gave it, the hurricane of magic came again, but this time, rather than trying to shred him, it flowed into him. He gritted his teeth against the torrent of power, standing his ground. It stung at first, as if his whole body were on fire. Then his reservoir, which had been sapped from its earlier use against Jack, claimed the incoming power.

Once, when he was a young child, Jefferson's family had gone out for a pleasure cruise with another family. The water in the Bay of Stars had been choppy, but none of the adults had paid any heed. Jefferson, always curious, had ventured too near the side of the boat, hoping to spy a dolphin. He was perched atop the railing and never had a chance when a swell dumped him into the bay. Foam-capped waters surged over his head and the current tried to drag him down. Blaise's magic flowing into him was just as overwhelming as the tide had been.

But then, a crewman had gone over to rescue him. Jefferson didn't have that now. All he could do was set his feet, hold his breath, and hope this wasn't his undoing.

After either an eternity or a few seconds the magical storm around him died down to nothing. The dream sky overhead cleared, leaving Jefferson in a grassy meadow. He felt a strange mix of exhausted and sated, as if he'd run a race and promptly stuffed himself with a fine meal during a solstice celebration. He flopped down on his back, staring at the azure expanse.

Jefferson heard a soft exhalation next to him. He turned and found Blaise nearby with his eyes screwed shut, trembling. "There you are. Are you okay?"

The Breaker's eyes flashed open. His breath huffed a few times as he calmed, but he seemed to come back to himself remarkably well for all that had just happened. "Maybe."

Maybe? Well, Jefferson would take a maybe. "What was that all about? You've never been like that before." He couldn't hide the concern in his voice.

Blaise was quiet for a moment, and while he gathered his thoughts, Jefferson shimmied closer to him. "Gaitwood is determined to make me into a weapon." He didn't shrink back from Jefferson's proximity but instead seemed to gain confidence from it. "They gave me a potion, and it did that." He gestured with one hand to the dreamscape. "Made my magic volatile."

"Not volatile," Jefferson corrected, thoughtful. "I mean, it was fierce, but there was *so much* of it. Like you were overflowing."

Blaise nodded. "That's how it felt until I gave some of it away." He sucked in a shaky breath. "I still have a lot—more than usual—but I can handle this. Barely." The Breaker angled a guilty look at Jefferson. "I'm sorry if giving you my magic hurt."

"It was...an experience," Jefferson said. If he had felt like he was drowning, then what had it been like for Blaise? Beside him, the Breaker was shaking with either exhaustion or fear. Perhaps both. "I'm fine, though, really. We're in the dreamscape. Everything's under control."

"I almost destroyed it. And you."

Jefferson schooled his expression to hide the fact that he'd shared a similar sentiment moments earlier. "But you didn't. I'm fine."

Blaise ran his fingers along the sides of his nose, following his mustache down into his beard, as if he were trying to soothe himself. "I don't want to hurt anyone I care about."

Jefferson swallowed, growing still at Blaise's soft admission. The younger man wasn't free with his feelings, not like Jefferson. He guarded them closely, as if he feared being rejected by the world. And with good reason, Jefferson reflected. There were no other assurances he could offer to Blaise—the fact of the matter was, his magic *could* hurt the people he cared about, if given another chance with whatever Gregor had planned. And that reminded Jefferson why he had come to the dreamscape in the first place.

With a groan, he sat up, eyes alight. "We're getting you out. Today."

Blaise stared at him for a moment, his mouth agape. "Really?"

"Really."

The Breaker's body slacked with relief. "I thought that would never happen."

"Hey." Jefferson slipped his fingers beneath Blaise's chin. "I keep my promises."

Blaise nodded. "It's just...after the potion they gave me, I think

I'm running out of time." His voice cracked, and he took a shaky breath.

Jefferson realized Blaise had not only worried about *Jefferson's* mortality, but his own. *Absolutely heartbreaking.* All it did was reaffirm Jefferson's drive to free him. "We're coming for you. You're going to be okay. You're going to be *free*."

Blaise stared skyward, the skin at the corners of his eyes crinkling with skepticism. "That sounds like a distant dream."

Jefferson chuckled. "Perhaps not so distant. We're in a dream right now, after all."

At the reminder, Blaise sat up gingerly, as if the overload of magic had bruised him. He met Jefferson's gaze and smiled. "I'll be waiting."

CHAPTER TWENTY-TWO
Impending Betrayal

Jack

*J*ack glared at Lamar. Lamar glared back.

"Would you two kiss already?" Flora demanded from her position beside the back of the unoccupied jail wagon.

Jack's lips curled into a snarl at the half-knocker's words. He patted the sixgun at his side. "Pucker up, Lamar."

The Commander sighed, rubbing his forehead as if he were second-guessing his agreement to their plan. "You can't carry a revolver into the Golden Citadel."

Jack crossed his arms. He didn't care if he looked like a petulant child. Lamar's inclusion in this had him riled up, and every fiber of his being screamed for blood before his former friend betrayed them. Sometimes Jack was impulsive, and at others, he was methodical and calculating. As much as he wanted to go with his gut instinct, he reined it in. He would wait like an ambush predator.

His eyes snapped to the revolver at Lamar's waist. "Fine." Jack turned and strode over to Zepheus, removing his gun belt and securing it to the saddle.

<Don't do anything stupid,> the palomino reminded him, nipping at Jack's sleeve.

The outlaw paused, pulling the palomino's head up so he could press his forehead against the equine's. Zepheus knew the storm of emotions that boiled within his rider. "Not making any promises I can't keep."

Zepheus's hide quivered as he shooed away a fly. <I'm serious. I can't bolt into the Cit and rescue you.>

A tiny smile tugged at the corners of Jack's mouth. Zepheus, loyal asshole that he was, would come after him if it came down to it, and they both knew it. But he was right—that wouldn't end well for him, not this deep in Confederation territory. "Yeah, I'm serious, too." He stalked back over, though he disliked the vulnerability of not having his sixguns. "Better?"

"Much," Lamar agreed, though his spine was stiff. Jack studied his old friend. Lamar was nervous about what they were going to do. Did his nerves point to an impending betrayal?

Well, if they did, Jack already had plans to derail it. He stepped up into the back of the jail wagon, relieved to discover the bars were the normal variety of iron. He flicked a finger against them experimentally. "Couldn't spring for the real thing, eh?"

"I didn't think you warranted it," Lamar replied. He had a last-minute discussion with Flora, then climbed into the driver's seat. The half-knocker vanished, using her own abilities to travel to the Golden Citadel.

Jack sat down on the floor of the wagon as Lamar got the mule team moving. He smiled. Lamar didn't realize he had his magic back. Or if he somehow did, he hadn't been able to arrange for one of the reinforced salt-iron jail wagons. That was fine. This worked for Jack.

As they traveled the short distance to the Cit, he readied his effigies and went over the plan. Malcolm should already be on the grounds, in the guise of Jefferson. Zepheus and Emrys were waiting a mile outside the Cit's walls, ready to come when called. Flora was...well, Jack wasn't certain about the half-knocker. She assured them she had her own ways of getting in. Lamar was the only unknown in the plan, and Jack figured out how to handle that.

The wagon trundled to the grimy courtyard where prisoners were regularly unloaded. Jack peered out through the bars, watching as guards approached to speak with Lamar. The Commander jumped down from the driver's box, gesturing to his captive as he spoke. A moment later, Lamar turned and unlocked the gate. The guards stood nearby, rifles out in case Jack got any ideas.

Oh, he had lots of ideas. He smirked as he came closer, allowing Lamar to clap shackles onto his wrists. Mundane iron shackles. But Jack kept his eyes averted, lest the guards suspect anything.

"Come on," Lamar directed, guiding Jack to the entrance.

As if the outlaw didn't know where he was going. He bit back a retort since that didn't fit with the image he needed to present until they got deeper into the Cit. Jack went through the motions of allowing Lamar to record his information with the registrar. Yeah, word was going to get out that the Scourge of the Untamed Territory had been brought in. Once the Salties figured out who was responsible for getting the Breaker out, they were going to be mad as a nest of hornets. But that was fine. Jack didn't mind adding more deeds to his legendary reputation.

Lamar grabbed his arm to urge him onward. Jack growled, staving off the urge to call up his magic and show the Commander exactly how helpless he was. *Wait. Stay focused.* But it was so damned hard with Lamar right there.

"Surprised you came back for the Breaker," Lamar murmured once they were away from anyone who might overhear.

Jack glanced at him. Did he detect jealousy? Disbelief? Interesting. "I'm not here to make nice-nice with you."

"That's obvious," the Commander agreed. "I want the Breaker

gone from here." He glanced at Jack. "Though I'm curious to see how you'll manage it."

"I'm always full of surprises," the outlaw said.

They continued in a stormy silence until they stood outside the hulking prison wing. Jack didn't need to touch the walls to feel the oppressive presence of salt-iron incorporated into the façade. He had forgotten about that. It meant this building wouldn't work for his purpose. Jack slanted a look across the courtyard. *The dorms might work.* "C'mon." He took a step forward, pausing for Lamar to follow.

"That's the theurgist dorms, not the prison," Lamar pointed out as Jack changed their course.

"Yep," Jack agreed with a smirk. Theurgist or prisoner, it didn't matter. He could work with that.

"What are you doing?" Lamar asked, suspicious, as Jack dug several effigies out of the pouch at his side. It was a challenge with the shackles, but he managed.

Jack chuckled. "And here I thought you weren't stupid."

The Commander cocked his head, his eyes troubled. "But you don't have magic."

He sounded baffled, and Jack enjoyed that. The outlaw said nothing, figuring a demonstration would be more informative. He pulled out four poppets—Jack had attuned three of them to targets already, but the last was not. "Unlock these cuffs, and then give me a strand of your hair."

Lamar's face clouded. "I will *not* remove those cuffs. You'll have to do whatever it is with them on."

He fears me. Because he's just now realizing he doesn't know what I'm capable of. Good. Jack smiled. "Have it your way. But I still need the hair unless you want to be caught up in my working."

"You don't have magic," Lamar repeated.

"That so?" Jack murmured.

"I was there when you were dosed with the potion," Lamar mused as he tried to figure out how Jack could possibly have magic now. He blinked. "How did you get it back?"

Lamar knew him well enough to know he wouldn't lie about his magic. Not after everything he'd endured. "That's on a need-to-know basis, and you don't need to know," Jack drawled. No way in Perdition was he going to tell Lamar that the *Breaker* had fixed him.

The Commander stared at him, then plucked a hair from his crown and offered it to Jack. The outlaw accepted and attached it to the fourth poppet, though it was a challenge with the shackles. He had doubted Lamar would agree to it. *You're mine now.*

"For the record, I don't like giving you that," Lamar said.

Jack shrugged. "I don't give a damn. The other option is to have you under the sway of *this* effigy." He hefted one of the diamond-shaped effigies for Lamar's benefit. "Now come on, I need to get these into place."

Lamar sighed but followed along. "What are you crafting?"

Jack ignored the question, reaching down to place the first effigy at the northernmost wall of the dormitory. He leaned down, whispering the words to prime it with a violent twist to his Rising Dread spell.

"*Jack.* Answer me." Lamar's voice was rife with warning.

The outlaw rose, the cuffs rattling with his movement. "Something to give us plenty of cover to get in and out."

Jefferson

JEFFERSON PRIDED HIMSELF ON HIS CALM AND PATIENCE, BUT HE HAD precious little of either while he sat in Grand Warden Kerney's office. Especially since the man was refusing to provide any information.

"I don't answer to you," Kerney said, not for the first time in their conversation. He sat on the other side of a broad desk, beefy arms crossed over his potbelly. "It doesn't matter that you know people on the Council."

Maybe if he had come as Malcolm, he would have received a different reaction. But Jefferson had an established history with Blaise's welfare, and he'd decided it was in his best interest to continue with this guise. It would spare Malcolm Wells from suspicion, especially since he had arranged for his impersonator to attend that day's Council session. He had confidence that actor Rex Godfrey would do an admirable job in his place.

And it was possible Malcolm wouldn't have had a better reception. As the public face of the Faedran faction, he certainly had no friends among those who ran the Golden Citadel. Because, of course, if Malcolm had his way, the Cit would no longer have reason to exist.

Flora stood nearby, ostensibly playing the role of diligent assistant for this encounter. She had dressed for the part in a tailored blouse and skirt, her pink hair pulled back into a severe bun that drew less attention to her. The half-knocker looked like a very short woman who didn't get enough sunlight, which meant that the Grand Warden ignored her presence.

"And as I said, I came to open a dialogue with you regarding the methods used on the mages here to see if any accords are being violated." Jefferson crossed his arms, matching Kerney's defiance.

The Grand Warden scoffed. "No accords are being violated. These are *mages* we're talking about."

Jefferson ground his teeth. Kerney said *mages* as if he were speaking of roaches or vermin. He would never understand how so many Phinorans refused to accept that those with magic were just as human as they. Unfortunately, he knew it wasn't a problem exclusive to Phinora. "And they're—"

"Stop." Kerney cut him off, lifting a hand. The Grand Warden tilted his head as if he were listening to something.

"Is something wrong?" Jefferson raised his eyebrows at the faint shouts echoing down the corridor.

The Grand Warden rose from his seat, striding with purpose to the door. He opened it and exchanged words with a guard who awaited him outside before glancing back to his visitor. "Mr. Cole, something has come up, and we'll need to revisit this topic at a later time."

Jefferson narrowed his eyes. While he suspected he knew what had come up, he wouldn't let the atrocities here off so easily. Especially after his encounter with Blaise last night. "My time is a precious commodity, Grand Warden. I expect you or one of your aides to compile the relevant files. I will send my staffer to retrieve them for review in three days' time." He gestured to indicate Flora, who gave a pert nod.

Distracted, Kerney flapped a hand at him. "Fine, yes. There are matters I need to attend to now."

"Then you won't mind if I take a look around."

Kerney's mouth worked as if he were struggling to find a response. He cut a look toward the door and seemed to reach a decision. Whatever was going on, Kerney was loath to tell a *magelover* like Jefferson. No doubt it would reflect poorly on the Grand Warden. He stalked across his office, picking up a paper from a tray on his desk. Kerney snatched up a pencil and circled something before turning to thrust it at Jefferson. "The Golden Citadel is, as always, open and welcoming to approved visitors. However, we have an incident near the dorms. I've circled the wings where you are free to travel, but for your own safety I ask that you not visit that wing."

Jefferson raised his eyebrows. That was much more than he had expected. He accepted the paper with a gracious nod. "I appreciate your concern for my welfare." And then, to maintain his role, he added, "I assume these wings will have your guards on hand in case I run into any problems?"

"Yes, of course, though there may be fewer as some will have adjusted to address our other issue." Kerney turned away. "Now, I must leave you, Mr. Cole."

"Thank you for your time," Jefferson said, and realized he meant it. Kerney had given him valuable information.

He stepped into the hallway after Kerney, watching as the

Grand Warden took purposeful strides down the corridor. Jefferson turned and walked the other way, glancing down at the map. Raised voices echoed down the hall, but he ignored them, instead focusing on the plan. *I'm coming, Blaise. Hang on.*

"That man is shiftier than a greased basilisk," Flora muttered. "I don't like him."

"He's hiding a lot," Jefferson agreed, voice soft. "Come on."

It was difficult to maintain a leisurely pace. Jefferson wanted to charge down the corridors of the Cit until he found Blaise and got him out. But instead, he walked as if he were observing. He pulled a small note-pad from his pocket, pausing from time to time to jot down notes before continuing onward. Flora trailed in his wake like an obedient aide. Once, a woman in a crisp uniform asked if he needed an escort to the exit, but he declined, telling her he was making observations and recommendations. It was accurate enough. There was a lot he would change about the Cit.

Jefferson's pulse raced as he finally reached the area that housed the older mages. The cacophony of a fight met their ears— crashes, shouts, and the solid thump of fists against flesh. He felt the insidious slither of something washing over his skin, like rain-drops trailing down water-resistant canvas. Jack's spell, turned away by the protections the Effigest had afforded them.

Flora swallowed, taking a deep breath. "Phew. Sounds like they're having a good time." She pushed her glasses up the bridge of her nose, shifting from one foot to the other as if the magic were trying to influence her, too.

"I don't know if I'd call it *that,*" Jefferson murmured. He glanced at the sign identifying the building as the dormitory. According to the map in his hands, the prison wing wasn't far. And then, at last, they would free Blaise. "Let's go."

As they passed by the last entrance to the dormitory, an armed guard rushed out of the door to stop them. "Identify yourselves!" His service revolver was out, though it quaked in his grasp. Jack's magic had him close to violence.

Before Jefferson could say a word, Flora stepped forward. She held up a finger to forestall him from using his magic. Their goal was for no one to discover that Jefferson Cole was a mage.

Flora batted her eyelashes at the guard, her voice dripping with honey-sweetness. "Oh sugar, I'd *love* to identify myself."

The guard stared at her, puzzled. Then something shifted in his expression, and Jefferson realized that lust was another flip of the coin of violence. The guard released a long, whistling breath as Flora minced closer. Jefferson rubbed the side of his face, debating if he should just leave Flora there with her prey and continue to look for Blaise or stay and watch her back.

When the guard was close enough to loom over her, Flora swept into motion. Her knee flew up into his groin in a brutal move that made Jefferson cringe in sympathy. The guard howled, dropping his revolver. Flora neatly kicked his knee out from under him, sending her victim crashing to the ground. She picked up the revolver and tucked it into her waist, then stripped off the guard's uniform jacket.

"Can I ask what you're doing?" Malcolm blinked as she ripped a sleeve off the uniform.

"Making sure he can't come after us." Flora was efficient as she tore a strip off the sleeve, using it as a gag that she stuffed into the guard's mouth. She used the other sleeve to create binds for his hands and feet, then used her considerable strength to shove him back into the dormitory. "That was fun."

"I'm a little concerned at how good you are at that," Jefferson said as they continued onward.

She favored him with a wide-eyed, innocent look. "I'm a woman of many talents."

He supposed that was true. Jefferson consulted the map, feeling a rush of victory at their proximity to the prison wing. He quickened his strides, but as he drew closer, a sudden ache developed in the back of his neck. Jefferson gnashed his teeth against the pain. "Gods, what *is* that?" he muttered.

"It's the salt-iron," Flora said, patting his arm with sympathy. "Keeps the prisoners compliant."

"Charming." Jefferson winced. No wonder mages hated the stuff. He didn't like the dull throb in his head, nor the way he could feel traces of his magic seeping away like water from a cracked cup. Minor things, he told himself, compared to whatever Blaise had endured here.

Flora skipped ahead as if she were out on a lark. She dragged open the heavy door to the prison, poking inside to check for any resistance. Flora waved him inside with an exuberant grin. "The coast is clear."

Jefferson slipped inside. A small desk crouched beside another door, the chair rocked back against the wall as if the prior occupant had left in a hurry. And no doubt they had if the guard had responded to Jack's distraction.

"This one's locked," Flora grumbled as she tugged at the door. Unwilling to relent, she planted her feet and gave the handle another jerk. Metal groaned from the strain, but otherwise didn't give.

"Suppose I'm already going to be in enough trouble," Jefferson reasoned, moving behind the desk. He pulled open the various drawers, sifting through the contents. Half-eaten apple. A wooden box filled with broken charcoal pencils. An envelope full of love letters. A deck of playing cards and a bag of dice. "Blast it. No keys."

"That's because I have them."

Flora whirled, her readiness for violence telegraphed in every muscle. Jefferson, too, was on alert, though he quickly calmed when he realized the speaker was Lamar. The Commander strode into the reception area, swinging a ring of keys on the index finger of his remaining hand.

"That's handy," Flora quipped, earning a scowl from Lamar.

"That wasn't very nice," Jefferson said.

"Nah, but I enjoyed it," Jack smirked as he came up behind them, the shackles on his wrists rattling as he walked.

Lamar ignored them with great dignity, turning to slip a key into the lock. There was a grating sound and then the mechanism within gave. Flora sprang forward, hauling the door open with renewed enthusiasm. Lamar pocketed the key ring.

The Commander led the way into the corridor, followed closely by the outlaw. Jefferson hurried along in their wake, struggling to fight off the effects of the salt-iron. Lamar and Jack seemed unbothered by it.

"Do you not feel the salt-iron?" Jefferson asked them.

Lamar shrugged. "I'm around it all the time."

Jack said nothing, though his eyes glittered dangerously. If the metal irritated him, he was hiding it well. The Effigest's chilling gaze flicked to Lamar, as if the Commander's presence was a distraction from the discomfort. Lamar paid no heed to Jack's vengeful look, instead focusing on each door as they strode down the long corridor.

"This one," Lamar said, stopping in front of a cell. The Salt-Iron Commander glanced up the hallway as he produced the key ring from his pocket.

Jefferson's attention snapped to the Commander. "This is Blaise's cell?"

"Yeah," Jack muttered, all the violence bleeding away for a moment. He pointed to the walls. "Didn't notice that, eh?"

Jefferson blinked in surprise as he saw what Jack meant. Someone had reinforced the stone walls with wood planks and salt-iron, but the whole thing was deteriorating. The wood was rotted and chipped. Sections of the stone wall had long, spider web-shaped cracks. Even the salt-iron had crumbled in some places, leaving shavings on the floor. Jefferson's mouth went dry. *Blaise did this?*

Jefferson swallowed, recalling the nightmare. "But...he can control his magic." He hadn't told them about last night. There hadn't been time.

Lamar finally found the proper key for the door and shoved it home into the lock. The cell door creaked open. Jefferson rushed over, peering inside.

He had prepared himself for many things, but not for this.

"Where in Perdition *is* he?" Jack snarled, giving voice to Jefferson's thoughts.

Lamar clenched his jaw. "We must be too late. Gregor must have moved him early."

"But moved him where?" Flora asked.

"To the Council."

CHAPTER TWENTY-THREE
Empty

Jack

*T*his mess was supposed to go differently. Blaise was *supposed* to be there. They were going to drag him out of this overgrown outhouse and get out. And then Jack would take his revenge on Lamar. He tightened his fists, staring into the cell as Jefferson stepped inside, snooping around as if hoping beyond hope that a grown man was hidden out of view in the small space. *Futile. Stupid.* But Jack was almost tempted to do the same.

"No. No, this can't be." Jefferson's voice was dull as his gaze swept the vacant cell.

Lamar shook himself like a wet dog, appearing as troubled as the rest of them. Maybe he *was* on their side. Or just a damned convincing turncoat. "The Council. They took him to the Council." He, too, sounded hollow.

Jefferson pivoted. His eyes were wild, as if he knew something he hadn't told the others. "They're going to use Blaise to kill the Council. We have to get him before he reaches the chambers." He consulted his pocket watch for the time.

What in Perdition? "How do you know this?" Jack snapped.

The Dreamer scrubbed at his face with a hand. "Last night. He was in a bad way in the dreamscape." Nearby, Lamar shifted, his eyes widening as he listened.

"Stop talking," Flora warned Jefferson, who blinked as he realized that perhaps he'd said too much.

Jack hid a smirk. *Don't you worry. I'll cover your tracks.* "You have an idea what route they'll take?"

Jefferson took a ragged breath, then nodded. "I do, yes."

Jack aimed a finger at him. "Good. Y'all start after him. I need to gather my poppets, and then I'll follow."

"No, absolutely not." Lamar shook his head. "I have to stay with you."

Please do. "Aw, didn't know your black heart cared so much."

Jefferson cast another forlorn look into the empty cell. "Yes, I'll start after him."

He sounded shaky and uncertain, shell-shocked. That wouldn't do. The dandy needed to *focus.* Jack stepped up to him, snapping his fingers. "Hey. You know what to do. You can do it."

Jefferson nodded, swallowing. "Right. Yes. Come on, Flora, let's go."

The half-knocker cast a suspicious glance at Jack over her shoulder but followed Jefferson after a moment. The outlaw watched her go, then pivoted to head down the hallway. Shouts and fighting still reverberated through the building, proof that his working was still in full force.

"What spell was that?" Lamar asked, keeping pace beside him.

Eh, at this point what did it hurt to tell him? "Modified Rising Dread." Jack shoved open the outer door, breathing a sigh of relief as he put a little more distance between himself and all that salt-iron. He needed to retain whatever magic he could before it bled away.

"I don't remember that one," Lamar remarked.

"You wouldn't." Jack had never used it around Lamar in his theurgist days. He made a beeline for the rear of the theurgist dormitory, scanning for the place he'd tucked an effigy. *There, behind that bush.* He picked it up, returning it to his pouch. As he started for the next one, he asked, "Where's my wife?"

The Commander hesitated at the steel in Jack's voice. "Your wife?"

"Kittie Dewitt. Don't play stupid like you don't know who she is."

Lamar blew out a breath as they walked. "I know who you mean. I was…surprised that you asked, is all. I don't know where she is."

Jack slowed. He had long suspected Lamar was part of the group that had tracked her down and taken her, but he had no proof. The outlaw chewed on Lamar's assertion as he picked up the next two effigies. As they walked toward the final effigy, Jack palmed a poppet from his pouch.

The last effigy lay just ahead, concealed by the branches of a bush in dire need of trimming. The protection afforded by the shrub would work in the outlaw's favor. The effigy was still draining some of his magic, so Jack needed to time things right. He plucked it from where he had hidden it, canceling the working. As soon as he sensed the magic wane, he flipped his attention to the poppet he had assigned to Lamar.

The Commander froze in place as Jack settled a paralysis spell over him. The outlaw smirked, content as a tomcat with a mouse beneath his paw. He had waited so long for this day. Jack cast a spell of strength onto his personal poppet. Strength was a huge magic drain, so he used it only briefly to rip the cuffs from his wrists. All the while, Lamar stared at him with growing horror as he realized the severity of his predicament.

"That's right. Trapped, like *you* trapped *me*," Jack crooned. "But I'm not bitter about *that*. Oh, no." He stepped closer to Lamar, liberating the revolver from the Commander's holster. "Nah, you see, I've been holding a grudge about you taking my *magic*. Stealing my *wife*." Jack's heart raced as his fury mounted. "Destroying my *town*. Kidnapping my *daughter*." He stalked in a circle around Lamar, hoping the other man felt every bit of the despair and terror Jack had endured.

A bead of sweat trailed down Lamar's forehead. Jack adjusted the paralysis spell enough to allow the Commander to speak. "*Jack*. Jack, *please*. Can't you see I'm *helping* you?"

"I *do* like hearing you beg," Jack said. "But if you think I believe your song and dance, you're a damned fool."

Lamar's eyes widened. "I'm telling the truth. We were friends once. Why won't you believe me? You *know* me."

"And that's why I don't believe you," the outlaw replied coldly.

"Jack, think about this. We have about two minutes before this area is crawling with soldiers. You won't be able to take all of them, and this will all have been for nothing."

As far as arguments went, it wasn't a bad one. Already, he heard the distant sound of soldiers arriving to bolster the guards, who must have been overwhelmed by the berserking mages. Jack glanced down at the revolver in his hand. It wasn't as familiar as his own sixgun, but it was serviceable. He hoisted it, pointing it at the Commander's forehead.

"No!" Lamar yelped, his protest silenced as Jack pulled the trigger. The world narrowed until it was only Jack, Lamar, and the sharp report of a bullet flying true.

The paralysis spell lost its grip, unable to work on a dying man. Lamar slumped to the ground, limp as a rag doll. Jack shoved the revolver into his waistband, staring down at the Commander's body. He had thought he would feel a sense of victory and justice, but instead, a hollow emptiness settled over him.

There was no time to analyze that now. Time to get out of the Cit while the getting was good.

CHAPTER TWENTY-FOUR
Damage Control

Jefferson

efferson had difficulty maintaining a sedate pace as he and Flora headed out of the Citadel grounds. Luckily, the place was in complete chaos, and no one paid attention to their exit. Once they left the walls of the compound, they broke into a jog. Jefferson whistled every few steps, hoping to catch the pegasi's attention.

The pegasi trotted out of the nearby forest, ears pricked forward. Emrys studied the pair, dark eyes worried. <Where is Blaise?>

"We were too late," Jefferson sighed as he hurried up to the stallion.

The pegasus's hide quivered. <What do you mean?>

"I mean, he's on the move, and we have to catch up." Jefferson glanced at Zepheus. "Jack will come behind us. Emrys, can you carry Flora and I?"

<I will,> the stallion agreed gamely.

Flora waved a hand. "Nah, don't worry about me. I'll be able to find them."

Jefferson stilled. "What do you mean?" She had already kept Lamar's involvement a secret until the last moment. What else had she not divulged? The half-knocker shifted under his focused gaze. "If it relates to finding Blaise, *tell me.*" Emrys loomed nearby, snorting his agreement.

Flora's shoulders tensed and her face fell. "I'll tell you, but…" She rubbed her face. "Promise me you won't tell anyone else."

Jefferson had never heard her so serious or worried before. "Yes, of course."

"I'm attuned to salt-iron."

He stared. Jefferson wouldn't have been more surprised if she'd turned into a tap-dancing jackalope. It was the last thing he had expected from her. "*What?*"

"You heard me." She frowned. "If they have him in a salt-iron jail wagon—which they will if they're smart—then he's that way." Flora pointed to the southwest.

Jefferson ran a hand through his hair. "That confirms they are taking him to the Council. Let's go." He climbed into Emrys's saddle, the stallion prancing in anticipation. Flora nodded, vanishing to follow the salt-iron trail.

The pegasus surged forward into a fluid canter, ears tipped back for Jefferson's guidance. The scenery sped by. Jefferson felt the nervous energy of the pegasus beneath him, and he wished they could take to the air to hunt for Blaise. But that would invite too much trouble. He had to trust that he was on the right track.

<Can you find him with your geasa too?> Emrys asked as they raced along.

Oh, if only it were that easy. "I don't think it works like that."

<Understood. I should be able to sense him when I'm in range.> Emrys plowed onward, lengthening his strides.

A few moments later, his ears flicked forward, slowing as his nostrils flared. The pegasus arched his neck, tail flagging behind him with joy. <I found him.>

Jefferson patted the stallion's neck. "Let's get him."

The pegasus charged up the road, and over the next hill, the jail wagon dawdled into view, pulled by a pair of mules lumbering along at a glacial pace. To Jefferson's dismay, he realized the wagon was under guard. *I suppose it makes sense. High-value prisoner and all.* Two armed outriders accompanied it, along with a sharpshooter perched atop the wagon beside the driver. He quailed as he realized they were about to attack Confederation defenders.

Emrys sensed his dismay, drawing to a stop. <Choose. Blaise or your Confederation.>

Blaise. He would pick Blaise every time, without hesitation. But he didn't know how they were going to do this. Flora appeared nearby, her eyes on the distant wagon.

"I don't think I can handle them all," Jefferson admitted. "They're armed."

The half-knocker rubbed her hands together in anticipation. "I can stop the wagon. I can even take out all of them if you want. But it's going to be bloody."

None of it was bluster. Flora was preternaturally strong and fast, with skin tough enough to deflect a knife, though bullets could still wound her. Yet here she was, offering to take on some of the Confederation's best on his behalf.

"Get the wagon to stop and distract the guards however you can. I'll do my part," Jefferson said. When her grin widened, he added, "But for Tabris's sake, don't kill anyone!"

"That all depends on you, boss," Flora replied, giving him an ironic salute. "You ready?"

Jefferson swallowed, patting Emrys's neck. The stallion bowed his neck, sidestepping as he awaited the command. "No time like the present."

Flora disappeared with a pop of displaced air. Emrys peered back at his rider. <Do whatever you need to prepare. I'll be ready.>

Jefferson took a deep breath, closing his eyes to calm himself.

He summoned his magic and found it ready to heed his call. At least he wouldn't have to fumble for it. Jefferson was aware of the pegasus slowing to a walk, then he felt Emrys's muscles bunch beneath him in surprise as a metallic crunch rang out.

"Shit!" a guard called.

"That the Breaker's magic?" another asked, voice loud and wary. Jefferson's eyes flashed open when he heard a gun being readied.

Jefferson swallowed. "Get me closer, Emrys." *Hope I don't fall asleep in the saddle because that would make for an awkward rescue.*

Emrys surged forward. Ahead, the wagon ground to a halt, pitched at an awkward angle. A dark, circular shape spun up the road—a wagon wheel, rolling free of the axle. Jefferson realized Flora's ploy inadvertently put Blaise in danger as his escort assumed the Breaker was responsible for the damage that had befallen the wagon.

The escort riders were focused on their current problem, ignoring the drum of hoofbeats as Emrys approached. Jefferson clung to the saddle for all he was worth, summoning his magic and focusing it forward. This had been so much easier when he had used his power against Jack or Emrys. He was more familiar with them, and they were easy to target. This was like trying to reach into a stream and grab a fish with bare hands. Jefferson missed his first attempt as the stallion drew closer to the wagon. And then he missed two more.

On his fourth try, he found the sharpshooter. Jefferson wasn't sure which of them was more surprised. He felt the soldier's presence and hastily summoned up the dreamscape, pulling him into it. One of his fellows, an outrider with a bushy mustache, made a cry of dismay as the slumbering sharpshooter slumped against the wagon.

"Smith! Are you dead?" Bushy Mustache demanded.

"Nah, he's snoring," the other outrider replied, rubbing his nearly nonexistent chin in bewilderment.

Jefferson sought Bushy Mustache but found Tiny Chin

instead. *Doesn't matter.* He shoved the outrider into the dreamscape.

Bushy Mustache was even easier, as Jefferson gained a knack for snagging his targets. Moments later, he had the driver ensnared as well. The man had gone to retrieve the errant wheel, collapsing to the road with a yawn as if he were seeking his bed.

Flora clapped her hands, impressed. "That was fun! You made it look easy."

"It wasn't." Jefferson's heart raced from the magical exertion. He dismounted, though as soon as his feet hit the ground, his knees nearly buckled beneath him. Emrys snorted, sidestepping to keep him from falling.

"You okay over there?" Flora asked as she tied one of the outrider's horses to the wagon.

"I've been better. Can you look for a key and get Blaise out?" Jefferson leaned heavily against Emrys, grateful for the support. "I need to do more than just dump them in the dream." He glanced at the nearest sleeping outrider.

"Why?" Flora asked as she perused the saddlebags.

He winced. Flora had already admitted her secret, so he supposed he might as well tell her what he thought he could do. He didn't like it because it was unethical and seemed like a violation. Just thinking of it made him understand why some of the populace feared mages and didn't want them to have a voice in government. "You know how sometimes a dream seems so real, you could swear it really happened? I think I may be able to influence their memories within the dreamscape."

<I can still taste the food from the Feast of Flight dream.> Emrys smacked his lips in agreement.

Flora whistled. "Give it a shot." She returned to her search for the key.

Jefferson nodded. He had done unethical things before. Why did this feel so different? He wrapped a hand around Emrys's mane to keep himself upright, steadying his breathing as he slipped back to the dreamscape. The men were still where he had left them, though he felt them trying to stir. Jefferson lulled them into a deeper sleep with his magic. They stopped struggling, content. Jefferson smiled. Their minds were malleable. Impressionable.

"Got it!" Flora crowed. Jefferson cracked one eye open to see her brandish a key and skip around to the back of the wagon to unlock the door.

Jefferson swallowed, splitting his attention between his dream and reality. Sweat beaded on his forehead with the effort, and the dull throb at the base of his neck reminded him that he was closer to salt-iron than he liked. Flora scuttled into the wagon and appeared a moment later with her arm around Blaise's midsection. Jefferson's heart broke when he saw the young man's scarecrow-thin frame and haggard face. Blaise's body shook violently, as if he were cold—*no*, that wasn't it at all. As if he were struggling to hold back an impossible amount of magic.

He let go of Emrys, abandoning the dreamscape for the moment. "Flora, step away." Jefferson slung his arm around Blaise, bothered by how feather-light he was. Emrys crowded close, nickering softly and sniffing Blaise all over.

The Breaker sagged against Jefferson, whimpering. "I can't. I can't…"

<What did they do to him?> Emrys's voice vibrated with cold fury.

"The outrider with the keys had a potion." Flora held the small amber bottle aloft. "Why did someone write '*administer on Council grounds*'?"

Jefferson shook his head. He didn't have time to explain, not right now. No time to tell them that little bottle was probably the last bit of an alchemical potion designed to send Blaise beyond the limits of magic he could contain. "Blaise, I'm here. It's okay. Give me some of that."

Blaise blinked, as if finally registering his presence. Jefferson felt a pulse of immense relief through their bond, followed by a frisson of fear. "It's too much. Too dangerous. Don't want to hurt you."

"Shh, you won't," Jefferson whispered, fervently hoping it was the truth. "Just like last night. *Remember?*"

The Breaker's lips twisted in a rictus of anguish, his entire body shaking so badly that Jefferson knew without a doubt how Gregor meant for Blaise to destroy the Council. He was a living bomb, about to shatter himself and everything around him. If he didn't siphon off some of that magic, they wouldn't last much longer.

"Jefferson?" Flora asked, concern in her voice.

He shook his head. Didn't have time for her right now. "Come on, Blaise. You don't have to bear it alone. And I can use the magic, anyway." Jefferson hazarded a glance at the guards. The sharpshooter was stirring. *Blast.* Spreading his power among multiple targets made it not as potent. Jack had slept much longer.

Blaise gave him a desolate look. "Don't want to kill you."

Gods, he doesn't realize he may do that no matter what. They were running out of time. If Blaise's magic didn't do them in, one of the waking guards might. "I trust you," Jefferson murmured, leaning in to kiss Blaise. If this was their end, he wouldn't die without doing that once more.

Blaise melted against him, something about their closeness breaking down whatever barrier he had up. A flood of magic swept through the geasa, pouring into Jefferson like a rising tide.

So much power. Jefferson had felt like he was drowning last night. That was nothing compared to this. He was drowning with every nerve ending on fire, every bone threatening to crack beneath the strain. Lungs crushing beneath the sheer might of the magic sweeping into him. Jefferson's vision swam, and he felt Emrys's muzzle shove against his spine to keep him upright.

How had Blaise contained it for even two minutes? Jefferson struggled against it, gathering the magic as best he could and lugging it to the dreamscape. It was difficult, almost impossible, to ignore the way the unfettered magic attacked his very being. But he had to, or he and Blaise would both be lost. Jefferson gritted his teeth, latching onto the sharpshooter and dragging him back into slumber.

Jefferson had a vague sense that Blaise was observing him somehow, but he was too busy constructing a new lie to replace their reality. He didn't have time to think it through, so made them believe that after the axle on their wagon broke, another wagon took their prisoner away. It was better than the reality of a well-known entrepreneur taking them down with magic.

When he finished, it took him a moment to realize Blaise was supporting *him*. The younger man's blue eyes were clouded with worry. "Are you okay?"

"I'm supposed to be asking you that," Jefferson replied, though he nodded. Exhaustion dogged him and he felt raw from the burn of magic, but Blaise was *free*. That was worth celebrating—once they reached safety. "Emrys? Can you carry the both of us?"

The stallion nuzzled Blaise. <I would normally say no, but Blaise weighs next to nothing. He's going to need to eat a lot of cake to fill out.>

"Maybe after he can keep down nourishing food," Jefferson muttered as the pegasus knelt so he could help Blaise into the saddle.

A few moments later, he was atop Emrys, with Blaise nestled behind him, the young man's arms around his waist. Thrilling as it was, Jefferson had no illusions about the severity of their situation. But they would focus on that later.

Blaise was free.

Malcolm

AGNES BENT OVER BLAISE. THE BREAKER SAT IN THE COZIEST CHAIR in the study, one of his arms propped on a pillow as the Healer applied an ointment to the gash that ran the length of his forearm.

She had been nervous of the young man at first, but her countenance changed to professional concern when she took in his ragged condition.

"I used a little of my magic on him, but he's been through a lot. I fear pouring too much into him and shocking his body," Agnes informed Malcolm once she had finished her ministrations. "I'll need to check that arm twice a day, if he'll allow it." She hadn't missed how Blaise had shrunk from her touch, though he was too tired to do more.

"Thank you," Malcolm told her, moving to sit near Blaise. Once Agnes left, he leaned forward. "Blaise? How are you?"

Blaise hadn't spoken since they'd arrived at the estate, and Jefferson had to change his appearance. He trembled, and Malcolm knew from their bond that it wasn't because of his magic, at least. The Breaker closed his eyes. "I don't know."

Malcolm pursed his lips. He wasn't sure how to make Blaise feel better. Perhaps it was something only time and distance from the trauma would heal. Or perhaps, Malcolm thought with regret, he might never heal. "It's okay to not know. But you're free."

Blaise shook his head and was about to say something when Flora and Jack boiled into the house like a pair of tussling gamecocks. The outlaw had never caught up to them, and the half-knocker had gone out to find out what had become of him while Malcolm got Blaise settled.

Flora screeched and Jack growled terse responses littered with creative expletives. Malcolm considered knocking them both out, but that would only delay their row. Blaise stared at the arguing pair, bewildered and worn.

"Stop this at once!" Malcolm commanded, pulling on his authoritative Doyen voice.

Flora and Jack paused, and the outlaw stopped short when he realized Blaise was there. His eyes narrowed to outraged slits as he took in the Breaker's rough condition.

"Care to explain what all this is about?" Malcolm gestured to the general madness of the pair. "Were you carrying on like that the whole way here from the Cit?"

"No. Found him on the road to your estate." Flora gave Jack her best death-glare. "What is *wrong* with you?"

"*Vengeance*," Jack rumbled, his hands fisted at his sides.

Flora whirled with an exasperated look, focusing on Malcolm. "We have problems because of this spawn of a syphilitic swamp rat." Jack lunged at her, but she was too fast and dodged out of the way, claiming a place on a chair beside Blaise. She focused on him for a moment, shooting him an encouraging smile. "Hey sugar, you've looked better."

"Don't call me that," Blaise said, staring at the ceiling as if he couldn't handle their drama right now.

Malcolm decided, all things considered, Blaise was taking whatever they were going on about very well. He, on the other hand, wanted to focus on anything else but their theatrics. Malcolm rubbed his forehead. "Either tell me what's going on or go kill each other outside so we can have a little calm. I just committed yet another act of treason, and I have other things on my mind."

"He," Flora declared, waving a finger at Jack, "killed Lamar Gaitwood."

Malcolm blinked in surprise. While that didn't sound like a *good* scenario in the grand scheme of things, it hardly sounded like the *worst* thing. Lamar had caused so many problems for Blaise that Malcolm didn't have any charitable feelings toward the man. But he had also helped to get Blaise out. Or at least tried to.

Blaise leaned forward, eyes on Jack. He looked like he wanted to say something, and his mouth opened slightly before he shut it again.

"I had *reason*. A *just* cause," Jack said, his shoulders tense. It sounded as if he'd been repeating the phrase over and over like a mantra. And like he didn't fully believe it anymore.

Malcolm didn't want to unpack whatever baggage went along with that right now. He looked at Flora. "Right. I agree that this is not the best ending for someone who was helping us. But it sounds like there's more to it than that?"

Beside Blaise, Flora straightened. She waved her hands around. "Just so you know, I didn't tell you because I was going to take care of the problem. *Quietly.*" She shot a disgruntled glare at Jack.

Blaise slowly rose from his seat, rubbing at his chin. He gave Malcolm an apologetic look. "I'm going out to the stables. This is...too much for me right now." The Breaker paused beside the outlaw before he made his way to the door. "Good to see you, Jack." The outlaw gave him a curt nod.

Malcolm watched him leave, frustrated that he couldn't follow and had to deal with this ridiculousness instead. But it was for the best. Blaise had been through so much. Emrys would keep tabs on the Breaker until Malcolm could check on him again. He rounded on Flora. "Continue."

The half-knocker put her hands on her hips, unapologetic. "Lamar discovered you were bound to Blaise. And I'm pretty sure he figured out you're also Jefferson. That information was surety for his life."

Jack's eyes narrowed, and his mouth moved with something that might have been a silent curse. A chill raced down Malcolm's spine. "Lamar arranged it so if something happened to him, that secret comes out?"

Flora nodded.

"We could have avoided this if you'd told us from the *start,*" Jack growled.

"Is that so?" Flora challenged. "I should never have trusted that you could behave any better than a rabid chupacabra."

"Yeah, well, that's on you," Jack agreed, crossing his arms.

Malcolm rubbed the bridge of his nose. "This isn't the time to argue. The fact of the matter is that now, not only has Gregor lost the mage he wanted to use for his plot, but he *also* has prime ammunition to use against me."

"*Your* fault," Flora hissed at Jack. The outlaw's shoulders tensed, fire in his eyes.

Malcolm shook his head. "We can't worry about who's to blame. It doesn't matter." He held up a hand to count off their issues. "One, they will accuse Jefferson in the plot to free Blaise. Two, Wildfire Jack will take blame as well—now not only for Blaise's escape but the death of Commander Gaitwood. And three, word will soon get out that I bound myself to Blaise." He paced the length of the parlor.

"I don't care about my reputation," Jack said. "I need to leave anyway."

Malcolm studied him, and he might have misread it, but he thought he saw a shadow of regret on the outlaw's face. Rather than comment on it, he nodded. "Just as well, since we'll present too big a target with all of us here."

"Oh sure, abandon us after *you* cause all the problems," Flora groused. "Where are you going, anyway?"

"None of your gods-damned business." Jack turned on his heel and stalked to the door, slamming it in his wake.

"Right," Malcolm sighed. "So we'll have to do some damage control." He tried not to think about how *much* damage control. Maybe if he feigned calm, it would be true. Or maybe he could hop on a steamer with Blaise, get new identities for them both, and start a new life in Thorn or Highhorse. Never mind that leaving Phinora right now would take nothing short of a miracle.

Flora eased back into her chair. "What do you have in mind?"

Malcolm sank down into the seat Blaise had occupied and put a hand over his face. "You flatter me by thinking I've gotten that far. No. I think this is going to be a late night. Call in my attorney—disasters like this are what I pay him for. Wait." Malcolm straightened, removing his hand as he snapped his fingers. A kernel of a plan was forming. "Get me Seledora, too."

Flora frowned. "But she's all the way in Rainbow Flat. That'll take time. And she's—"

"Doesn't matter. You heard me." Malcolm pursed his lips. "I

think we can buy a little time. They can't just force their way onto my estate and drag Blaise and I out." That was one of the small perks of being a Doyen. His home was, effectively, an embassy. "Oh, and reach out to Doyen Jennings's wife."

Flora studied him. "Thirty seconds ago, you didn't have an idea, but I suspect you do now. What is it?"

Malcolm smiled. He was tired, a little panicked, but he felt better now that an idea was fermenting in his mind. "We're going to get ahead of the narrative."

CHAPTER TWENTY-FIVE

Impulsive as a Weasel in a Hen House

Jack

J ack stormed out of Wells's overstuffed temple of opulence, stalking to the stables. Circumstances forced him to make an abrupt pivot when he realized that in his anger, he had forgotten his saddlebag of clothing and supplies. He avoided Malcolm and Flora as he traipsed to the guest quarters, irritated as a flea-bitten manticore. Once he had the bag slung over his shoulder, he made his way back out to the stables.

He blazed a path to Zepheus, although the pegasus was pissed at him, too. The stallion called Jack *rash* and *impulsive as a weasel in a hen house.* "I wasn't *rash.* I'd been planning this for years," the outlaw grumbled to no one in particular.

"I understand," a soft voice said from a nearby stall.

The outlaw tensed. *Blaise.* He had forgotten the Breaker had fled before the rising tide of his argument with Flora. Blaise rested his forearms against the top of Emrys's stall, peering at him with haunted eyes.

Blaise was the last person he expected to understand, but then again, Blaise had been imprisoned in the Cit for months. Jack knew firsthand how the treatment foisted upon mages could twist and blacken a person's soul. Jack had hoped Blaise would prove more resilient. "Do you?"

The Breaker lowered his head until his chin rested atop the wood of the stall. "I understand, but I don't agree with what you did."

Jack didn't let the relief that flickered through him show on his face. Maybe they hadn't broken Blaise to the core as he had feared. "Didn't expect you would."

Emrys walked up beside Blaise, thrusting his head out and snorting at Jack, as if to emphasize that Blaise was a better person than him in every way. The stallion wasn't wrong.

"Did you come for me?" Blaise asked.

Jack frowned. Damn it, of course Blaise would ask that, all the while looking like a kicked puppy.

"It's okay if you didn't. That would be a stupid move on your part, and you're not usually stupid."

Jack set his jaw, then realized that the Breaker had sassed him on purpose. Even fresh from the torture of the Cit, he was trying to help someone else. That was good. He wasn't broken. Jack was tempted not to let the barb go uncontested, but he wasn't foolish. Blaise was a Breaker, and after the abuse of the Cit there was no way to know how he might respond. So Jack held his tongue. He went the route of the truth because if anything Blaise would appreciate that. "I came because Emmaline ran off."

That caught the Breaker's attention. He straightened, the corners of his eyes creased with concern. "Then why are you *here?*"

Jack couldn't help it. He chuckled because Blaise had the right of it. "I found her. And she humbled me." He rubbed his forehead. "Here I thought she ran off to free you. She wanted to, by the way."

Blaise smiled, though the corners of his mouth quivered with the effort. "I was afraid she might. She's brave."

"I was going to go with *overly confident teenager* but then the apple doesn't fall far from the tree," Jack said dryly. "Anyway, she's tracking down her mother." He couldn't help it; his voice cracked on the last word. He'd tried to keep his mind off Kittie so he could focus on the task at hand, but now that he had kept his promise and Blaise was free, the thought of her dug into his brain like spurs.

"That's all you ever wanted," Blaise observed, getting to the core. "You going after them?"

"Yeah."

"Good luck," Blaise said. "I hope you can finally be happy."

Jack nodded, turning away from the Breaker before hesitating and spinning around again. "Something I need to tell you. You restored my magic."

Blaise's brow knit in confusion. "I did?"

"You did," Jack confirmed. "When you freed me from Lamar's trap. You're like a gods-damned miracle worker." He shifted in place. What he wanted to say next didn't come naturally. "Thank you."

The Breaker straightened, rubbing his chin. "You're welcome." He swallowed. "And...thank you. For helping to free me."

Jack was about as used to being thanked for a good deed as he was returning the favor. He touched two fingers to the brim of his hat and inclined his head. "I better get."

Jack had just opened Zepheus's stall door when the young man spoke again. "What's going to happen to me?"

The outlaw pursed his lips, urging the palomino out into the broad aisle so he could recheck his equipment. "Don't know, kid. But Wells seems less of a self-absorbed peacock than I thought, and he might actually have your best interest in mind."

Blaise twitched at his use of *kid* but didn't protest. "I want to go to Itude." He paused, shaking his head. "I mean, Fortitude."

So Wells had told him about the town's name change. Jack pulled a burr out of his pegasus's mane, tossing it aside. "If you can get there, you'd be welcome back. The Gutter needs more mages like you." Blaise stared after him as Jack ambled out the door, Zepheus's hooves ringing on the hard-packed dirt.

CHAPTER TWENTY-SIX
Machinations

Gregor

Gregor picked up the ladder-back chair, flinging it against the wall with a resounding crash. *Unbelievable.* He had been so close, and they had stolen the Breaker from his clutches at the last instant. Fists curling at his side, he stared at the broken ruins of the chair.

One of the miscreants involved had to be Lamar's hated outlaw. The Effigest's name had been recorded in the Cit's logs that day, but now the man was nowhere to be found. And then some of Gregor's best men had been discovered asleep along the road, beside a broken-down jail wagon empty of the Breaker. None of them remembered how they had fallen asleep, but they were certain they had transferred the Breaker to another wagon. Except there *was* no other wagon.

Gregor didn't believe a word they said. Just in case they were in league with either the outlaw or one of those bleeding-heart Faedrans, he made certain the failed guards were flogged.

The most curious, mind-boggling part of the entire thing was

Lamar's involvement. He had been the one to turn the outlaw mage in to the Cit. And then he had been found dead, slain by his own revolver. Had he somehow played a role in the bid to free the Breaker?

Perhaps he should have felt a pang of sadness, an emptiness from the death of his brother. But Lamar was a mage. Gregor's only regret that he could no longer take advantage of his sibling's position as Commander.

A knock sounded on his office door. Gregor hunched his shoulders, sneering at the idea of answering it. He was in no mood to deal with anyone else. The knock came again. "Go away!"

And yet, it came a third time. Gregor growled to himself, stalking over and slinging it open, prepared to berate whoever dared interrupt his brooding. He stopped when he came face to face with a woman in the uniform of a Confederation soldier. The pin on her chest marked her as one of Lamar's lieutenants.

"Pardon the interruption, Doyen Gaitwood, but I have something you'll want to see." She inclined her head, deferential, though she otherwise maintained her perfect posture.

He studied her, frowning. "I'll allow it. Come in."

The soldier slipped inside, glancing at the destroyed chair but wisely keeping any comments to herself. She revealed a carry pouch at her side, opening it to pull out an envelope wrapped in crinkling wax paper. "To protect it from the elements," she murmured, offering it to him. Gregor noted a glistening dew on her clothing. In his preoccupation, he hadn't noticed it had started to mist outside.

He nodded sharply, taking it from her and opening it. He chewed on his bottom lip, thoughtful, as his eyes took in Lamar's cramped handwriting. When he reached the end of the missive, a smile curved onto his lips. His one-armed sibling wasn't so useless in the end. Gregor met the soldier's gaze. "Do you know anything about the contents of this letter?"

She shook her head, her expression stony. "No, sir. But I presume it's related to our Commander's murderer?"

"It is." At his words, she tensed, rage growing in her eyes. Rage was something he could work with. "Lieutenant...I apologize, I didn't catch your name."

"Lieutenant Davis."

Gregor offered her a hesitant smile. "Thank you, Lieutenant Davis. Can I count on your support to bring the perpetrators to justice?"

"Yes, sir. And those I command. Say the word and we are yours."

Perfect. Yes, Lamar's death was proving to be infinitely useful. "Our first step will be to bring in Doyen Wells. He's the mastermind of this plot." He crumpled the letter meaningfully in his hand.

Davis frowned. "That will be difficult if he's gone to ground at his residence."

Blast, she was right. But maybe Malcolm would slip up. "Send a contingent to surround his estate, in that case. If he so much as sticks his nose out, grab him. He can't stay in there forever." She nodded. Gregor took the opportunity to sift through the papers on his desk. He had a stack of *Wanted* handbills somewhere...ah, there. Wildfire Jack Dewitt's mean eyes stared up at him from the topmost paper. "And I want this man. Do you recognize him?"

Her eyes flickered with suppressed anger. "He was at Fort Courage. I was there."

Good. That would offer her ample motivation. "I want him, too."

CHAPTER TWENTY-SEVEN

Blaise Bloody Hawthorne

Blaise

*B*laise rested his cheek against Emrys's warm neck, eyes closed as he inhaled the comforting scent of equine, hay, and dust. The stallion said nothing, simply offered his bulk as a much-needed anchor from the whirlwind of emotions and thoughts swirling through Blaise's mind. He was a confusing mix of relieved, frightened, angry, and smitten. That last one was, strangely enough, the hardest to cope with. There were so many complications.

It had been easier to grasp in prison. Jefferson's dream visits were a respite, a balm after his hours of mistreatment. And while they were so very real, they were still a dream, which made them safe. But now he was here in reality, in Jefferson's—no, Malcolm's —home. That made things real and a little frightening in a way that differed from the terrors of his time in the Cit.

He realized, when he came face to face with Malcolm, that he was nervous around the man. Which made little sense because he was *also* Jefferson. At the same time, he *wasn't*. It was stupid to think of it like that. But since when had his thoughts ever made any sense? He sighed into Emrys's mane.

<He's coming,> the stallion advised him. No need to specify who.

Blaise heard the grate of wood as the stall door opened. "How are you doing?" Malcolm's voice was like sunshine on a winter day, welcome warmth in the bitter cold.

"I'm here," Blaise said with a shrug, turning to face him, though he stayed close to his pegasus, hungry for reassurance and Emrys's protection.

"That's not an answer, you know." Malcolm leaned against the feed trough, studying him. "Agnes wants to check your arm again. But it can wait."

Blaise nodded but didn't say anything.

Malcolm adjusted his posture so that he met Blaise's lowered eyes. "Are we okay?"

And that was the real question. The one Blaise didn't know the answer to, and it was frustrating. "I don't know."

Malcolm's chin dimpled with concern. "Why not?"

Why not? Blaise shook his head, then regretted it when the move made him dizzy. He had to be more careful. "Because...because just *look* at us." For emphasis, he gestured between them. "You're a *Doyen*. I'm...I'm a..." He squeezed his eyes shut. Blaise didn't want to say *prisoner* or *war criminal*, even though they both described him. *Breaker. Sorcerer.* "I'm *me*. You're my handler."

Malcolm blinked at him, and it was clear from his startled expression he hadn't seen it as such. "Is this because I had to use the geasa to stop you last night?"

Blaise shivered at the mention, his gut clenching as he staved off the reminder of the dark alchemy surging through him. He didn't want to think about that ever again. But maybe that was a part of it. Jefferson had made it clear he could use the geasa, if he chose. "You have *power* over me."

"But it's not like that," Malcolm protested.

Blaise crossed his arms. "Isn't it? Because that's how it seems."

Malcolm took a tentative step closer. "But that's not how it is *here*." He slapped a hand against his chest, over his heart. His big brown eyes pleaded with Blaise, full of so much emotion that the Breaker couldn't help but uncross his arms, some of his tension bleeding away.

Emrys bumped Blaise with his nose. <He doesn't look like Jefferson, but his heart is the same.>

Blaise glanced back at the stallion, lips pursed. The pegasus always had keen insight into people, and it was clear Emrys not only liked Malcolm but had worked with him. *Trusted* him, even.

"I didn't know how else to get your attention. To save you," Malcolm whispered.

Blaise sighed. "You won't use the geasa against me again?"

Hurt flashed through Malcolm's eyes, but he shook his head. "I didn't use it *against* you, I used it to *help* you. To help *us*."

Blaise raked a hand through his unruly hair. He needed a haircut, a shave, and a bath—probably not in that order. A change of clothes, too. He was a walking disaster.

"Blaise?" Malcolm roused him from his thoughts. "I promise you. My position...the geasa. I would *never* use any of it against you. I'm sorry if you think I did. That was not my intent. I just want to be *me* with you." His voice was tinged with such raw distress that it shook Blaise. He met Malcolm's eyes again, momentarily surprised by the veiled pain he read in their depths.

Maybe Blaise wasn't the only one with old wounds. He thought back to the glimpse of Malcolm's old life revealed in the dreamscape. He nodded, understanding. "You can be you."

Relief reflected in Malcolm's eyes, and he took another step closer. Something about the tilt of his head reminded Blaise of Jefferson, and the very thought stirred his core. Malcolm brushed a hand against the healing wound on Blaise's cheek, his touch tender. The corners of his eyes crinkled, and Blaise thought he was about to speak, but he didn't.

Blaise knew what he wanted to ask, though. He answered the unvoiced question, because after all he'd endured, he *needed* to feel wanted. He leaned into Malcolm, breathing out a soft sigh as warm and welcoming arms wrapped around him.

Salty tears ran down Blaise's face, dampening Malcolm's shoulder. Malcolm pulled back. "What's wrong?"

Blaise shook his head. He didn't know how to answer that. How could he explain that for the first time in what felt like forever, he felt safe? And loved? He closed his eyes, breathing in Malcolm's minty fragrance. Then his wandering mind recalled why he had left the house in the first place. *Jack and Flora.* "Why was Flora so angry at Jack for killing Lamar? I mean, I generally frown on that sort of thing but...again, *Lamar*."

Malcolm made a face. "Can we not talk about that?"

Blaise shook his head, his worries swooping back into place. "I couldn't stay in there to hear their yelling. But I want to know. I don't want to be left out." Because at the heart of it, he felt like he was the reason this had all happened. Whatever bad thing had transpired wouldn't be so if not for him.

Reluctantly, Malcolm explained the issue. Emrys listened too, ears pricked with interest but keeping his thoughts to himself as the Doyen outlined the situation.

Blaise chewed on his bottom lip. "What's going to happen to you? You're a Doyen. And I'm..." He winced. He was a war criminal. A *murderer.* And Malcolm had so many plans to help the mages throughout the Confederation. All his plans were going to be shattered, another casualty of Blaise's destruction.

"You're *Blaise bloody Hawthorne*, and you're amazing and kind and literally the best person I have *ever* met," Malcolm said with conviction. "Don't worry about me."

Blaise crossed his arms. "You don't know me very well if you think I won't worry about you. Anxiety should be my middle name."

Malcolm chuckled. "Fine, fine. I should have said I'm coming up with a plan."

Blaise cocked his head. "What can I do to help?" Mention of a plan put him at ease.

"First things first, focus on getting well." Malcolm brushed a hand against Blaise's too-thin chest. "You worry about that. I'm buying us some time before my plan comes to fruition."

"Are you going to tell me this plan?"

Malcolm smiled. "Once I have it all figured out, absolutely."

"I thought you had it figured out."

"I said I'm coming up with a plan. Though I appreciate the amount of faith you have in me, even I need a little time to work in my wondrous ways," Malcolm clarified with a grin.

Malcolm

"Mr. Wells!" Marta wailed, indignant, as she burst into Malcolm's study. One of Marta's many charms was that, like Flora, she was overly comfortable around him and discarded the usual social niceties like knocking. "The Breaker is in my *kitchen!*"

Her appearance and level of upset momentarily alarmed Malcolm, but as he absorbed her words, he leaned back in his chair, a grin spreading across his face. "Oh. Is that so?" That was excellent news. Something to take his mind off the fact that the Confederation had his home surrounded, eager to snap him or Blaise up if they so much as stuck a toe beyond the gate.

Marta marched up to his desk. "Sir, with all due respect, *that is my kitchen.*"

He chuckled. She was protective of her domain, and he would have supported her under other circumstances, but not this time. Malcolm eased forward, folding his hands atop the desk. "Marta, please allow me to explain something. I know you think he's dangerous."

She gave a sharp nod, her eyes catching the slew of newspapers arrayed on his desk. She scowled at the headlines: *Traitor Jefferson Cole Missing. Breaker on the Run: Soldiers Surround Wells*

Estate. Malcolm shuffled the papers away. He didn't want Blaise to see those, either.

He aimed a winning smile at Marta. Malcolm appreciated that she had held her tongue against Blaise, but he knew her, and read the unease in her body whenever Blaise was around. "He's a *Breaker*, Mr. Wells. *A Breaker in my kitchen.*"

"No harm will come to anything in there, I assure you." Malcolm rose from the desk. "That may be the safest place for him." She glowered at him, dubious. "He loves to bake, Marta. It calms him."

At that, her brow furrowed with thought. Then she nodded. "I can understand that."

"To put you at ease, I'll check on him to be sure all is well." Malcolm headed to the door. Little by little, Blaise was creeping out of the shadow cast over him by the Golden Citadel. Venturing into the kitchen had to be a positive sign, by Malcolm's judgment. He edged past Marta and hurried down the hall, ignoring her *hrmph* of annoyance. She didn't like others going into her kitchen —including him.

As Marta reported, Blaise was there. The young man was a sight to behold, his hair cut and slicked back, his beard neat, and skin clean. He wore a set of Malcolm's clothes from years ago, and they hung baggy on his slender frame, but all the same, it was a happy improvement from his garments of the previous day. He had sugar and flour stationed on a nearby counter, bowls and pans surrounding him. Fragrant, freshly-washed berries and a bowl of cream loomed near tins of spices. Blaise moved more slowly than Malcolm was accustomed to seeing when he was at work doing what he loved, but it was to be expected. Blaise glanced over his shoulder when he heard the door open, a guilty look crossing his face.

"I think your cook is mad at me."

Malcolm smiled, waving a hand in dismissal. "Marta's not used to sharing her space. She'll get over it." *Probably.* "What are you making?"

"Cookies." He gestured to the other assortment of ingredients. "And a berry cream cake."

Oh, that was promising. Marta had a sweet tooth to rival a pegasus. "If you give her a cookie, she'll definitely get over it." Malcolm eased over to a section of the counter that wasn't covered in supplies and leaned against it. "How are you feeling?"

Blaise closed his eyes for a moment, taking a deep breath and then exhaling slowly, as if centering himself. He was having a tough time adjusting to life outside the Golden Citadel. Malcolm was glad for the high walls around his home—it shielded Blaise from the fact that the Confederation knew he was there. Malcolm was gambling they would respect his position as a Doyen and the sanctity of his estate. It was also very possible they wouldn't.

"Feeling like I needed to come and do this," Blaise answered after a moment, jutting his chin toward the ingredients. "I needed to take my mind off things. Sometimes it's like I'm drowning in my thoughts and in my magic. Or like they're both eating me alive." He scrubbed at his face, leaving a trail of flour along one cheek and dusting his beard. "And Emrys said that while you have been very nice and given him sweets, they're not up to the quality he prefers."

Malcolm studied Blaise, wanting to turn him back to the discussion about how he was faring. It had become difficult to read anything through the geasa, as if Blaise had discovered a way to avoid broadcasting through it. But poking too deeply at the question might force him away, and Malcolm was unwilling to take that risk. "Yes, well, I'm sorry that my award-winning chef is not up to your stallion's standards." If Blaise wanted to keep things light, Malcolm would match him.

The younger man set back to work, though his movements lacked the certainty and precision they'd held before. His hands trembled as he poured ingredients, a sign of how much he was struggling. "Thank you for taking care of Emrys, by the way."

What else could Malcolm have done? Emrys had become an

ally, wanting Blaise free as much as he did. "You're welcome. He's a good pegasus. And a good friend."

Blaise looked down at the flour, which he had been about to measure when Malcolm came in. "He is." He picked up a tin measuring cup and gave it a contemplative look, as if he had lost his train of thought.

"You're going to be okay." Blaise's quailing uncertainty thrummed through their bond, the first thing Malcolm had detected in a while. "I know it."

"Maybe," Blaise whispered, dubious.

"No maybes," Malcolm corrected. He straightened, stepping closer to rest a hand gently on Blaise's shoulder. "Want me to ask Marta if she has chocolate around here somewhere?"

Blaise blinked, surprised by the question. Then he nodded. "Semi-sweet. Not baking chocolate."

"There's a difference?"

"*Of course* there's a difference."

Malcolm hid his smile as he turned away. One way or the other, he was going to make sure Blaise was okay.

Flora

THE ARBORETUM WAS ON HIGH ALERT AFTER THE SHENANIGANS AT the Golden Citadel, but that wasn't about to stop Flora. She was on a mission of compassion. After all the things that had been botched, she decided that Marian, at least, deserved to know Blaise was free. And she had a troubling question for the alchemist—one that hadn't occurred to the others yet.

It took some doing, but she found Marian in the small quarters that served as her room. The alchemist was playing cards to pass the time, though she looked up abruptly as soon as the half-knocker made her appearance. She gathered the cards up and set them aside, her shoulders tense. "Well?"

Flora grinned. "We got him. He's safe."

"Blaise won't be safe until he's off Confederation lands," Marian replied, though her shoulders relaxed at the news. She swallowed. "I wish I could see him."

Flora gave a sad shake of her head. "Too risky. This place is being watched closely, and things didn't go according to plan."

Marian's back straightened, steel glinting in her eyes. "Where is he? They can't get him again." The alchemist fisted her hands, bony knuckles standing out like the spines of a dragon.

"The estate," Flora answered. "He'll be safe there for a time." Marian's brow knit, as if the response wasn't to her satisfaction. But there was little to be done. When the alchemist didn't give voice to her concerns, Flora addressed her own. "You said that Blaise's blood can spawn new mages."

Marian nodded, weary. "Yes."

"How likely is it that Gregor Gaitwood will have magic?" Flora steeled herself for an answer she wouldn't like.

To her surprise, Marian started laughing. Flora wondered if maybe the stress had gotten to her, but after a full minute of mirth, the alchemist quieted with a savage grin. "Doyen Gaitwood is as magical as a boar going to market."

Flora's eyes widened as she caught on to what the woman was implying. "You switched the Ink?" *With pig's blood of all things. Oh, that's grand.*

"The second batch, yes. You nabbed the first batch before I could complete the swap." Annoyance crossed Marian's face for a moment before evaporating. Flora wondered if Marian had been the presence she'd sensed that day. "No one would listen to me about Blaise, so I took matters into my own hands." The alchemist licked her lips. "If there is *anything* I can do in the future to help keep him safe, let me know." She met Flora's eyes.

The half-knocker nodded. "And is there anything I can do for you?" Because blast it all, Flora *liked* this gutsy woman.

Marian offered a sad, reflective smile. "You've already done it."

CHAPTER TWENTY-EIGHT

Echoes of Jack

Kittie

"What is this place?" Emmaline asked as she walked beside her mother. They strode down the main street (the only street) to the corral on the outskirts of the town, where Emmaline's pegasus awaited her. The overuse of magic had drained the girl, and she slept for days once she had gotten settled.

"The only bolt-hole for mages in the Confederation," Kittie answered, tamping down her impatience. She brimmed with questions she was eager to ask, but her daughter had just as many. Maybe more. "You sure stirred up the fire ants by punching through our wards like you did."

Emmaline gave an unapologetic shrug, a move that reminded Kittie almost painfully of Jack. "Didn't know what I was going against, but I'd do it again if I had to."

You even sound like your father. "I'm glad you did." *Ugh. Blasted headache.* Kittie licked her lips, struggling against the urge to take a swig from the flask at her side. It was a losing battle. The hazy comfort of liquor had been her solace for too long. Emmaline frowned as she took a sip of brandy.

And then they arrived at the corral, Emmaline's attention drawn by the striking spotted pegasus who trotted to the fence, thrusting his head over the railing. Kittie would be the first to say the stallion was handsome, and she was fiercely proud that her daughter was the one who rode him. She watched as Emmaline fussed over the pegasus, climbing the fence and dropping down to the other side.

A gaggle of children raced over, eyes wide and curious. They climbed on the fence nearby, though they all had enough sense not to go into the corral. Kittie watched them out of the corner of her eye.

"Miss! Miss!" A freckled girl with red hair waved a carrot in her hand. "My ma said that's a pegasus! But I thought they had wings?"

Emmaline put an arm around her stallion's neck, turning to the curious group. "Your ma is right." She combed her fingers through Oberidon's mane, whispering something to him, and a moment later, a pair of long, speckled wings unfurled from his shoulders. Even Kittie sucked in a breath of wonder, captivated by the magnificent sight. The spotted stallion ruffled his wings, twisting his neck to preen a feather in place before folding them neatly at his sides.

"Oooooh," the children chorused.

"Can I give him a carrot? What's his name?" the red-head asked, her face scrunched in delight.

Emmaline grinned, the pegasus following as she walked closer to their audience. "Sure. You can call him Oby."

"Here, Oby!" the girl dangled the carrot in her hand.

Oberidon's lips curled daintily around the vegetable, tugging it into his mouth with a crunch. <Thank you. It's delicious. Do you know what I like even more?>

The children squealed in unison as the pegasus's voice

resonated in their minds. Kittie smiled. She had forgotten that the equines could do that.

"What?" the girl squeaked, rapt.

"Oby, don't be greedy," Emmaline corrected the stallion, bonking him on the muzzle. He lipped at her in mock retaliation, and their interplay made Kittie's heart sing. "He's going to tell you to bring cookies, and then he's going to get so fat and sassy he won't be able to fly."

The children howled with laughter. Oberidon laid his ears back. <One cookie never hurt.>

Kittie watched as Emmaline bantered with the children a little longer. A boy broke away from the group, returning a few moments later bearing a cookie like a hard-won prize. Emmaline allowed them to break it into tiny pieces and take turns feeding the pegasus, and afterward, the children drifted off, happy.

Emmaline's interaction with the children was another heartrending echo of Jack. She couldn't hold her questions back any longer. Once the children were out of earshot, Kittie climbed onto the top rail. "Em, I have to ask. Only because…" She drifted off, shaking her head as she fought back the emotions she had bricked away so many years ago. "I thought you were dead. I was *told* you were dead." The yawning emptiness of those words opened a deep gulf between them, and Kittie trembled. She took another drink from her flask to settle her nerves.

Emmaline flinched, her mouth dropping open. "*Oh.* What do you want to ask? Ask me anything." She scurried up the fence and sat beside her mother, rubbing Oberidon's forehead.

"What happened to your father? Is he…?"

Emmaline blinked. "Daddy's alive. At least the last I knew." She looked chagrined. "He…well, it's a long story. After you got stolen away from us, he kept me safe." Emmaline scraped at the wood with a fingernail, thoughtful. "Daddy never stopped trying to find you."

Something inside Kittie crumbled to ash. *Jack tried to find me.*

He wasn't dead. He just couldn't get here. She swallowed. "How did you find me when he couldn't? And where is he now?"

Her daughter pulled the tiny doll-like figure from her pocket. "My magic is better at finding people than his. I'm an Effigest. Like *him*." Something about the way Emmaline emphasized the last word told Kittie that there had been strife between the pair. Not surprising in the least. "And Daddy...he's helping a friend of ours. He let me look for you by myself." Her voice softened as she pulled back some of the vitriol.

A smile tugged at Kittie's mouth. "And you succeeded. Now what?"

Emmaline chewed on her lower lip. "I should find him once my magic's replenished. Let him know I found you." She fixed an imploring look on her mother. "And maybe you'll come back to the Gutter with us?"

Kittie blinked. Jack had settled in the Gutter? She tightened her grip on the top rail. "There are some things I need to take care of here."

"Please, Mom. I...I missed you." Emmaline's voice cracked, crestfallen.

As if Kittie hadn't missed her child and husband with every fragment of her being. As if the easiest path hadn't been to drown her sorrows. "I missed you, too. That doesn't mean I won't go. I only need time to handle something."

"What?" Emmaline asked.

Kittie studied the churned dirt in the paddock. Would Emmaline hate her? "I have to tell my husband."

Emmaline stared at her, and Oberidon snorted. "What...what do you mean? What about Daddy?"

Kittie jumped down from the fence, stumbling and almost fell her knees. She straightened, trying to preserve her dignity. "What else was I supposed to do? I thought he was *dead*. That *you* were dead." She gestured to herself. "Was I to just wither away and die?" There had been a time when she'd wished for that—the time before she had cured her grief with liquor and the first comforting arms she fell into.

Her daughter sighed. "No. it's just that..." She shook her head. "Daddy's a jackass but he waited for you."

Of course, he had. Jack was far from perfect, and Kittie wouldn't have blamed him if he sought comfort from the soiled doves of the Untamed Territory. But that wasn't his way. He would only fall into bed with someone he had an emotional connection to. "That's why I need time, Em. Just a little." Kittie swallowed. "I love your father." But would Jack feel, as Emmaline did, that Kittie had betrayed them? It was impossible to know. Was he still the man he had been, or had he changed as much as Kittie herself?

Emmaline nodded. "We don't have much time. I left him in Izhadell." She stuck her hand into a pocket, pulling out a tiny doll. "And he's on the move."

Izhadell. Kittie tensed. Jack was in Phinora? She seldom left the limits of Bitter End's wards, but she knew very well that he would be a wanted man. Jack was no innocent, and she couldn't imagine the years doing anything to change that. "Why is he in Izhadell?"

Emmaline licked her lips. "It's kind of a long story. But it's about that friend I told you about."

Kittie nodded. "I have all afternoon. Tell me."

CHAPTER TWENTY-NINE

Puppeteer

Jack

Soldiers and guards patrolled Izhadell like a murder of chupacabras on the hunt. Maybe killing Lamar had been a miscalculation, but Jack didn't regret it. Not really. Zepheus reminded him that the increased presence of guards and soldiers in the streets of the capital city was a direct result of his actions.

"Not as if freeing a war criminal from the Cit played a part or anything," Jack muttered.

<Doesn't help that the murderer of a Salt-Iron Commander is running around free.>

The outlaw huffed out a breath, fingers tight on the reins. The last few days had been rough, requiring the use of Obfuscation more frequently than he liked. By night he bunked in abandoned buildings and by day he skulked through the outskirts of Izhadell, searching for leads.

He had exchanged his usual clothing for the nondescript, professional clothing of a merchant again. Though the hair dye had washed out, a check in his small hand mirror proved he had cleaned up well and only bore a passing resemblance to his Wanted posters. Those always somehow made him look meaner.

<You *are* a mean son of a plucked griffin,> Zepheus reminded him.

Jack shrugged, not about to deny the truth of the statement. He nudged the palomino onward, heading to a tavern. Wells probably hadn't noticed it with his concern over Blaise, but Jack had relieved him of some of his wealth. Just enough to get some jaws yapping so that he could find out what he needed.

The customers in the tavern were on edge, alarmed by the heightened presence of guards and the rumors racing through the streets about the Breaker holed up at the Doyen's estate. Jack grabbed a barstool and listened in. Their fear of Blaise was damned annoying. Not that they used his name. No, to the public at large, he was the Breaker. The outlaw who had single-handedly destroyed Fort Courage and injured or killed scores of Confederation men and women. *I never get any credit.*

But the mysterious murder of Commander Gaitwood was also a hot topic for debate. The only problem was that the idiots suspected Blaise of that, too. Jack nearly slapped a hand to his forehead. *Bunch of beef-headed coots.*

<You're on your own if you correct them.> He could imagine Zepheus pinning his ears back in annoyance.

No, Jack wouldn't correct them. His current guise wouldn't have such knowledge. *Unfortunately.* Instead, he flagged over the bartender. "Any young, blonde girls come in here?"

The bartender, a stocky, middle-aged woman with her hair pinned into buns, glowered at him. "We don't cater to such appetites here, you blighter."

Jack tilted his head. "If that's the case, you're one of the few."

She glared at him, baring her teeth in an unfriendly smile. "If that's what you're after, then you'd best be on your way."

The outlaw tapped a finger against the bar, taking a moment to decide how he wanted to play it. *Figures I'd walk into the one place in all Phinora that isn't happy to offer innocents up for the taking.*

"I apologize, but you misunderstand. I'm looking for the girl for *other* reasons."

At that, the bartender gave him an assessing look. She had probably heard all the lies before. "And?"

"She has a horse—a particular one I'm interested in." Yeah, maybe focusing on Oberidon was the smarter way to play it. "I run a breeding operation."

The bartender studied him, then nodded. "Right. Anything particular?"

"Spots. Unusual for a Phinoran-bred."

The bartender licked her lips. "The sort with the blanket patterns on their hind end, like the Mellan Spotted? Or the piebald type like the Petrian Trotter?"

Jack shook his head. "Not like either of those." He racked his brain for the name of the spotted breed native to Oscen and the northern Untamed Territory.

"Pelushan?"

The outlaw snapped his fingers. That was it. "Yes, spots all over the body like a Pelushan. The particular one I had my eye on had liver brown spots."

The bartender gave a small smile. "There's someone I can ask." She rubbed her fingers together with meaning.

Jack reached into his coin purse and drew out two golden eagles, sliding them across the bar. She dropped them into a pocket, holding up her index finger in a *wait* gesture. She saw to another customer, then slipped into a room behind the bar. Jack took another sip of his drink as he waited.

<You've got guards incoming.>

Jack stayed on the barstool, though he turned just enough to have an eye on the door. True to Zepheus's warning, a trio of guards entered, surveying the tavern. The common area grew quiet, save for a rowdy group at the billiards table too absorbed with their game to notice. Jack ignored the guards when they approached the bar. The bartender returned, frowning at the newcomers.

"Don't want any trouble from you lot," she warned the leader.

The man shrugged. "Answer my questions, and we'll be on our way. You seen any mavericks or strange doings around here?"

Jack took another sip of his beer. Technically, he wasn't a maverick.

The bartender rolled her eyes. "I work with the public. There are always strange doings." One of the newcomers snickered, though he stopped when his neighbor elbowed him. "You need to be more specific."

The lead guard sighed. "I don't know the name of 'em. The sort that messes with dolls and stick figures?"

"Puppeteer?" one of his cronies guessed.

"No, those are the ones who do the plays for children. They're entertainers, not mages," the guard who had snickered corrected.

Gods. I'm surrounded by half-wits that couldn't teach a hen to cluck, and I don't dare correct them. Jack sighed and took another swig.

"Eff...effer...oh fuck, I don't know." The lead guard spread his hands in exasperation.

"Effigest," Jack muttered.

The guards brightened. "Right! Yes, that. What this fine man said." The leader gave Jack a grateful nod before returning his attention to the bartender. "We're looking for one of those. But a girl, long blonde hair. We think she's the one who killed the Commander. Found one of the little doodads at the scene."

It's a poppet, you fiddlehead. Jack stared at his mug, troubled because he didn't think he'd left any evidence behind. And he knew for a fact the Cit had a record of his alleged capture. Unless they were dumber than he thought, they would also know he was no longer on the grounds. So why look for Emmaline? She hadn't been at the Cit.

Oh. Then he realized why. As far as the Confederation knew, Jack had no magic. It was documented that Lamar had Jack's magic stripped. And Emmaline had been in their custody for a time. They had a record of her magic. And she, like Jack, had a compelling reason for wanting Lamar dead. Lamar had seen her in Izhadell. *Damn it.* Now it was even more urgent that he track her down before the Salties did.

The bartender gave a noncommittal shrug. "Lots of girls on the streets around here. Gonna need more than that."

The lead guard nodded. "She rides a spotted horse. Like one of them Pelushans."

The bartender smiled, canting her head. "That so? Boys, then I have somebody you should meet. This gentleman here is looking for that horse. Perhaps you can work together."

All eyes turned to Jack. He took another drink as the lead guard shifted to face him. *To Perdition with this bartender!* And here Jack had thought she might be a reasonable person.

"Is that so?" the leader asked, suspicious.

Jack rolled his shoulders in what they might construe as a lazy shrug. "Maybe. Got an eye out for interesting horseflesh."

"And why is that?"

The outlaw met the guard's eyes. Jack wanted to plant a fist in the man's face, but that wasn't something his current persona would do. At least not without good reason. Jack himself needed little cause. "Breeding stock."

"How did you know about this horse?"

Jack rolled his eyes. "Because I'm not blind or stupid like you boys." Maybe he shouldn't have said that. The guards tightened up their ring around him. Yeah, he definitely shouldn't have said that.

<I can hear you being stupid. I'm around the back if you can get out.>

"You must be new in town. No one insults the guard around here," the leader growled. "We keep the peace, though we're not afraid to remind rabble like you of what we can do."

<Oh, they're going to regret that,> Zepheus commented.

Jack ignored the stallion, lifting his chin in defiance at the young man's words. Judging by their youth, Jack estimated he had between fifteen and twenty years of age on them. They were all young and eager to prove themselves. No doubt they saw him as a man past his prime. None of them knew they were dealing with an outlaw, much less a mage.

"I think it would be in your best interest to leave me alone to finish my drink," Jack advised them, turning away. As much as he was spoiling for a fight, the odds weren't in his favor in these close-quarters, outnumbered as he was. At least without using magic or a sixgun. But those would give him away. *Please show you have the common sense of a drunk goblin and don't poke the monster.*

They chose violence. A hand clamped on Jack's shoulder. "That's quite enough from you. A night in a cell will teach you some respect." The guards laughed, foreshadowing that getting Jack to the aforementioned cell would include some roughing up first.

Jack sighed. He met the bartender's eyes. "This is on you."

She shrugged. "I have no regrets."

Yeah, well, she was going to regret the clean-up that her tavern would require. He glanced back at the guard, palming his personal poppet as he attempted to shrug his shoulder free. "This is your last warning. Get your Garus-besotted *Saltie* hands off me."

The guard's mouth opened to make a retort, then snapped shut as he and his cohorts digested the insult Jack had hurled at them. The bartender goggled at him, too. No fine, upstanding Confederation citizen would call another a *Saltie* or disparage Garus, their precious god of wisdom. Which meant that he wasn't a fine, upstanding Confederation citizen. Jack smiled as they connected the dots.

Fingers tightened on pistols. A handful of customers who sensed trouble brewing skulked out, but others were now on alert, eager at the promise of bloodshed. "You're coming with us, outlaw."

"Nah." Jack took a last sip of his drink, simultaneously pulling on the magic of his primed poppet for a burst of strength and speed.

He rammed his mug into the leader's face, his hand a blur as it smashed into the man's nose. The guard sprawled backward into one of his fellows.

The remaining guard dodged out of the way, aiming his pistol at Jack. For half a second the outlaw thought the guard might hesitate and not shoot, but by the determined slant of the man's brow, he realized that was an incorrect assumption. He had the advantage and whipped his leg out, kicking the guard's knee so that his shot fouled, the bullet slamming into a wall.

And just like that, fights boiled out across the room. The remaining customers, out of boredom or inebriation, started a melee of their own. Billiard balls flew across the common area like cannonballs, a cue ball sailing past Jack's nose. Beer bottles shattered as enthusiastic brawlers broke them on the edge of tables. A giggling dancehall girl jumped off the bar and landed on the back of the guard who had tried to shoot Jack, whooping as if she were astride a half-broke unicorn.

Jack slid beneath a table, avoiding a guard who had recovered and lunged after him. He leaped up on the other side, hurling the table into his pursuer and, in the process, taking out a burly man who howled with rage. Jack was distracted, trying to track the other guards.

He didn't realize until too late that the burly man had jumped to his feet and was barreling at him like an angry bull. Jack turned when he caught a glimpse of a shadow in his peripheral vision.

A beefy fist smashed into his right cheek and eye. Jack's head cracked backward, and he saw stars. It wasn't the first time he'd taken a punch, but this one had poor timing. His eyes watered as he staggered away from his new assailant. The punch served as a great comeuppance, smacking Jack right in the pride—where it hurt the most.

Jack pulled out his sixgun, sighting it on the big man who had his hand cocked back for another punch. His vision blurred, but this close Jack wouldn't miss. "Try that again." The man backed off, realizing his brawn was no match for a bullet.

The outlaw turned, slipping out into the streets while the

guards were distracted by the chaos, skirting around the building to the back where Zepheus was waiting. The palomino eyed his shiner as he mounted. <What happened to the guards?>

"They fucked around and found out," Jack growled, rubbing at his tender cheek. "Now let's get out of here before more arrive."

<Where to?>

"Anywhere but here."

CHAPTER THIRTY

The Power of Baked Goods

Malcolm

Sunlight filtered through the window, chastising Malcolm for his lateness. He shifted in his bed, pausing when he noticed the contours of a dark shape on the other side, curled up. Blaise's eyes were closed, his face slack and hair a wild nest from whatever restlessness had possessed him. But he was peaceful in his slumber, and all Malcolm wanted to do was stare at him and try to figure out how he had snuck in here during the night without him realizing.

In the days since Blaise's release, Malcolm had kept himself away from the dreamscape at night, giving the Breaker the space he needed. Or at least, the space Malcolm suspected he needed. Blaise didn't talk about it and had closed himself off, spending most of his time with Emrys. But maybe Malcolm had been wrong. He frowned, considering his options. *Nothing ventured, nothing gained.*

Malcolm rolled over to face him, the mattress jarring with the movement. It shook Blaise awake, as was his sneaky intent.

Blaise's eyes flashed open, and Malcolm detected a shiver of panic and embarrassment through the geasa.

"Um, howdy," Blaise murmured. "Sorry."

Why are you apologizing? Malcolm would gladly wake up like this for the rest of eternity. "Nothing to be sorry about."

Blaise relaxed at his words. "I just...being alone...I..." He faltered, shaking his head against the pillow.

Not for the first time, Malcolm had to rein in his anger at what the Cit had done to Blaise. He reminded himself that this was part of his gambit. It was a systemic problem he was going to address and correct. But for the moment, Blaise was the priority. "Hey, you never have to be alone here. Not when I'm around. You know that, don't you?"

Blaise swallowed. "Yes, but..." He closed his eyes. "I know the Confederation is outside your walls. Waiting. For *me*."

"Not just for you, love." Malcolm hid a secret smile when Blaise's eyes flew open at the endearment. "You give yourself too much credit. They want me, too. And I have business to attend to regarding that issue today."

Blaise adjusted, braced upright on his elbow. His hair was still an adorable mess, which Malcolm wanted to point out but didn't want to risk embarrassing him. "Did you come up with a plan?"

Malcolm nodded. "Mostly. I had some parts of it confirmed late last night. Very late." Technically, it had been morning. Blaise must have come in once Malcolm collapsed from exhaustion. He read the hunger for information on the Breaker's face, so he sat up. "I'll tell you, if you like."

"Please do."

There was a knock at the door, followed by Flora's voice. "Hey, Mal! You better get your tail down here because company's coming in a half hour!"

Malcolm groaned. "Change of plans. Let's get dressed and I'll update you as we choke down a quick breakfast." He swung his legs over the side of the bed, glancing over at Blaise. As much as he adored that man, he had no taste for clothing. "I'll pick something out for you." Malcolm had splurged and bought a small wardrobe of clothing he hoped might fit Blaise. "Come on. To the closet in your guest room!"

Blaise raised his brows but dutifully trailed behind him out the door.

Flora saw the pair exit the master bedroom and whooped. "It's about time, you two!" She blew air kisses at them.

Blaise's cheeks flamed, and Malcolm scowled at her. If it were anyone else, he wouldn't have cared what Flora thought about their nocturnal activities. But with Blaise he cared very much. "It's not like that."

Flora snorted, favoring them with a skeptical look. "If you say so, boss."

Malcolm clenched his jaw, hoping Flora hadn't dimmed the spark of Blaise that had shone through this morning. He hazarded a glance at the Breaker, who hung back a step behind him. Something flickered in Blaise's eyes that Malcolm couldn't read, and then he ducked his head and whispered, "Thank you."

"Of course," Malcolm said, voice soft. Flora was right, though. He wanted more, *longed* for more. But he cared for Blaise too much to force the issue. Malcolm clung to the hope that perhaps some day, Blaise might change his mind. Until then, he would wait. And dream.

He laid a gentle hand on the younger man's shoulder, guiding him to the neighboring guest room so that Malcolm could peruse the array of clothing.

A short time later, Blaise stared at his reflection, dressed in fresh, well-tailored clothes. Malcolm had helped him tame the mess of his hair with a comb and scented oils. The Breaker didn't say a word but shook his head at himself in disbelief. Malcolm smiled, rather pleased with the results.

Once Malcolm himself was dressed, he met Blaise downstairs for breakfast and laid out the plan. Which, predictably, Blaise was dubious of. "How sure are you this will work?"

"Not sure at all," Malcolm replied, trying to stay upbeat. It was an audacious gamble, but it was all he could come up with. "My back-up plan is that we sneak out, get on a steamer, move to Theilia and start a new life as goat herders."

"No offense, but you would last less than five minutes as a goat herder," Blaise said seriously.

"Yes, and this is why it's the back-up plan." Malcolm nodded, pleased that Blaise was willing and able to banter.

"But I don't like the part where I have to, you know, *meet people*." Blaise worried at his bottom lip.

Malcolm gave a pained sigh. "My darling little introvert, you know meeting people is one of my favorite things to do, right?"

"You can do that, and I'll stand in a corner and pretend not to be there."

Malcolm chuckled. Blaise had no idea he would be the star attraction. But he would never think that of himself. "It's going to be fine. You'll be great."

Blaise

IT WAS NOT, IN FACT, FINE OR GREAT. IT HAD BEEN EASY TO BELIEVE Malcolm when he spoke with such confidence, but quite another thing when Blaise faced the reality. He knew from Emrys about the Confederation forces amassed outside Malcolm's gates. Malcolm pretended like it was nothing to worry about. Anxiety clawed at Blaise's insides.

Blaise braced himself for some sort of sneak attack or ambush from the Confederation ranks when the front gates opened to allow entry to Malcolm's guests. Nothing more threatening than staffers with dour faces accompanied the carriage that came up the drive. Blaise relaxed as he watched Malcolm greet the new arrivals. He had found a corner to skulk in (he hadn't been kidding about that), and Flora was nearby, though she said that she would have to duck out soon. She didn't want to be seen.

Blaise wished he could do the same.

He slipped into the parlor, noticing that Malcolm's staff had laid refreshments out on a table. Finger sandwiches and fresh-squeezed lemonade. "No cookies? Everything's better with cookies." Not to mention the berry cream cake. He huffed in annoyance.

Malcolm was still greeting their guests outside. Blaise hurried to the kitchen and grabbed a tray, arranging an assortment of cookies. He was afraid of running out of time, so discarded the idea of bringing the cake to the parlor. Cookies would have to do. He couldn't help his satisfied smile at the sweets.

A few moments later, Malcolm led his guests inside. When they entered the parlor, Blaise was already seated in a chair in the farthest corner. Maybe Malcolm would realize he hadn't been joking.

Malcolm's eyes slid to Blaise as he entered, making a little *get over here* gesture with one hand as he and his guests swept into the room. Blaise frowned and shook his head.

"There he is, just as I said!" Malcolm's voice rang with false cheer, and he stepped over to Blaise, leaning down. He lowered his voice. "Please. We need all the allies we can get."

The sincerity and worry in Malcolm's brown eyes won Blaise over. With a soft sigh, he nodded and rose from the chair, rewarded by the Doyen's relieved smile. Malcolm turned back to their guests.

"Doyen Seward Jennings and Mrs. Lizzie Jennings, it's my pleasure to introduce you to Blaise Hawthorne."

Blaise had to admit it warmed his soul that Malcolm hadn't mentioned his magic at all. Even though he knew it was going to be discussed. It was just a tiny, precious nod to the fact that his magic didn't define him, and Malcolm believed that. It was a part of who he was, but not the sum.

Doyen Jennings was shorter than Malcolm, and he beamed as he stared at Blaise. He extended a hand, then grunted as he corrected himself. "Oh, my apologies, I don't know what's proper."

That was a little surprising, since aside from Malcolm, everyone with any power in the Confederation assumed Blaise's touch would destroy them. They weren't wrong. "We can shake. If you like." Blaise focused on keeping his magic under wraps and calm, though he was anything but. He extended his hand, and Jennings took it with a clammy and cool hand, as if he were a little nervous, too.

The woman at Jennings's side watched Blaise with rapt attention, thoughtful. She glanced at Malcolm. "He's easy on the eyes. I think we can work with this." She tilted her head, dark ringlets cascading to one side.

Easy on the eyes? Blaise glanced at Malcolm, whose lips twitched at her assessment. He couldn't offer a comment, however, as Doyen Jennings interceded. His gaze flitted between Blaise and Malcolm with keen interest.

"I will admit, Mal, the revelation shocked me. You, the figurehead of the Faedrans, betraying us to bind to a mage?" The words surprised Blaise. He hadn't thought of it from their political perspective. He was about to speak up, but the Doyen continued. "But now I see your argument. You're right. He wasn't treated well, and not even a prisoner deserves that."

Blaise had put on a little weight, but his cheekbones were still prominent, and the stone bruise on his cheek stubbornly refused to retreat. Self-conscious, Blaise rubbed at the underside of his arm, though the wicked, still-healing gash was concealed by his long sleeve.

Jennings didn't even know about Gregor's plans for him. Didn't know anything about the potion that turned him into a destructive force. Malcolm had said that was something they couldn't reveal, not yet. Baby steps.

"Still," the Doyen mused after a moment, "surely you could have gone about it a better way than binding to a mage?"

"Not while obtaining actual evidence," Malcolm lied.

Meanwhile, Mrs. Jennings snatched a cookie and nibbled at it, walking around Blaise in contemplative circles. He might have found it annoying, but her first bite elicited an *ooh* of pleasure, and he did like when people enjoyed his baking. "You said this was a two-pronged attack, Doyen Wells. What's *my* role?"

Malcolm smiled. "Excellent question, Lizzie! As you heard, I'm going to demand an Inquiry into the conditions of the mages at the Cit."

"Going to be difficult with Gregor leveraging an Inquiry against *you* for binding to a mage," Doyen Jennings pointed out. "As the rumor mill predicts will happen."

Malcolm waved a hand as if this were inconsequential, keeping his focus on Lizzie. "Play the sympathy angle. Seed whatever rumors you can to buy our plight as much favor as you can."

"Only rumors, or can I...be more creative?" Her eyes flashed, eager.

"What did you have in mind?" Malcolm's voice rose with interest. Blaise slunk a few feet away so he would no longer be the literal center of attention.

"Remember when I told you I was interested in penning a play about him?" She gestured to Blaise with the remains of her cookie. *Wait, what?* Before he could catch up, she plowed onward. "I have a draft ready. I can rewrite the third act however you like."

"Er," Blaise protested. *A play? About me?* "What in the blueberry muffins are you talking about?"

Lizzie snapped her fingers, trotting across the parlor to pick up a napkin. She pulled out a pen and started writing. "I love that expression! Let me jot it down."

Malcolm was doing a poor job of hiding an amused smile. "I didn't agree to this," Blaise hissed.

"Come on," Malcolm said, sidling up beside him, voice soft. "We need every advantage. Even the smallest bits of propaganda will help."

"I think we need to brush up on your goat-herding skills." Yes, that sounded more and more tempting.

Malcolm put a companionable arm around him. Blaise almost shrugged it off but he liked it, much to his own chagrin. "My goat-herding skills will remain woeful. What if I promise to never drag you to the play about yourself?"

Blaise sighed. He wasn't sure why a play about himself would be anything but a terrible idea, but Malcolm seemed to think it was worthwhile. And Malcolm was doing so much to help him, he couldn't be a heel and fight everything. "I might live with that."

"Thank you," Malcolm whispered, his breath warm as he leaned close to Blaise's ear. He turned back to Lizzie. "Madame, if you'd like to discuss this with Blaise, I'll go over strategy with Seward."

"Wait, I have to *discuss* it?" Blaise fought back a wave of panic. He wanted to go out to the stables and bury his face in Emrys's mane and not be here.

Malcolm paused in front of him, meeting his eyes. "Lizzie is here to help. It's going to be okay. You can do this." Then he added a wink for good measure before abandoning Blaise to the playwright while he and Seward retired to the study.

Oh well. At least he still had cookies.

"WHAT DID YOU DO?" AS SOON AS THE JENNINGSES LEFT, MALCOLM rounded on Blaise, his eyebrows raised so high they brushed against a curl of his dark hair. "Lizzie was *purring* with joy when they left."

Blaise offered the last cookie to him. "Cookie."

Malcolm eyed it, tempted but undeterred. "Later."

"No, I mean, you asked what I did, and that's the answer." Blaise waved the cookie with meaning. "You're not the only one who can come up with ideas, you know."

Malcolm's expression softened. "That's true. But you were supposed to talk to her so she can finish her play about you to gain support."

"Did that, too." Blaise couldn't help the pride that bloomed in his voice.

Malcolm glanced from the cookie to Blaise, giving in to temptation. He snagged it and took a bite. "So it went well?"

Blaise winced. He wasn't good at reading people, and Lizzie Jennings was no exception. "Probably? She asked a lot of questions. Including who made the cookies, and it surprised her when I said I did. Then we got off topic for a while, and she tried to get me to come work for her until she remembered that was a bad idea."

Malcolm blinked. "Are you seriously telling me Lizzie Jennings tried to steal you away from me for your *baked goods*?"

"You'll be happy to hear I told her no."

Malcolm snorted at that. "I should hope so. Why does it seem as if you're leaving out a *but*?"

There it was. Blaise was rather proud of this next bit. Malcolm was so much savvier than him at this political business, but Lizzie had given him an irresistible opening. "That's what I was trying to tell you. The Jenningses are hosting a party in a few days."

"Gala," Malcolm corrected absently. "Yes, Seward mentioned that to me in passing. But we can't go. If you leave the grounds of my estate before the Inquiry, we'll be right back where we started."

Blaise grinned. "I have no intention of leaving this estate until it's safe for me to do so. My desserts, on the other hand…"

Malcolm slanted a wily look at him. "Wait. I see where you're going with this. That's…that's *brilliant*."

"You once told me my cakes could stand up against the best of the best in Ganland." Blaise hoped that was still true. He was out of practice, and that worried him.

"I meant every word." Malcolm sounded fiercely proud. He rubbed his hands together as he considered the idea. "That's quite the coup. I wish I had thought of it myself."

"You've had a lot on your mind," Blaise murmured. Then he paused, thinking back to something Malcolm had said. "Hold on. You think I would willingly go to someone's fancy party? You're familiar with the fact I'd rather hide in a corner, right?"

Malcolm chuckled. "It's a *gala*. And I may have a long-term goal of taking you to one."

Blaise snorted. "Did you miss my failed attempt at invisibility earlier?"

"And aren't we lucky that's not your magic?" Malcolm grinned.

"It's a pity. Would be so useful." Blaise shook his head, then rubbed his hands together as he turned his attention back to his new goal. "I need to take an inventory of your kitchen. Do you mind?"

Malcolm studied him, a tiny smile curling his lips. "Do what you need to do."

Turning, Blaise strode to the kitchen, and for the first time in a long time, he felt more like himself. He had a purpose, and it was something he could *do*. Now he just had to hope Marta would allow it.

CHAPTER THIRTY-ONE
Not All Monsters Are Alike

Jack

Jack spent days lying low, though he bridled against the delay this put in his search for Emmaline. He considered doubling back to Wells's place, but that wouldn't solve anything. Not to mention the estate's perimeter was crawling with guards. The Doyen and Blaise had enough on their hands without his added complications. While he waited, he did everything he could think of to aid his search. Emmaline herself had a knack for finding people with her Effigest magic. Jack figured if she could do it, maybe he could, too. He tried, but nothing did the trick. His poppet for her only told him she was out there somewhere, with no sense of direction. It was damned frustrating.

"And I'm the fool who didn't plan far enough ahead to figure out a rendezvous," Jack groused to himself. Although he had half-expected Emmaline to track him down by now. It made him worry that something had gone wrong. That she had been captured or hadn't found Kittie.

Besides the guards and soldiers Jack originally encountered, bounty hunters had taken up his trail. The fools were eager to cash his head in for gold and fame, though they were more an inconvenience than a threat. At first, he had worried the Confederation might send out a pair of theurgists, but he soon realized most of those coming after him were norms, without a lick of magic. They had youth and weapons, but those didn't hold a candle to a seasoned outlaw mage partnered with a pegasus.

In other circumstances, Jack might have found the constant interruptions entertaining. As it was, they were pissing him off, so he decided at last to see if he could make them *useful*.

He stood over the latest bounty hunter, a spirited young woman with red hair who reminded him of Vixen Valerie. Maybe the resemblance was why he didn't kill her outright, like the rest. *Nah, not really.* He hoped she had information. She lay sprawled in the boggy clearing, panting through the pain of a broken arm, Jack's sixgun trained on her.

"May as well shoot me, you bastard," she spat.

Jack canted his head, amused. "Mighty rude of you. You attacked me first, after all." And it was true. He wasn't a dunderhead, and he played the innocent traveler card until the hunters came at him.

The huntress glared at him. If she had magic, he would have recruited her for the Gutter in a heartbeat. He liked her spunk. "Of course, I attacked you. Who wouldn't? Your mug is plastered on *Wanted* posters all over the place."

"Yep," Jack agreed, spinning his revolver for show. "So you know I have no qualms with putting a bullet in someone's brain. That's enough to make you wonder why you're still alive, eh?"

"Because you're a monster. You probably want to force yourself on me." She struggled into a sitting position, whimpering when she jarred her arm.

The outlaw spat in the dirt, jaw jutting as he holstered his sixgun. He knelt beside her, meeting her eyes. "I'm not gonna argue that I'm a monster. But not all monsters are alike."

Zepheus stood nearby, wings mantled and ears flattened. <Not sure how that's going to convince her of anything.>

Yeah, he was getting to it. Jack kept his focus on the huntress. "Ask yourself what the Scourge of the Untamed Territory is doing this deep in Confederation lands."

"Assassinating good Confederation men and women, I assume," she shot back.

<I mean, she's not *wrong*.>

Annoying pegasus. Jack frowned. "I'm trying to find my *daughter*."

She blinked, taken by surprise at his admission. Then her face shifted to suspicion. "How do I know that's true?"

"Because you're still alive." Jack shifted to sit down cross-legged nearby. His sixgun was still handy if needed. "What's your name?"

"Lauren."

He nodded, accepting it at face value. Might not be her real name, but it was something. "Well, Lauren, pleased to make your acquaintance. I'll make you a deal. You tell me anything you know that might help me find my daughter, and you get to live."

"How generous," she muttered.

He smirked. "I have my own code of honor, thank you kindly. Now, tell me if you have any information on a girl with blonde hair who rides a spotted stallion."

Lauren twitched at the description. "I know she's *Wanted*, same as you." She licked her lips, some of the fight leaving her as she asked, "That your daughter?"

Jack tilted his head. "You're a smart woman and can probably figure that out. Where was she last sighted?"

The huntress stared at him, as if considering whether she would answer. She glanced down at her limp arm. "I can do you one better, if you let me live."

"How's that?"

"I can give you the handbill."

Jack's pulse quickened. When the Confederation really wanted someone, they distributed individual handbills to bounty hunters. Often the handbills included information not found on a general *Wanted* poster. "Deal. Where is it?"

"If you can find my horse, it's in the pannier."

<Just a moment.> Zepheus trotted off, returning shortly with the reins of the woman's bay gelding between his teeth as he led the steed back. The gelding smacked his lips as he walked, incriminating evidence that he had fled the scene not out of fear but greed for the surrounding foliage.

Jack rose and rifled through Lauren's saddlebags, nodding with satisfaction as he found the missive. He slipped it into his own saddlebag, then shoved his boot into the stirrup to mount. "It's your lucky day, Huntress Lauren. You get to live to tell the tale of how you survived an encounter with Wildfire Jack."

"You're an arrogant bastard, and you can go straight to Perdition."

He smiled, giving her a little salute. "All in good time, darlin'. Thanks for the help." And with that, he rode off.

CHAPTER THIRTY-TWO

Rekindled

Kittie

*K*ittie glanced at the calendar on the table. *He's due back today.* She hadn't told Emmaline much about Hugh Fasig, the man she had married. What was there to say, besides he had served the purpose of distracting her from past pain with his own sort? She didn't love him, and it wasn't something she was proud of.

After she and Emmaline shared a quiet breakfast, they set into the cadence of their day. Kittie served as one of the town laundresses, cleaning and mending clothing for the other citizens. Not a glorious occupation, but it had given her something to do. And it ensured she always had a full flask and needn't rely on her husband for that.

Emmaline plucked a sock in need of mending out of the nearby basket, holding it up as if it were offensive. "Mom, why?"

Kittie selected a needle from her sewing kit. "Why what?"

Her daughter gestured to the domestic scene around them, tossing the sock onto the top of the basket. "I don't understand this. You're a *mage*. A Pyromancer, even. Aren't you meant for more than this?"

Kittie swallowed at the question. She didn't want to answer it, instead focusing on threading her needle. "I don't know what you mean."

"This...this isn't *you*." Emmaline frowned.

"I don't know what you expect of me," Kittie replied, picking up the discarded sock. She found the hole in the toe and set to work mending it.

Emmaline rose from her chair, pacing the small laundry room. Even the way she hunched her shoulders reminded Kittie of Jack. "Daddy told me stories about you when I was little. Before he..." She turned away, toeing a pile of dirty laundry thoughtfully. "Before it hurt him too much to talk about you. He called you a firebrand. Said you wanted to change things. Change everything for mages. Find a way to lead them to freedom."

Kittie bowed her head. That felt like it had been a lifetime ago; dreams that had belonged to someone else. "That was another time, Em."

"What changed?"

"*I* changed." Kittie sighed. She focused on finishing the sock, then found its mate. "I discovered it was futile. One person can't take on something as big as the Confederation and win."

Kittie couldn't bear to go into detail about how her time in the Golden Citadel had hammered that message home. They had made certain she knew that it was because of her fight against the Confederation that her loved ones were gone. That was all it took to snuff out her fire. *What use is magic if it can't protect the ones you love?* Why fight, only to face more pain?

Emmaline pursed her lips and said nothing for a few minutes. Kittie kept to her work, though she sipped from the flask to bolster her nerves.

"What if it wasn't just one person, though?" Emmaline asked at last.

Kittie glanced at her, shaking her head. "I wouldn't do that again." Not now that she had her daughter back. It wasn't worth the risk, especially if they found somewhere they could live in peace.

"Why not?" Emmaline asked, challenge ripening her voice. "What if you had something worth fighting for?"

The needle stabbed into Kittie's index finger, so distracted was she by Emmaline's question. With a hiss, she drew it back and set the sock aside. "I had something worth fighting for, and I lost it *all.*" Kittie swallowed, focusing on the tiny blossom of red on her fingertip. "I don't think I could survive that happening a second time." Sometimes she wasn't so sure she had survived the first occurrence. Maybe she was a banshee, cursed to walk the land, not knowing her soul was already in Perdition.

"Daddy would keep fighting," Emmaline pointed out.

That made Kittie smile. Gods, but she missed that man. "Faedra didn't grant him the sense to know when to quit."

Emmaline pursed her lips. She still struggled to speak well of her father, bothered by something she hadn't divulged yet. But she shook her head. "Nah. He'd change his strategy. That's what he would do."

Kittie thought about that as she took up the troublesome sock again. "What are you wanting me to do?"

"To be *you.*" Emmaline's voice was a whisper, and something about it reminded Kittie of quiet voices on warm summer nights. Sitting on a porch watching fireflies with a wide-eyed toddler on her knee. "To be my mother and the firebrand I *know* you can be."

"I never stopped being your mother," Kittie said. And that was true, even when she had mourned her daughter as lost. But the *firebrand*...she was dead and gone. She had no more illusions of leading the mavericks to freedom as she had as a starry-eyed young woman. Foolish.

Emmaline settled down, getting to work on the laundry. Their conversation died, and Kittie lost herself in the routine. But shortly before their lunch break, a voice shattered the peace.

"Katherine!"

Kittie dropped the pants she was patching, hands trembling. Gods, this day was taking a toll on her. She took a swig from her flask, returning it to her side. Beside her, Emmaline shot her a questioning look. "Mom?"

"It's my husband," Kittie said, putting a hand on Emmaline's shoulder. Her daughter glanced at her quaking fingers, frowning. Kittie pulled her hand away, hurrying to the door. "Wait here. *Please.*"

Hugh Fasig was ten paces from the door to the laundry, closing the distance like a fast-moving squall line. "Katherine! What's this rumor I hear about your *daughter* showing up?" His voice was like a peal of thunder. "How in Perdition do *you* have a daughter?"

Kittie lifted her chin. She wasn't proud of the fact that she had omitted mention of her past, but there it was. She needed to do better, even if it hurt. But maybe, just maybe, things would hurt a little less now that she knew her family hadn't made the long walk to Perdition. "Welcome back, Hugh. Surprise, I have a daughter. I thought she was dead." Kittie laughed humorlessly. "Turns out my first husband isn't dead, either."

Hugh stared at her, stunned by her announcement. "What do you mean?"

"It means we're done."

He was many things, but Hugh was not a compassionate man. Selfish and mean-spirited were better descriptors. His lips curled into a snarl. "I don't see what claim he has to you. *He's* not the one who's been here with you all these years."

Claim. Jack had no claim to her, but he was the fire of her heart. "This topic isn't open for debate. I'm only doing my part to let you know, as a kindness." She wouldn't cower before him as she had in the past. She wasn't going back to the old ways, the ways of *Katherine*—vulnerable, seeking comfort in the bottle and in his arms. In Bitter End, she was Katherine Larue, too heartbroken to bear the name Kittie Dewitt.

Hugh scowled. "You're not going anywhere. You're *mine.*"

"I don't belong to anyone."

His face became thunderous, and he was upon her faster than she could react. Hugh's fingers dug into her shoulders, and Kittie yelped. Her magic roared up, demanding release. She held it back, writhing against him as he wrapped a hand around her throat, spitting obscenities into her face.

And then his shout turned into a scream of agony as he released her. Kittie staggered away, massaging her neck with one hand. She stumbled against the wall, gasping for breath.

"Mom! Are you okay?" Emmaline asked, sliding to a stop beside her. Something small was in her hand, but Kittie was too distracted to figure out what it was.

"I will be," Kittie rasped after a moment, mopping at her forehead. She stared at Hugh. He was squealing like a hog going to slaughter, his hands clasped to his groin as he rolled around on the ground. "Did you do something to him?"

"Yep." Emmaline didn't sound apologetic at all. She hefted the thing in her hand, and Kittie realized her crafty daughter had made a poppet out of a pair of socks. Three sewing needles pierced the tiny doll's lower abdomen. "When I heard what you called him, I remembered seeing a basket with his name on it, and I pulled the socks out. Didn't have time to do much more than a simple hex."

A simple hex. Kittie was shaking from her close encounter with Hugh, but *she* had almost done more than a simple hex. She whooshed out a breath. "Release him so I can speak to him, please."

Emmaline frowned. "You sure?"

"*Please.* He won't try to hurt me again." At least Kittie hoped he wouldn't be that stupid. Hugh was a coward at heart.

The young Effigest sauntered over, arms crossed. She loomed over the downed man, removing the needles one by one. When she finished, he lurched into a sitting position, bracing his arms behind him in preparation to vault to his feet.

"*No sir,*" Emmaline snapped, her braid whipping as she planted a boot firmly in his chest, pinning him back down. She held up the makeshift poppet. "Next time it'll be more than a prick for your little prick." Emmaline stared at him until he looked away, then removed her foot.

Hugh scrambled to his feet, hands curled into fists. "You little —" He doubled over as Emmaline rammed a needle into the poppet's stomach.

"*Ah, ah, ah.*" Kittie shook a finger at him, flames dancing on the tip of her fingernail. "I would choose your next words with care if I were you." Emmaline pulled the needle out, allowing Hugh to straighten.

He glared between the pair, eyes alight with fury. He wasn't stupid, and while Hugh was a mage, his ability to change eye color had him at a disadvantage. But he was a fair shot with a pistol, which Kittie was glad to see he kept holstered. "I'm leaving town this afternoon for another sales trip, Katherine. When I return, you best be out of *my* house."

Kittie met his gaze, unblinking. She had no claim to the home and didn't plan to fight him on it. "That won't be a problem."

"Just remember, you were *nothing* without me, Katherine Larue!" He jabbed a finger in her direction.

"When you found me, I was nothing but ash. But even ashes can be rekindled with a spark," Kittie replied. She had a staring match with him for another minute before he turned on his heel and stalked off. Kittie shook her fingers, dismissing the flame. She wiped her face with one hand, exhaustion tugging at her after the tense standoff. "Thank you, Em."

Emmaline watched until Hugh was out of sight, then turned away. Her shoulders slumped, and Kittie noticed her daughter was shaking. "I thought he was going to kill you. Why would you be with someone like that?"

Kittie shook her head. "Sometimes, when we're hurting, we do stupid things."

Emmaline followed her mother back inside the laundry. The Effigest stuck the needles back into Kittie's pincushion and untwisted the sock poppet, tossing them back into the basket they originated from. "Daddy's the king of doing stupid things, then."

Kittie wondered about that. Emmaline seemed to be at war with her feelings about Jack, vacillating between love and disdain. Maybe that was typical for her age. Kittie picked up a pair of pants in need of hemming and found her seam ripper. "We all make mistakes."

Her daughter snorted. "He'd never admit to that."

It sounded like, in some ways, Jack hadn't changed. Kittie tore out the seam. "Want to tell me what has you so mad at him? I see he's taught you some of his magic, so it can't be that."

Emmaline rubbed her arms, frowning. "It all started with Fort Courage..."

CHAPTER THIRTY-THREE

Razzle-Dazzle

Blaise

<*B*laise!> At first, Blaise thought he detected alarm in Emrys's voice, but he realized it was excitement. <You won't believe this! There's a pegasus *mare* here.>

Blaise turned over, jostling the bed so that beside him, Malcolm jerked awake. It was still early, the window untouched by dawn's fingertips. Malcolm's hand brushed against his arm, only a brief touch to reassure each other.

"Something wrong?" Malcolm mumbled, drowsy.

"Emrys says there's a pegasus mare here."

Malcolm yawned. "Oh. Is that all? That's Seledora. Smart of her to fly in during the night." He rolled over and pulled the blanket up over his shoulders.

That Malcolm knew about a pegasus mare's impending arrival was enough to shake the last vestiges of sleep from Blaise's mind. He tugged at the blanket. "You can't just pass this off like it's normal for a pegasus mare to be here. Even *I* know that's not normal."

"Can we talk about it at breakfast?" Malcolm dragged the blanket back into place, snuggling into its soft depths.

They both had stayed up far too late the previous evening, each working on their separate projects. Malcolm busied himself with the voluminous amount of paperwork he needed for his Inquiry. Blaise had been hard at work on the desserts for Lizzie Jennings's gala. But Blaise was awake, and sleep wasn't going to revisit him soon. Maybe he should have let Malcolm sleep, but he wanted answers.

He shifted closer, leaning over until he was near the other man's ear. "I need you to tell me about it now."

Malcolm yawned, then unwound from his blanket cocoon. "Should have left it at the first three words of that sentence."

Blaise snorted. He nudged Malcolm's shoulder, ignoring the flirtation. "Why is there a pegasus mare here?"

Malcolm rolled onto his back, reaching over to flick the mage-light on the bedside table. "Seledora is one of my attorneys. She flew in from Rainbow Flat."

Blaise blinked. "You have...a pegasus attorney?"

"I'm rather progressive that way." A slow smile slid across his face. "She handles affairs for Jefferson, but I saw no harm in calling her in to represent us. She's the one who approved all of our original paperwork for our business agreement."

Blaise sat up, frowning, as he tried to work this out. "There's such a thing as pegasus attorneys?"

Malcolm rubbed his eyes. "I believe she is the only one, but yes, that means there is such a thing. And Seledora is here because she's part of my strategy."

"And that is?"

Malcolm sat up, coming to the realization Blaise wouldn't let him get back to sleep anytime soon. They had both been so absorbed with their work, they hadn't taken the time to discuss the details of their joint campaigns. "Razzle-dazzle. Part of the gamble I'm making. If this goes wrong, this may be the last big impact I can make on my long-term goals."

Blaise nodded, understanding. He hated being the reason that Malcolm might have to abandon his ambitions.

"Don't you blame yourself for that," Malcolm said quickly, leaning over to peck Blaise on the cheek. "I decided that for this effort, I'm going all-in. Turn this Inquiry into such a circus that anything they believe we've done wrong is minor by comparison."

Blaise mulled that over. "I guess that's one way to do it."

Malcolm grinned. "I'm going to hit them with everything I've got. Turn the world on its head if I can."

And that, right there, was why Blaise found himself falling for this man. His fervent desire to create meaningful change, to make the world a better place. And it had started with his determination to love Blaise, no matter who he was.

"I THOUGHT YOU WERE BRILLIANT, BUT NOW I'M HAVING MY regrets," Malcolm commented to Blaise from across the kitchen. He had two bowls in front of him: one containing pear he had already peeled and sliced, and another with fruit he still needed to attend to.

Blaise grinned at him. "You were the one who told Marta we didn't need any help." He couldn't help ribbing him on that bit. Malcolm had blatantly done it as a bid to give them more alone time, which Blaise appreciated. Malcolm had made an unfortunate miscalculation, however. Blaise was determined to make a good showing for Lizzie's gala. As much as he loved the unfettered joy that baking brought him, he was also serious about it.

"Yes, and that's one of the stupider things I've said in my life. I'm not cut out for this." Malcolm added another slice of pear to his completed bowl.

Blaise slipped over to him, peering into the bowl. "You'll be ecstatic to hear that you don't need to peel or slice any more pears, then."

"Overjoyed," Malcolm agreed, setting the knife aside. "What next?"

"Hmm." Blaise gave him a contemplative look. "Want to try your hand at decorating?"

Malcolm brightened at that. Blaise had hoped he might—he had a keen eye for detail, and while he wasn't as enthusiastic about basic tasks like slicing fruit, this would play to his strengths. "Show me what to do and I'll try it."

As he suspected, Malcolm was a quick study, and before long, he was piping frosting onto one of the cooled cakes. Blaise focused his attention on the audacious bread monstrosity he was wrangling into shape.

"Blessed Tabris, what are you *doing* over there?" Malcolm asked when he took a break to select a new food coloring to mix into his frosting.

"Eight-strand plaited loaf," Blaise murmured, concentrating on weaving the long tendrils of dough together. It looked, he decided with a little chagrin, like he was trying to wrestle an octopus into shape. "Who's Tabris? I've heard you say that before."

Malcolm kept his attention on the cake he was working on. "Oh, I suppose he's not as known in Desina, hmm? Tabris is the Gannish god of wealth and fortune."

"That makes a lot of sense," Blaise said, then paused, frowning at the array of dough before him. Oops, had he lost track? "Seven under six and over one." He untangled the tentacles and corrected the braid.

"I think I underestimated your enthusiasm for this." Malcolm glanced over at his squid-like loaf. "But I have to say, this haul is going to be impressive."

Blaise coaxed the last tendrils into place. He studied the loaf before him, then tucked the ends beneath it to give it a tidy look. *Not too bad.* "That's the goal. Win them over like a sugar-starved pegasus."

Malcolm paused, watching him. "I wish everyone could see you like this. Doing what you love."

Blaise was quiet for a moment. He knew what Malcolm meant, but it turned his thoughts to the upcoming Inquiry. Malcolm had told him what to expect, and Blaise wasn't confident of their chances. He would have to attend and speak. Answer questions in front of *people*. Feel the judgment of a thousand eyes on him. Everything he had endured, all his wounds and flaws, would be unveiled and on display. And they would no doubt bring up Fort Courage. *I'm a killer. A threat.*

Blaise swallowed, pushing away that thought, and instead, stared at the plaited loaf. "I'm kind of glad that only a few people see this side of me."

"Why is that?"

Blaise shook his head. "Because I don't want to share this with everyone." And he couldn't help it, but the grin that lit Malcolm's face made his stomach flop. He cleared his throat. "Now, back to the serious business of baking."

"Stick to the strategy," Malcolm agreed with a wink.

CHAPTER THIRTY-FOUR

Overdue Credit

Jack

J ack should have known things were going too well.
Things always had a way of getting mucked up sideways to Perdition, but he had been hopeful. The
handbill, enchanted by a Confederation Scryer, displayed the
latest information on the target. It even included a perfect image
of Emmaline, so lifelike he couldn't help the tears that stung the
corners of his eyes. Crisp text laid out the pertinent information:
her name, approximate age, magic type, and last known location.
It terrified him to see his daughter as the subject of a bounty. Her
life wasn't meant to be like this.

But, he supposed, it was inevitable. She was his daughter,
after all.

He and Zepheus set off to the northwest, the direction the
handbill suggested. As helpful as the handbill was, something
about it rubbed him the wrong way. He and Lamar had never
used them in their work, but then again, they'd had no need. The

handbills were helpful to the mundane bounty hunters without magic to call on or unicorns to stalk their prey.

<Are you forgetting the Confederation had an airship wrapped in magical protections?> Zepheus pointed out when Jack mulled it over with him as they stopped for a drink at a creek.

The outlaw shook his head. "Not gonna forget that anytime soon." Emmaline's face peered up at him from the parchment surface. "This reminds me of some of the books in the Archive at Highhorse."

The pegasus tilted his head to peer at the handbill. <I've been to Ravance with you. I think they would consider that inferior work.>

Jack snorted, amused. "You're probably right. They'd have a little map on there, enchanted by a Scryer, showing exactly where —" He stopped short, jaw agape as he folded the handbill up and threw it into the creek. It splashed, floating for a few seconds before sinking below the surface, curious tadpoles darting over to investigate.

Zepheus snorted, lowering his head to watch it sink. <What was that for?>

Shaking his head, Jack rose and put a foot in the stirrup. "I was a fiddlehead to take that."

The pegasus danced in place as Jack settled in the saddle. <Why?>

As Zepheus broke into a steady trot, Jack shook his head, mentally kicking himself. "Because it's magic. Can't believe she bamboozled me."

The palomino's ears pitched back, listening. <Are you saying...*oh*. I see.> And at that, Zepheus said no more, instead, shifting into an urgent lope to put more distance between themselves and any pursuers.

Jack balanced in the saddle, trusting Zepheus to continue onward as he scanned their surroundings. He had a poppet primed and ready to go if needed, but he didn't have any beneficial spells for the stallion. It had never occurred to him to try a working on the pegasus before. He thought about it as they continued, and after a few miles, he asked Zepheus to stop.

<You seriously want to stop now?> Zepheus asked as Jack slipped down from the saddle, striding over to the perimeter of a marsh.

"It won't take long, and it may be worthwhile." Jack stooped over, breaking off several stems of tall grass. He plucked a handful of willowy sticks from the spongy ground. The pegasus watched, puzzled, as he used the grass to tie together a very rough semblance of a stick horse. Jack held it up for the stallion's assessment.

<Is that...is that a poppet of *me*?> He sounded flattered.

"Yep," Jack replied. "I just need a bit of hair or a feather, if you don't mind."

<Feather,> Zepheus said, craning his neck around. The hide over his shoulders twitched as wings popped back into existence. Zepheus turned and nuzzled a loose covert feather. He wrapped his lips around the quill, plucking it out and presenting it to the outlaw. <Here.>

Jack accepted, attaching it to the equine poppet as Zepheus dismissed his wings from sight. He ran a hand over it to prime the unusual poppet, grinning as magic flooded through it.

Zepheus prodded the likeness with his nose. <What are you planning?>

"Salties were probably tracking us with that spelled handbill. We need stealth," Jack said, reaching up to balance the poppet on the pommel of the saddle. "I think I can muffle the sound of your hooves to give us the advantage. Sort of like a poor man's Dampener." Nowhere near as good as a Dampener, since they were experts at shutting down whatever was their specialty—sound or vision, sometimes both. But it was worth a try.

It took a few tries to get the spell right. Each time he attempted the working, he had Zepheus walk in a circle around him. The first two times, it had no impact on the sound—instead, Jack himself was muffled, a classic case of (luckily harmless) spell misfire. That was a hazard of devising a brand-new spell. The third time made Zepheus's hooves louder, which was jarring, but at least now the magic wasn't bouncing back to Jack.

The fourth time was the charm. He grinned, satisfied as Zepheus moved around him, hooves whisper-light. "I still got it," Jack murmured, mounting.

<If you mean an ego, then yes, you certainly do.>

The outlaw grunted a reply, but he couldn't hide his pleasure with the result. He'd have to remember that spell. Might be handy in the future. A sort of modified Obfuscation. *Maybe it would work with a sixgun.* Yeah, that would be handy.

They started on their way again. Jack grimaced as the afternoon wore on, and he discovered the magical toll of the new spell. Perhaps it was because of Zepheus's sheer size, but it packed a wallop and drained him fast. By comparison, his own Obfuscation was cheap. Jack held the line as best he could, not wanting to relinquish the advantage this gave them. But by the time dusk fell and a small town came into view, he was ready to call it a day.

Jack dropped the spell on the outskirts. It would be telling for him to ride in on a "horse" that made no noise. Relief washed over him as the magic dissipated. Jack flipped open a saddlebag and stuffed the poppet inside for safe keeping. Zepheus plodded to the livery, where Jack rented a stall for the night and untacked the stallion.

"Gonna grab a bite and see if I can learn anything new. Then I'll be back here for the evening," Jack murmured as he rubbed Zepheus's forehead. Sleeping in stables wasn't glamorous. Or comfortable. But Jack was on edge this deep in Saltie territory, and he stood a better chance with his pegasus. Not that he would say that aloud.

But Zepheus understood. He leaned into the caress, blowing out a hay-scented sigh. <But first, feed me. *Priorities*, mage.>

"Priorities," Jack agreed with derision. But he saw to it, going out and bartering for a bucket of sweet feed which he delivered to the stallion.

<And stop by the mercantile and get a bag of sugar for the water bucket?> Zepheus bumped his nose against it. Jack had carried a little with them, but it was all used up.

"You're a blasted hummingbird," Jack griped, good-natured. They both knew he would.

But first he had to see to himself. Jack needed fuel to keep his own fires burning, and he was spent from the new spell. He strode into the lone tavern, pausing at the entry to assess the room. He saw nothing that meant trouble. Well, trouble aside from the normal variety that haunted a place full of inebriated blowhards.

Men and women laughed uproariously over a card game in the corner. Billiards balls clanked together. A pianist played a tune on a piano in sore need of tuning as a woman with a voice like warm honey did her best against the odds. Jack ambled toward the bar since his preference was to chat up the barkeeps first—even though that hadn't worked out the best for him last time.

He paused halfway to the bar as a customer sitting alone at a table caught his eye. It took every bit of discipline he had to not turn and race over to her. Emmaline sat at the table, hunched over as if trying to avoid notice. But he recognized the sweep of her hair and the angle of her cheeks. Jack faltered. He corrected his course, heading for the table.

Jack stood behind the chair opposite her. "Anyone sitting here?"

Emmaline lifted her head, eyes widening in surprise. She bit her bottom lip for a moment, then shook her head. "All yours."

Jack claimed the seat, putting his elbows on the table. *Why is she acting guilty?* "Any luck?"

A server slipped over, and Emmaline wisely said nothing. "Welcome, traveler! Here's our menu. Can I get you a drink?" She thrust a menu at the new arrival.

Really, Jack wanted nothing more than for the server to vanish into a pit. He accepted the menu, though, knowing there were certain social niceties he needed to uphold. "I'm good for the moment." The server gave a bright smile and walked off.

"How—?" Emmaline started.

"Answer me first." Jack couldn't rein in his tension. The hand-bill had him unnerved. He wanted answers, and then to get Emmaline out of here and to safety.

"Any luck with what, Father?"

Jack stilled. *Father?* Since when did Emmaline call him that? *Since never.* Jack's mind raced as he took stock of the situation. No spotted stallions in the livery. It was possible Oby might be hiding outside town, seeing as he stood out like a sore thumb. He wanted to be damn sure before he made his next move.

He pulled on the last dregs of his magic, drawing his sixgun lightning-fast. "Maybe you should tell me, *daughter*. What were you supposed to be doing?" Alarm bells were ringing in his head. *This isn't her. Can't be her. This is wrong. She would know.*

She swallowed. "What are you doing? We're in *public*."

Yeah, perhaps she had a point. All around the tavern, eyes shifted to their tableau. Interest and menace. Jack weighed the options: 1) shoot her, 2) keep the sixgun aimed at her until he had some gods-damned answers, 3) holster the sixgun.

"Put it away, Papa," Not-Emmaline urged, holding her hands up in a placating move, eyes pleading.

That decided it for him. *A liar wears her face.* He pulled the trigger, the muzzle flashing as the bullet tore through Not-Emmaline's skull. She hadn't been expecting his volatile response and only made a soft exhalation as he snuffed out her life. No, *his* life, Jack corrected as the Illusionist's guise melted away, dispelled as the theurgist could no longer maintain it in death, revealing a young man.

Across the room, someone shrieked as if pained by the loss. *The handler.* He whipped around, trying to find the Illusionist's handler, but instead was greeted by the sight of half the occupants of the tavern turning on him. Too late, he realized it was a trap. Power rippled through the air, proof that some of those surrounding him were theurgists. And Jack was on their shit list for killing one of their own.

<I heard a shot. I'm coming!> Zepheus called.

Jack couldn't focus on the stallion. He swung his gaze around, tugging at his magic again, but that damn spell he had used all afternoon left him hung out to dry. He had gotten out of similar scrapes before, though.

Jack rolled his shoulders. Sixgun in hand and another at his back. Knife in his boot. He grinned. "If you wanna start a fight, you better throw the first punch," Jack advised them, making a rude gesture with one hand. Then he didn't give them a chance as he charged.

The melee was a blur, and that was by Jack's design. Most theurgists required concentration and space to work, and he wasn't about to give them any advantage. The problem was the handlers on the scene, who were trained for combat against mages. Jack focused on the theurgists first, or at least the ones he pegged for theurgists. It was hard to tell without them using their magic. They were the ones more likely to flinch when he came at them, and he took out three in quick succession with a mix of bullets and fists to the face. Jack dove beneath tables and hurled chairs to keep the handlers away, though he knew that risked giving the theurgists an opportunity to work.

And he was right to be concerned. They must have had a Telekinetic, which spoke volumes for how wanted a man Jack was. A table jerked up from the floor and flew right at his chest, slamming the outlaw against the wall. Jack hissed out an agonized breath, then shook off the sensation. He couldn't afford to let pain be a distraction.

Jack ducked as the Telekinetic sent a bottle at him, the quick motion shooting sparks of agony through his chest. He was too disoriented by the pain to avoid the chair that battered him next. It worked in his favor—or so he thought—because it shoved him closer to the door. Gritting his teeth, poppet curled in his fist, Jack tried to call on his magic to stave off the pain, but he had nothing left.

Gotta do this the old-fashioned way, then. He staggered to the threshold, his spare sixgun in hand as he brandished it at the menacing knot of assailants. "I didn't start this," Jack snarled at them. "But now you know why *I'm* the Scourge of the Untamed Territory."

"You killed our *Commander*," a theurgist spat, eyes blazing.

"And you killed more of our number at Fort Courage," another added, stepping forward with hands that crackled with power. The Telekinetic.

Sure, now *they give me overdue credit.* Jack narrowed his eyes. So his pursuers had been under that jackass Lamar's command at Courage. Their ferocity and determination to take him down made that much more sense.

<I can't get out. And they have salt-iron!> Zepheus punctuated his fear with a piercing whinny.

Shit. They knew about Zepheus, too. Jack tucked one arm against his aching chest to stanch the stabbing pain, spinning on his heel to sprint for the stables to help his pegasus. He drew up short, a gleaming brass muzzle pointed at him.

Gregor Gaitwood studied him, eyes full of disdain. "You're the one Lamar went on about for years? You don't look so impressive." He pulled the trigger of the hexgun.

That was the last thing Jack had been expecting. He was so surprised he didn't even flinch as the pellet splattered against him, releasing the spell housed in the casing. Sleep tugged at him, darkening his vision, and Jack collapsed.

HE AWOKE TO THE GENTLE SWAYING OF A WAGON BENEATH HIM, THE steady clop of hooves and the rumble of wheels on the road the best clues to his fate. Jack kept his eyes closed, suspicious of being watched. His wrists itched, and he felt the oppressive weight of salt-iron shackles on them. *Blast them all.* That was something he'd hoped to never experience again.

While he waited, he cataloged his condition. Aside from the

hives on his wrists caused by the shackles, his midsection was tender. And his magic was as dry as the Gutter in a drought. *Let's look on the bright side. I'm not taking the long walk to Perdition. Look at me, being all optimistic and shit.*

After several more minutes passed, he cautiously opened the eye pressed against the floorboards. He didn't spy any boots or other potential signs of watchers, so he opened his other eye and discovered he was alone in a jail wagon. *Yeah, that's not surprising.* Jack eased into a sitting position, trying to push away the grogginess caused by the sleep spell. He cursed his luck that Gregor Gaitwood had somehow gotten his slimy hands on a hexgun. Probably one of Jack's missing hexguns at that. *Insulting.*

He idly rubbed at the inflamed skin beneath the shackles, bridling against the salt-iron. They were taking no chances with him this time, he noted. They had figured out he had his magic back and were responding in kind.

Jack sighed as he braced a hand against the wall and rose, moving to peer out the tiny window. Gods, but his chest hurt. Cracked ribs, probably. He closed his eyes as the very act of breathing stabbed at his innards. *Maybe not just cracked.* He needed a Healer after the abuse the Telekinetic had hit him with, but that didn't seem likely to happen anytime soon. The outlaw forced his eyes open to figure out where he was.

They were trundling into Izhadell already, which meant that he had been out for quite a while. Maybe that accounted for why he had foolishly thought he wasn't hurt as badly as he was, too.

Where was Zepheus? If the pegasus was free, he had half a chance of getting out of this mess. But if the stud was captured... Jack swallowed, refusing to think the worst. *This isn't the first terrible scrape we've been through. And I'll be damned if it's the last.*

Colorful lanterns and banners for the Luminary Festival still decorated the businesses and homes they passed. *Huh. With everything else going on, I forgot it's still that time of year. How lucky.* No doubt he'd end up the finale in the hangman's noose.

As he stared at the column of theurgists riding behind the jail wagon, Jack's stomach soured when he saw a familiar flash of gold at the end. *Zepheus.* Beaded salt-iron rope looped the stallion's neck, blocking his mental speech and effectively clipping his wings. There would be no help from the pegasus. Jack's only remaining solace was that, as far as he knew, Emmaline was still free. Jack hoped fortune favored her and that she found her mother. *Alive.*

The outlaw settled back on the floor with a grunt, probing at his chest with one hand. *Yeah, that's tender.* He wasn't willing to admit defeat. Not yet. As long as he was alive and kicking, he was going to fight.

To his surprise, the jail wagon didn't take him to the Cit. Jack expected to be taken there and reintroduced to the maximum-security wing. Instead, the wagon continued, rolling through the city and to the other side, eventually coming to a stop in the driveway of a sprawling plantation.

Jack rose with a grunt, biting the inside of his cheek to distract from the intense pain caused by the movement. Armed men and women approached the wagon, and he took a step backward into the dark depths. No sense giving up any advantage he had.

With a click and a grating of metal, they threw the door open, flooding the interior with light. Jack entertained the idea of launching himself at them, but without access to magic or weapons, they outmatched him. He could probably strangle one with his shackles, but that would leave him vulnerable to attacks from the others. He took a step forward, and his ribs promptly reminded him that he'd be doing no such thing.

"Get out," a familiar voice snapped. "I see you in there analyzing how to murder the guards."

Jack allowed himself a savage grin as he fought off the pain. "Can't blame a man for trying." He took another step closer, the grin shifting to a snarl when a pair of guards reached out and grabbed his arms to drag him out.

Their harsh handling sent waves of anguish through him, and as they stood him before Gregor Gaitwood, it was all he could do to remain upright and not whimper. Every whistling breath was agony. Through slitted eyes, he saw a pair of theurgists lead Zepheus away. The pegasus balked, but after shouts and the slash of a whip from his handlers, the stallion plunged forward.

Gregor Gaitwood stood ten paces away, the hexgun holstered at his side. "Oh, are you hurt? That's unfortunate." He clucked his tongue, looking to one of the men who stood nearby. "Call the Healer. This state won't do for him."

A wizened older woman arrived on the scene, favoring him with a deep scowl as she assessed his injuries and muttered about idiot men. She turned to Gregor. "Two broken ribs." She uttered a wheezing laugh. "It would be a simple thing to pierce his lung with a bit of bone. Do you want this man alive or dead?"

Good question. Jack tried to take a deeper breath to test her assessment concerning his ribs, and his vision swam with the effort.

"He's worth more to me alive. Do what you need," Gregor commanded the Healer.

Why does he want me alive? Jack didn't have long to wonder before the soldiers were in motion, removing the shackles to allow the woman to work her magic. She laid her hands on him, and nothing about her power was gentle. Maybe he was too used to Nadine, who had awe-inspiring command of her magic. This Healer's power was like being dragged behind a runaway wagon. It seared over his entire body, assaulting his aches and pains as she repaired the damage that had been done.

It was painful but effective. When she pulled her magic away he felt raw and achy, but could fill his lungs with sweet air again. He choked out a curse. "Gods-damn you. Your Healing is the worst ever."

"But did you die?" she asked, giving him a rude gesture before striding away.

Gregor watched her go, then waved a hand. The soldiers replaced the shackles on Jack's wrists. "Come along without a fight. Easier to have you walk than drag you if you're asleep."

Or a corpse? The fact that he was still alive was concerning. To be sure, he was thankful for it and shouldn't look a gift pegasus in the mouth, but it was odd. The theurgists who had ambushed him had been furious. No one would have faulted them for killing him, especially after he had taken out some of their number. But they acted with discipline and had kept him alive, which meant they had orders from someone on high to do so. Someone like Doyen Gregor Gaitwood.

He trailed along with the guards as they followed Gregor up the winding alabaster staircase and into the manor. They made their way to a parlor where an afternoon repast awaited. Jack frowned, wondering what was going on as a guard pushed him down into a chair. Gregor sat nearby, picking up a glass of iced tea and taking a sip. He didn't offer Jack anything, but that was no surprise.

The outlaw studied the parlor. They must be at Gregor's home, which was interesting. A pity he didn't know the layout of the place, but he would pay close attention now that he was feeling more like himself. "What do you want, Gaitwood?"

Gregor set the glass of tea down, his gaze venomous. "I *wanted* the Breaker, but I suppose you'll have to do." A calculating smile slid across his face. "But there's a certain brand of justice in my brother's killer being brought to heel. Though I appreciate you taking care of that familial embarrassment, seeing how he was ready to betray me."

Pin prickles of regret bit into the back of Jack's neck. Lamar had been telling the truth. But he shook away his misgivings. He couldn't bring back the dead, even if he wanted to. He focused on Gregor. Jack didn't trust anyone who celebrated the death of a family member. Even if that family member was scum like Lamar. And he didn't like the wording of *being brought to heel,* either. "So hang me and get it done with."

The Doyen smirked. "That's too simple. No, I'd rather use you until you've been run into the ground. But cheer up. I know how much you enjoy killing members of the Confederation. You'll get to try your hand at the other Doyens."

"I'm not an assassin," Jack shot back.

"You were once, and you will be again." Gregor rose, pacing around the parlor with fluid strides. He paused to cast a contemplative look at Jack, lips curling with glee. "It's going to be poetic when word gets out that a Gutter rat has slain most of the Council. Especially those starry-eyed Faedrans."

Jack stared at him, his mouth going dry. Gregor was right. There was a time when that would have pleased Jack to no end, and he would have slept well at night after doing the deed. And under the right conditions, he still might do that now. But not at Gregor's behest. "You're crazier than a drunk Knossan if you think I'll do that for you."

"I'm not asking." Gregor rolled up his sleeve, revealing a tattoo. He tapped it with a finger. "I meant this for your friend, but as I understand it, we can make it work for you, instead."

How? Jack narrowed his eyes. He wouldn't have suspected that Gaitwood himself would attempt to become a handler, but maybe after Malcolm's stupid move, he shouldn't have been surprised. The Doyens were a spectacularly egotistical lot. "Good luck binding to me when you already have a tattoo keyed to someone else."

Gregor smiled. "Alchemy has made strides since you were last a theurgist. I don't need luck." He snapped his fingers to get the guards' attention. "Please, escort our *guest* to his quarters and call for the alchemist."

CHAPTER THIRTY-FIVE
Words Matter

Blaise

<I don't think she even knows I exist.> Emrys sighed heavily as Blaise loosened clumps of dirt from around the frog of the stallion's left hoof.

The *she* he referred to was Seledora. Blaise was still figuring things out for himself regarding relationships, but it was apparent Emrys wanted a mate. Seledora was an eye-catching mare, a dark dapple grey with wings that reminded him of a dove (when she showed her wings, which wasn't often at their current location). She spent much of her time in a box stall that had been repurposed into an office, either consulting with Malcolm or reading over texts and drafting documents with the help of one of Malcolm's staffers who served as her hands.

"To be fair, she's kind of busy right now," Blaise pointed out. "Did you forget she's here to help with my, er, situation?"

"Speaking of that!" Malcolm piped up, peering into the stall and grinning at Blaise. "When you're done, would you join me in the house? I have something to show you."

Blaise released Emrys's hoof from between his knees, setting it down on the ground. He tucked the hoof pick into his back pocket. "I hope you're more serious than the last time you wanted to show me something." Emrys snorted with amusement.

Malcolm chuckled. "I assure you I was serious then, too. But no, I want you to see the fruits of our efforts so far."

The fruits of...oh. The propaganda. He followed the other man up to the house and into the study, newspapers and magazines stacked on the desk.

"Look! Every newspaper Flora could get her hands on from the last several days. Some are more sensational than others." Malcolm pulled one off the top to display the headline *Mages: Misunderstood and Mistreated*. He shuffled it to the bottom and held up another, featuring an article titled, *BREAKER to Debut at the Legend Theater*.

Blaise narrowed his eyes at the title. "Um, is that the play Lizzie was writing?"

Malcolm grinned. "It is."

"And she named it *Breaker*?" Blaise rubbed the bridge of his nose.

"She had to name it *something* to attract attention," Malcolm pointed out, infuriatingly reasonable. His eyes softened when he saw Blaise's tension. "Look, I know you hate being called that. But trust the process."

"Trust the process," Blaise repeated, unconvinced. "Okay. What else?" Malcolm still had a large stack of papers.

"Now, before you lose your mind, these next few headlines are from some of the yellow papers." Malcolm brandished the next one. *The Doyen and the Breaker: Secret Love Affair Revealed.*

Blaise cupped a hand over his mouth. "What is *that*?"

Malcolm coughed. "I warned you some of them are...sensational."

Blaise snagged the paper from his hands, reading over the article. It *was* sensational, citing details that weren't true. Except maybe for the bit about them being in love, though he was still figuring out how he felt about that. His stomach flopped with nerves. "It's ridiculous," Blaise muttered, folding it up and slapping it down on the desk. "Is this the sort of thing you have to deal with as a Doyen?"

Malcolm laughed, then mulled his question over. "I'll let you in on a little secret. When I became the youngest Doyen to hold a seat, one of the papers reported it was due to my charms as a half-dragon."

Blaise blinked. "Wait, what? You're not half-dragon." His face scrunched, uncertain. "There's no such thing...right?"

"I'm not an expert, but I think that would be biologically impossible." Malcolm snickered. "But yes, this is something I've dealt with before. Jefferson's had his share as well. The yellow journalists love *all* of me."

"Of course they do." Blaise sighed. He plucked another paper from the pile, making a face. *Doyen Seduced by War Criminal Breaker*. "Oh, come on. That's unfair." He glared at *Love Triangle: The Breaker, the Doyen, and the Entrepreneur*. His cheeks warmed at how close to the truth *that* particular rag came.

"Alas, too bad Jefferson's on the run himself," Malcolm shook his head at the headline. "He'd have been quite flattered. You know, there used to be rumors about Jefferson and I having a thing."

That brought Blaise up short, and he stared at Malcolm. "How would that even work?"

Malcolm's eyes danced. "Oh, that's right. You haven't been introduced to Rex."

"Rex?"

"Rex Godfrey. He's an actor I have on retainer to portray Malcolm when needed. Sometimes Jefferson and Malcolm are invited to the same events, and it would be suspicious if they never appeared together, don't you think?"

That made a fair amount of sense, and leave it to Malcolm to have it all figured out. Blaise folded up the paper with the bold love triangle headline and shuffled it to the bottom of the stack.

"Don't let that one get to you. They're not all that bad." Malcolm flipped through, demonstrating that many headlines kept the romantic inclination but read more favorably.

"Bad enough that I may just die of embarrassment," Blaise muttered, tugging at his collar. Already his face was hot, and he wished the ground would open up and swallow him, never to be seen again.

Malcolm studied him, sympathy in his eyes. "I know. I'm sorry —I should have realized that the more sensational journalists might take the rumors Lizzie planted in this direction. But what's done is done. On the positive side, I think this only supports one of my arguments for the Inquiry."

Blaise glanced at the stack, wondering how the sordid headlines could possibly help. "And that is?"

Malcolm smiled. "That mages are every bit as human as non-mages. Look, most of those articles read like absolute trash, but here's the thing: you will never see an article like that written about a mage or a theurgist. They're not considered worth writing about. But *you* are."

"Lucky me." Blaise blew out a sigh.

Malcolm put an arm around him. "I know this is so far outside your comfort zone it's like you've gone to the moon, but I promise it will be okay."

Blaise's gaze fell on the stack of papers. All those things printed about him. About *them*. Some of them were true, but so many were skewed. Some outright lies. But really, was it any change from the rumors that had plagued his life before? He picked up one of the newspapers, eyes flicking over the article. It made very little mention of his magic or the dangers associated with him. That was a difference from the rumors of the past.

"I don't think I'll ever get used to this," Blaise admitted.

Malcolm bumped against his shoulder gently. "I don't expect you to. And I promise to shield you from it in the future when I can. But for now, this is just another tool that we can use to our advantage." He paused. "There's one more to show you. I saved the best for last."

Blaise gave him a skeptical look. "Why am I filled with dread when you say those words?"

"Trust me," Malcolm said, digging out something that didn't look quite like the other newspapers. A magazine. "This is an advanced copy, but it will be in homes across Izhadell tomorrow." He flourished the cover, showing that the magazine was *Hale's Ladies' Book*. Blaise had never heard of it, but from the cover he gleaned it was aimed at women. "Look at this." Malcolm tapped an article with his forefinger.

Breaking Bread: Desserts by Talented Mage the Star of Gala. Blaise snatched the issue from Malcolm, his excitement growing as he read. His desserts and breads had been the breakout stars of Lizzie's gala, with many high-profile women in attendance demanding to know who had crafted the treats.

"They called me *talented*," Blaise said, staring at the glossy paper. "There were so many other words they could have used, and they chose that one." Words mattered. He traced it with his fingertip, almost afraid it wasn't real.

Malcolm gave him a fond look. "Of all the things I just showed you, that is the one with the most truth." He picked up the papers and tucked them under his arm.

"I'm keeping this one." Blaise held the magazine protectively.

Malcolm chuckled. "I thought you might. That's fine, you more than earned it. Between Lizzie's gala, the rumors, the play, and the actual evidence we'll bring to the Inquiry, I think we can win the court of public opinion."

Blaise rubbed his chin. "Is that what matters, or will it matter more how the other Doyens vote?"

"Both matter," Malcolm answered. "But with the public in our favor, it will make it that much harder for anyone to vote against us."

Blaise glanced down at the magazine, hope kindling in his heart. Maybe, just maybe, they stood a chance.

CHAPTER THIRTY-SIX
The Talk of the Town

Malcolm

$\mathcal{H}$aving Seledora around gave Malcolm an unfair advantage. The walls of his estate were under constant observation by Confederation troops, eager for him to slip up and set foot outside his gates. They failed to appreciate the fact that they should watch the sky, too.

And so it was that Malcolm made an early start to the day, heading out on the mare's back before the sun was even a casual suggestion on the horizon. It had been hard to get out of bed with Blaise in a contented slumber so close to him. It still amazed him every morning when he woke up and found the younger man there. Blaise kept space between them as he grappled with whatever was going on in that head of his, but he was *there,* and that was what mattered.

<Not very observant, are they?> Seledora remarked as she touched down on the road a mile from the estate, briskly hiding her wings as she continued at a trot.

"And for that, I'm grateful," Malcolm replied. For him to

demand his Inquiry, he had to get to the Council chambers in person. Council rules stated he couldn't use a surrogate or correspondence. It had to be him, and Gaitwood and his fellow Mossbacks were doing everything they could to prevent it. He reached around to check the straps on the carry satchel on his back. *Still secure.*

He kept an eye out as they trotted along. Malcolm wished he could ride into town in the guise of Jefferson Cole, but his alter ego was in just as much trouble. He missed being Jefferson for so many reasons. Not only was he more comfortable in his second skin, but Blaise had always seemed more at ease with Jefferson. But for now, he had to sustain the narrative that Cole wasn't around. He hoped that none of the guards would recognize him. It would be a simple thing for them to arrest him outside of the diplomatic immunity provided by his residence as a Doyen, and then this would be all for naught. Unless he used his magic...

<That's something we need to avoid,> Seledora mentioned, as if she had been monitoring his train of thought. Which was likely. She didn't miss much.

The mare had noticed the change in him when she arrived. She had been quick to ask about the circumstances, citing that she needed all the information on hand about her client. He had told her, and she hadn't outright judged him, but he got the sense from the way her ears pitched back that she didn't approve. But what was done was done, even if it made life more challenging. It pleased her that very few others knew, at least.

"That's the plan," Malcolm agreed. He still had conflicted feelings about his use of power to free Blaise. Would he do it again in a heartbeat? Absolutely. But as a Doyen, it bothered him.

Seledora kept a sedate pace, and they arrived in the city proper at mid-morning. It wasn't until they neared the complex where the Council met that someone recognized him.

"It's him! It's Doyen *Malcolm Wells!*" The voice of a female admirer rang out, the elated pitch both flattering and worrisome.

"Oh my gods, it *is* him!" another called out.

<This is *ridiculous*. Is this because of those absurd newspapers?
> Seledora demanded, lengthening her strides to carry them
closer to their goal

"Either that or because I was voted the Confederation's most
eligible bachelor for two years in a row," Malcolm said, wincing as
a cry went up and a nearby patrol went on alert.

Up ahead, he saw another group of guards on the move,
attempting to block the path to the complex. If Malcolm set foot
on the Council chamber grounds, he had authority there, and the
guards couldn't hold him. But out here, it was a different story.

Seledora slowed, her head high with uncertainty as she spied
the looming blockade. <Is there another route?>

Malcolm smiled. There was. "Up and over, my lovely."

<First, *never* call me that again. Second, are you certain?> Her
black-tipped silver ears flicked back.

Everything he had done for the last several days was an enormous gamble, so what was one more? And besides, her nature was
going to be revealed at the Inquiry, regardless. "Yes. Let's make a
flashy entrance."

Seledora arched her neck, nostrils cupped as she snorted with
determination. Malcolm blinked as her wings flowed out from
her shoulders, silvery dust wafting off her wingtips. The
bystanders cried out with a mix of wonder and fear. No one knew
what to make of a pegasus in their midst. Seledora tore toward the
guard formation, Malcolm leaning low over her neck.

The guards had their rifles up, ready to fire.

Malcolm didn't think they would shoot, unless it appeared she
was going to strike them. He hoped she saw that, too. They were
moving too quickly for him to point it out.

He felt the muscles in her hindquarters bunch as she surged
skyward, wings spreading to catch the air. She tucked her forelegs
neatly beneath her as she sailed over the blockade with twenty
feet to spare. The guards yelled something unintelligible, and then
Seledora coasted to the ground to land delicately, tail arched
behind her.

That was magnificent. Not for the first time, Malcolm wondered why Blaise disliked flying on his pegasus. It certainly got the blood pumping. "Nicely done!" He patted her neck as she pranced in a tight circle, staffers flooding out of the hall to see what the commotion was all about. It wasn't long before the Doyens on-site joined them.

Seward had a huge grin on his face as he strode out, pounding Doyen Aaron Thatcher, Malcolm's cohort from Ganland, on the back. "I told you that scoundrel was up to something! See? Didn't I?"

Leonora Peppers studied the scene as Malcolm dropped out of the saddle, allowing the reins to dangle. "You've been the talk of the town for the past week, Malcolm, and now you're treating us to more of the show. To what do we owe the pleasure?"

Malcolm unstrapped the satchel from his back and pulled it around, opening it to remove a folder stuffed with documents. "I'm here to lodge a formal Inquiry into the treatment of mages at the Golden Citadel." He presented the folder to Leonora, who accepted it as the senior-most Doyen present.

She tucked the folder beneath her arm. "Accepted. Do you have counsel?"

<He does.> Seledora stepped forward to stand beside him as an equal. The mare tipped her head in amusement as people all around them gaped at her mental speech.

Seward's jaw seemed to nearly unhinge, eyes bugging at the spectacle of pegasus telepathy. Malcolm had forgotten how shocking it could be to "hear" one of the equines for the first time. "Did she just speak?" Seward shook his head, remembering to shut his mouth.

<She did,> Seledora confirmed for the startled Doyen, her dark eyes glinting. The mare arched her neck, legs squared neatly beneath her. <I am Seledora, attorney-at-law. I shall represent Doyen Wells for this Inquiry, so long as Senior Doyen Peppers finds it permissible.>

Leonora didn't bat an eye. It took more than a talking pegasus lawyer to fluster her. Moreover, she seemed pleased that Seledora had identified her as the one in charge of the proceedings. "It is, Counselor Seledora. Thank you. We'll start—"

"Hold!" an imperious voice called out. Malcolm turned, annoyance growing as Gregor Gaitwood stalked in. "I, too, wish to lodge a formal Inquiry—into Doyen Wells and his corruption by fraternizing with a criminal."

Leonora's gaze cut to Malcolm, expecting a rebuttal. She appeared surprised when he merely nodded. "Very well. While it's highly unusual to invoke two Inquiries at once, we'll accept them. However, as Doyen Wells brought his about first, it will have priority."

Gaitwood clenched his jaw. "Priority? There is higher priority than corruption of an elected official? This is an outrage."

"No, it's the rule," Seward piped up. "Should have lodged yours sooner, Gregor. Better luck next time."

Malcolm aimed a brilliant smile at Gaitwood. "Yes, it's unfortunate."

The glare Gregor aimed at him would have stripped the paint off a building. Gregor wasn't going to like Malcolm's show at the Inquiry one bit. He smiled at Gaitwood, touching two fingers to his forehead in a cheery salute.

CHAPTER THIRTY-SEVEN
Voice for the Voiceless

Blaise

"*A*re you *sure* I can leave?" Blaise asked, not for the first time, as he stared at his reflection in the mirror. Now that the day of the Inquiry had arrived, his stomach churned at the thought of going. Public opinion of him might be favorable, but he was painfully aware there were still a chunk of people out there who hated him and what he was.

"Of course, I'm sure," Malcolm reassured him, slipping closer to adjust his collar. "The soldiers are gone. Nothing can happen until the Inquiry is complete."

Depending on if it ended in their favor. Blaise rubbed the back of his neck, worried. "And what happens if we lose?"

He expected Malcolm to declare that they wouldn't lose, but he didn't. The Doyen shook his head, and his voice was raw when he spoke. "I'm trying very hard not to think about that."

Malcolm's admission brought Blaise up short. It was so easy to assume Malcolm thought everything would work out somehow because he pressed onward as if it would. It was the face he showed to the world, but in that moment, he made himself vulnerable to Blaise, his own fear bright in his brown eyes.

"I've done some audacious things in my life, but this tops them. And I don't know if it's going to work. I promised I would fight the Confederation for you." Malcolm's voice was apologetic.

You promised to fight. You never promised to win because we both know that might be impossible. Blaise licked his lips. "I didn't mean to bring you down. It's just...this is a lot. And it's only going to get harder today."

Malcolm took his hand, though his grasp was loose, allowing Blaise to escape if needed. Blaise tightened his grip as the Doyen spoke. "I know. But you can do this. You're not the only one hurt by the Cit. Be the voice for the voiceless."

And how could Blaise refute that? He knew in his heart that others had been through the same. And were still going through the same. He studied his reflection in the mirror again. His face had filled out a little since he'd gone to ground at Malcolm's estate. He looked less haggard and more like the person he had been. Blaise wanted to pretend that everything in the Golden Citadel had happened to someone else. But that wasn't being true to himself.

"I'm sure we could find someone to teach you the finer points of goat-herding in Theilia," Blaise hazarded.

Malcolm chuckled. "That ship has quite literally sailed. We're committed to this course now." He studied his reflection, rubbing his chin. "Besides, Theilia is difficult to get to. It would make more sense to start a new life in the Untamed Territory. Maybe I could learn how to hustle billiards and card games."

"To think I assumed you'd prefer to start your own dancehall," Blaise commented.

Malcolm winked. "Jefferson already has one of those." He cleared his throat and flashed a reassuring smile. "Back to the matter at hand. The Inquiry will host *more* than the Salt-Iron Council. This is a big event, and I have it on good authority that many a high-profile lady will be in attendance to see the magical baker who created those scrumptious desserts for Lizzie Jennings. You're going to have people rooting for you."

Blaise ducked his head. That was overwhelming in a different way. So many eyes on him. Watching his every move. Judging him. "I don't think I can do this."

Malcolm bumped against his shoulder, eyes mischievous. "You can absolutely do this. And if you get nervous…"

Oh gods. Blaise frowned at him. "Don't say what I think you're about to say."

"Just imagine that everyone in the crowd is naked."

Blaise blew out a frustrated breath. "Not helping."

"Fine. Then just imagine that *I'm* naked." Malcolm spun in place, spreading his arms with a flourish and a tempting grin.

Blaise's face flamed. "This is the exact opposite of helping."

Malcolm raised his brows, looking quite satisfied with himself. "Are you sure? Because now you're not thinking about being in front of all those people. You're thinking about *me*." The fact that he was right was downright annoying. Blaise crossed his arms. Malcolm licked his lips, his countenance softening again. "I promise that you're going to be fine. You're not doing this alone. And I *know* you can do it."

It was reassuring to hear the conviction in Malcolm's voice. Blaise relaxed a little. "Really?"

"Indeed. Now come on, you're as ready as you'll ever be. Let's go make history."

SOMEHOW BLAISE SURVIVED THE FIRST DAY OF THE INQUIRY. HE treated it like his time at the Golden Citadel, confining it as an experience separate from himself. He didn't recall any of the questions they asked him, though he knew he answered them in as much depth as he could, reliving painful memories he wanted to keep buried. Even the now-healed scar on his forearm burned with remembered pain when he had discussed it.

They asked, too, about the fateful day at Fort Courage that had led to all this. That was another topic Blaise preferred to shy away from. The mere thought of it made him queasy and light-headed. But it was relevant to the discussion as most of the Doyens demanded to know why he'd chosen to destroy the airship. And Blaise told them, because Malcolm was right about one thing: they were asking him questions and treating him like a human, as well as a mage.

The stresses of the day took their toll, and he was bone-tired and done with being around humans by the time they arrived back at the estate that night. He had ridden on Emrys, who was pleased to appear, wings and all, beside the lovely Seledora. Emrys quickly keyed into the mood of his rider, refocusing his attention to keep Blaise from mentally falling apart.

Now Blaise leaned against the stallion in the stable, having already untacked and groomed him. He knew he should go up to the house, but he couldn't bring himself to do it. Malcolm was already there, no doubt waiting for him. Wondering about him. Maybe even worried about him.

Emrys huffed out a comforting breath scented by sweet feed. Blaise didn't know if Emrys had been close enough to scrape the details of his ordeal from his mind as he spoke. If he did, the pegasus didn't remark on it. He simply offered himself to Blaise as a balm for a wounded soul. <You should go up soon. He cares about you,> Emrys said.

"I know," Blaise whispered. "But he might want to talk about it. And I don't want to talk about it."

<Give him more credit than that,> Emrys rebuked. <And if he asks, then tell him you don't wish to discuss it. He'll respect that.>

It was solid advice. Blaise's gut knew it, but his mind disagreed. Ever since he had been freed from the Cit, Jefferson no longer visited his dreams. A nagging part of Blaise suggested it was because Malcolm finally realized how neurotic and broken he was. And today had bared his problems to the entire audience of the Council chamber. No one would want anything to do with that.

Emrys froze, ears flicking as something caught his attention. He moved away from Blaise, trilling a whinny.

"What is it?" Blaise asked

<Zepheus.> Emrys nosed him aside, using his nimble lips to manipulate the bolt on his stall door and striding out with purpose. Blaise blinked and then followed along.

They found the golden pegasus in the stable courtyard, limping and riderless. His wings were bedraggled, as if he had been in a fight, and his eyes were white-rimmed. He was bare of saddle and hackamore.

All thoughts of the day's events fled from Blaise. He rushed over to the pegasus. "Zeph! What happened? Where's Jack?" Blaise's mind raced. Jack had gone after Emmaline and his wife...

<They have him.> Zepheus hung his head. His coat was dark with sweat, and he trembled from exertion.

"Who has him?"

<Gregor Gaitwood. They had me, too, but I escaped.>

Blaise rubbed his forehead. He recalled Gaitwood sitting in the Council chamber earlier, though he had made every effort not to look at the man. Bad enough he had felt the searing heat of the Doyen's eyes on him all day. Why did Gregor Gaitwood have Jack? This didn't bode well.

First things first. Blaise focused on the stallion. "Come on. Let's take care of you, then I'll go tell Malcolm, and we'll figure something out."

<I'm worried about Jack.> Zepheus's voice was weary with defeat.

Blaise urged the pegasus into the stables. "He's a fighter. Whatever's going on, we'll figure something out." At least he hoped so. He settled Zepheus into a stall and saw to his needs before steeling himself to head to the house and alert Malcolm to this new problem.

Malcolm

H E HAD NEARLY GIVEN UP HOPE THAT BLAISE WOULD COME UP FOR the night. It had been an arduous day for him. The younger man's blue eyes were haunted from reliving his hardships and misuse. Malcolm knew he didn't want to talk about it, and he understood. All the same, it stung that Blaise hadn't even come up so they could spend time together. Malcolm reminded himself that Blaise was still working through things, and he would come up when he was ready. But it was hard. Malcolm wanted to be a part of the healing process.

And then Blaise pushed open the door to the master bedroom, striding in with a resolve he'd lacked earlier in the day. There was a spark in his eyes again. Something had him worked up. Malcolm straightened. "What is it?"

"Jack. I mean, Zepheus came back. Without Jack." He made a circular gesture with one hand. "They were ambushed, and Zeph says Gregor has him."

"Gregor?" Malcolm frowned. That made little sense. While it wasn't by any means good that someone had caught the outlaw, logic and protocol dictated he would have gone to the Golden Citadel to be held and eventually hung. "Are you sure about that?"

"Zeph was sure," Blaise answered. "I believe him."

Malcolm studied Blaise, thoughtful. The Breaker had come up to him for a purpose. "Right. What are you thinking?"

Blaise looked him in the eye. "Do you think we could find Jack in his dreams? The same way you found me?"

At that, Malcolm blinked. It wasn't something he had thought about—didn't even know if it was possible. But Blaise was so earnest and hopeful that Malcolm didn't want to disappoint him. "I could try," Malcolm agreed after a moment. "But I'm not as good with my magic as you are with yours."

Blaise raised his brows, incredulous.

"What?" Malcolm asked.

"Sorry. I thought you were joking. I don't consider myself *good* with magic." Blaise shrugged.

Well, at least he had shaken off the haze of his recounted trauma. Malcolm was content with that. "I know you're good with it." Blaise was something the Confederation hadn't seen in living memory: a Breaker in control of his power, not the other way around. "I'm still figuring mine out. Some parts, like the dreamscape, just naturally developed."

Blaise stepped closer and grabbed his hand, which was a welcome surprise. "We'll figure it out together, then. We need to find Jack, if we can, and figure out what's going on."

Mmm, pushy. I like this. Malcolm kept that to himself. Didn't want to scare off this feisty side of the Breaker. "What's the plan?" He quite enjoyed the way Blaise tugged him over to the bed.

"What do you think?" Blaise asked.

Malcolm bit his lip to keep from saying aloud what he really wanted to say. Blaise was on a mission, and it wouldn't be welcome. So he settled for quirking a brow suggestively.

"You're hopeless," Blaise grumbled, but he said it with fondness.

"Hope*ful*, you mean," Malcolm corrected softly, meaning it. He sat on the edge of the bed and peeled his shoes off, tucking them below. He unbuttoned his shirt, pleased when Blaise cast a furtive glance his way. "Are you proposing we go to the dreamscape and search from there, or what? I've not done anything like this before." *Though, I'm always up to try new things with you.* Should he tell Blaise that? No, that would be too much.

"I'm a Breaker, not a Dreamer." Blaise sat down on the opposite side of the bed, his back to Malcolm. There was a soft thump as he took off his boots, dropping them on the floor. "But that would be my guess. How did you do whatever it was when you found me in the dreamscape?"

Malcolm frowned with thought. "I think I found you because of our connection through the geasa. Though I think even without it, I had plenty of motivation to find you." He glanced back and found Blaise watching him, so he threw in a wink for good measure.

"I'm motivated to find Jack, so that will have to do," Blaise said, a hint of a smile curling his lips.

Malcolm flopped down on the bed. "Sugar, I'll do just about anything you ask me to." He patted the space on the bed beside him.

Blaise studied him, and Malcolm was certain the young mage was going to chide him about the nickname. Instead, he dropped onto the bed. "I'm going to remember you said that."

Malcolm grinned, pleased. *I hope you do.* He rolled onto his side, facing Blaise. "Very well. Let's do this." Blaise shifted to face him, and the sight of those blue eyes watching him made his heart race.

"Do I have to be asleep? How does your dreamscape work?" Blaise asked. The Breaker adjusted his pillow. "I think I'll have a hard time falling asleep after..." He squeezed his eyes shut, and Malcolm caught the glimmer of a tear in one eye.

Nightmares. Blaise feared being consumed by nightmares after revisiting his memories. Malcolm found his hand beneath the covers. "You don't have to be asleep. I've learned that I can make people sleep. I can pull you to the dreamscape."

Blaise's fingers relaxed. "And you said you weren't good with your magic."

Malcolm's heart soared at the compliment. "Are you ready?"

"Yes."

"Sweet dreams," Malcolm murmured, pulling on his magic.

It was easy to focus it on Blaise. *So* easy. His Dreamer magic settled over the young man like a blanket, lulling him into a peaceful sleep. Malcolm smiled, watching as Blaise's face slackened. He reached over to brush back an errant coil of hair that had fallen across Blaise's forehead. Malcolm sighed with contentment, then burrowed into his pillow as he sent himself to slumber.

The dreamscape swelled around them, and Malcolm—no, he

was *Jefferson* here, he corrected himself—discovered Blaise by his side, where he belonged. The world around them was different, a grey void. Blaise turned in a circle, inspecting their surroundings.

"Why does it look different?"

"The Itude dreamscape is *ours*." Jefferson didn't want anyone else intruding on that particular space. "Besides, it takes magic to build all of that and I don't know how much it will take to find Jack."

Blaise slanted him a look. "If you run low, I can share."

Jefferson swallowed. He tried not to let Blaise see how much he would like that. He coughed and then realized the corners of Blaise's mouth had tugged upward. "You said that *on purpose*."

"I said what I said." Blaise's tone was flat.

"You're being quite unfair," Jefferson complained. Then he realized something. "Hold on. You flirt with Jefferson and not Malcolm. Why is that?"

Blaise blinked. "Wait, what?"

"Just an observation," Jefferson murmured, coy.

Blaise cleared his throat, crossing his arms. "I don't know *how* to flirt."

"Trust me, you've figured it out." Jefferson couldn't help the grin on his face. He rubbed his hands together, refocusing. "All right, let me figure out how to find Jack."

CHAPTER THIRTY-EIGHT

Hypocrites

Jack

O f all the things to dream about, that pompous peacock Jefferson Cole was the last thing Jack wanted. His waking life was terrible enough without his dreams being plagued, too. But there he was, sauntering out of a grey mist like some damned fashion icon, greatcoat slung over one shoulder.

"I found him, Blaise!" Jefferson called.

The Breaker appeared through the mist, and Jack set his jaw, narrowed his eyes, and glared at them. Blaise spotted him and hurried through the strange nothingness, stopping when he was ten feet away. "Jack?"

"Get out of my dreams," the outlaw growled. "It's the only place I can catch a damned break." And then, because it was a dream and he figured why not, he lunged at Jefferson. And stopped in his tracks.

He couldn't move. Gods, he hated the sensation of trying to run or move and being immobile in a dream. Jack writhed against the invisible force that held him in place, furious.

"Saying this will only make you hate me more, but my world, my rules," Jefferson said, his hands clasped behind his back.

"Jack, it's *us*," Blaise added, daring to come closer. "Zepheus found me and told me what happened. That you were captured. This was the only way we could think of to help."

Jack stared at him. He had thought—really thought—that this was all a frustrating trick of his subconscious. But maybe it wasn't. For Blaise to know those details and to speak them aloud...he swallowed, his fists uncurling. As his tension left him, the invisible bonds slackened, and he was free. "Zeph got loose? This is real?"

"Yes, and sort of?" Blaise shrugged.

"It's complicated." Jefferson lagged back, keeping Blaise between them. "Is it true that Gregor Gaitwood has you?"

Gaitwood. The name set Jack's blood afire. "Yes."

Jefferson pursed his lips. "What does he want with you? I thought an outlaw like you would go straight to the Golden Citadel."

Jack crossed his arms. "Especially this time of year." He shifted his weight, shaking his head. "Nah. He has more games afoot. He's pissed that Blaise slipped his grasp."

Blaise paled and stared down at the ground, as if the kid felt guilty. "Sorry."

The outlaw snorted. "Nothing to be sorry about. I don't regret my part in freeing you." He meant it. Blaise lifted his chin, surprise shining in his eyes.

"What does he intend with you?" Jefferson asked.

Jack pinched his lips together. He angled away, shoulders tense again. Really, he didn't want to say it because to speak it was to make it true. And the truth hurt. "Gaitwood bound me with the geasa."

Soft footsteps approached behind him. A hand settled on his shoulder. "I'm sorry." Blaise's voice was soft, and even in the dream, his hand trembled. Jack wondered what it had cost him to reach out to make that contact. The outlaw wasn't normally one for softness, but in that moment, it meant the world to him.

"*No*," Jack insisted, his voice gruff. "You don't apologize for that, damn it. It wasn't *your* fault."

The Breaker pulled his hand away, as if he expected Jack to whirl around and attack him. Like he would have done before. Jack longed to lash out at a more deserving target. Preferably Gregor Gaitwood. "Gaitwood's a damned hypocrite." Jack eased around to face them again, allowing his eyes to fall on Jefferson. The other hypocrite among them.

"He is that," Jefferson agreed, his tone even. "And I'll ask again, what does he intend to use you for?"

Jack shifted his weight from foot to foot, absently rubbing at his throat. In his waking hours, the geasa controlled his words and actions. It didn't seem to impact his functions in the dream, though. Would he be able to warn them? "Same thing he was planning to use Blaise for, I reckon. Kill the other Doyens. Probably the Luminary, too. I don't know squat beyond that. A man like Gaitwood won't tell me everything. I'm nothing. A tool." None of the normal geasa restrictions came into play. He was unfettered in the dream. Maybe the Dreamer was worth a damn after all.

"A weapon." Blaise's voice was little more than a whisper, but somehow it reverberated through the surrounding grey expanse.

"Yeah," Jack agreed, dour. Gods, he hated the geasa. The only time he felt like he had any freedom at all was when he slept. *Freedom.* He pointed a finger at Cole. "And he wants you in the bone orchard. The *other* you, I mean."

Blaise's jaw tightened, hands clenching. Jefferson only nodded, as if that hadn't surprised him. "There's no love lost between us. He disliked me before my stunt with Blaise, and the Inquiry has only made it worse." He paced in a small circle. "Is there any way we can free you?"

Jack stared at him. Did he hear that right? Jefferson Cole wanted to free *him*, an outlaw? He glowered, not about to show that it made him feel a little less hopeless, a little less forsaken.

Yeah, he had warmed up to Blaise, but he wasn't about to call that dandy a friend. Regardless, Jack had analyzed the situation, looking for every possible way out of it. "You couldn't get Blaise out of the Cit without me."

"But now I'm in the mix," Blaise said, his blue eyes meeting Jack's.

The outlaw should have realized Blaise would pony up. He wasn't a fighter, but he wasn't a coward, either. Jack shook his head. "Gaitwood knows I have my magic back. I'm locked up with salt-iron."

Jefferson wrinkled his nose at that. "Vile stuff." He ran a hand through his hair. Jack had seen him enough recently to know the gesture for what it was: a tell for unhappiness. It genuinely bothered him he couldn't help Jack. That was…strange.

The outlaw made a dismissive gesture. Curse them for giving him all these feelings in a damned dream. "Blaise is free. That was always the goal. I'm an old man. Not as if I matter." *Lie, lie, lie.*

Jefferson raised a brow. "I have it on good authority you're ten years my senior. That's hardly old."

"By outlaw standards, it is," Jack muttered, hoping they would take his meaning. Damn them. He liked Blaise, and he didn't want the idealistic kid to wander into something and end up trapped. Again. He seemed to have a penchant for that. Although maybe Jack shouldn't point that out since he didn't have a sterling record, either.

Blaise's eyes were troubled. "But you *do* matter. What about Em? And Kittie?"

He had hoped his family would escape mention. The outlaw whirled away so that neither of them saw the way his face crumpled at the thought that he had been *so close*, and ultimately so far, from what he had always wanted. The people he had made himself vulnerable for. "If you come across them, tell them what happened to me." *Tell them I'm sorry. Tell them I love them. That they're my entire world.* His throat constricted, and even in the gods-cursed dream, the words wouldn't come. It was like the geasa, choking his words back. But it wasn't the geasa. It was him.

Behind him, Blaise's boots scuffed the hazy ground. "We'll come for you."

The outlaw spun, shaking his head. "No. *No.*" His voice was almost hoarse with emotion. "Don't be stupid. Gregor still wants you. Both of you."

The Breaker smiled. "I'm not stupid. But I *am* your friend."

Jack sighed. Yeah, Blaise was stupid.

CHAPTER THIRTY-NINE

Pour Some Sugar On Me

Blaise

Blaise hadn't realized that the Inquiry was going to last as long as it did. He had expected that it would be over in a day or two. Never would he have imagined that they would draw it out over several weeks, but to his dismay it did. Every staffer or guard who served at the Cit was called in to speak and examined at length. Weeks of traveling to the Council building each morning with Malcolm to see what awaited them. Weeks of being on the alert, not knowing when Gaitwood might try to use Jack against them.

"He's probably waiting things out to see how the first Inquiry ends," Malcolm advised Blaise. It made a little sense, but Blaise couldn't help but be on edge. He spent every minute within the chamber tensed for danger, not knowing what Jack might be capable of with his magic restored. The outlaw was a merciless killer without magic. Blaise assumed he would only improve with his special brand of power.

Malcolm (as Jefferson) and Blaise reached out through the

dreamscape almost every night, though Jack was either contrary in his typical fashion or had no additional information for them. Blaise pitied the outlaw. He had escaped from this before, and his gloom over his predicament shrouded the dreamscape with thunderheads as Jefferson subconsciously drew on the outlaw's mood.

Despite Jack's situation, the nights in the dreamscape helped Blaise more than anyone else would ever know. Not only was it a much-needed distraction from the Inquiry, but it served as a sure-fire way to chase away the nightmares that were certain to follow. It was also much more than that for Blaise. It gave him the opportunity to reconcile Malcolm and Jefferson as the same person in his mind. Blaise came to grips with the fact that he loved that very confusing man.

Three weeks into the Inquiry, Blaise was almost accustomed to the spectacle. Seledora transformed from a fantastical to an ordinary sight (which, he supposed, was Malcolm's point all along) and the pegasus lawyer was as sharp as any of the humans in the chamber.

Blaise himself had gained a steady flow of curious admirers, which would never cease to amaze him. They came and asked him questions during recesses, with topics ranging from his relationship with Malcolm (*awkward*), to his magic (*even more awkward*), to baking (*best topic ever*). When his fans (that was what Malcolm called them) left, their whispers didn't escape his hearing. They were witnessing history, they said. They had met a living legend. Blaise didn't feel like a legend, though. He was afraid, and stressed, and in the grand scheme of things, he felt tiny and insignificant.

After a final long day of arguments, witnesses, and stacks of documents taller than Seledora, Malcolm's cohorts from the Faedran faction invited them out to a celebratory dinner. The next day was a scheduled break for everyone involved, with the Doyens reconvening the day after that to deliberate and reach a verdict. The end was near, and everyone was relieved.

And that was how Blaise found himself in the private room at a posh restaurant, being toasted as some sort of hero. As glasses tinkled, he certainly didn't *feel* like a hero. Blaise said as much to Malcolm, who was at his side.

"But you are," Malcolm insisted, raising his chalice in yet another toast. There had been many toasts already, and the Doyen appeared pleasantly sloshed. "You think you're nothing. A zero. But you're wrong." He took a long swig before settling the crystal goblet on the table. Blaise sighed. Malcolm usually unwound with a glass of wine in the evenings. But not *this* much.

"He's right, you know," Lizzie agreed with an emphatic nod. She sat across from Blaise, declaring that it was only right as she had done so much for their cause. "And oh, you should come to opening night at the Legend tomorrow!"

"Opening night?" Blaise asked, puzzled. He sipped his blackberry ginger switchel, enjoying the rich flavor.

"For *Breaker*, of course!" Lizzie announced with pride, her dark eyes dancing. "The timing couldn't be better, especially with the Inquiry ending this week! Anyone who's *anyone* is going to be there, and you simply must come. It would be an absolute windfall for you to attend." She aimed an endearing smile his way. "You *will* come, won't you?"

In all the frenzy of emotions surrounding the Inquiries, Blaise had forgotten about the play. He was certain he didn't want to see whatever fantastical fiction she had created about his unfortunate life.

"Nah, he won' go," Malcolm said, slurring uncharacteristically. Blaise froze beside him, alarmed. He'd never seen Malcolm drunk before—he held his wine well, but certainly never had this much. "Too embarrassed, even though there's not a *damn* thing to be embarrassed about."

Blaise rubbed the bridge of his nose. "I'm not embarrassed." Maybe if he said it out loud, it would become true.

"Are so."

"Am not."

"You are. E'rything embarrasses you. Even *me*." Malcolm's

voice dipped into an octave of sadness Blaise didn't know he was capable of. "And I put all of myself out there for you. I've risked everything for you."

Blaise swallowed, something inside of him torn by Malcolm's drunken words. He had been hesitant to divulge his changing feelings, distracted as he was by the Inquiry. *Later*, he had thought. *When things are settled. When I'm more certain.*

But Malcolm's words also stirred something deep within, his old hurt regarding the geasa. "I never asked you to do that."

Malcolm stared at him, eyes bleary. "I couldn't leave you there. Couldn't allow someone *else* to have you."

Lizzie's eyes were owlish at the conversation. Her mouth dropped open as if she were trying to come up with something to say to turn the tide, but Blaise wouldn't have any of it. *Stupid, drunk Malcolm.* "I'm *not* a charity case. *Not* property. *Not* a commodity to be bought or sold."

Hurt flashed across Malcolm's face, as if Blaise had wounded him. Perhaps he had. The Doyen averted his gaze. *Shame.* That was shame etched across Malcolm's handsome face. It only riled Blaise's agitation further, validating his words.

Blaise's palms itched, his magic rising. He shoved it down. The last thing he needed was for his power to break loose here, in front of all the Faedran Doyens. He rose from his seat. "I need some air."

If anyone spoke to him as he beat a quick retreat, he didn't hear it. Blaise found an exit that led to a back alley and walked into a darkness only punctuated by the light coming from windows and the stars overhead. He shut his eyes, releasing a whistling breath as he leaned against the restaurant's wall. He stayed that way for several minutes until he felt his magic unwind and seep back to his core.

"You know he wouldn't have said any of that if he were sober," a familiar voice pointed out. Flora dropped to the ground from the roof.

Blaise pushed away from the wall. "And that's what makes it worse."

The half-knocker studied him for a moment. He wondered how well she saw in the dark. All he could see was her face angled to look at him, her pink hair nothing more than a darkly gleaming curl in the night. "You know he's stupidly, madly in love with you, right? I can see you're dense about the whole courting thing, so I thought maybe I should spell it out for you."

Blaise snorted. "You're not wrong about the dense part, but... yeah, I know how he feels about me." He rubbed the back of his neck. "What would you do if you were me?"

Flora laughed. "That's the wrong question to ask. I would have shagged him back in Itude."

Blaise cringed. He had forgotten that Flora wasn't shy about her emotions and drives. Well, and she actually *had* drives. "Okay, that was a stupid question. I deserved that answer. What do *I* do?"

"Him, obviously." Flora bleated a laugh at her own joke, then stepped closer to pat his arm. "Sorry, I don't have filters sometimes, and you have to admit, you were asking for it. How do *you* feel about him?"

Blaise sighed. "I don't know." *Lie. Liar.* Why was it so hard to admit aloud that he loved Jefferson?

Flora was quiet for a moment, and Blaise shifted uneasily in the silence that hung between them. After a bit, she said, "If that's true, that's fine. But don't go breaking a good man's heart because you're afraid of the unknown. Nothing about you has *ever* scared him. He's never thought for two seconds about turning away from you. Even when it was in his best interest to do so. That's a rare and precious thing." She patted his arm again, this time more forcefully, as if she were trying to hammer some sense into him, before letting go and scaling the side of the restaurant to perch on the roof.

Oh, biscuits. She was right. Why did emotions and relationships have to be so messy? Life had been simpler when he thought he had no prospects. But his existence then had lacked the color and verve it had now. Flora was right. *Rare and precious thing*, indeed. He steeled himself and started back toward the restaurant.

He took a quick step back as the door opened, and Malcolm stumbled out. The Doyen didn't seem to see him, instead wobbling unsteadily before bracing an arm against the wall.

"Malcolm? Are you okay?" Blaise wished he could see better in the darkness.

"Dandy. Was lookin' fer the quincy. Need to vomit." It was followed by the sound of splatter as he made good on his words. Blaise winced in sympathy. And hoped that none of it had gotten on his boots.

"Well, this is certainly not that," Blaise advised him. Overhead, the moon peeked out from behind a cloud, revealing that Malcolm had aimed beside a trash can. Inside would have been better, but sometimes close counted. Blaise's boots had survived, at least. "Do you need help? Can I get you something?" What helped someone when they were drunk? He had absolutely no idea.

"I nee'...I nee'..." Malcolm fumbled over the words, then retched again. "I nee' to go back in time and tell my idiot self to not drink so much after you left. And before that, too." He wiped his mouth on his sleeve, an appalling move he would never have done sober. "But you know what? I love you. Like, *love*-love you. So much." He took a step closer and would have fallen had Blaise not swooped in to keep him upright. Malcolm giggled.

Blaise sighed. "I love you, too."

Somewhere above them, Flora cackled. "I *knew* it!"

"Not fair," the drunk Doyen complained, ignoring the hidden half-knocker. "Not fair sayin' that right now."

Blaise paused, trying to figure out where the stables were from their current position. Silent as a wraith, Flora hopped down and pulled out a mage-light, crooking a finger. Blaise steered Malcolm in her wake, wondering if Seledora could keep an unsteady rider on board. They would cross that bridge when they got there.

"Shut up," Blaise muttered as they walked. "I do love you, idiot. I just don't show it like you do."

"If you love me, then kiss me. Wait, no. My mouth tastes like warm garbage right now." Malcolm grumbled with disappointment.

"I *have* kissed you before," Blaise pointed out, patient.

"That's all, though." Malcolm's voice reflected a small measure of his earlier hurt—and his longing. "You don't know how much I want *more* of your attention. *More* of you." He wove on his feet, leaning heavily against Blaise. "Do I need to let you pour some sugar on me? 'Cause I will, you know."

"Oh my *gods*," Blaise muttered. "Just when I thought one conversation was the most embarrassing in my life, another appears."

"Kinda like cutting the head off a hydra." Flora spun, the magelight dancing in her palm tinting her grey skin with a bluish haze. "I don't know what's going on between you. Or what you've said to one another in the past. But you both need to figure this out. *Soon.*"

I thought I had more time. "We will," Blaise promised, because there was no other answer. She was right. They needed to figure out what they were to one another. They both deserved that much.

Relief washed through him when they reached the stables. Emrys snorted, reading his rider's tension. But the stallion didn't comment, though his ears flicked whenever Malcolm giggled. That was happening far more frequently now, along with the formerly dignified Doyen murmuring terms of endearment.

<I'll keep my client on-board,> Seledora assured Blaise, even though Malcolm almost faceplanted twice just getting into the saddle. At least someone in their haphazard group had confidence.

By some miracle, they reached Malcolm's estate without disaster. Flora found a groom to tend to the pegasi, and Blaise helped Malcolm into the house. He was still giggling, muttering something about royal icing. Blaise eased him down on the bed, prying off his shoes so that he would be comfortable. Malcolm flopped backward onto the bed, eyelids drifting closed.

Blaise worked the sheet and blanket out from beneath him, then pulled them up so he wouldn't get cold. Malcolm snored softly—another unusual trait brought about by his current state— and for a moment, Blaise considered leaving him alone for the night so he could sleep in peace. But he thought about how Malcolm had already given up so much for him. The least he could do was sacrifice a night of sleep. Blaise prepared for bed and then settled down beside the sleeping Doyen.

"I do love you. But I love Jefferson more," Blaise whispered, touching Malcolm's slack cheek. That was the source of his true embarrassment: he realized that, even though they were the same person, he had a preference. He didn't want to hurt Malcolm with the revelation. But he needed to be honest, so he resolved to find a way.

But first, he had to wait for Malcolm to sober up. He closed his eyes and went to sleep, disappointed to discover that a hungover Malcolm was incapable of summoning his Dreamer magic.

Jack

JACK REFUSED TO ADMIT IT TO JEFFERSON OR BLAISE, BUT HE looked forward to their intrusions into his dreams. They didn't happen every night, and he was fine with that, but their appearance gave him hope. Hope was all that he had left. Hope was *everything*.

And now he didn't just want to see them, he *needed* to see them. He had actual information. Gregor Gaitwood had realized that the tide of the first Inquiry was against him, and he was ready to remove pieces from the game board. From what Jack gleaned, there was going to be a week-long break before the new Inquiry began, and Gaitwood was justifiably concerned about Wells continuing to work his political magic.

"Where in Perdition *are* you?" Jack stared at the dark ceiling. He picked up a poppet he had left on the bedside table, tossing it from hand to hand. Malcolm's poppet. He wanted to destroy it, but the geasa wouldn't allow him to act against something connected to his magic. And the poppet was still active, tied to the Doyen.

Jack was thankful Gaitwood was ignorant in the ways of his power. Real handlers learned the ins and outs of their theurgist's magic, so they could unleash it to the best of their ability. It was like the working relationship Jack had observed between wranglers and their ponies, where the rider had an almost innate ability to guide their steed's movements with the pressure of a knee or the flick of a rein. The ponies knew their job, and the cowboy let them do it, within reason.

Gregor was nothing like that. He treated Jack, and therefore the geasa, like a servant. He had a set of commands, and that was it. Much of it was left up to Jack's interpretation, which was all the free will he had. Gregor didn't care if he used bullets or magic. They were all the same to him. He had no clue about the depths of the outlaw's magical potential.

He stared at the poppet. "Means you're lucky, you feckless dandy." Jack dropped it onto the table again, rolling onto his side to stare across the darkened room. He kept waiting for the sudden pull of sleep, the insistent tug of Jefferson drawing him into the dreamscape. The Dreamer had lulled him into it before, and Jack hoped against hope that he would do so now.

The dreams never came.

CHAPTER FORTY

The Most Confusing Person Ever

Blaise

"I'm feeling personally attacked right now by the fact that the sun is up." Malcolm winced, raising a hand to shield his eyes from the offensive ray of sunlight that slipped through the curtains.

Blaise glanced over from where he sat in an armchair in the corner, reading a book. He marked his page and placed the book on the bedside table, then clasped his hands in front of him as he studied Malcolm, whose hair was mussed and face pale. "How are you feeling?"

Malcolm winced. "Like I made a very poor life choice last night. Fortunes of Tabris, I haven't drunk like that for years. And definitely not as *me*." He rolled onto his side with a groan. "I think I need to vomit."

"Wouldn't be the first time," Blaise remarked, rising from the chair to help.

Malcolm appreciated his aid and, from what Blaise could tell, had very little memory of the previous night. He asked how the festivities with the other Doyens had gone, and Blaise danced around the topic, saying that it went well. He wanted—no, *needed*—to get to the heart of their fight last night. Because that's what he realized it had been, and it didn't sit well with him—even if Malcolm didn't remember it.

Marta brought up breakfast for them—though the food she provided for Malcolm was bland: toast, bananas, and ginger tea, which she told Blaise would help him recover from the nasty effects of the hangover. Malcolm sat cross-legged on the bed, sipping the tea and nibbling toast, muttering that he didn't want to see any other company until his head stopped pounding. It was a little disconcerting to see the sophisticated Doyen sitting in bed with toast crumbs raining down beside him, but Blaise decided he liked how it made him more *real*.

"Apologies if I was awful last night. I haven't drunk like that in a very long time," Malcolm said once he polished off the first piece. He wiped his fingertips on a linen napkin, frowning at the crumbs. He busied himself sweeping them into the napkin with one hand.

Malcolm's not stupid. He knows something happened but doesn't know what. Blaise wished the other man knew, to prevent the need for explanation. But this was something Blaise couldn't hide from—not if he really cared about the other man. And he did. Or he thought he did, anyway. Blaise hadn't slept at all last night, too busy examining how he felt about Jefferson and Malcolm and where to go from there.

"There *is* something we need to talk about," Blaise said after a beat, trying to keep his tone neutral. "Last night you said some things that made me think." Malcolm opened his mouth to interject, but Blaise held up a hand. "Let me finish, please. It's important. You put yourself out there for me and you show me constantly how you feel. And that's harder for me..."

Malcolm nodded. "I know. It's okay."

"No, it's really not." Blaise rubbed at his face. Everything made more sense in his head, but suddenly he was at a loss for the right words. He wished he could just throw his jumbled thoughts at Malcolm so he would understand. Sadly, it wasn't that simple. "We need to decide what we are to each other."

Malcolm reached for his cup of tea and took a sip, though Blaise saw it for what it was: a delaying tactic to allow him a moment's thought. His forehead puckered. "What did I say that brought this about?"

"That you wanted more than kisses."

"*Oh.*" The single word held the sharp edge of regret and truth. Malcolm swallowed, and he gave an abrupt nod. "I remember what you told me before—how you feel about that. That doesn't stop how *I* feel about *you.* When you're near, you're all I can think about. But not *only* because of how I want you. You make me feel *loved.* Something I never had with...with anyone before." He raked a hand through his hair, mussing it further.

He's afraid of losing that. Blaise studied Malcolm from the tendrils of black hair standing at attention atop his head down to his legs curled on the mattress. His stockinged toes poked out from beneath the sheets. "I love you, too. But..."

A range of emotions flickered over Malcolm's face, and Blaise's stomach cramped. The Doyen had years of practice at schooling his expression, and his face briskly turned neutral, though the corners of his eyes crinkled with uncertainty. "But what?" His voice was soft and a little husky, as if he were afraid of something but denying the fear.

Blaise rubbed the back of his neck. "I'm *attracted* to Jefferson."

Malcolm's eye-crinkle disappeared, replaced by confusion. "You realize *I'm* Jefferson, right?" He sounded more amused than hurt. "Quite literally two sides of the same coin."

"I know it's stupid." Blaise swallowed, tension creeping into the base of his neck. He shouldn't have said anything. Why couldn't he be normal? "But I wanted you to know."

Malcolm licked his lips. "It's not stupid. As they say, the heart knows what it wants."

"Who says that?" Blaise had never heard such a thing, but that didn't mean much.

"Heard it at the theater," Malcolm said, rolling his shoulders in a casual shrug. He gave Blaise a curious look. "May I ask how you came to that conclusion?"

"I just..." Blaise faltered. He didn't want to tell Malcolm he'd been thinking about him—and Jefferson—all night. Puzzling through his feelings. Struggling to identify what separated Jefferson from Malcolm in his mind. "I don't know."

"We can test your theory, if you like." Malcolm reached over, opening the drawer of the bedside table, and pulling out a velvet box. His ring nestled inside, the scarlet stone glinting in the morning light. He plucked it from the velvet and held it between his thumb and index finger, an invitation. "What do you think?"

"I thought you were trying to keep up the image that Jefferson is in Ganland right now. You know, since he's a wanted man," Blaise said, though his pulse raced. For weeks he had only seen Jefferson in the dreamscape, where he was Malcolm's preference, too.

"A wanted man, you say?" Malcolm's mouth twitched, teasing.

"You know what I mean," Blaise muttered, though he only feigned his annoyance. And judging by the way Malcolm's eyes danced, he was aware. "Isn't this inviting trouble?"

"No one's going to know." Malcolm slipped the ring onto his finger, magic sluicing over him as he changed. Obsidian hair brightened to tawny brown, and his five o'clock shadow faded away. Brown eyes shifted into an intense green. Jefferson aimed a crooked smile at him. "Better?"

Blaise swallowed. "Um, I think so."

"Gods, you are the most confusing person ever."

That was accurate. Even Blaise knew that. He couldn't take his eyes off Jefferson, and even though logically he *knew* he was still the same person, he couldn't deny the draw. Because Jefferson had been the one to first show interest in him back in Itude. Jefferson had been kind and talked to him. "Oh. It was Jefferson first," Blaise murmured to himself.

"What?"

Blaise shook his head, sitting down on the bed, close enough so that his shoulder brushed Jefferson's. "If you thought I was confusing thirty seconds ago, please don't ask me to explain what just went through my head."

"If your thoughts were about me, then no explanation necessary," Jefferson replied, a rumble in his voice.

The heat in his tone made Blaise feel giddy, like the prospect of trying a new and challenging recipe. He thought back to Flora's words. *Rare and precious.* This man loved and treasured him, not caring that he was a walking mess of a human being. No matter his magic. There was no judgment. Jefferson didn't ask him to be anyone else but who he was. And that was...liberating.

He turned, leaning in, until his lips met Jefferson's. Their arms entangled, and for an instant, Blaise fought back against the old panic of someone so close. *This is okay. This is safe.* Jefferson's hands were as tender as his lips were demanding. He ran a finger along Blaise's jaw, scuffing the edge of his beard with his nails. His touch was bliss, a kindness that Blaise hadn't felt in the Cit outside of the dreamscape.

Blaise quivered, pulling away with a soft sigh. He closed his eyes as Jefferson stroked the short hair at the nape of his neck.

"Are you okay?" Jefferson asked, his hand light on Blaise's neck.

"Yes," Blaise murmured, meeting the other man's eyes. Did he know what he was doing? No. But he was with Jefferson, and that meant things would be all right. Blaise traced a hand up Jefferson's chest until he reached the top button of his shirt, still rumpled and unchanged from the previous evening.

Jefferson rested a hand atop his, green eyes pensive. "What are we to each other?"

Blaise paused beneath his touch. He had been so focused on Jefferson's presence that he'd forgotten his earlier hesitation.

"Safety. Acceptance." The words felt right as he said them, ringing with truth. "I *do* love you."

A shiver swept through Jefferson, one that Blaise felt beneath his hand. "And I love you. But this..." Jefferson curled his hand around Blaise's. "Is this what you want?"

Is it? Blaise swallowed. He knew he was standing on the edge of a cliff. This had the potential to change things between them, and his inexperience with relationships was a detriment. He cared about Jefferson—when they were together, he felt whole. Someone who made him the man he wanted to be, not the man everyone else thought he was. "I want you to know how I feel about you." He toyed with the top button.

Jefferson swallowed. "You just told me. That's a treasure in itself. As much as I want you, I'm afraid I'll drive you away if we do anything more." The skin on his brow puckered with indecision.

Blaise touched Jefferson's cheek, smooth as if he had just shaved. Jefferson shuddered, leaning into the caress. "You won't drive me away. Not with this."

Jefferson froze beneath his touch, though Blaise suspected he was like a coiled spring, ready to be released in an instant. "You were crystal clear about your stance on sex before. What changed?"

How could a question be both difficult and easy to answer? Blaise tipped his head as he thought. "I realized that when you care about someone, you want to make the other person happy."

Conflicting emotions warred on Jefferson's face, a mixture of anticipation and uncertainty. "Not at the sacrifice of *your* happiness, though."

"Who says I won't be happy?"

Jefferson hissed out a breath, studying him. "Gods, Blaise. You certainly know how to tie me in knots. I—"

Blaise crushed his mouth against Jefferson's, cutting off whatever protest he was about to make. The Dreamer tensed for a heartbeat before melting against Blaise with a low moan. Jefferson's hand found the back of Blaise's neck again, fingers winding around a lock of his hair.

Blaise looped his arms over Jefferson's shoulders when they parted. "You were saying?"

"I have no idea what I was saying," Jefferson murmured, resting his forehead against Blaise's. He closed his eyes for a moment. "Wait, I remember now." Jefferson's eyes flashed open again. "This. *Us.*" He shook his head, as if annoyed that his usual eloquence had fled. "What I mean to say is, I think I can make you happy, too."

Blaise smiled. "I'm counting on it."

———

BLAISE'S BACK NESTLED AGAINST JEFFERSON'S CHEST, WARM AND welcoming. He breathed out a soft, contented sigh, turning over when a familiar hand brushed against his arm.

Green eyes flashed a greeting as a satisfied smile slid across Jefferson's face. He had shed his earlier fears, emboldened by Blaise's change of heart. "I must say, all that kneading bread does wonders. The way you rubbed my—"

Blaise touched a finger to his lips. *Great, now he's downright cheeky.* "Don't ruin this."

"I was going to say *back*," Jefferson replied, eyebrows raised, the very picture of innocence. "Why? What did *you* think I was going to say?"

Blaise couldn't help it. He laughed because everything about this was ridiculous and wonderful. Jefferson grinned, his expression one of unfettered delight.

"No, really. What did you think? I'm genuinely curious." Jefferson rested his chin on one hand, inviting an answer.

"I won't dignify that with a response," Blaise mumbled, shaking his head. He couldn't even be annoyed at the question. Jefferson was nearly effervescent in his joy, and it was infectious.

Jefferson planted a gentle kiss on his cheek. "I was only teasing. And trust me, it was a compliment."

Blaise's cheeks heated for a new reason at that. "Oh." He swallowed as Jefferson draped an arm over his bare side, pinning him with a serious look.

"Are we okay?" Jefferson asked, his voice soft. "Because as much as I've wanted this, I don't want to harm what we have."

What we have. Blaise turned those words over in his mind, enjoying them. They had something he'd never expected to have in his life. It was new, and a little frightening, but it was *his.* Blaise discovered it was something he wanted to protect, this love he had found.

Blaise realized he hadn't given Jefferson any sort of response, lost in his thoughts. "I'll be honest. I'm still figuring things out, but I think we're going to be okay."

CHAPTER FORTY-ONE

Breaker: The Musical

Blaise

"I can't believe you actually agreed to this." Malcolm's voice reverberated with excitement as he and Blaise found their seats in the Legend Theater. A grin lit his handsome face as his eyes feasted on the sights and sounds all around them.

Blaise gave a small shrug, tolerating the hubbub because it made Malcolm happy. After the revelation that the Doyen had forgotten most of the previous evening, Blaise had, much to his surprise, reminded him of their invitation to the debut of Lizzie's play. "I know you enjoy this sort of thing."

"I do," Malcolm agreed, grasping Blaise's hand and giving it a quick squeeze.

They were both in a pleasant haze. With the Inquiry recessed for the day, there was no need to hurry anywhere. Malcolm's staff cleared his schedule so that Jefferson and Blaise spent most of the day together. The more time they were together, simply *being*, the more certain he was that they would be okay. Blaise hadn't felt like he would be okay for a very long time.

An usher seated them in a private box along with Doyen Jennings and his wife. Lizzie was radiant, beaming with pride. Blaise couldn't help but smile as people stopped by to chat with her. It was a bonus that the admirers focused on her rather than him. As the titular Breaker, he was interesting but not as influential for the sycophants as the talented Lizzie Jennings. Blaise was fine with that.

The house lights dimmed as orchestral chords wafted through the theater. An *orchestra*. They had an entire orchestra. Blaise shook his head, overwhelmed at the opulence. Lizzie's admirers retreated to their own seats as the lights came up on the stage, illuminating a young man strutting to the center. Music swelled as a chorus dressed in scarlet filed onto the right side of the stage.

Blaise groaned. "Wait. Is this a musical?"

Malcolm chuckled. "Yes. Did you miss that part on the program?" He held it up for Blaise's inspection. "Look, none other than *Edward Monroe* is playing you."

"I don't even know who that is." Blaise wondered if he could burrow so deeply into his seat that no one would see him. The seats in the theater were exceptionally plush.

"All you need to know is that you should be flattered," Malcolm assured him. He craned his neck to get a better look at Blaise's face. "What's wrong? Afraid the songs will be so catchy that you'll hear people singing about you?"

"Actually, yes." Blaise rubbed the side of his face as the young man on stage belted out a song about his life. "Do you think it's possible to die of embarrassment?"

Malcolm glanced at him but otherwise kept his attention focused on the stage. "Don't be ridiculous."

"All I'm saying is we might find out if it's possible."

In the darkness, a hand pressed against his, warm and reassuring. Malcolm eased closer. "If you're truly upset, we can leave."

Oh. Blaise hadn't meant that. "We can stay. Um, sometimes I just like to complain about things." Though he thought this was a valid complaint. Sweet Faedra, had the actor just sung the line *A stalwart Breaker, who would rather be a baker?* The chorus echoed it a moment later, so yes, he absolutely had.

The reflected stage lights illuminated the hint of a smile on Malcolm's face. "Noted." His hand roved to Blaise's knee, settling there like a comforting weight.

The worst part was the fact that the songs *were* catchy. And fun. Did it divert from reality? It did, to the point where Blaise sometimes forgot it was about him. Which, all things told, made it more palatable. The musical's storyline was engaging and often over-the-top.

A few minutes before the intermission, an usher delivered a note to Malcolm. He unfolded it and read it, brow furrowed. He leaned over to whisper, "I'll be back in a few moments."

Blaise nodded, though he didn't want to be left alone. Well, he supposed he wasn't alone. Seward and Lizzie were nearby, watching the production. They had become sort-of friends, so he had the reassurance of their combined presence until Malcolm returned. He nibbled on his bottom lip, keeping his attention on the current musical number in which the actress playing Vixen was helping to train actor-Blaise's magic. Lovely aerialists swung around on billowing silks in the background. Blaise couldn't figure out what they had to do with anything, but they made for a striking scene.

Intermission came and went, and still Malcolm hadn't returned. Blaise clasped his hands in his lap, constant worry distracting him. He licked his lips, glancing around for any sign of the Doyen. A few more minutes passed, and he poked at the geasa bond between them, but it was quiet. And quiet was unusual. Wrong. He should have felt something there, Malcolm's steady presence as sure as the beating of his own heart.

Blaise closed his eyes, swallowing. Just because he didn't feel Malcolm didn't mean that the worst had happened. His hands itched with his rising anxiety. All he had to do was find Malcolm and assure himself that he was fine. No big deal. He rose from his seat, giving Seward a small nod as he exited the box.

Blaise peered down the long corridor, trying to decide which way Malcolm might have gone. Was Flora around? She had a penchant for lurking near Malcolm when he was in public. Blaise wouldn't have been surprised to discover her somewhere nearby. That thought made him feel better.

He walked along the concourse, almost wandering behind the scenes to where the actors and actresses did whatever it was they did behind the curtain. Still, there was no sign of Malcolm. What had been in the note that had drawn him away? Blaise should have asked more questions. He rubbed the back of his neck, torn about what to do next. Maybe he had gone outside? That was the only other place he hadn't checked.

Gas-powered lamps lit the streets outside the Legend Theater, fending off the encroaching darkness. Blaise peered up and down the street, unsettled that he found no sign of Malcolm. He started a loop around the theater complex.

The chill of danger tickled Blaise's spine as he stepped into a back alley, and he knew without turning around who made him feel that sense of impending doom. Blaise froze, swallowing. "Howdy, Jack."

Boots scuffed the ground as Blaise pivoted, slow and careful. The outlaw stood at the other end of the alley, his sixgun holstered. He somehow looked older than his years, as if the geasa had sapped the fight out of him. Blaise couldn't imagine that Jack, who seemed to exist on pure spite alone, would lose any of his fighting spirit. But Jack was being *used*, and Blaise knew that was one of his greatest fears. A part of him had wanted to deny Jack's situation in the dreamscape, but now it stared him in the face.

Jack didn't speak, simply touched a finger to his broad-brimmed hat.

"I'm going to guess you're why I can't find Malcolm?" Blaise asked, somehow keeping his voice calm.

The outlaw stared at the ground at Blaise's feet, then gave a sharp nod. "He's not dead." Jack's voice was a pained rasp, as if it had cost him to even say that much.

Somehow, Blaise knew there was a *yet* attached to that. There was no guarantee for Malcolm's safety at this point. He stood still, thinking. Jack was a man of action. If he were here to fight, Blaise would already be a bloody pulp. But instead, the outlaw remained in place, like a reluctant marionette. He had an idea. "Jack, what if I broke the geasa?"

Cold blue eyes snapped up to Blaise's face. "*No,*" the outlaw choked out. One of his hands reached out like a claw, and he shook his head, adamant. "Wells."

Oh. The geasa shackled Jack's tongue, but he'd bought enough slack to warn Blaise. The Breaker trembled, his magic swarming as fear swept over him. Jack had done something with Malcolm but couldn't tell him what. Malcolm was in danger. Jack was trapped. And there wasn't a thing Blaise could do about it.

"You have to come with me," Jack said finally, resigned. As if he had been hoping that Blaise would somehow come up with a plan to save them all. "It's the only way anyone gets out of this alive."

Blaise froze, trembling. He was about to speak when Flora rained down on them like a rabid goblin. She landed on Jack's back, knocking the outlaw down with surprising force. Blaise stumbled backward as they fell in a cursing, spitting tussle. Flora screamed with such enthusiasm Blaise thought his eardrums might burst, and he wondered why the city guard didn't come running. Though if Gregor were behind all this, he had likely arranged for them to either not be around or ignore whatever they heard.

Jack was not at the top of his game or full of fight. Their battle was short and ended with the outlaw flat on his back, Flora perched atop his chest with her knives at his throat. "Where's Malcolm, you cold-hearted bastard?"

"Flora, stop," Blaise called, walking closer with caution. Jack was breathing hard, eyes closed. "He can't help it. He's under Gaitwood's control."

She glanced up at him. "Hrmph." Flora put away her knives and crossed her arms, maintaining her position over Jack. "Can I just stab him a little?" Jack's eyes flew open, and he bucked beneath her with a furious growl.

"Please don't," Blaise said quickly. He ran a hand through his hair, tugging at it. "Let him up. I have to go with him."

The half-knocker shook her head. "No. How will I ever explain to Malcolm that I let you go with Killhappy Murderface here? There has to be another way." She climbed down from her position atop Jack's chest, though she brought her blades back out.

"Gaitwood wants Blaise," Jack said, groaning as he adjusted into a sitting position. He winced as he moved, a thin trail of blood seeping from a gash on his forehead. He didn't seem to notice it.

Flora's pink ponytail whipped around as she shook her head. "Exactly! This is what you were trying to avoid. What *Malcolm* fought so hard to avoid."

Oh, Blaise knew. And he didn't like it, but he couldn't go on if he became the reason Malcolm no longer drew breath. And besides... "I trust Jack. We'll figure something out."

"Okay, let me point out that putting your trust in someone under the sway of the geasa is a poor life choice." Flora put her hands on her hips. "He's already got Malcolm! You want Gregor to collect the whole set?"

If Jack had input, he was quiet, unable to voice it under his current compulsion.

Flora was right. It was stupid. Blaise didn't have any sort of plan besides the drive to know that Malcolm was okay. But maybe... "Jack, Flora can leave here with no harm done?"

"Long as she doesn't come at me again. Might have to kill her then."

"I'd like to see you try!" Her knives glinted in the gas-lamp light.

Blaise sighed, holding up a hand. "Wait." He approached Jack, who stood as still as a statue. Blaise reached up and plucked a hair from beneath the outlaw's hat, receiving no response aside from frigid eyes watching him. Blaise plucked a few hairs from his own head for good measure, then wrapped them in a bandanna before handing the strange package to Flora. He knelt down close to her and whispered in her ear, "Can you find Emmaline? She can help."

The half-knocker scowled, then pocketed the precious bandanna. "I'll try. Stall for as long as you can." She stepped back, glancing between Blaise and Jack. "Outlaw, if anything happens to Malcolm, I'll be the last thing you'll ever see." Jack made no response, further proof that the man wasn't in control.

Blaise rose, turning to face the outlaw as Flora hurried off. "All right. Let's go."

JACK ESCORTED BLAISE TO A DARK CARRIAGE WAITING NEARBY. Once the outlaw opened the door, Malcolm was visible, slumped across one of the bench seats. Blaise gasped, vaulting inside to check for a pulse.

"Told you he wasn't dead," Jack grunted, climbing up and closing the door behind him. The outlaw claimed the seat opposite the Doyen, crossing his arms as he waited for Blaise to finish his assessment.

Malcolm's eyes were open, but he was motionless aside from involuntary blinking. Blaise chewed his bottom lip with worry, brushing a hand across Malcolm's cheek. Magic pulsed through the downed man.

"Don't," Jack urged, though his voice was neutral.

"What did you do to him?" Blaise drew back from Malcolm, taking a seat next to Jack.

"Paralysis spell." Jack pulled a poppet from his customary pocket, turning it over in his hands. "He's fine." The muscles in his jaw worked, as if he wanted to say more. Instead, he shook his head, eyes burning with frustration.

Blaise nodded, rubbing the side of his face as he shot another glance at Malcolm. As tempting as it was to ignore Jack's command and break the spell, Blaise figured that wouldn't end well. Magic against magic, he could probably beat the outlaw in a fight. But he wasn't a fighter. Besides, Jack was armed and had a lifetime of experience. Blaise sat, fervently wishing he and Malcolm were watching the ridiculous musical instead of this.

"Why haven't you done that to me?" Blaise asked, shifting his eyes from Malcolm to Jack.

The Effigest was quiet for so long that Blaise didn't expect an answer from him. After several long moments had passed, Jack finally said, "There's no need."

Blaise nodded, since Jack had the right of it. While Malcolm was at risk, he would behave. Blaise was more likely to fight if Jack used his magic against him. The outlaw respected the power of a Breaker.

The carriage rolled into the night. Jack glanced out the window, a resigned expression on his face. He touched his throat, as if testing his limits. "How was the play?"

That wasn't a question Blaise had been expecting. Jack clearly had directions for topics he could and couldn't discuss. This one must not have been off-limits. He shrugged. "It's not a play, it's a musical. And the part I saw wasn't bad, considering that I had to watch a bunch of people singing and dancing about me."

"Musical, huh?" Jack sounded almost normal for a moment. "Am I in it?"

Weird conversations with Jack weren't unusual, but this ranked up there among the strangest. "Um, yeah. There's an entire number about you punching me in the face, in fact."

"Is that so? I might have to check that out." Then a silent sneer curled his lips. No doubt he was thinking, *If I ever get free.*

"It was a distressingly catchy tune," Blaise agreed, which turned Jack's sneer into an almost-amused smile.

They grew quiet, watching the dark scenery scroll past their windows. Blaise frowned, wondering where they were going. He considered asking Jack, but he figured the outlaw wouldn't be able to answer, even if he knew. So he waited, and a half-hour later his question was answered by their arrival at a train station.

Blaise had never seen a train in person before, and the size of the hulking metal leviathan crouched on the tracks at the head of a dozen railway cars was surprising. The station house was lit by pools of golden gas lanterns arrayed around it, casting it in a haunting light. The carriage bypassed the station house, and the horses drew to a halt near the last passenger car.

There was a scrape and thump as the driver got down from the box. A moment later, the door opened. Jack glanced from Blaise to Malcolm. "I'm going to remove the working. Don't try anything. My instructions are clear if you do."

"Got it," Blaise whispered.

Jack cupped the poppet in his palm. Blaise couldn't quite make out if he did anything special or said something, but Malcolm made a great gasp and struggled upright, shaking. He sagged against the velvet seatback for a moment, rubbing his forehead. Blaise wanted to rush to him, but he wasn't sure if that would set Jack off, so he froze where he was. "Are you okay?"

Malcolm offered Blaise a brave smile. "I'm functional, so we'll leave it at that."

"Let's go," Jack ordered, jutting his chin toward the door.

Blaise reached out and helped Malcolm up. The bond between them shivered at the touch, and he relished Malcolm's presence again. The Doyen flashed a grateful smile and together they stepped down from the carriage, goaded by Jack toward one of the passenger cars.

They mounted the steps into the rail car. It was lavish, all polished dark woods, beautiful draperies on the windows, and paisley-patterned, velvet-covered seating. Voluminous rugs with a floral design cushioned the floors, and the coach had the look of a fabric shop that had vomited its contents into a train car. He was so busy gawking he didn't realize they weren't alone until Malcolm growled.

"Good to see you again, Doyen Wells," Gregor Gaitwood said from his seat on a couch, camouflaged among the ridiculous patterns like Iphyria's gaudiest predator. "How was the show?"

"What are you *doing*, Gregor?" Malcolm demanded, furious. For a moment, Blaise thought he might rush across the car and attack the other man. He wouldn't have blamed him.

Gregor smirked. "Winning." He glanced at Jack and must have issued some sort of silent command because the outlaw took out his poppet, and Malcolm froze, staggering before Jack grabbed him and eased him down to a safe spot on one of the awful rugs.

Blaise balled his fists at his sides, magic swimming beneath his skin. He wanted to do or say something, but not if it risked Malcolm. He settled for glaring at their smug captor.

Gaitwood rose from his seat, moving to what Blaise guessed was a mini-bar set up at the other end. He pulled something out and poured it into a glass, then ambled over and offered it to him. "Drink up."

Blaise curled his lips, turning away. "I don't drink."

"You'll drink *this*," Gregor replied, holding it out again. "I'm not stupid enough to risk being in a locomotive with a Breaker after what you did to the *Retribution*."

Blaise took the glass and peered at its contents. He didn't want whatever it was, but he didn't see any other options. "I'll drink it, but I think I deserve to know what it'll do."

Gregor stared at him. "You deserve *nothing*."

Was that so? Blaise tapped a tiny vein of his magic, shooting it through the glass. A spider web-thin crack shimmied up one side. "You're threatening me and someone I care about. It's not unreasonable for me to ask. Because if I think this is going to kill me, I may just decide to take you out with me."

The Doyen glared at him, then heaved a put-upon sigh, relenting. "It won't kill you. It's a sleep potion."

Sleep? Blaise cast a glance at Malcolm. He didn't know where they were headed, but maybe, just maybe, they still had a chance. He drank.

CHAPTER FORTY-TWO

Boss Mares

Kittie

C ursing and the sounds of a skirmish carried across the short expanse of Bitter End. Kittie's head jerked up from the work shirt she had been mending as Emmaline packed their meager belongings. Jack hadn't come to find them, and whether it was from lack of ability or something else, they didn't know. She and her daughter had resolved to find him, instead.

Emmaline traded looks with her. "Are we under attack?" Her hands tremored, a tell that made Kittie frown. Her daughter had spoken of the assault on Itude, and it was evident she hadn't forgotten the trauma.

"Let's find out." Kittie slipped her needle into the shirt she had been working on, placing it in a nearby basket for safe-keeping. She rose, heading for the door.

"Hang on, don't you want a pistol or something?" Emmaline called as she grabbed her revolver and stuck it into her waistband.

Kittie shook her head. "I don't need it." Not now, with the incentive to have full control of her fire. But it was nice to know that her daughter was armed. That would allow Kittie the chance to focus.

They followed the sounds of fighting to a copse of trees bordering the wards. Other citizens of Bitter End had heard the commotion as well, though they elected to retreat, guiding children away from town. A furious screech echoed through the woods, causing birds and squirrels to burst away, and both women broke into a jog. Through the branches, Kittie spotted a shock of bright pink hair weaving between the trio of men struggling to fight off the invader. An invader, Kittie realized, who couldn't be over four feet tall. *A child?*

Emmaline's eyes widened, and she accelerated into a run. "Wait! I know her!"

Kittie raised her brows. *Must be something related to Jack, then.* The sentries hadn't heard Emmaline's revelation, too embroiled in their frantic fight against a surprisingly agile and slippery foe. It was unlikely they would cave to Emmaline's command, anyway. Kittie strode forward, tucking her chin and rolling her shoulders. She didn't know if a young Effigest could stop a brawl, but as a Pyromancer, she had a few compelling tricks up her sleeve. Kittie rubbed her hands together in anticipation, glancing at her daughter. "Stay back."

"But—"

"*Do as I say.*" Kittie's urgency ended Emmaline's protest, allowing her to turn her attention to the combatants. The pink-haired terror was holding her own against the men, faster and tougher than they were. It was as if they were trying to capture a greased pig. Kittie snapped her fingers, and a line of flame sprung up from the ground, forming a dancing wreath around the group. Emmaline gasped, taking a hesitant step backward, but Kittie ignored her. Everything around them was very, very flammable, and it took all her concentration to restrain the fire's drive to consume.

The primordial force roaring around them got their attention. Few creatures alive would ignore flames in their vicinity, even in the fever of battle. The pink-haired woman untangled from the melee, edging a few paces back from the men who clustered together, sweaty, bruised, and bleeding. Kittie had the distinct impression the invader had been doing her best to neutralize the sentries and nothing more.

"Who is she?" Kittie barked to Emmaline, glancing over her shoulder.

"Flora," Emmaline answered as the little woman waggled her fingers in greeting.

"*How* did she get past the wards?" Basil panted, stomping the ground. He flashed an angry look at Emmaline, no doubt blaming her for this.

"Honey, it's gonna take more than a little hocus pocus to contain me." Flora winked, then turned her attention to Kittie and Emmaline. "Hey kid, is Sparky there your mom?"

"Howdy, Flora," Emmaline drawled. "You bet she is. What are you doing here?"

Flora twirled her knives and sheathed them, ignoring the humiliated sentries glowering at her. Kittie dropped her wall of flames with another snap of her fingers, allowing the small woman to cross to them.

"We need—" Basil started.

Flora held up a hand, all four feet of her rigid and commanding. "Don't care. Not listening." She looked to Kittie and Emmaline. "We need to talk, but I've got some friends on the outside who need to come in. Can someone drop that ward?"

Kittie blew out a breath. She looked to Basil. He was going to be delighted. "Can you?"

He stared at them as if they had lost their minds. Maybe they had. "What?"

"Listen, there're three annoyed pegasi out there. I'd do it quick-like if I were you," Flora advised.

"Pegasi?" Emmaline asked, on alert.

Flora frowned, giving a tiny shake of her head. Her eyes were on the menfolk, who she clearly didn't trust.

Basil scowled. "I would need to check with the mayor—"

"Faedra's tits, I hate bureaucracy sometimes," Flora muttered.

Kittie decided she liked this woman. "Basil, it's *pegasi*. Not humans. Do it quickly and bring the wards up again. No fuss, no muss."

Basil complied, though he grumbled the entire time, and a few moments later, three equines trotted in. Kittie assumed they were pegasi with their wings hidden. Emmaline had told her about Jack's pegasus, and she recognized the palomino stallion immediately.

He froze as he entered the clearing, nostrils quivering as he picked up her scent. Then he released a soft, throaty nicker and trotted over to her, shoving his exquisite head against her chest.

<You are my rider's mate.> The stallion's voice resonated in her mind, part declaration and part reassurance. <I am called Zepheus, and I am honored to finally meet you.> He blew out a warm breath, tickling her chest.

"And I'm honored to meet you," Kittie murmured, marveling at the magnificent stallion. The scars that laced his coat might have made him unappealing to others, but Kittie knew an old warrior when she saw one. He was a good match for Jack. But if the palomino was here without his rider, what did that mean? Her heart squeezed in her chest. "Where's Jack?"

Zepheus flattened his ears. <We will explain.>

"We need to go somewhere to talk," Flora announced as Basil sealed the wards again. "Privately." She gestured to indicate that the pegasi were to be included as well, leaving Kittie to wonder how that would even work.

Emmaline studied the trio of pegasi and made connections that Kittie could only guess. "What happened? It's not right for Emrys and Zeph to be here without..."

Flora's face turned more serious than it had been moments ago. "That's what we need to talk about. They need help." Her gaze shifted to include Kittie. "From both of you."

Jack should have been the one sitting on Zepheus's back. Kittie imagined that astride the pegasus, he would look like a legendary warrior, rough and ready. A smile touched her lips as she thought about how his blond hair would be gilded by the setting sun, Zepheus's coat shining like a newly-minted coin.

Her smile evaporated as her mind turned back to the information they had brought. The news that Jack had been bound by the geasa again settled in the pit of her stomach like a rotten meal, and the way she saw it, no one would fault her for the flask she had at her side. She took a swig of liquid courage.

They were an odd group. A washed-up Pyromancer, a pink-haired half-knocker, a teenager looking to prove her mettle, and four ornery pegasi. After their strategy session, they had decided it would be wisest to travel at night, when the equines could reveal their wings and take to the skies, as long as they had moonlight to navigate by. But first, Flora suggested they make a brief stop in Izhadell.

"What for?" Emmaline asked, fidgeting with Oberidon's reins.

"Got one more ally to pick up," Flora answered, and didn't elaborate. She simply encouraged Emrys to surge forward with an exuberant shout.

As they neared the outskirts of Izhadell, Kittie realized they were headed for the Arboretum. She liked alchemists about as much as goats liked chupacabras. Kittie treated herself to another draw from the flask as the pegasi fluttered to a ground halt a half-mile outside the walls of the garden.

Flora dropped down from the huge black stallion's back, landing nimbly. "I need to go in and have a word with someone. I won't be long."

"No. We're going with you." Kittie shook her head.

The half-knocker frowned. "That's not a good idea. I'll have an easier time going in unseen. This," she gestured to their group, "is a circus."

"We can handle ourselves." Kittie slid down from Zepheus's back, cursing at the shock of her boots hitting the ground. She nearly stumbled but caught herself at the last moment and covered it with a smile that promised more confidence than she had. Emmaline raised her eyebrows, dubious, but followed suit with a much more graceful dismount.

<We'll stay nearby and keep an ear out in case you need us.> The palomino pegasus arched his neck, ambling off a few strides.

Flora shrugged and pivoted, heading for the Arboretum. "Fine. I was trying to avoid going in the big dumb human way, but we'll figure something out."

"I could just burn a hole in the wall," Kittie offered.

Flora aimed an index finger at her as they walked. "I like that energy, I do. But that would announce our presence and hinder our ability to find who I'm looking for."

"Who *are* we looking for?" Emmaline asked.

The half-knocker pursed her lips, reluctant to respond as she studied the wall in front of them. Flora laid a hand against the bricks before continuing. "Blaise's mother is here."

Emmaline's eyes widened. Kittie glanced between them. All she knew of this Blaise was that he had been a friend of Emmaline's and was a powerful and rare breed of mage. "This place is for *alchemists*."

"Yep." Flora found whatever she was searching for. "Be right back." She vanished in a way Kittie thought must be particular to knockers, then reappeared a moment later, opening a rusting gate twenty feet ahead. "C'mon. The coast is clear."

Kittie wrinkled her nose in distaste, thinking of the ill effects of alchemy. But for whatever reason, the pegasi trusted Flora, so Kittie followed along and hoped that their faith wasn't misplaced. Emmaline trailed after the smaller woman without hesitation, though as soon as they made it to the other side of the fence, her head swiveled as she took in the sights.

"You know, it's really more of a botanical garden than an

arboretum," Flora commented as they passed a stand of moonlit maples with darkened beds of flowers planted around them.

"It was just an arboretum, years ago." Kittie couldn't help but admire the pearly white flowers on a nearby magnolia tree, illuminated beneath the nearly full moon.

"Before the Salties got all grabby." Flora nodded. She paused outside what looked like a storage area. "Okay, I know you're big on following me, but I need you to wait here a moment." She opened the door and gestured to the interior of the room. Shelves lined with neat rows of vials holding liquids and jars containing powders filled the room.

Kittie nodded, summoning a tiny flame in her palm to light the area while Flora went off in search of their mysterious ally. It danced across her skin, cheerful and obedient as she read the labels on the containers.

"What are these?" Emmaline asked.

"Months, if not years, of work," Kittie murmured. She narrowed her eyes when she came to the Inkwells, organized alphabetically by surname. Her pulse sped as she brought her light closer to read the cramped script on the labels. None of them bore her husband's name, but that meant very little. The door opened, and Kittie spun, the flame flaring as she went on the defensive.

"Just me, Sparky," Flora said, holding up her hands. A curly-haired brunette loomed behind her, rubbing sleep from her eyes. The half-knocker grinned at them. "Quick introductions! This is Marian Hawthorne, Blaise's mother. Also a scary-effective alchemist. The walking fire hazard is Kittie Dewitt, Pyromancer, wife of blowhard outlaw Wildfire Jack, and an all-around badass." Kittie raised her brows, deciding to take the litany as a compliment as Flora turned to her daughter. "Emmaline Dewitt, Effigest-in-training, the daughter of the badass and the blowhard, and friend to Blaise. Are we all good?"

Kittie licked her lips, trading hesitant looks with Marian. She didn't want to trust an alchemist. They had harmed too many mages. Emmaline glanced between them, uncertain.

Flora blew out a breath. "Make nice, boss mares. The clock is ticking."

Emmaline was the one who broke the standoff. "She's Blaise's *mom.*" Her voice trembled with emotion.

Marian nodded. "I am. And I'll do anything to protect him." Her eyes were haunted by old regrets that Kittie understood on a primal level, even if she didn't know exactly what they were.

Kittie cocked her head, releasing a pent-up breath. "An alchemist working with mages. Will wonders never cease?"

"Gonna be a lot of ceasing if we don't get to your manly men in time," Flora commented. "Let's go."

"Wait." Marian's command froze them in place. Kittie turned to face her slowly, ready to pull on her magic if needed. Something gleamed in the alchemist's eyes. *Tears.* "I need to do something first. I failed at it the last time I escaped from this place."

Escaped? Years ago, Kittie heard rumors of an alchemist who had escaped the Confederation. All information about the topic was quashed as quickly as it appeared. Maybe there was a grain of truth to the rumors. Marian squared her shoulders with determination, studying the contents of the nearest shelf.

The half-knocker sighed. "How long is this gonna take?"

Marian continued reading the labels, pulling a handful of tiny bottles from the shelves. "Not long. I'm just going to make sure they can't use any of my discoveries again."

That caught Kittie's attention. She stepped closer. "What do you mean by that?"

The alchemist didn't look at her. "I don't want my work to hurt anyone. I've done enough harm." Her expression was stricken. A mother would only wear an expression that wounded if she thought she had harmed her own child.

"Need a drink?" Kittie offered her flask, commiseration from one mother to another.

Marian blinked, surprised. Then she laughed. "I don't drink, but after all this I should consider it." She focused on Kittie, thoughtful. "How would you feel about turning all this to ash?"

Marian made a sweeping gesture to encompass the room they were in—and presumably the entire Arboretum. She glanced at the half-knocker. "Do we have time for that?"

"I like arson as much as the next person, so I guess it depends on how fast it is." Flora considered the laden shelves around them. "But first let me gather a few—"

Marian caught her hand before she touched any of the potions on the shelves. "No. I made the mistake of not being thorough the last time I left. I won't be sloppy again. *Everything burns.*"

The half-knocker's eyes widened with understanding, and though it had to be difficult for her, she stepped away from the temptations. "Gotcha."

A thought occurred to Kittie, and she held up a hand. "Wait. Is there anything in here that *breaks* a geasa?"

Marian narrowed her eyes, crossing her arms. "None of these potions leave here."

Kittie met her eyes. "Please. The geasa has snared my husband. I know how to break it, but…" What if his handler wasn't around to be burned to a crisp? What if he was protected, and she failed to get to him? Failure had so many ways to rear its head.

The alchemist matched her stare for stare but was the first to turn away. Marian sighed, drifting across the room to scour the shelves. She picked up a vial, turning it over in her hands. "It's rare and expensive. No records exist documenting how to make it. Except here." She tapped her temple. "*I* will carry it. I will use it. This doesn't leave my possession."

Kittie wanted to argue, but Marian had drawn her line in the sand. She nodded. "Thank you. Now what?"

"Now," Marian said as she wrapped the precious potion in a cotton wrap, tucking it into a pouch at her belt, "we burn this place to the ground." Her tone went flat.

Kittie swallowed. She had no qualms with attacking the Confederation, not after everything the Salties had taken from her. "What about the other alchemists?"

Marian grimaced. "I may regret it later, but we should only

take out anyone who tries to stop us." She stepped over to the small window, peering out into the darkness.

Kittie nodded, hiding her relief. She didn't like to use her magic to kill, but she wouldn't hesitate if it was necessary. She glanced at Emmaline. *My child, who witnessed the destruction of her town. Her home. She doesn't need to see this.* "You should go back to the pegasi."

Emmaline shook her head, adamant. "I'm staying with you." She straightened with determination. "This isn't my first fight."

Kittie wanted to argue, wanted to protect her daughter from the horrors of the world. But it was too late for that. Emmaline had as much as told her so. Sometimes it was hard to reconcile this Emmaline with Kittie's last memory of her child, little more than a wide-eyed toddler chasing butterflies. The child was gone, replaced by a woman hardened by the hand life had dealt her. Kittie inclined her head in acquiescence.

Flora nodded. "Back up isn't a bad idea. I suspect fire is going to cause a swarm of testy folks."

Kittie cracked her knuckles, striding to the door. All things considered, support was welcome. Pyromancy on this scale was a massive power drain, and it wouldn't be long before she was defenseless. She took a drink from the flask to fortify herself, capping it with a sigh. "Time to release the dragon."

CHAPTER FORTY-THREE

Welcome to the Dreamscape

Blaise

"I thought you'd never fall asleep," Jack griped as the dreamscape swirled into life.

Blaise breathed a sigh of relief as Jefferson and Jack walked toward him from different paths. The surrounding land shimmered into an endless field full of brilliant wildflowers.

"You try falling asleep when your body has been paralyzed for hours," Jefferson replied, massaging his arms, as if doing so while dreaming might help his physical body. He paused when he saw Blaise, a smile curling his lips. He quickened his pace until he was mere inches away. "There you are."

"Howdy," Blaise said, breathless, as he studied Jefferson's face. He closed his eyes for a moment, recalling the shelter of his embrace. He felt arms wrap around him, and then Jefferson's forehead gently pressed against his.

"Are you okay?" Jefferson whispered.

"I should be the one asking you that," Blaise murmured, opening his eyes. His pulse raced at the memory of Malcolm helpless, caught in the web of Jack's spell. *Jack*. He turned toward the outlaw, though he didn't shrug out of Jefferson's embrace. "What's going on?"

Jack's arms were crossed, shoulders tensed with false bravado. "We're fucked, that's what." Disappointment shone in his eyes. "If you'd come in a gods-blasted dream the other night, none of this would have happened. You bother me every other night but not the one that counts."

Jefferson coughed, releasing Blaise. "Oh. That was my fault."

Blaise shook his head. "No, it was my fault."

Jack glared at them. "I'm more than happy to blame both of you, but that won't do shit to help us. And that's what I would rather focus on."

"You're insightful when you're angry," Jefferson observed, earning another glare. He put an arm around Blaise. "And you're right. We missed the opportunity to prevent this. Now we need to figure out what to do about the situation."

Blaise studied the distant horizon—bluebonnets, primroses, and paintbrush flowers spread as far as the eye could see. It was easy to ignore reality in this idyllic dream. "Can someone update me on our situation? I don't know anything beyond when Gaitwood forced me to sleep."

The outlaw paced in a circle, trampling wildflowers beneath his boots. "I caught a look at Gregor's schedule. I think we're bound for Ganland. By train, in case you forgot that detail." When Blaise nodded, he continued, "I don't know what we can do. At least not yet. It was smart of you to send Flora to look for Em, but I don't know how they'll catch up to us in time."

"Ganland," Jefferson repeated. "With stops, it'll take us a week and a half to get there. If Flora can find Emmaline and they come after us with the pegasi, we may have a chance."

"*If* Flora can find Em," Jack pointed out.

"A lot of ifs." Blaise rubbed his chin, thinking.

"Don't doubt Flora. She'll come through. Always does." Jefferson was unshakeable in his confidence.

Something occurred to Blaise. "Jefferson, can you pull her into a dream, too?"

"Hmm." His face scrunched in thought. "If I can find her. I've never had reason to visit her dreams, so it's a bit like trying to catch a specific fish in a big pond." Jefferson rubbed his cheek. "She would be easy to locate if she were close. But I've known her for years, so perhaps she won't be as difficult to find as Jack."

"I do enjoy being difficult," Jack agreed. Blaise noticed he had relaxed a little more over the past few minutes, letting some of his agitated guard down.

Jefferson excused himself, wandering off to one side of the meadow, leaving Blaise and Jack alone. The Breaker shifted where he stood, glancing at the outlaw. "How are you holding up?"

Jack shot him a stony look. "I'm not."

Blaise rubbed the back of his neck. Guilt roiled over him, even though he wasn't responsible for Jack's predicament. "Hey, if you need someone to talk to, I'm here."

"You think I want to talk about any of this?" Jack gestured to his head, and Blaise knew he was referring to the geasa and the control it wielded over him.

"And I'd rather not talk about what I endured in the Cit. So if you ever want to not talk about it together, I'm here."

The outlaw snorted. "How can you make no sense and a great deal of sense at the same time?"

Blaise managed a small smile. He was about to reply when they heard Flora's indignant yell as she appeared in the dreamscape. The half-knocker came in on the defensive, knives out (how did she have knives?). She crouched a few yards from Jefferson, then straightened as she recognized him, regarding him with suspicion. Flora narrowed her eyes, scanning the area before turning back to Jefferson. "Is this your magic, or is my subconscious giving me a guilt trip for napping during our break?"

Jefferson chuckled. "Welcome to the dreamscape, Flora."

She put her knives away—or rather, they vanished from existence. She relaxed, giving Blaise a nod and sticking her tongue out at Jack. "Well, this is handy." Flora held out her hand, and a box of popcorn appeared. Blaise wondered how she managed that, or if Jefferson made it appear for her. Too much was happening to worry about the weird details.

"We certainly hope so," Jefferson agreed. "I heard what you were asked to do. Any luck?"

Flora grinned, gulping down a mouthful of popcorn before speaking. "Actually, yeah." She angled an index finger at Blaise. "You're cleverer than I gave you credit for, so good for you. I found Emmaline." At her declaration, Jack lifted his chin, relief flooding his face. Flora turned to focus on the outlaw. "And she was with someone else." Jack froze, his body atremble. Blaise knew who he was hoping for. "You know someone named Kittie?" Flora asked, coy.

Blaise had not expected Flora's words to drive Jack to his knees. But they did. He went down, his face slack with disbelief and eyes crimped shut. He made a sound that was half-whimper and half-sob. Blaise didn't know if he was relieved or upset. Maybe both.

The half-knocker grinned, enjoying the impact she was having. She glanced at Blaise. "And that's not all. I've got someone else with me that'll particularly interest you."

Blaise swallowed. What? "Who?" He couldn't imagine who it could be.

"Marian Hawthorne."

CHAPTER FORTY-FOUR
Meet the Parents

Malcolm

For Malcolm, it was not the luxurious train ride he was accustomed to when traveling from Izhadell to his homeland. Gregor had Jack keep him paralyzed most of the time, though he was allowed short breaks three times a day to see to his bodily needs. Each time Jack released him, Malcolm looked for some way to gain advantage of the situation, but Gregor had the outlaw in line like a well-trained hound. He always loomed nearby, a tangible menace.

Malcolm worried about Blaise as they traveled. Because of the sleep potion, he drowsed most of the time, and Gregor compelled Jack to help see to the young man's needs. But Blaise drank and ate very little, and by day Malcolm couldn't help but fret about his condition. He wasn't sure how he would have made it through the interminable days without the ability to check in with the Breaker through the dreamscape.

"I've been through worse," Blaise admitted quietly one night.

"That doesn't make it right," Malcolm responded, remembering the scarecrow of a man he'd rescued from the Cit. Blaise had only recently filled out again. Malcolm didn't know how much malnutrition a body could take.

Malcolm lost track of the days, but it didn't surprise him when the train pulled up to a station and Gregor prepared to disembark. The Doyen barked at Jack to release Malcolm, and the next thing he knew, they'd hustled him into a carriage. His legs nearly gave out from under him as he tried to negotiate the steps, and Jack growled with irritation as he thrust him onto the bench seat. Malcolm knew what was coming next. He sighed as his muscles locked up, and he lost command of his body again.

Jack brought Blaise to the carriage next, gentler, as he guided the groggy young man inside. Blaise blinked owlishly at Malcolm, struggling to stay awake, but the potion won out, and he curled up on the floor. Jack shook his head and sat down, soon followed by Gregor.

Malcolm had a thousand questions he wanted to ask the other Doyen. But they remained trapped within, locked away as he stared at Gregor's knees, which were the sum of his field of vision with his body paralyzed. Unremarkable scenery, as far as he was concerned.

Gregor said nothing as the carriage started forward. Malcolm wished he would say something. It was surprising, as he would have assumed Gregor was the gloating sort. But he seemed content knowing that *he* had won and Malcolm had lost. The Inquiries didn't matter one lick in their current situation.

If not for poor Blaise nestled on the floor, Malcolm wouldn't have been able to withstand the uncertainty. Even Jack's sullen presence, puppet that he was, helped. They were a team—a hamstrung, ineffective team, but a team nevertheless.

They traveled for another hour or two, the fabric of the seat chafing his cheek. The carriage turned down a road, and the horses slowed. Gregor's knees moved, as if he anticipated rising soon. They must be near their destination. Malcolm patiently waited. What other choice did he have?

The carriage ground to a halt. Gregor rose and exited, leaving Jack to watch them. Malcolm heard Jack shift and curse softly. The dull vibration of male voices carried through the shell of the carriage, but Malcolm couldn't identify them.

A few moments later, the door to the carriage opened. "Bring out Malcolm," Gregor ordered.

Jack obeyed without comment, releasing the spell. Malcolm gasped with relief, bracing an elbow beneath him to lurch into a sitting position. The next thing he knew, Jack clamped a hand onto his shoulder, launching him past Blaise's prone form and toward the exit. Malcolm stumbled down the stairs, falling to his knees when he reached the ground, as his legs revolted from lack of use.

"Up," Jack growled, hoisting Malcolm to his feet.

His mouth dried as he realized where he was, the discomfort all but forgotten. Horror and panic vied for his attention. Malcolm looked over his shoulder, trembling at the sight of the backward wrought-iron letters that spelled out *Wells Estate*. Ahead, the villa loomed at the end of the manicured drive, the stately columns guarding the entry covered in creeping ivy. To their right, fanciful topiaries reared up, bringing back dreadful memories. "No," he whispered, hoarse.

"Home sweet home, hmm?" Gregor asked, smirking.

That was why Gregor had been careful to withhold any information. He wanted to see Malcolm fall to pieces when faced with his past. The past he had resolved to turn his back on. And it was tempting. Nausea roiled in his stomach at the very thought that not only was *he* here, but *so was Blaise*.

"And here I assumed you wanted Blaise just so you could murder all the upper echelons of the Confederation in one go," Malcolm commented, narrowing his eyes. He wouldn't let Gregor see him wilt, not here. No, he would leave all the panic and worry for later.

Gregor scowled at him. "The *Breaker* told you, didn't he?" He realized he had admitted too much and gritted his teeth. After a beat, his lips twisted into a smile. "Never mind, that doesn't matter. That was the original goal, yes. But then you and that outlaw interfered and ruined my plan." Gregor paused, and Malcolm feared he would stop talking. He wanted to know what had motivated this change. The other Doyen shrugged. "I thought all was lost, but my dear brother's death brought me gifts I hadn't expected." He chuckled.

Nearby, Jack tensed, anger radiating from the lines of his body.

Gregor studied Malcolm. "I didn't know we were so alike. I would never have guessed that *you* would be one to use a mage."

Malcolm swallowed, lifting his chin. Gaitwood was baiting him. He pressed his lips together, refusing to react.

He waited a moment, but Gregor gave up on his bait and continued. "I'll admit, your Inquiry had me worried. But then my men delivered the outlaw to me and..." Gregor scuffed a heel against the cobblestones. "And then someone made me an offer that was hard to refuse." He glanced ahead to the house with meaning. "Let's go meet the parents, shall we?" Gregor's eyes glittered with malice, his gaze sliding back to the carriage where they'd left Blaise. "What will they think of you prigging a *sorcerer?*"

"*Do not,*" Malcolm rumbled, trembling with fury, "*ever* speak of Blaise like that." As soon as he spoke, he realized he had taken the bait like a foolish pegasus colt stepping into a sugar-snare.

Gregor chuckled. "You really *are* a magelover, aren't you? I thought maybe those rumors you had Jennings's wife spread were just that. But I suppose not." He licked his lips, as if savoring a fine meal. "Undoing everything you fought for is going to be so gratifying."

And he would, Malcolm realized. He swallowed, wanting to say something else, to fight back. But there was no way he could win this, not right now.

Gregor turned to Jack. The outlaw waited nearby, his shoulders rigid. "See that the Breaker is secured, then join us inside." Jack's eyes narrowed, but he moved to obey.

There would be no help from Jack. Malcolm sighed, ducking

his head as he followed Gregor up to the villa, resigned that the ghosts of his past were about to haunt his present.

By the time they reached the elegant, curved staircase leading to the entry, Malcolm's muscles were more or less compliant to his commands. At least he wouldn't stagger in front of his parents like a drunken sailor. A grey-haired butler opened the door, inclining his head to Gregor and not at all surprised to see either of them. Malcolm didn't recognize the man, but that wasn't unusual. His parents had always gone through the hired help as if they were expendable.

"Doyen Gaitwood, what a pleasure to see you again." Malcolm's father, Stafford Wells, posed in the middle of the foyer. He nodded towards the grand room behind him. "Come and be welcome."

Stafford didn't so much as acknowledge his son's presence. Malcolm had expected nothing less. Gregor gave him a meaningful look, so Malcolm turned and preceded him into the grand room, as obedient as a child. It looked much the same as he remembered, wallpapered in an awful salmon-pink floral design with matching furniture. Not for the first time, Malcolm wondered if he was adopted because there was no way he would have picked such a hideous design. He consoled himself with the knowledge that, since he had left home, the offensive area rug had been removed, exposing lovely hardwood floors.

Malcolm realized belatedly that his father was staring at him, as if aware that his son was judging his beloved decor and finding it detestable. Malcolm hoped he did.

"Have a seat," Stafford invited, speaking more to Gregor than to Malcolm.

Gregor claimed a place on the pink sofa. Malcolm glanced around before settling upon a wingback chair that gave him a little distance from his father and the Doyen. Gaitwood made himself at home, leaning forward to pick up a finger sandwich from a tray laid out before them. As hungry as Malcolm was, he would rather eat charcoal than anything from his parents' house.

Stafford and Gregor exchanged benign pleasantries, as was customary during a business transaction. Malcolm knew the song and dance. He sat and waited, stoic, and thankful that at least Gregor hadn't had Jack paralyze him again. The outlaw had joined them after presumably seeing to Blaise and now waited nearby, a silent sentinel. The hate rolling off him was almost palpable. If Jack ever slipped the chain of the geasa, Gregor was in serious trouble.

Stafford nodded to his son. "I see you brought him as we agreed. Do you still believe he can be coerced to our side?"

What? Malcolm glanced from Gregor to his father, uncertain where this was going. He wanted to speak up, but until he knew more about the game they were playing, anything he said or did could jeopardize not only himself but Blaise.

Gregor smiled. "I think with the proper persuasion, anything is possible."

Stafford's eyes shifted to Malcolm. He hadn't been beneath that gaze for years, and he had forgotten how his father assessed everyone as if he were studying a price tag. Even his own flesh and blood weren't immune to the look. "Is that so?"

"You know I will *never* support the cruelty you engage in." Malcolm met those calculating eyes, unflinching.

The way his father smiled reminded him of the alligators that called the swamps of Phinora home. "Fine words for someone who has *bound* a mage to him. But then you always were a hypocrite."

Anger surged through Malcolm again, and even his magic took notice. For a breath he thought about using it, but he didn't know what had become of Blaise. He pushed the magic back down, the thought of his father discovering it a new aspect of horror. Malcolm trembled with rage. His father laughed, sonorous and mocking.

Gregor took a sip of iced tea, for all the world looking like he was enjoying the entertainment. "You have all the coercion you need to encourage your son to work with you, Mr. Wells." He raised his glass in a salute.

Stafford raised a brow. "Do I?"

Gregor smirked. "I think he would do just about anything to keep that Breaker of his safe. Treason, for one." He spoke casually, as if they were discussing an innocuous topic like the weather. But somehow, Malcolm suspected Gregor knew just how deep in the mire he was.

Stafford studied his son, revulsion spreading across his expression. "Really, Malcolm? You could have done so much better than that. We could have paired you with a *normal* man or woman—whoever you desired." Before Malcolm could respond, his father plowed onward. "The regulations and laws that you and your Faedrans have squeaked through the Council ever since you took your seat have caused no end of problems for my bottom line. You're going to set things right and change them back."

Malcolm gaped. "But...no! There is no way I will do that. Absolutely *not*." His father referred to all the trafficking legislation he had worked on tirelessly. Malcolm knew very well the impact it had had on his family's *shipping business*. "And even if I could, the other Doyens wouldn't allow it."

"They have to be alive for that," Gregor murmured, a reminder and warning.

His father leveled a stern look at him. "You've run roughshod over the family business long enough. You're going to step back into line *or else*."

There was no need to ask what he meant. Stafford had ways of bending others to his will. And now that he knew the strings to pull for his son, Malcolm would have no choice but to dance to his tune. *But Flora is coming.* She had never failed him before, and she was bringing help. All he had to do was stall. Malcolm bowed his head. He met his father's gaze. "I understand."

MALCOLM STARED AT THE CHARTREUSE CEILING OF HIS ROOM, HIS
mouth a thin line. His parents had left it much the same as the day
he had left. They had not allowed him to express his own tastes
and interests in the interior, so there were no touches that made
the room his. And in the current circumstances, he was fine with
that. He laced his fingers over his midsection, a vain attempt to
quell the sickening ache spreading through him.

To say dinner that night was awkward was an exaggeration.
His mother had been there in body, but not in mind. Malcolm
couldn't remember a time when she hadn't depended on drink or
her favorite hallucinogenic herb to make it through the day. Once,
he had felt sorry for her, knowing it was a crutch to survive
married life. But she had never fought against her dependencies to
rally for her children, and there came a time when Malcolm realized the nanny who raised him was the closest thing to a mother
he'd ever had.

Belinda Wells hadn't acknowledged her eldest child's presence,
either. But then, she didn't seem cognizant of much of anything.
Not for the first time, Malcolm wondered how his father could
allow his wife to just wither away beside him. Likely his father
didn't care. Belinda was just another possession.

None of that had been the worst of it. No, the worst came
during the humiliating dessert course, when everyone else chose
from an array of fine desserts. But not Malcolm. Instead, his
father rose from the table and strode to his bar, pulling out a
small amber bottle. At first, Malcolm thought it might be some
sort of liquor, but the savage smile his father aimed at him forced
him to reconsider. Stafford pulled out a bottle of bourbon,
pouring it into a glass before adding the contents of the amber
bottle. He brought it over to Malcolm and set it before him on the
table.

"Only time I'll ever fix you a drink."

Malcolm stared at it, fighting down panic because he knew
this was not a gesture of kindness. It was one of dominance. "I'm
fine, thank you."

His father took his seat and stared at him. "You'll drink every last drop. That potion costs more than the finest racing unicorn."

Malcolm stilled. *A potion?* He was so troubled by the significance of the potion, he hadn't noticed some of his father's muscle slip into the parlor. "I think not."

Stafford's visage turned stormy. "I won't have my son bound to a mage. Makes the both of you worthless."

What? Fresh fear blossomed at his father's words. He intended to break the geasa. "No!" Malcolm lunged at the glass, hoping to spill it and render it useless, but the thugs were quicker. They were on top of him in an instant, as if Stafford had warned them what to do if he refused. Malcolm thrashed against them as they hauled him down to the floor. A part of him wondered why Gregor didn't have Jack paralyze him, but that wasn't how Stafford worked. Malcolm's father preferred to dominate as physically as possible.

Malcolm panted as he struggled against them. He wasn't a brawler, but he knew where a man's tender bits were. He scored a strike against the groin of an assailant, not feeling the least pang of sympathy at the howl that followed. Then someone smashed his face against the cold wood floor, and he couldn't move. Malcolm's vision swam, and as a last-ditch effort, he tried to call on his magic. He didn't care if they discovered he was a mage. They weren't going to take Blaise away from him.

But the magic shied from him, like trying to catch an eel with his bare hands. Malcolm couldn't focus on it, not like this. He cried out as they held him down. Someone forced his mouth open. Malcolm tried to shake his head, but they braced him, so he couldn't even do that as they poured the concoction down his throat.

It burned as it went down, leaving a cloying taste like oil and copper. Malcolm nearly vomited it right back up, desperately hoping to do so. Restrained as he was, they didn't give him the option. Woozy and miserable, the thugs held him down for what felt like an eternity.

"The first part of our deal is complete," he heard Gregor say. "Is it to your satisfaction?"

The heavy sound of footfalls nearby belonged to Stafford. He peered down at Malcolm, who regarded him with bleary eyes. "I believe so. As agreed, I'll give you half of the payment now. The other half will be deposited to your account in Thorn once Malcolm has done his part on the Council."

Thorn? Gregor had accounts in the Untamed Territory? Malcolm moaned, struggling into a sitting position as his father's goons released him. "What makes you think I'd ever help you after you've done this?" It was difficult to speak. His tongue felt fuzzy and strange.

Gregor smiled. "Because you've already proven you would do anything for the Breaker."

Malcolm clambered to his feet, swaying. "Blaise won't let you get away with this."

Stafford regarded him with a stony expression. "The jeopardy is mutual, son. If he misbehaves, *you* will be the one to suffer."

"I don't think we need the geasa to control either of you." Gregor's smile was downright predatory. And blast it all, but the greasy Doyen was right.

They escorted him to his room after that, locking him inside. Now he was alone—truly alone because he didn't even have the geasa. The alchemical potion churned against his insides, and he thought he was being torn in two. He curled into a ball on the bed, eyes watering against the pain. Malcolm agonized at the knowledge of everything he had ever fought for coming undone. Including his scheme to save Blaise.

CHAPTER FORTY-FIVE
Weakness and Strength

Blaise

*B*laise's head throbbed. He swiped a hand across his closed eyes, groaning as he tried to figure out where he was and what he last remembered. His mind was foggy, and as he sat up, he realized he had been lying on a dirty blanket that someone had charitably thrown on the floor beneath him. Wherever he was, it was dimly lit and surrounded by salt-iron. He felt it in his bones.

He rolled onto his back, staring at the ceiling. Something about the place tickled the recesses of his brain, though it was strange, like a memory that didn't belong to him. *Where have I seen this place before?* Blaise slowly rose into a sitting position as his eyes adjusted to the gloom. Swallowing, he recalled why it was familiar. He had seen it in Jefferson's dreamscape. It was the holding area beneath the Wells family gardens.

But was this a dream or reality? Blaise took stock of the situation. Based on the hunger gnawing at his stomach and his pounding headache, he assumed it was reality. Jefferson never allowed his dreams to harm him. If it wasn't a dream, then where was Malcolm? He was nowhere in sight.

He shut his eyes, taking a calming breath. A new prison was not something he wanted to wake up to, and it would take very little for him to give in to the depths of despair. Blaise rubbed at the long scar on the tender skin of his forearm. He didn't want to use the geasa, but he knew Malcolm had used it before to check on him. And that wasn't an abuse. He pushed against the geasa, trying to get a sense of Malcolm's condition. Nothing was there but a yawning emptiness, like a string that had lost its kite.

Blaise trembled, hugging himself as he tried to look at the situation logically. A lot of things could cause that, probably. Maybe the salt-iron was interfering? He quickly discarded the idea since all the salt-iron in the Cit had never touched the geasa. All he knew was he was alone, afraid, and worried. None of those were good things for a Breaker. His magic rose as his anxiety grew, his palms itching as he rubbed them together. The dungeon was reinforced with salt-iron, but the Golden Citadel had been, too. Salt-iron was no match for a motivated and distressed Breaker. He got to his feet, stretching a hand toward the bars.

"I wouldn't do that if I were you." Jack stepped into the single pool of light, his tone resigned. "I got sent to babysit you in case you pulled something."

Blaise quelled his power. The outlaw was still under Gregor's thrall, but at least Blaise didn't feel alone anymore. And maybe, just maybe, Jack could provide some information. "Where's Malcolm?"

"Alive," Jack growled.

Blaise cocked his head, pursing his lips. Something had Jack's hackles raised, and it wasn't Malcolm. Maybe something related to him, though. "Are we at the Wells Estate in Ganland?"

Jack gave a curt nod. Whatever restrictions Gregor had placed on him, he could discuss this. "Yeah. How did you know that?"

"That's an explanation for later." Blaise rubbed his cheek. "Do you know what they're planning?"

The outlaw licked his lips, as if trying to figure out how much he could say. Blaise wondered if Jack had more rein now because Gregor was distracted elsewhere. "Bad business all around." He tried to say more but instead looked as if he were gagging on the words, shaking his head with frustration.

"It's okay," Blaise said softly, not wanting Jack to suffer any more than he already was. "What time is it? For that matter, what day is it?"

Jack relaxed. He pulled out his pocket watch. "I don't even know what day it is anymore. Whatever day it is, it's just after noon."

Blaise nodded in thanks. He couldn't recall the last time he had spoken to Jefferson. Certainly not since they had arrived at the Wells Estate. Why was that? He had been a constant, reassuring presence before. "Do you know why I can't feel Malcolm through the geasa? Is it the salt-iron or...something else?"

The outlaw twitched at the question, and for a moment, Blaise thought he might be unable to answer it. Then Jack tilted his head, eyes narrowed. "Not salt-iron. Only reason would be if the handler was dead, but that ain't the case." He frowned, shaking his head as if a fly were annoying him.

Blaise waited to see if Jack would finish the explanation, but he never did. The outlaw paced the length of the dungeon, then found a bucket and turned it upside down, sitting atop it, lost in whatever thoughts he was allowed. Blaise sat down on the dirty blanket, making a silent vow that if anything had happened to Malcolm, he would tear this place down brick by brick.

WITH ONLY A LEASHED THEURGIST FOR COMPANY, THE AFTERNOON and evening lasted an eternity. Relief washed over Blaise when Jack announced it was time to get shut-eye. The blanket provided little protection from the hard ground and negligible warmth, but Blaise had grown accustomed to dozing in terrible conditions.

The dreamscape curled in around him like a cat snuggling against its master. As the grey took shape, Blaise realized two things: first, it was only him and Jefferson for the moment, and second, they were in what looked like Malcolm's home in Izhadell.

They were in the master bedroom, which was one of their last happy memories together. Jefferson sat on the edge of the bed, head down and shoulders hunched. He looked up, green eyes latching onto Blaise. Then he shoved up from the bed, crossing the room in a handful of long strides as he pulled Blaise close against him as if he would never let go. Jefferson's chin rested against Blaise's shoulder, fitting like a missing puzzle piece.

"Jefferson?" Blaise returned the embrace, needing it just as much. "What happened?"

Jefferson's heart thumped against Blaise a dozen times before he answered. "It's gone."

Swallowing, Blaise pulled back just enough to see Jefferson's face. A single tear slid down one of his cheeks, leaving behind a luminous trail. He wasn't used to seeing Jefferson fall apart. He was the sturdy one, the one who had everything figured out. Blaise licked his lips. "What's gone?" Though he had an idea. It would explain his inability to detect Malcolm through the bond. "The geasa?"

Jefferson nodded, then sagged against him, lifting a hand to scrub at one eye. "I tried to fight them, but it was too much. They overpowered me."

A jolt of protective anger shot through Blaise. "Are you hurt?"

Jefferson slipped out of the embrace, moving back to the bed and sitting down on its edge. Blaise followed, determined to stay close. "In the only way that matters. My father gave me some sort of potion that took away the geasa."

His father. Blaise had suspected something like that, based on where he had awoken. That was alarming, but something to face later. Right now, he needed to mend Jefferson however he could. He didn't know what to say. Blaise wanted the joyful, ebullient

Jefferson back. How could they have gone from so happy, so victorious, to this? He put an arm around Jefferson, resting his head on his shoulder.

Jefferson glanced at him, sniffling. "I don't want to lose what we have. Our connection."

"The geasa is *not* our connection," Blaise pointed out gently. "It never was."

Jefferson sighed, scrubbing at his face with his free hand. "That may be so, but..." He trailed off, angling to face Blaise better. "You were right about me, before. I treated you like a possession. I wanted you to be mine, to belong to me." Jefferson laughed, but it was hollow and devoid of humor. "Look at me. I'm more like my father than I care to admit. I was foolish to think I could escape his influence."

"*No*," Blaise said, shaking his head, surprised at the sudden ferocity in his own voice. "If even half of what you told me about Stafford Wells is true, you're nothing like him. You *care* about people. You love me for *who* I am, and not because of *what* I am." Jefferson was staring at him now, like a man seeking rescue. "And if I'm yours, then *you* are mine. There's no geasa or power in this world that can take that away."

Blaise backed up his words with action, pulling Jefferson into a proprietary embrace. Their lips crushed together, Blaise tasting the salt of his love's tears. Jefferson shuddered against him. After a moment, the tension in his muscles ebbed at Blaise's touch.

"For someone not keen on intimacy, you certainly enjoy kissing," Jefferson remarked.

"I enjoy kissing *you*," Blaise corrected. He loosened his grip on Jefferson. "Every word I said was true."

"Thank you for that." Jefferson rubbed at the tattoo on his bicep as if it bothered him. It had faded a little, perhaps as an effect of the potion. "I forgot how much power he could wield over me. My father, I mean." He shook his head. "And now he has you, and it's all my fault."

Blaise kissed his cheek. He wished there was something he

could say, but he didn't fully grasp their situation yet, aside from knowing the outlook was grim. So he took Jefferson's hand in his, because that felt right.

Jefferson glanced down at their entwined fingers. "My father plans to use us. Both of us. Not just you."

Blaise frowned. "Why would he use—oh, *Malcolm*." The Doyen. The man with political power.

"My father and Gregor are going to force me to undo everything I've ever fought for." Jefferson rubbed at the bridge of his nose.

"How?" Blaise asked. Jefferson angled his head to look at him, and Blaise suddenly knew what would force his hand. "Oh." He wasn't sure how he felt, being Jefferson's weakness. He met Jefferson's eyes. "You can't do that."

A sad smile flickered across Jefferson's lips. "I don't want to, no. But I would, for you."

Blaise shook his head. "But your legacy..." All of those innocent people who would suffer if the changes Malcolm Wells had fought for were removed. The Confederation was far from perfect, and it needed more people like Malcolm fighting for the right path.

"My legacy means *nothing* without you." Jefferson exhaled an unsteady breath. He shook his head. "Stafford Wells has never loved anyone in his life, but he knows how to use it against others. Against *me*."

Malcolm never stood a chance with a father like that. Blaise wrapped one arm around Jefferson, their shoulders bumping with the motion. "Does he know about your magic?"

Jefferson managed a wan smile. "No. That's one of the few things in our favor."

"Then we'll figure something out," Blaise said. "Have you tried contacting Flora? Is that why you didn't come to me last night?"

Jefferson grimaced, looking embarrassed. "No. I...I didn't call up any dreams last night. I was too upset." He glanced downward, swallowing hard. "And afraid."

It was difficult to imagine Jefferson afraid of anything. Blaise only thought of him as bold and charismatic. But everyone had something that would make them come undone. Blaise was going to have to pretend to be the strong one. "Even more reason you should have." He leaned over and gently kissed Jefferson, a token of affection and support.

Jefferson relaxed, sighing when they parted. "I'm sorry. It's hard to think sensibly right now. I feel like my father and Gregor have stripped me of all my authority, all I've ever worked for and earned. I'm just the child expected to grow into my father's shadow again. To become a thing I don't want to be."

"I won't allow that," Blaise replied, and it was true. He didn't like to fight. Didn't *want* to fight. But he would fight for that.

"So this is the Breaker?" Stafford Wells peered at Blaise through the salt-iron bars as if he were assessing livestock at a sale.

And perhaps, Blaise thought with annoyance, that was how he felt. When the elder Wells had arrived in the dungeon, his silhouette lit by a lantern, Blaise mistook him for Malcolm. As he drew closer, Blaise realized his error. Stafford Wells possessed the same athletic build and chiseled face, and without a doubt, he was what Malcolm would look like in another thirty years. But there was not so much as an ember of kindness in his eyes, only cold calculation. Blaise understood why Malcolm was uncomfortable staring at that face in the mirror and preferred to be someone else.

"Yes," Gregor answered, sounding bored. Jack stood nearby, eyes downcast. Malcolm was nowhere to be seen, and if not for the dreams, Blaise would have fretted over his absence.

"Doesn't look like much," Wells observed. "I doubt this scrawny slip of a boy could break a twig in two."

Blaise's head snapped up at that. He smirked, stepping up to the bars. "Come closer and find out." At his words, Jack lifted his chin, surprise registering in his eyes. *See, Jack? I've learned a thing or two from you.*

Gregor's head whipped in Blaise's direction. "Don't make me reconsider dosing you with the sleep potion."

Blaise was tired of bullies. This place was full of them, and it was even worse with Malcolm and Jack hanging in the balance. He bit his tongue because he really wanted to invite Gregor to try that. But he would send Jack, and Blaise had no desire to fight the outlaw. Instead, he met Gregor's challenging gaze. Every impulse within tore at him, telling him to look away, but he couldn't help the thrill of satisfaction when the Doyen dropped his gaze first.

"He cracked a salt-iron-reinforced airship like an egg. Don't let his unremarkable looks fool you." Gregor's voice was sour as he turned his back on Blaise.

Stafford continued to study him, as if Blaise were a puzzle he couldn't figure out. "Normally, I would prefer to use a mage such as this. Or better still, sell to the highest bidder." He rubbed his chin as he mused.

"The more fruitful long-term option is to use Malcolm first." Gregor's greedy eyes slid to Blaise. "Once he's done his part, I'll take care of him, and you can do as you like with this one."

His words set Blaise's nerves on edge, but he remained still, listening. Malcolm's father nodded in agreement. "You're right. That is best for the bottom line. And that will give me ample time to grow interest in the purchase of a Breaker."

That was too much. Blaise crossed the cell in three quick steps, wrapping his hands around the bars, his magic boiling at their callous words. The salt-iron bit into his palms, but he didn't care. His power roared up and crackled through him, crashing against the barrier. A high-pitched, eerie squeal assaulted their ears as Breaker magic corroded the metal.

"Tabris help us!" Stafford leaped backward. Gregor, too, was shaken and stumbled away, though he recovered quickly. With resignation, Jack pulled his sixgun and stepped closer, his piercing eyes pleading for Blaise to stop.

Blaise relented, pulling his magic back as he unwrapped his hands from the bars. Metal flaked away. He dusted his hands together, not regretting his show of force.

"He *is* a monster, isn't he?" Stafford murmured, though he sounded awestruck. And greedy.

A year ago, Blaise would have shrunk back at being called a monster. But he knew now that there was strength in being misperceived. He stood his ground, unmoving, hoping that he looked intimidating and not like the frightened ball of anxiety he truly was. Stafford and Gregor considered him for another few minutes before turning to leave him alone. Night couldn't fall soon enough.

CHAPTER FORTY-SIX

Where There's Smoke, There's Fire

Malcolm

Sleep eluded Malcolm. Frustrated, he paced the length of his room, pausing with each pass before the bay window to stare out into the darkness. He wanted—no, *needed*—to sleep. He'd had no luck contacting Flora through his dreams over the past few evenings. If it was because of some failing of his magic, he didn't know. But with each passing day that he and Blaise were in his father's custody, his hopes for their escape diminished.

Blaise wouldn't speak about his conditions in their dreams, but Malcolm knew he wasn't treated well here, either. If Stafford Wells was smart—and he was when it came to dealing with the precious commodity of mages—he would keep Blaise weak and vulnerable. Minimal food and salt-iron would do it. Malcolm put his face in his hands, distraught. At least he knew they wouldn't physically harm Blaise. As long as Malcolm cooperated, anyway.

He settled onto the seat of the bay window, back against the wall and legs folded as he gazed at the twinkling stars. And that was the thing, wasn't it? For Blaise, he would absolutely walk back all the changes he had fostered in the Confederation. And they would revile him for it. If it meant that Blaise lived...well, then it would be worthwhile. He thumped his head against the wall. But what sort of life would that be for either of them?

Malcolm wished he could at least fall asleep. Maybe he could talk to Blaise more about their limited options. Or maybe Jack had information. Restlessness and worry still seized him, and he knew that his mind wouldn't rest.

He yawned, rubbing at his eyes. When his vision cleared, he thought he saw something in the distant darkness. A strange disruption in the starry sky. Malcolm squinted, not daring to hope. A multitude of large birds called this part of Ganland home. Seaside, where the Wells estate was located, was near the coast, and those faraway shapes might be herons or pelicans. Except he didn't think those birds were active at night.

On the horizon, a wing clipped the edge of the full moon, followed by an unmistakable equine shape. Malcolm whistled out a breath, blinking in surprise. *Am I really seeing that?* A pegasus. No, not just one. *Four.*

"Flora Strop, you beautiful little miscreant," Malcolm murmured to himself, hope surging.

Blaise

"Get up. Blaise, wake up."

Blaise grunted, rubbing at his bleary eyes. He had been asleep, but not in the dreamscape. *Disappointing.* He sat up on the thin blanket. Something in Jack's voice was borderline frantic, and he couldn't figure out why. "Huh?"

"Smoke. I smell smoke." The outlaw stood at the base of the staircase that led to the surface, peering up. He braced one hand against the wall, as if he wanted to go up to investigate.

Smoke? That got Blaise's attention, and he rose. There was a tremor of excitement in Jack's voice. And Blaise suspected he knew why. He knew about the type of magic wielded by Jack's wife.

"Definitely smoke," Jack whispered, shifting his weight from foot to foot. For a moment, Blaise almost forgot that the geasa bound him. Then a change flowed over him, his muscles tensing as Gregor put his call out. The outlaw growled with frustration, blue eyes wild and angry. Blaise winced in sympathy as Jack bowed his head and trod up the stairs, boot heels slapping a resentful cadence against each stone step.

"Oh good, I don't have to kill him."

Blaise jumped, heart pounding, and defensive magic crackled beneath his palms. His terror was short-lived, though, when he recognized the voice. Flora somehow stood in the cell with him, face creased with disgust. Her gaze fell on the bars he had damaged, and she walked over, poking them with a finger.

"You do that?"

"Um, yeah," Blaise answered, rubbing the back of his neck. "I wasn't expecting you. How did you even get in here?" Knockers were mystical creatures, and he was in a salt-iron cell. There was no logical explanation unless... His eyes widened.

She put a finger to her lips. "Our little secret. I mean that, got me?"

He nodded. "I understand." Gods, if anyone knew of her attunement to salt-iron, of all things...she would never be safe. Or free. Flora risked everything by coming here, and gratitude flooded through him. "I'm glad to see you."

Flora beamed. "Now that's what I like to hear. Where does that grass-bellied sidewinder have Mal?" Her visage skewed dangerously with each word, and a knife was in her hand by the end of the question.

Blaise shook his head. "I...I don't know. All I know is he's on the estate somewhere. They don't let us see each other."

"Of course not." Flora sighed. She licked her lips, eyeing the damaged salt-iron bars. "Can you get yourself out? I need to find

Mal. Going to be disappointing if we come all this way for him to burn up in friendly fire."

Her words spurred his panic. "Fire? So there *is* a fire?"

Flora nodded. "Jack's wife. I swear, I think he married a blasted dragon. It's impressive." She bounced on her heels. "Anyway, are you good? Because if so, I should hop out."

Blaise swallowed, glancing at the bars of his prison. He was weary and not at his best, but there was no one else to save him unless someone nabbed the key from Stafford Wells. Blaise nodded, cracking his knuckles. "I'll be fine."

The half-knocker raised her eyebrows, detecting his uncertainty. She blew him a kiss and vanished.

Blaise closed his eyes for a moment. Help had come. His palms still stung from his display of force, but that was something that could be tended to later. He had to get out. Blaise moved over to the bars he had assaulted earlier, grimacing as his raw skin met the detestable metal. His magic roared up, defensive against his pain. He poured it into the bars, grimacing against the combination of his magic being leeched away and the force it took to shatter salt-iron.

Gods, the potion they'd given him in the Cit was awful, but the amount of sheer power it gave him would have made this child's play. He didn't have that now, but maybe he didn't need it. Blaise was the Breaker of Fort Courage. He had taken out an airship reinforced with magic and salt-iron. *I can do this.* He hunched his shoulders as the salt-iron grated away at him, hollowing him out.

The metal fractured beneath the onslaught of his magic. He heaved a ragged sigh as the two bars shattered to the point where he could kick the remnants out with his booted foot. Blaise angled his body and slipped out through the opening. He reached the other side, shutting his eyes with relief for an instant. He wasn't out of the woods yet, but now he could do his part. *I'm coming, Jefferson.*

Blaise took the stairs two at a time, though he revised that to one at a time when he stumbled and almost fell face-first. He had enough enemies without his own feet betraying him. At the top, a small landing crouched beneath the trap door that led to freedom. Blaise pushed against it, discovering that it was locked from the outside. It was going to take more than some old wood to stop him now. He rested the flat of one hand against the panel, ramming his magic into it. Wood cracked and whined as it shattered before him.

He climbed out, grime and dust clinging to his clothing. *Hard to believe I once looked presentable enough to go to the theater.* Blaise winced as a splinter bit into his arm, but that was a minor complaint. Smoke drifted across the garden, choking the air. In the moonlit haze, fire ravaged a beautiful estate home. Shouts rang out in the chaos, the silhouettes of men and women shifting like grotesque specters. A few fled, but most of them were involved in fighting the fire or—

Mages. They were fighting mages. And pegasi.

<Blaise!> A desperate voice slammed into his mind. Emrys landed in the garden, his wings clipping a pair of topiary dragons. The stallion surged over to him, his massive hooves ripping up the turf, shoving his muzzle against Blaise's chest. <Get on my back. Let's go. *Please.*>

Blaise bit his lip, glancing at the temptation of the saddle on Emrys's back. Every instinct clamored for him to climb aboard and go. Emrys's own panic and guilt at having left him behind at Fort Courage were clear in the stallion's white-rimmed eyes. Blaise wrapped his arms around Emrys's thick neck. "I can't. Not yet. I'm sorry. I have to find Jefferson."

<I understand,> Emrys said with resignation, hanging his head. <But I will not leave you.>

Blaise smiled, warmed by the pegasus's devotion. "Thanks. I—"

"Blaise!"

The unexpected voice made him freeze, and he turned slowly, not believing his own ears. He trembled as his mother strode over and swept him into a hug, alternately laughing and crying. Blaise understood since he felt the same. He had forgotten that Flora had mentioned she was coming, too. Or maybe he hadn't dared to hope. It was ridiculous and made no sense, but he couldn't help the feeling that his mother was there and everything would be okay. Because that was how Marian Hawthorne worked.

"Mom, I..." Blaise faltered. He wanted to tell her so many things, but they would have to wait. "I have to go help."

She smiled at him, pressing her forehead against his. "I know. So do I."

Emrys snorted, arching his neck. Blaise knew the stallion still wanted to whisk him away to safety. When his mother released him, he turned to the pegasus. "This isn't Fort Courage, Emrys."

"No way in Perdition," Marian agreed, surprising Blaise with the ferocity in her voice. She squared her shoulders, glancing at him. "I'm so proud of you. Of the man you've become." Marian licked her lips, as if she wanted to say more, but she shook her head and stared at the burning house.

He rubbed the back of his neck, shrugging. "Thanks." Blaise patted Emrys's shoulder. "Come on, let's see what we can do." He had a boyfriend to find.

CHAPTER FORTY-SEVEN

The Dragon

Jack

Kittie wasn't anywhere in sight, but Jack felt her presence in the marrow of his bones. How could he not, when she'd left her signature so clearly across the battlefield?

The flames that clawed at the house shifted and swelled, sometimes taking on the shape of a massive reptilian head and at others a whip-like barbed tail. Kittie had once told him that among Pyromancers, she was a dragon. As ever, Jack believed every word. His geasa-trapped heart rattled at the bars of his cage. His wife was here, and there was nothing he could do about it.

Except fight her if it came down to it.

He took a silent mental count. *Kittie, Emmaline, Marian Hawthorne, and probably Flora.* Four brave women against Gregor's minions, himself included. And some of the elder Wells' servants, he added with chagrin, as he recognized them among the armed defenders.

A fluting scream split the air, followed by the crunch of hooves colliding with an unyielding body. *And the pegasi.* Zepheus's golden form strafed overhead. The stallion circled around, coming to ground nearby. He trotted toward Jack, tail flagging like a banner, nostrils wide and questing.

Jack suspected he was trying to communicate, but the geasa allowed nothing through. The outlaw shook his head. Sometimes Zepheus was a pain in the ass, but he loved that stallion and missed his meddlesome ways.

A command seared against his brain. Jack winced, closing his eyes before snapping them open. He strode past Zepheus with determination, ignoring the stallion's querying whinny. Gregor wanted his guard dog by his side. Gunshots rang out, testament to the genuine threat. *Good.* He hoped Gregor was so scared he pissed his pants.

"Daddy!" Emmaline's voice was like a shot to the heart. He slowed. Gregor's new command bade him to fight anything that was identified as a threat. And gods, Emmaline was a threat.

She stood twenty feet away, her hair crimson in the firelight. Smoke curled from the muzzle of the sixgun in her hand, a fallen combatant groaning nearby. The girl who had run away from Fortitude was gone, replaced by a competent warrior woman. A gust of hot wind tousled her hair, her brow slanted with determination. She strode toward him, every step deliberate, her head held high.

Sweat trickled down Jack's brow. He didn't want to fight her, but if she came any closer, he would be forced to. Emmaline crossed whatever invisible threshold he had, and Jack pulled his sixgun.

His brilliant daughter, Faedra bless her, was ready. She holstered her sixgun, swapping it out for a poppet. Emmaline was nowhere near as practiced as he was, and he regretted that they hadn't added more to her repertoire. His finger caressed the trigger of his sixgun as she cast her spell. He stumbled, losing his target as his left arm pinwheeled to keep his balance.

But the geasa wouldn't let him back down, and Jack was too

wily for a simple hex to undo him. He straightened, adjusting his grip as he squinted at Emmaline through the sights.

A gust of wind unbalanced him as Zepheus swooped in, the stallion skidding to a halt inches from the outlaw. The pegasus slammed his wings into Jack, long primary feathers gusting the revolver from his grip. It went spinning toward Emmaline, who lunged and snagged it from the ground before Jack could react.

The stallion backed off, folding his wings and loping away to another part of the battle where he was needed. Emmaline stared at her father, tucking his precious sixgun into the small of her back.

Jack gritted his teeth. Though she'd claimed his sixgun, it wasn't his only weapon. The geasa was out for blood, and he had a knife in his boot. His fingers twitched, and he almost reached for it. But instead, his fingers found her poppet.

Emmaline knew it on sight. "Daddy, no!"

He struggled against the geasa, mentally rifling through the catalog of spells it would allow. It was fortunate Gregor didn't know his full potential, or they would be in dire straits. Jack was capable of some spells he wasn't proud of. Breathing hard, he settled on one that was benign but would keep her out of the action.

Sorry, sweetheart. She collapsed with a gasp as he invoked the paralysis spell.

Somewhere nearby, Oberidon screamed, bolting away from his own battle to come to her aid. The spotted stallion saw him, ears pricking forward as he debated if Jack was friend or foe. His ears swept flat against his skull an instant later as he realized Jack wasn't on their side, not right now. The pegasus stood over Emmaline, stiff-legged and teeth bared, a threat to anyone who came too close. Jack backed off, able to give the stallion room since Oberidon hadn't attacked him.

At least someone would watch over Emmaline. Not for the first time, Jack hated himself. He pivoted, the geasa reminding him of the command to get to Gregor. A new voice stopped him in his tracks, his heart pounding.

"Jack Arthur Dewitt."

Kittie

THE SMOKE AND THE CRACKLING OF THE SURROUNDING BLAZE muffled Kittie's voice. But it still made her husband quiver like he'd heard the primal bellow of a dragon. If she was less of a realist, she might have thought that the sound of her voice, absent from his life for so many years, was all it took to shatter the alchemy that ensnared him. His face contorted as if he were grappling against the geasa. And maybe he was. But they both knew it was a losing battle. The will of a human—even a stubborn mule of a man like Jack—was no match for alchemy.

"Jack," Kittie tried again, though this time her voice faltered. Exhaustion from keeping her flames compliant tugged at her. Charred corpses littered the ground in her wake, a testament to the amount of power she had already spent. Fire was a simple thing to call, but took an incredible amount of will to keep leashed and obedient. This inferno was no exception. Sweat trickled down the side of her face as she walked toward him.

He made a strangled sound, as if trying to warn her off. His eyes—oh, she had forgotten how beautiful his blue eyes were, like a placid lake in winter—met hers, pleading. Kittie wouldn't let him warn her away. She wasn't going to back down. Licking her lips, she cast a glance at Emmaline, torn between worry for their daughter and annoyance at her husband. He had almost shot their child, and would have, if not for Zepheus. As much as she loved Jack, Kittie hated to think of what she might have done if Jack had pulled the trigger. At least whatever spell he had cast seemed harmless. Emmaline's pegasus stood vigil over her, and Kittie was confident she could count on him.

Jack's full attention was on her. He stood so still it was almost possible to think that he was a magnificent statue, bathed in the glow of her inferno. Kittie spared a glance to ensure that her husband was her only opponent. Somewhere nearby, the little half-knocker had rejoined the battle, shrieking as she moved with frightening speed and ferocity. The grey mare was a looming shadow in the smoke, striking out with wicked hooves, battering with her wings, and harrying her attackers with snapping teeth.

Kittie knew Marian was out there somewhere, too. She had seen evidence of the alchemist's handiwork: a man with a face melted from a caustic potion, sobbing as he struggled to breathe, and a woman screaming that she couldn't *see* as she ran into the fire, clawing at her eyes. Kittie decided perhaps alchemists weren't so bad when they were on *her* side.

"Oh, Jack. I never thought I'd see you again." Kittie drew back the flames threatening the stables. She didn't know if there were animals within, but if there were, they didn't deserve a fiery tomb. Then she returned her attention to Jack, taking another step. "Emmaline told me that you never gave up. You never stopped believing that you would find me." Another step. And another.

Jack stared at her, breathing hard, as if he were in the fight of his life. Maybe he was. Kittie swallowed at the thought, her resolve flagging. Her hand found the flask at her side, and she took a quick swig to renew her courage. "It doesn't have to be like this." Kittie clipped the flask back onto her belt. "Do you want to be free?"

He couldn't speak because the dark alchemy that bound him had its hooks in too deep. But those eyes she had lost herself in before tracked her every move, and Kittie was almost certain she saw him tremble.

"Who do I have to kill to free you, Jack?" Kittie asked, raising her hands as the flames leaped skyward behind her, fanning out like wings. *Come on, Marian. Where are you?*

She took another step, and combined with her question, it set off whatever trigger he had to launch an offensive. With a roar, all recognition vanished from his eyes, replaced by the fury of a monster. He lunged forward and attacked.

CHAPTER FORTY-EIGHT
The Death of Malcolm Wells

Malcolm

*G*lass exploded as Malcolm slammed a ladder-back chair into the window. He tossed it aside, grabbing a throw pillow and using it to brush away shards of glass that had landed on the windowsill. The night air carried the telltale sounds of fighting and the threatening crackle of flames, accompanied by acrid smoke. He wrapped his hands around the bars on the outside of the window, rattling them. They weren't salt-iron, so didn't hurt or leech his magic, but that didn't matter a bit if he died from smoke or flame.

"Damn." The bars were secure, and he had little hope of getting them to budge. He ran a hand through his hair, laughing at the hopelessness of the situation. The Confederation feared the might of mages, and here he was—a *mage*—utterly helpless. What good was his magic?

Frustrated, he shook his head, weighing his other options. The door that led to the hallway was locked. Malcolm sized it up, wishing that his education had included helpful topics such as escaping dire circumstances. He gave it an experimental kick, driving the heel of his shoe into the unrelenting wood. The door shuddered slightly but otherwise didn't give. "Why does the theater make that look like such a good idea?"

Malcolm paced back over to the window, peering out. The pegasi were engaged in the battle below, their shadows distorted by the flames. Maybe one of them could help? He clutched the bars, watching as two of the equines coordinated their attacks. "Help! I'm up here!" In the dancing firelight, he spotted his attorney's telltale dappling. He whistled. "Seledora! Help me!"

The mare was amid her own battle with an attacker, hooves flying and teeth raking. One of her black-tipped ears flicked his way, and she squealed. Maybe she had heard him? Malcolm rubbed his face, sweat dripping down into his collar.

The door rattled, and he spun, thinking that surely rescue had come. He gasped when his father entered, a little sooty but otherwise uninjured. Stafford glanced around the room, then motioned to Malcolm. "Come on, son. We need to get out of here."

His father hadn't come to rescue him out of the kindness of his heart. No, it was all self-serving. He still saw Malcolm as the key to removing political roadblocks for his business. "I'm not going anywhere with you." Malcolm crossed his arms, taking a step back.

A scrape outside the window distracted Malcolm for an instant, but his father was speaking, and he couldn't split his attention. "Then you'll *die* here," Stafford stormed. "Set aside your foolish pride and come with me."

Foolish pride. Malcolm might be guilty of that in other areas, but not here. Not when it concerned the family business. He shook his head, backing closer to the bay window.

The jarring clang of breaking metal startled both father and son. Malcolm thought for a moment the fire had eaten away another crucial part of the home, further dooming him. But no. He turned and realized the metal bars were gone. A familiar form climbed through the wreckage, a phantom in the haze. The heavy flap of departing wings signaled the fly-by of a pegasus. Blaise yelped as a shard of glass slashed the palm of his hand.

"Blaise!" Malcolm shouted. At the same time his father cursed, taking a step back and glaring at the Breaker as if he were a fiery demon. Malcolm glanced from his boyfriend to his father, shock chilling him when he saw the gleaming pistol aimed at Blaise. "No!" Malcolm screamed, lunging at his father, but it was too late.

Someone else was faster. Stafford reeled wildly, his shot striking the ceiling. The pistol fell from his grip, dropping to the bed as he wheeled in confusion and pain. A pearl-handled knife was lodged in his back, blood already soaking his shirt. Flora stood in the doorway, panting.

"Guess you found him first," Flora said with a wave to Blaise, leaning against the threshold. "I got distracted."

Stafford groaned. "Help me, Malcolm!" He stumbled closer to the bed, shaking as he sat, spatters of blood on the floor marking his path.

"Want me to finish what I started?" Flora asked casually, pulling out her other knife. She twirled it in her hand, meaning every word. Not that Malcolm had ever doubted.

Malcolm stared at his father. Blaise came up beside him, slinging an arm around him. The Breaker held his injured hand tight against his chest, blood seeping between his fingers. The younger man stared at Stafford, swallowing.

Malcolm glanced at him, uncertain. "What should I do?" Stafford was a horrible human, but he was still Malcolm's father.

Blaise was quiet for a moment. Regret clouded his eyes. "I don't know what to tell you. I prefer not to hurt anyone, but he had no issues with hurting me. Or you." His eyes turned stony at that. "He signed off your death. After you changed whatever laws they needed, the plan was to kill you and sell me."

Flora's grip tightened on her knife. "Mal?" She had no qualms with this brand of justice.

Malcolm swallowed. He knew his father was callous, but this…this was unbelievable. Or was it? He shook his head. No, he had known the depths of his family's depravity from the day they had sold his sister. His father would never change. Greed and the hunger for power burned brighter in his heart than anything else, including love. Flora shifted her weight, waiting for the verdict.

He crossed the room to where his dirty, discarded greatcoat was folded atop the dresser. He picked it up and removed the lapel pin that represented his status as Doyen. Malcolm dropped the pin on the bed beside his father, who gave a damp cough as his son drew near. He met his father's eyes. "The Wells legacy dies today."

"You can't be serious," his father rasped.

"I am. I no longer wish to be a part of this family. Goodbye, Father." Malcolm fumbled in his pocket as he turned to face Blaise.

The younger mage peered at him with concern. "What do you mean?"

"Traitor to your bloodline!" Stafford roared.

Somehow, the old man had steadied enough to pick up the pistol from the bed. Malcolm had missed it, consumed with other worries. Blaise tugged him close as the weapon discharged. The Breaker grunted and rocked on his feet, and Malcolm panicked. "No, no, *no!*" He pulled Blaise aside as another gun boomed, punctuated by a soft cry from Stafford.

Malcolm sat Blaise on the bench of the bay window and glanced over his shoulder. His mother stood in the doorway, her arm braced against the frame. A tiny pistol was in her hand, and she cackled as she brandished it before dropping it to the floor. Flora scooped it up and took a dozen cautious steps backward.

"*Worthless bastard,*" Belinda spat, the pupils of her eyes dilated as she stared at her dying husband. Her gaze drifted to Malcolm. "My son. I'm sorry. So sorry. Couldn't protect you until now." She blinked, and her moment of lucidity vanished. Belinda stared at him as if he were a stranger before wandering into the smoke-filled corridor, muttering to herself.

Blaise sagged against Malcolm, returning him to the reality of what had just happened. "Oh gods, are you hurt?"

The Breaker shook his head, though he trembled. "No."

Malcolm stared down at a smear of red on his sleeve, pursing his lips at a matching drip from Blaise's hand. "What do you *mean*, *no?* You're bleeding!"

"Oh. I guess I'm hurt, but I wasn't *shot*, which is a noteworthy difference." Blaise gingerly lifted his hand, blood welling from a jagged slash across his palm. "I haven't had much luck with stairs or windows tonight."

Malcolm allowed himself a near-hysterical laugh. "I don't know how you weren't shot. Fortunes of Tabris." *My father was going to shoot me. He almost did. And he almost killed Blaise.*

Blaise licked his lips. "I thought he was going to kill you. I didn't know if it would work, but I had to try."

Malcolm blinked, almost afraid to find out what he meant. "What did you do?"

They both made it a point not to look at the gasping, dying man on the bed. Blaise pointed at something that looked like metal shavings littering the floor, along with a worrying amount of the young man's blood. "Um, I did that."

Blaise had shattered a *bullet*. Malcolm didn't even know that was possible. Didn't care. They could worry about the implications later. "Thank you."

Flora poked at the ruined shrapnel with the toe of her boot. "You stopped a *bullet*."

Blaise shrugged, bowing his head and curling his injured hand against his chest.

"You. Stopped. A. Bullet," Flora repeated, her eyes wide.

Malcolm clapped Blaise on the shoulder, deciding to change the topic. He took a shaky breath. "Malcolm Wells dies today."

Flora had moved to use a blanket to clean her gore-covered blade, and she froze, scowling. "Come again?"

Blaise stared at him, swallowing. "What do you mean?"

Malcolm revealed the cabochon ring he held in the palm of his hand. "The masquerade is over." He slipped it onto his finger, the magic settling over him like a mantle as his features shifted.

Blaise's brows rose with understanding. He nodded. "What about your mother? Should we go after her?"

Flora waved a hand before Jefferson could even consider answering. "Parts of the house are starting to fall in. Too dangerous. As far as I'm concerned, she made amends for her wrongs and can go to Perdition in peace now."

Jefferson sighed. It was harsh, but Flora was right. He nodded, but still felt the yawning pit of emptiness within. It was heartrending that his mother hadn't stepped up for him until the end. "We should get out while we can." He paused, alarmed by the amount of blood seeping into Blaise's shirt from his hand. "We need to do something about that."

The young mage shook his head. "After we get out of here." He jerked his chin to the open window. "Come on. Emrys and Seledora are on standby."

Jefferson turned to Flora, trying to keep his father's body—no, *Malcolm's* father's body—out of his field of view. "Can you get out safely?"

"I'm dandy. You're the one I'm worried about." She gave an ironic salute, then stuck her tongue out at Stafford's corpse.

Blaise had already moved over to the window, whistling for Emrys. Jefferson came up behind him, peering over his shoulder. "Wait. Is that Jack?" A shadowy figure faced off against a woman and a pegasus, the trio wreathed by flames.

"Yeah," Blaise rubbed at his forehead, smearing blood and soot across it. "I need to get down there."

Jefferson put a hand on his shoulder. "I would expect nothing less."

CHAPTER FORTY-NINE
Fury of the Ghost Riders

Jack

*J*ack decided that a quick death was too much of a mercy, *too kind*, for Gregor Gaitwood.

The cowardly Doyen had called off his summons, instead making the deliberate choice to engage the outlaw in a pitched battle so he could make his escape. Jack found himself fighting against his long-lost wife and his pegasus, internally cursing Gaitwood with every passing moment. The utter loss of free will was bad enough, but as he fought them, he was little more than a spectator within his own body. He couldn't stop it. He was glad that Zepheus had disarmed him earlier—otherwise he would have already taken them down, and he couldn't have lived with that.

All he had was a knife, his brawling skills, and magic. Against most other opponents, he would still have the upper hand. But Zepheus knew him well, and the stallion was as much a fighter as his rider. And Kittie...well, he knew immediately that she had lost her fighting trim, and maybe she was a little drunk. But she was a

Pyromancer, and until the flames died, she was a threat. Fire was a merciless destroyer. There was a reason most sensible creatures fled before its fury.

He assessed the situation, calculating. The charred corpses gave him a solid idea of the amount of raw magic she had expended to control the burn. Her attention was split between fending off Jack and watching for any new attackers so that she and Zepheus weren't caught unawares. Kittie was flagging, between the enormous amount of power and her careful sallies against Jack. She hadn't come to kill him.

But Jack, with the geasa in command, had no such compunctions.

She danced through the flames, deceptively light-footed as she hid the drag of her magic. Jack was thankful he didn't have a poppet to represent Kittie with him. His primary was tucked away safely at home in the Gutter. As it was, he had to use his magic in a more general way, which made her more challenging to target. And Gregor didn't know shit about Effigests to coerce him to use the magic properly.

Something about the way Kittie and Zepheus coordinated their attacks made Jack suspect they were herding him some-where. He didn't know where—or care, for that matter. That meant they had a plan, which meant there was hope. He knew hope was as fragile as a dandelion, blown away by the slightest breeze. Jack couldn't help it. He clung to the glimmer of hope because it was all he had left. It was a buffer against the horror of the things the geasa was making him do.

Jack lunged at Kittie when he saw an opening. A corona of flame surrounded her, but the geasa forced him to ignore it as he wrapped his hands around her neck, crashing down to the ground with her. Kittie kicked him in the groin—and oh gods, but that *hurt*, and he wanted to curl up into a ball, but the damned geasa wouldn't allow it, overriding the pain with the drive to kill. Kittie's flames extinguished with a surprised hiss as he tightened his grip.

His world exploded into blinding stars. Jack tumbled away from Kittie, his fingers scrabbling for purchase and only finding empty air. The air whooshed out of his lungs as he hit the ground, and his right arm and shoulder screamed with pain. He caught a glimpse of gold. Damn, Zepheus had kicked him. Jack staggered to his feet, even though his body was ready to give in. The geasa wouldn't stop until he was dead...or they were. He charged.

Something—no, someone—smashed into him from the side, sending him spinning off his path and down to the ground again. Jack snarled as his attacker's hands fumbled against his upper arms, outstretched fingers clawing at his sleeve. He spun, catching the other person in the stomach with a brutal kick, sending him hurtling. A distant part of him realized it was Blaise. He had just kicked away his best chance at breaking the geasa. *Damn it.*

More reinforcements had arrived. Two newcomers dogpiled onto him, flattening him to the ground as they pinned his upper body and legs. Pink hair gleamed in the eerie light. Flora. Jack writhed beneath them, howling as someone rammed something between his lips. His teeth clanked against the glass lip of a bottle, and an oily liquid dribbled into his mouth. Jack tried to turn his head, but they wouldn't let him. He swallowed the concoction down, gagging at the sensation of it oozing down his throat like a slug.

The potion hit his stomach with a twisting, stabbing sensation. Jack gasped as something within him seemed to loosen and snap, like a chain breaking. No, like a *geasa* breaking. Jack's heart pounded as the fetters fell away from his mind. His eyes widened as he searched for any lingering remnants of his leash. It was gone. He was alone with his own thoughts and drives again.

Well, not really alone. Jefferson sat on his chest, breathing hard as he glared down at the prone outlaw. Flora had her long arms wrapped around his legs.

"Get off me before I punch you in the face," Jack growled at Jefferson.

"You're sounding more like your charming self," Jefferson

remarked, though he didn't budge. He shifted his gaze, concern etched on his face. "Blaise, are you okay?"

A short distance away, the Breaker pulled himself into a sitting position, clutching at his midsection. In the firelight, his face was pale. "Great. Never better." He shook his head. "I didn't get to break the geasa, though."

There had been a time when Jack would have enjoyed kicking the young man, but that time had passed. Now he just felt bad about it. Blaise had been trying to help him, and Jack had kicked him in the stomach for his troubles.

"It doesn't matter because I did." Marian Hawthorne strode over to her son, kneeling beside him to check his injuries. She licked her thumb and rubbed a smudge of soot from his cheek before glancing back at Jack. "It should have worked." The alchemist pulled something out of her hip bag, gently taking her son's hand and sprinkling a powder onto his bloody palm.

"It did," Jack agreed, staring at the smoke wafting overhead as his actions during the battle caught up with him. He needed to get up, to break Emmaline free of the paralysis. And Kittie...gods, he had fought her. Something he never wanted to do. "*Get off.*"

<He's free. I can speak to him again.> Zepheus's voice was a welcome addition after so long. Jefferson gave Jack a dubious look but climbed off. Flora followed suit, eyes twinkling with mischief.

"Not a *word*," Jack warned the half-knocker, though doing so only made her giggle.

His body hurt in places he didn't know could hurt. Jack cataloged his injuries to make sure it was safe to move. His shoulder and upper arm were going to be one massive bruise, but Zepheus hadn't broken anything. One of his hands was blackened, but he thought it was more from soot than a burn. Or so he hoped. Jack didn't feel fully connected to his body. He was bleeding in several places, and his head felt like it was wrapped in cotton, but he was alive. It was more than he had expected.

With a ragged sigh, he pulled out Emmaline's poppet and dropped the paralysis hex. Jack didn't look at Kittie. He couldn't.

She had seen the monster he was, and there was no coming back from that. Tears prickled the corners of his eyes as Emmaline rose and dusted herself off, grimacing.

"I'm sorry," Jack muttered to her, eyes downcast. He had almost shot her. *Gods, I almost killed my daughter. And my wife.* He shook his head.

"Daddy." Emmaline's voice was soft, and she came closer, taking his hand. She shifted her position until he couldn't avoid looking at her. "I know that wasn't you. All you ever wanted is to protect me because you're like a dragon with a hoard." He swallowed at her words, nodding. His daughter opened her palm, revealing a poppet. "But you can make it up to me by teaching me that hex."

He blinked, relief washing over him at her forgiveness. "I will."

She smiled. "Now there's somebody you need to see. She came a long way for this." Emmaline turned, looking expectantly at her mother.

Jack followed her gaze. Kittie stood a dozen paces away, bleeding from a few gashes and scrapes she had picked up during all the fighting and rubbing at the red lines on her throat. Soot smeared her right cheek, and her brown hair hung in bedraggled hanks as the inferno calmed behind her. She was the most glorious and welcome sight he had ever beheld. Jack strode over to her before he even realized he was in motion, a moth to her flame.

His mouth went dry as he stared into her eyes, all the things he longed to tell her dying on his lips. But his lost words didn't matter as her face drew close to his and their lips met, seeking and exploring.

Kittie smelled of hickory smoke, a scent that clung to her even when her magic was quiet. It was part of her and gods, how he had missed it. He melted against his wife, pulling her close. She burned against him with the fire of her love and forgiveness. It made him temporarily forget about all his new aches and pains.

"So you want me to kill Doyen Sleazypants while you make

out or what?" Flora asked from somewhere nearby, interrupting an otherwise legendary kiss. She held a mage-light in her hands that bathed the area with its glow now that the fire had died.

Jack pulled away from Kittie with regret, glancing over his sore shoulder. Emmaline stood nearby, her smile grim. Blaise and Jefferson were watching as well, supporting each other. As were four pegasi. Jack had forgotten they might have an audience. And did he care? Not really. He was going to savor this moment, though the half-knocker was right. They had unfinished business.

"He's mine." It was Jefferson who spoke, his tone brooking no arguments.

The outlaw wanted to ask what business the entrepreneur had, but the answer was in his eyes. Deep-seated anger burned in their depths, a fury that demanded justice. Jack almost felt sorry for Gaitwood because he suspected Jefferson didn't deal in merciful death.

"I'll stand in your place, if you need," Jack offered. He could make the Doyen suffer, too.

Jefferson blew out an angry breath. "He has done nothing but turn the lives of those I care about into a living nightmare. I intend to do the same to him." His shoulders tensed, and even Blaise looked at him with uncertainty.

Could he do that? Jack wondered if it was just righteous bluster. But he didn't know the full capabilities of the man's magic. And honestly, it was a little disturbing if that was the case. And fitting. Jack nodded, pulling out a poppet. It had taken some doing, but he had snagged a napkin Gregor used once and incorporated it into a doll. He whistled to get Emmaline's attention and then tossed it to her. "Hunt him down."

She blinked at the tiny form, then nodded. Emmaline leaned over the doll, whispering words of power to activate it. A moment later, she narrowed her eyes, pointing to the northwest. "That way." Oberidon trotted over to her, snorting.

<We will join the hunt. He can't be far,> Zepheus announced, rearing and pawing at the air. Emrys and Seledora snapped to

attention, nostrils dilated and muscles quivering. The palomino whinnied a challenge.

The grey mare trotted over to Jefferson, prancing in place. She must have said something to him because a moment later, he climbed into the saddle.

Blaise limped over to Emrys, tender from Jack's kick. It took him longer to get into the saddle, but when he finally settled, he pinned Jefferson with an insistent look. "Not letting you go without me."

Zepheus's haunting cry split the air as he bolted into the starlit sky. In a flurry of wings, the other pegasi took to the air, the moonlight reflecting off their glossy feathers and sweaty coats. Jack smiled, savage. Surely Gregor had never imagined that his foolishness would end with him being hunted down by a herd of bloodthirsty pegasi, an enraged dandy, a liberated Breaker, and a teenage Effigest.

Jack turned back to Kittie, satisfied that Gregor was going to be taken care of. "Wanna go for a walk in the moonlight?"

She choked out a ragged laugh, glancing behind her at the smoldering estate. "Is that what you call fleeing this?"

"I was trying to be romantic." Jack attempted a charming smile, though he supposed it was probably ghastly, covered as he was in soot and blood, stinking of sweat and death.

"I didn't know you did romantic. I thought you only did surly or arrogant and there weren't other options," Flora commented from nearby, watching them with intense interest. Marian stood beside the diminutive woman, looking weary but amused.

Kittie looped her arm through his, ignoring their audience and mindful of his injuries. "I would love to go for a moonlit walk with you."

Jefferson

CHILDREN THROUGHOUT IPHYRIA GREW UP HEARING STORIES OF THE Ghost Riders. Legend had it that the revenants and their dragon-winged equines served the goddess Nexarae, rounding up the souls of the guilty and dragging them to Perdition to face justice.

As Seledora flitted through the star-dappled sky in Oberidon's wake, the pegasi trumpeting their fury with every wingbeat, Jefferson fancied their group looked like the living equivalent. He hoped so. He wanted Gregor to know fear when they descended upon him.

Jefferson tightened his grip on Seledora as the mare changed course to follow the spotted pegasus. Who was he to have these savage thoughts? A quick glance at Blaise, off to his right on Emrys, was the only reminder he needed. Jefferson wasn't doing this out of vengeance, even if it felt like it. No, he was doing it out of the need to protect those he cared about. Blaise, most definitely. But he was just the tip of the iceberg. If Gregor remained unchecked, he would do more damage to the vulnerable. And Malcolm Wells was no longer around to block him.

Emmaline shouted something, but her words were lost to the wind. <We are close,> Seledora informed him, descending. Her ears were flat against her head, and the tight bow of her neck radiated anger.

The first grey rays of dawn tempered the sky at their backs as the pegasi crashed through the underbrush, squealing challenges. Sleepy birds and a family of deer fled before them. Jefferson peered straight through the arc of Seledora's ears, though in the dim light he couldn't see as well as their mounts. Emrys plowed along beside the mare, Blaise's face unreadable in the grey light.

Zepheus and Oberidon broke off to either side. <He is near,> Seledora reported, and Jefferson wondered at the bloodthirsty note in her mental voice. The mare might be for law and order in her profession by day, but now that was not on her mind. She was as furious as the stallions. A distant part of Jefferson knew that might be a problem for her later, if anyone could prove she was complicit.

"*No*. No, no! Get back!"

A dozen yards away, a beautyberry shrub thrashed as Gregor bolted around it. Zepheus and Oberidon slipped around behind him, cutting off his only escape route. Gregor stood in the ring of irate pegasi, his hands up as he frantically searched for a way out. Emrys mantled his wings in a threat, the ground quaking beneath the force of his great hooves. Zepheus half-reared, forelegs slashing the air.

Gaitwood swallowed, turning in a slow circle as the sunlight broke through the clearing. He realized the pegasi had riders, and his face slackened with relief, especially when he saw Jefferson. "Mr. Cole, thank Garus you're here! Please, tell the mages to call off their monsters."

"I only see one monster here," Jefferson replied from his seat on Seledora's back.

Blaise remained on Emrys, face impassive, though his stallion snorted at Gregor's insult. Jefferson dismounted, his hands behind his back as he approached the Doyen. He made a show of smoothing his bedraggled greatcoat. He canted his head, regarding Gaitwood coolly. Jefferson smiled as Gregor took in the state of his clothing, connecting that it was the same as Malcolm Wells had worn.

"What...? I don't understand..." Gregor sputtered.

Jefferson studied him. "There's nothing to understand. By all rights, this should be your end." Hooves drummed behind him, and Seledora snaked her neck for emphasis. "But that would be too simple. Too merciful after what you put us through. After what you did to *him*." His voice shook with emotion as he glanced back at Blaise.

Gregor shrank back. "I'll give you whatever you want, Cole. *Anything*. Name it, and it's yours."

Jefferson's green eyes glinted with barely suppressed anger. He shook his head. "You can't give me anything I want." Trembling, he balled his fists at his side. Boots crunched through dry leaves and grass, and a hand rested on his shoulder. Blaise arrived to steady him.

Another pair of boots hit the ground. Emmaline, dismounting from Oberidon. Jefferson glanced back and saw her crouching low, rubbing the poppet's legs into the dirt. "He ain't gonna move till I let him. Do what you need."

"What? No!" Gregor protested, struggling where he stood. He tugged his right leg, but his foot refused to budge from the ground. With a cry, he sat down, trying to pull off his shoes. "Wicked sorcery! To Perdition with you, b—"

Blaise closed the distance to him so quickly, Jefferson hadn't registered he was in motion. He held his hands up, palms aglow with magic the color of moonlight. "Not another word." His shoulders squared, chin tucked. The Breaker had reached the limit of his tolerance.

Jefferson stepped beside Blaise, and the young man relaxed. Gregor was fortunate that even when angry, Blaise had incredible restraint. But he might wish otherwise once Jefferson was done with him. The trapped Doyen stared at him as he found a clear place to sit down, crossing his legs.

"What are you doing?" Gregor asked.

Rather than answer, Jefferson shook his head. Gregor would find out soon enough. Blaise sat down beside him, and even Emmaline moved to join their small group, lending her own assurance.

Jefferson closed his eyes, drawing in a deep breath. He needed to find a place of calm to control his magic, and his previous failures daunted him. A warm hand found his, and he smiled. And then, to his surprise, he felt magic surge from Blaise and into himself, granting him a wealth of power. It wasn't the wild, painful torrent Malcolm had helped Blaise ease from the alchemical potion. This was a gentle lending of strength. The geasa was gone, but Blaise was right. They didn't need it.

"Do what you need to do," Blaise murmured, though the

Breaker didn't know Jefferson's intentions. But he believed in him, nevertheless.

Jefferson squeezed his hand in gratitude, calling up his Dreamer magic. Gregor had made Blaise's life a nightmare. It was time to return the favor.

CHAPTER FIFTY

New Beginnings

Jack

J ack closed his eyes, savoring the warmth of Kittie's body tucked against his. It had been so long since he'd shared a bed with anyone; he had forgotten how comforting it was. How it made him feel human and wanted. He wouldn't admit it to anyone—aside from maybe Kittie if she asked —but that was something he sorely needed after his time in Gaitwood's thrall.

It had been a rough few days since the Wells estate had gone up in flames, and Cole had left Gaitwood a gibbering shell of a man, tortured by nightmares. A little concerning to know the Dreamer was capable of that, but he had been utterly drained after the effort and good for little else besides using his name and connections to smooth things over when local officials became involved. He had the connections to bring in a Healer to tend to the worst of Jack's wounds. He was still bruised and sore, but he could work with that.

Before long, their dogged little group made their way to the entrepreneur's home outside the Gannish capital to recover and assess their options. Jack especially enjoyed it because, at long last, he had his wife all to himself, with no prying eyes or listening ears.

Kittie shifted beside him, rolling onto her back. Something made sleep elude her, and he knew it wasn't guilt for the lives she had snuffed out with her gift of flame. She could be as fierce and merciless as he. With a soft exhalation, she turned to face him.

"What is it?" Jack murmured, stroking her lustrous chestnut hair.

Kittie propped herself up on one elbow, hazel eyes searching his. She traced a hand over his bare chest, caressing the scar of the wound that had almost claimed his life the previous year. "You waited for me all those years. But I didn't wait for you."

Her voice was ripe with guilt, and it sent a shiver down his spine. This was something he had feared; he had been out of her life for so long, it was reasonable for her to move on. Even if he couldn't. He knew the basics of her life after the Confederation had stolen her away—those had been things they could discuss openly as they traveled. But this was more private. Personal.

"Do you love him?" Jack asked, his voice a growl. He couldn't help it. This was his wife, the woman he had relentlessly searched for.

Kittie frowned at the question, as if it were the most ridiculous thing she had ever heard. "No. I said I didn't wait for you. That doesn't mean I loved someone else. There's a difference."

The outlaw held his peace because he didn't know what to say to that. In his mind, love and intimacy were as tightly bound as a vine climbing around a tree. And he feared that if he said the wrong thing, he would lose her forever. After all he had endured, that would unmake him. So rather than trust his words, he curled her closer against him, her hand hovering over his beating heart.

"I thought you were dead," Kittie continued when she realized he was holding his silence. "You and Em both. I...I was in a bad spot when I escaped from the Cit."

"I was in a piss-poor spot when I got back and found you taken," Jack whispered, trailing kisses along her shoulder. He didn't know where the information she was laying out would lead them, so he made the most of the opportunity.

Kittie sighed softly and shivered at the gentle brush of his lips. "I found a lover and I was fool enough to marry him, but that's all it was. I was hurting and needed comfort." She shook her head. "He was an asshole."

Jack raised a brow. "How fortunate that I'm not." Kittie snorted in derision. They both knew that was a lie. He chuckled; he couldn't help it.

"You're a lot of things," Kittie pointed out after a moment. "Look at you. You made something of yourself. All I did was tuck my tail and run to the first safe harbor I could find."

He couldn't blame her for that, not really. All he had to do was think about the Golden Citadel...Jack suppressed a shiver, deciding to keep the conversation light. He gave a lazy shrug. "Won't deny it. You *are* fadoodling the Scourge of the Untamed Territory, after all."

"Jackass," Kittie muttered at him, but it pleased him that his flippancy distracted her. "Here I am trying to be serious, and you're showing off your big ego."

He propped his head up with one hand. "That's not the only big thing I'm showing off." He added a leer for good measure.

Kittie smacked him on the shoulder with her fist, annoyed. Jack winced when she found the remnants of the deep bruise Zepheus's hooves had inflicted. He didn't mind, though. Not really. This banter was gloriously like old times. It was *right*. He wanted this back.

"I hate you sometimes," she growled.

"No, you don't."

Kittie surged against him, pinning him down so she was on top with her hands to either side of his head. He grinned up at her. She made a frustrated sound.

"I'll behave," Jack drawled, though he hoped she kept her

current vantage point. She disappointed him by drawing back to a
sitting position, arms crossed.

"I'm trying to tell you I'm not proud of what I became." She
blew a tendril of hair away from her face. "I started drinking
and...I felt so empty. Why have all this magic if it's worthless to
protect the people I love?" Kittie shook her head, a single tear
trailing down her cheek. He reached out and brushed it away. "I
was desperate for something to fill that void, and I found
someone."

He fiddled with the edge of the sheet, thoughtful. Was it so
different from the approach he had taken? Jack had filled the hole
in his heart in other ways. Searching for her. Picking fights. He
nodded. "You sure you don't love him?"

The face she made was all the answer he needed. "Gods, no.
He really *was* a piss goblin. Ended things with him as soon as I
could."

"Good," Jack murmured, pulling her close again. "Means I
don't have to hunt him down." He paused, mischief in his eyes.
"Though if you have any of his personal effects and want me to
work my particular brand of magic..."

Kittie snorted. "Hugh's an ass, but I think he's below the notice
of the Scourge of the Untamed Territory." Her nails rasped against
his skin as she ran a hand up his arm. "Besides, Emmaline terror-
ized him enough."

Jack nestled into the pillow, pleased. "Did she now? That's
music to my ears. I reckon this means you might come back to the
Gutter with me?" He hoped he kept the raw need out of his voice.
But even if he failed, it didn't matter. He needed her, and that's all
there was to it.

Kittie beamed at him, and it was like the sun had come out
after a never-ending winter. He basked in the glow. "I was going
to, whether you asked or not, Wildfire Jack Dewitt. A herd of
pegasi couldn't keep me away."

Jack's pulse raced, and he feared his heart might explode like a
misfiring sixgun. He pulled her close, and their lips met. Unbound

joy poured through Jack—he couldn't recall the last time he had felt like this.

Their kiss began tame, like a candle, but in moments it scorched them both, spreading like an inferno. His fingers curled against her soft skin, exploring her with wild abandon. She was his, and he was hers. It reminded him of their first night together, only better. Now they were firmly rooted in one another. More mature. More grateful for the gift of each other.

After another interlude of exploration, Kittie snuggled up against him. "Wildfire Jack, hmm?"

"Huh?" he murmured, drowsy and sated.

She poked his chest. "Your outlaw name. You picked it because of me, didn't you?"

Oh, that. He rolled onto his side. "Sounds tough. Impressive. Like someone you don't wanna mess with." Jack flopped onto his back again. "Wildfire Jack."

Predictably, she saw through his dragonshit. "It sounds to me like a man who was pining for his flame-calling wife."

"Does it?" he asked with a wink. "Guess the world will never know."

Jefferson

IT WASN'T A SIMPLE TASK TO FIND JACK ON HIS OWN, BUT JEFFERSON was no stranger to getting someone alone so he could discuss delicate political dealings. All it took was a word to Flora, and she was on the job. His only regret was that he had to make up an excuse to keep Blaise away. That didn't sit well with him. Once he had more of the details worked out, he would go over them with Blaise. No sense in getting his hopes up.

The echo of boots on Eskelan tile announced the outlaw's arrival. Jefferson leaned against the balustrade of his veranda, smiling a greeting.

"Should have known it was you," Jack commented, though he said it with no real rancor. His wife's presence was reformative for him. He had lost some of the jagged edges that defined him, though Jefferson suspected if he said as much, the outlaw wouldn't appreciate it.

"I know I'm not your favorite person, but there's something I wanted to discuss without distraction." Jefferson pulled back from the edge of the veranda, crossing to a grouping of wicker furniture. He gestured to one of the chairs as he sat, and the outlaw followed him over. "I've been thinking about the Gutter."

Jack stiffened at his words. "What about it?"

Jefferson watched him for a moment, wondering what had set him off. "That's where Blaise wants to go," he explained after a beat, to which Jack nodded. "But it's already proven to be vulnerable to the Confederation."

The outlaw's expression turned stormy, and Jefferson regretted his phrasing. "Only *vulnerable* because—"

He held up a hand to quell the outburst. "Hold on, I apologize. But you know what I mean." Jack's frosty eyes met his, though that was the only agreement Jefferson received. "The Gutter is vulnerable because it's wild land, belonging to no one."

Jack's hackles were up. "What are you playing at?"

Jefferson was walking on eggshells, and he hoped the outlaw didn't take his next words poorly. He suspected Jack still had a poppet of him and could make his life miserable. "What I'm trying to say is that the Gutter should be its own nation."

The outlaw's jaw dropped, but he snapped it shut an instant later. His eyes narrowed, cynical. "What is this, a ploy so we'll join the Confederation?"

Jefferson almost laughed. That was...ridiculous. He shook his head. "Have you forgotten what I *am* now?"

Jack studied him. "No, I haven't, *Dreamer.*" Somehow he made it both an insult and an honorific.

The wicker furniture creaked as Jefferson leaned forward. "Look, all it takes is a single established nation to recognize it.

Well, that and all the other trappings of a new nation, but we can work that out."

"No nation in the Confederation is going to recognize the Gutter," Jack said, crossing his arms.

"Ganland might," Jefferson persisted, ignoring the dubious shake of the outlaw's head. "I promise you, it's true. I may not be Malcolm Wells anymore, but Jefferson Cole has just as many connections." He smiled as Jack's brows raised in tentative interest. "I only need the go-ahead to approach the Gannish leadership about it."

Jack rose from his chair, striding over to the edge of the veranda and staring out at the distant Gulf of Stars. Gulls called overhead, riding on the sea breeze. "What's in it for us?"

That was the opening he'd hoped for. Jefferson seized it. "Trade. Mutual protection."

The outlaw snorted. "I see why Ganland would have an interest in trade. Mutual protection, though?"

Jefferson crooked a finger. "Don't think of the Gutter as it is now. Think of it as it *will be*." He grinned. "A nation of free mages."

Jack shot him a sharp look, and Jefferson knew the idea had hooked him. "Like Ravance." The outlaw ran his hands over the balustrade, thoughtful. "You realize I'm only a single Ringleader of Fortitude. I can't speak for the entire Gutter."

"I'm aware, and I don't expect you to. But the spark of a fire has to start somewhere." The outlaw's eyes cut to him at the metaphor, and Jefferson smiled. "Talk to the other Ringleaders, see what they think. If you can, send a query to Asylum. I can test the waters of Rainbow Flat."

Jack canted his head, eyes narrowed. "You're thinking to claim that much land?"

"*I'm* not claiming anything. This is for..." Jefferson hesitated. He wanted to say *us*, but Jack would argue the point that Jefferson wasn't an outlaw. Not yet, anyway. "This is for people like Blaise and Emmaline."

Jack studied him, then gave a curt nod as he accepted the

answer. "We were planning to head out to the Gutter soon, anyhow. I'll broach the topic with the others when I arrive and have Hank deliver our response." He paused, angling a shrewd look at Jefferson. "What's in it for *you?*"

He frowned. "Does it have to be self-serving?"

To his annoyance, the outlaw smirked. "With you, it normally is."

Jefferson tilted his head. He couldn't argue. On the surface, it was mostly true. "I admit, it hits several of my goals. A place where mages can be free, for one." And he wanted a place where Blaise would be happy and safe, but that was too private to share. He suspected Jack already knew, though.

"As long as we're honest," the outlaw drawled, ironic. He rubbed his hands together. "Let's do this."

"There's one more thing I want," Jefferson said, earning a disgruntled look. "But I think you know what that is."

Jack studied him, and for a few heartbeats, Jefferson feared the outlaw would deny him. But instead, Jack asked, "It's not really for you, is it?"

"Not this time."

CHAPTER FIFTY-ONE
Revelations

Blaise

The last few weeks had been strange, but compared to the circus that had been the Inquiry, it was sedate. Blaise didn't mind hunkering down at Jefferson's estate outside Nera. He was far from Izhadell and surrounded by people he was comfortable with. Jack, Kittie, and Emmaline had headed back to Fortitude. But Blaise still had Jefferson, his mother, and Flora—though by day Jefferson was busy, absorbed in a task he assured Blaise he would tell him about soon.

One afternoon, his mother sought him out in the massive kitchen, where he was cutting a small pumpkin in half. The oven was already warm, awaiting the sliced gourd that Blaise planned to set inside to roast. Emrys had asked for a treat, and Blaise had all the time in the world to make a delicious pumpkin pie happen. He glanced up at Marian's arrival but otherwise kept working, scooping seeds into a bowl. "Howdy."

His mother assessed the nearby collection of spices. Cinnamon, ground ginger, nutmeg, and cloves. "I'm glad to see you haven't lost your passion."

Blaise placed the pumpkin halves in the oven, checking the time on his pocket watch. *Take them out in an hour.* "Baking still relaxes me." Though his first few baking sessions had been hard. He banished the memories of those early, difficult days of freedom, turning to face his mother. Marian had been distant, lost in thought over the past few days. "I don't think you came to ask after my baking."

Something flitted across her face, a lightning-quick expression he couldn't identify. Regret? Pain? Fear? Marian shook her head, and she crossed the kitchen to stand beside him. "No. I'm glad to see you're happy with someone."

Blaise allowed himself a small smile. Jefferson had revealed the secret of his dual identity to Marian, insistent that she knew *Malcolm* had cared about Blaise, and he didn't want her to have any misgivings about *Jefferson.* As Blaise predicted, the news made her suspicious. She had been displeased that Malcolm had bound Blaise in the first place, and the duplicity only made things worse. Blaise thought perhaps she had spent the last few days reconciling her son's relationship. Blaise had argued on Jefferson's behalf, assuring his mother that he'd shared her concerns in the past, but no longer did.

"I *am* happy with him," Blaise agreed, enjoying the aroma of roasting pumpkin. He crossed his arms, studying her. Marian lifted her chin high, reminding him of a high-strung horse. Something was on her mind, and it wasn't Jefferson. "You have that look."

She raised her brows, questioning. "What look?"

"The same look you had on your face the day you were told I couldn't go to school anymore." Blaise recalled how difficult that day had been. She'd had the look of someone who knew she was about to lose a fight then, and the same expression was stamped across her face now.

Marian licked her lips, her shoulders drooping. "There's something I need to talk to you about."

He nodded, though old fears tried to take root. It was a difficult thing, shedding the memory of being a shunned outcast. He had friends—*real* friends—now. Someone who loved him. *None of this will be taken away from me.* "What is it?"

Marian rested her forearms against the counter, locking her gaze on the assortment of spices carefully arranged in their tins. "I should have told you long ago, but I..." She took a deep breath, lifting a hand to her face. "I've never pretended to be the perfect mother. I know I'm not. I tried to make up for my mistakes, to do the best for you."

Her words sowed nothing but confusion in Blaise. He couldn't even act like he understood. None of it made sense. "And you did." It was the only thing he could think of to say, and he knew his uncertainty bled into his voice.

His mother shook her head. "No, I didn't. I was foolish to think anything could ever make up for what I'd done to you." Her words were tremulous, and the sheen of tears in her eyes startled Blaise.

What she'd done to me? "Mom, I don't understand." He picked up the tin of cinnamon, if only to give him something familiar to cling to.

"I'm not your mother."

Blaise stared at her, the world around him seeming to slow down, everything contracting to that single, devastating sentence. He dropped the cinnamon, the metal clattering as it struck the counter and rolled against the cloves. Blaise wanted to deny it, to insist what she said simply wasn't true. But the regret reflecting in her eyes spoke the truth.

He blew out a long breath, as if he'd been punched in the stomach by the news. There had to be a reasonable explanation. Marian Hawthorne had raised him as her *son*, for Faedra's sake. "I'm adopted?"

His mother—he refused to think of her as anything else,

because she *was* his mother—swallowed a lump in her throat. "Not quite." She glanced toward the small table in the corner of the kitchen. A tray of muffins sat in the middle—one of his earlier projects. Marian moved to the table and pulled out a chair.

Blaise followed, sitting on the opposite side. He plucked a muffin from the tray. He wasn't particularly hungry, but he suspected he might eat his emotions before too long. "If I'm not adopted, then what am I?"

"An experiment."

Blaise felt light-headed, like he couldn't breathe. This couldn't be. But at the same time, he knew it *could* be. *It's what alchemists do. Transmute. Transform.* Mixed components to do the impossible. His magic, stirred by his agitation, flowed up like a protective wave. The muffin crumbled in his hand, raining down on the table. "Tell me what that *means*."

Marian bit her bottom lip. "You know by now that I was a Confederation alchemist. I was full of myself, thinking I could tackle any challenge. Solve any problem with alchemy." She sighed, rubbing her cheek. Marian suddenly looked older than her years. "They tasked me with creating mages."

"Mages are *born*. You can't—" He stopped, realization hitting him. *Jefferson* hadn't been born a mage. That had been attributed to...what? Blaise frowned, struggling to put the pieces together. *Alchemists create the geasa tattoo with blood.* He idly rubbed at the long, pale scar on the soft underside of his arm.

"I can, and I did." Marian's voice was soft. "You were one of the orphans in a test group." She wet her lips, as if the very act of speaking her truth parched them instantly. "You were the only one to survive."

"I wasn't born a Breaker?"

The question hung in the air between them. Marian shook her head. The only sounds punctuating the silence were the ambient noises of the oven, soft pops and crackles. It didn't seem fair, the way that the kitchen was redolent with the warm, comforting scent of roasting pumpkin. Not when Blaise was learning that his life was a lie. His shoulders shook as he braced his arms against the table, his head sinking down until his forehead thudded against the surface.

"I'm not your mother, but I've always loved you as my own," Marian whispered. "Never doubt my love for you."

Blaise squeezed his eyes shut. He wanted to lash out, to yell...*something*. Instead, he felt hollow, like he didn't know who he *was*. He heard the scrape of Marian's chair and then she was there, her arms around him. Blaise thought about shrugging her away. He *hurt*, and *she* had caused this pain. One of the people he thought he could trust.

"Blaise?" she asked.

He shook his head. It was impossible to find the words to say what he wanted to say. Blaise didn't even *know* what he wanted to express. Nothing was adequate to describe the soul-shattering revelation. He lifted his head, rubbing at his eyes.

Marian was watching him, tears glistening on her cheeks. "I'm sorry."

Apologies changed nothing. Didn't change the fact that his life could have—*should have*—been different. He blew out a ragged breath. He wasn't willing to accept her apology, not with this wound so fresh. "Who *are* my parents, then?"

Marian shook her head. "All I know is that they died from the redrot pox going around Izhadell. We had easy pickings among the surviving children." She sighed. "I *am* sorry, Blaise. And I *do* love you, even if you don't believe me right now."

He swallowed, meeting her gaze. "I believe you." *And that's why it hurts so much.*

"I'M SORRY I WAS AWAY LONGER THAN EXPECTED TODAY," JEFFERSON apologized as he stepped out onto the veranda. "How have things been here?"

Blaise reclined on a wicker settee, staring up at the twinkling stars overhead. "Just peachy."

Jefferson's green eyes flicked over him, narrowing with concern. "Flora tells me your mother set out to rejoin your family in Rainbow Flat." His inflection at the end almost made it a question.

My family. Were they ever really my family? Blaise levered into a sitting position, running a hand through his hair. It was a mess, but he didn't care. "Did you know?"

Jefferson walked over and sat down beside him, perplexed. "Know what?"

Blaise gestured to himself. "About me. I was born without magic. I could have been *normal*." He put his face in his hands. *I could have avoided so much pain. So much suffering.* Marian had been right. The knowledge stung. He still loved her, but he was allowed to ache from the news she brought.

Jefferson made a soft sound of understanding, and a hand settled on his arm. "Your mother told me after Flora enlisted her help. And I'm sorry I didn't tell you, but it was not my secret to share."

Blaise looked up at Jefferson. "She's not my mother, either." Somehow, he said the words without breaking.

"Oh." The settee creaked as Jefferson settled onto it. His eyes never left Blaise, brimming with so much love and...shared grief? "I had wondered how..." He paused, composing himself. Jefferson started again, his tone neutral. "I had wondered how a mother could do that to her child. I suppose that explains it."

Blaise nodded. He was glad Jefferson was here, glad that he had someone to talk to who knew what it meant to be betrayed by a parent. *But, unlike Malcolm's situation...* "She said she loves me. And I believe her."

"I think she does, too." Jefferson's voice was soft, though also protective. "People can change. However, you're also allowed to be angry."

"I don't want to be angry, but I am." Blaise mopped at his warming face with one hand. "I wasn't supposed to *be* this."

Jefferson wrapped an arm around him. He was quiet for a moment, and Blaise drew comfort from his presence. "Forgive me, but that's where I disagree." He pressed a kiss against Blaise's forehead. "I think you are *exactly* who you need to be."

"The world doesn't need a Breaker."

"Maybe not. But it *does* need you." Jefferson met his eyes. "It's made you who you are today. And for that, I am thankful."

Lips pursed, Blaise wanted to argue, but then he realized what Jefferson was getting at. His life had been riddled with pain, but the brilliance of his best times outshined the shadows of darkness. The friends he had made and the love he had found.

He rubbed at his nose, nodding. Blaise wasn't sure how to respond. *Thank you* seemed too small, so instead, he squeezed Jefferson's hand, earning a smile in response. Blaise straightened, deciding to change the subject. He didn't want to think about what might have been anymore. "Are you going to tell me what you've been up to?"

Jefferson smiled. "Actually, yes." The breeze rolling in from the Gulf of Stars tousled his hair. "I finished tying up Malcolm's loose ends."

Blaise winced. It was easy to forget that as far as they were concerned, Malcolm was dead. He thought it must feel strange to have such a large part of your life *gone*. "I'm sorry." It was more condolence than apology.

Jefferson put an arm around him again. "Don't be. It must be done, and I'm content with who I am now. Happy, even." And he was, that much was clear. It had been no lie when Malcolm claimed he was happier in the guise of Jefferson. It provided a clean slate without the sordid family affairs of the past. "Seledora is executing the will. Oh, and be aware that you now have a house in Izhadell."

"I *what* now?" Blaise stared at him.

Jefferson flashed a mischievous grin. "Malcolm bequeathed the house to you. Seledora found an archaic loophole to take advantage of to make you a very rare land-owning mage in Phinora."

Was that so? Blaise wasn't sure how he felt about that. "But...I don't want it."

Jefferson shrugged. "You can sell it if you like. We rather enjoyed upsetting the apple cart one last time." He winked, his good humor restored by the prospect of defying Phinora's policies.

Blaise shook his head. "No, I won't sell it." He didn't think he could ever sell something like that. But he didn't want to live there, either. How was he going to take care of a place so far away?

Jefferson read the question on his face. "You also were granted a large sum of money for its upkeep."

Blaise relaxed. "Okay. Is that all you're taking care of then?"

"No." Jefferson shifted on the cushioned seat, turning to face Blaise. "Madame Boss Clayton asked if I would put my name in for consideration to replace Malcolm as Doyen for Ganland."

Blaise swallowed. He hadn't even thought about who might fill the empty seat on the Council. Hadn't cared, really. "Oh?"

"I told her no," Jefferson said softly, fiddling with the cabochon ring on his finger. "But I had her ear for something else."

Blaise raised his brows. "And that is?"

Jefferson rose from the chair, moving to lean against the balustrade. Blaise watched him, lips pursed. "Thought I might try my hand at an ambassadorship. Specifically, to the Gutter."

The Gutter? Blaise's face scrunched as he tried to figure out what Jefferson meant. "But the Gutter isn't a country."

"It will be soon. I hope." Jefferson chuckled. "Boss Clayton will certainly agree—she's eager to forge a strong relationship with the Gutter. You're looking at Ambassador Cole." He canted his head to one side. "I mean, I *will* be, at any rate."

Well, then. Blaise rose, closing the distance between them again. "I'm not even going to pretend to know what goes into that. Tell me what it means for us." He was afraid to find out. After his mother's revelation, he was waiting for the other shoe to drop.

Jefferson licked his lips, and Blaise realized he was nervous.

"Do you still want there to be an *us*? You've been through a lot and..." He shifted his gaze to the horizon. "I know I come across as too much sometimes."

"You can be *overwhelmingly* intense," Blaise agreed, his stomach fluttering. "If you can handle me and all of my oddities, I can handle you."

Jefferson's shoulders sagged with relief. "I wouldn't have it any other way."

Blaise clasped his hands together. "So, the Gutter? Would we go there?" Excitement laced his voice.

The future Ambassador bumped his shoulder against Blaise. "Yes. As Ambassador, I'm expected to live where I'm assigned. You know, so I can learn the customs. Become better acquainted with the people." He waggled his eyebrows suggestively.

"As long as I'm the only one you're getting *acquainted* with," Blaise muttered.

Jefferson grinned. "Ooh, you *do* get jealous." His eyes twinkled at the glare his words earned him. "I assure you, my life of debauchery is behind me." With all the practice of a politician, he flipped the conversation. "I was hoping to settle in Fortitude. What do you think?"

Blaise swallowed. He had hoped for that, but he wasn't sure. Until this conversation, he hadn't known what prospects he might have. His voice was husky with emotion as he said, "I'd like that a lot."

"I hoped you would," Jefferson murmured, his face close to Blaise's.

They stared into each other's eyes. Blaise's heart thundered in his chest. He was still awkward when it came to love, and intimacy would never be a simple thing for him. But Jefferson accepted that, and it was all he could ask. Blaise grinned, leaning in to close the gap between them.

Jefferson's green eyes sparked with joy as their lips brushed. *Maybe he's right*, Blaise thought as he lost himself in Jefferson's embrace. *I'm exactly who I need to be.*

CHAPTER FIFTY-TWO
Something to Fight For

Blaise

ormerly Itude, Fortitude perched on the canyon wall overlooking the Deadwood River. From Blaise's vantage point on pegasus-back, it looked to have recovered in the time since the attack launched by Lamar Gaitwood. He scratched his head as he tried to think of when that had been. After last year's Feast of Flight. They had missed this year's celebration, still in Ganland at the time while Jefferson finished his final arrangements.

Emrys and Seledora touched down outside the town. The last time he had been here—outside of Jefferson's dreamscape—the town had been in ruins. Blaise swallowed a lump that formed in his throat as he took in the sight. The town was whole and beautiful, the wind-pump towering over the smaller buildings with its long blades spinning lazily in the afternoon breeze.

"Home sweet home, hmm?" Jefferson asked, grinning as he lifted his flight goggles and snapped them against his forehead. He had taken to pegasus flight like it was in his blood, reveling in the opportunity. Blaise was still content to keep his feet on the ground, but everything seemed more palatable with Jefferson by his side.

"Something like that," Blaise agreed, patting Emrys's sweaty shoulder. The stallion folded his wings, the feathers whispering against his rider's legs. A handful of unfamiliar buildings had sprung up along the main streets of the town, and in the distance, frames of new homes were visible. He pulled his own flight goggles off, hanging them on the saddle horn. "Is this a dream? I feel like I'm dreaming."

<If it is, then I'd like to eat my weight in cherry pie,> Emrys suggested, his enormous pink tongue slurping out at the thought.

Jefferson laughed. "Not a dream, so let's not founder any of the pegasi."

<One cherry pie, then. That's reasonable.> The stallion glanced over his shoulder at Blaise. <Oh. We have something to show you.> A zing of delight accompanied his mental words as he flowed forward at a ground-eating trot. Seledora burst after him.

Blaise shot a furtive look at Jefferson, but the other man kept his eyes straight ahead. They were up to something. Emrys nickered with amusement, neck arched as they paraded into the town.

The black stallion drew to a dusty halt in front of a familiar building. The exterior, previously gutted by fire, had been repaired and painted a cheerful yellow. A handful of people stood outside, watching their approach. Jack leaned against a post that supported the porch shade. Emmaline stood nearby, bouncing on the balls of her feet. Clover's forearms rested against the porch railing, her tail flicking at their approach. Vixen whooped a greeting.

Seledora sidled alongside Emrys. Jefferson crossed his wrists over the pommel of his saddle, grinning at Blaise. "It's all yours."

"What?"

<Look up,> Emrys advised.

"Up here!" Emmaline couldn't help adding, gesturing to the name painted above the awning.

Blaise's Bakery.

He stared at it, wondering if he was reading it right. The former building only had the word *Bakery* painted overhead. It was Jack's building. He couldn't imagine the outlaw liking this one bit. Blaise glanced at the Effigest for confirmation.

"It's yours now. If you want it," Jack said with a nonchalant shrug, as if he didn't care one way or the other.

Did he want it? What sort of question was that? Blaise slid out of the saddle, marching up the steps and peering inside the window. A key clinked in the lock, and Emmaline pushed the door open. "Go on in."

Blaise stepped inside, trembling as he took in the interior. Everything had been restored and even improved. The original oven still stood in place, though care had been taken to make sure it was in proper working order. Blaise opened the cabinets, finding new bakeware and utensils. It was too much. He leaned against the island workspace in the middle, face in his hands.

"Is something wrong?" Jefferson's voice was soft as he stepped inside.

Blaise lifted his head, wiping away a tear from one eye. "No. It's...I can't believe it's *mine*. Is it because of our contract?"

Jefferson moved around the island, a puzzled expression on his face. "The contract...oh, *no*. Believe it or not, with all that's gone on, I forgot about that. No, this is because it makes you happy."

<Also because we require delicious treats,> Emrys added, ever helpful.

The stallion must have broadcast to Jefferson as well. The other man gave a small shake of his head and sighed. "Does it make you happy?"

Blaise smiled. "It does." He bowed his head, almost at a loss for words. Everything he had ever wanted—but thought he would never have. It was here, and it was his. All because someone cared about him. He met Jefferson's eyes. "But you know what? *You* make me even happier."

Jefferson stared at him, tapping his fingers against the countertop. "That's music to my ears." He drew closer, heat in his gaze.

<Excuse me, but your pegasi still have full saddlebags and haven't been compensated with cookies yet,> Emrys reminded them.

<You're contractually obligated to provide cookies upon arrival,> Seledora added.

With a laugh, Jefferson pulled away from Blaise, rubbing at the bridge of his nose. "I suppose it's in our best interest to keep my attorney happy."

<Always,> Seledora agreed.

"I'll get them settled if you want to look around a little more," Jefferson offered, putting an arm around Blaise. "Are the leftovers you made in Ganland still in your saddlebag?"

Blaise nodded. "Yes. And...Jefferson? Thank you. For everything." His voice broke at the last. *A bakery.* He had a bakery again, and it was *his.* He ran a hand over the cool smoothness of the counter, already imaging how it would look when he was back at work. Errant crumbs and escaped dustings of flour scattered across the surface.

Jefferson walked to the door, pausing to touch two fingers to his forehead in a salute. He looked as if he wanted to say something but gave a small shake of his head and hurried out to tend to the pegasi. Sometimes no words were necessary.

Jack

JACK SAT ON A SANDSTONE OUTCROPPING OVERLOOKING THE Deadwood River as the setting sun painted the horizon like a dazzling canvas. Gold and ochre rays pierced the feathery clouds dappled with violet and crimson. Zepheus grazed nearby, the stallion snorting a warning as someone approached.

"What are you doing brooding over here?" Kittie settled down beside him.

He chuckled. "Not brooding."

She raised her brows. "Are you sure? You certainly look the part, with the thunderous expression on your face."

Had it really looked like that? Jack shook his head. "Nah. Just thinking."

Kittie pressed something cold and flat against his palm. He glanced down, spotting a coin. "Golden eagle for your thoughts?"

Oh, that was a loaded question. He grunted. "I'm thinking about the future. About this thing we want to do." Jack gestured to the yawning canyon before them.

"Your outlaw nation?" Kittie asked.

"*Our* outlaw nation," Jack corrected. He might butt heads with Jefferson, but the dandy was right about who it was for. Folks like Blaise and Emmaline—yeah, they were outlaws in their own right. That couldn't be denied. But they needed a place that would allow them to just *be*. "Even if Ganland has the balls to recognize us, nothing about this is gonna be easy."

Kittie gently lifted the coin from his hand, tucking it into the pouch at her belt. "Since when does *Wildfire Jack* do easy?"

She liked to tease him about his nickname. He didn't regret selecting it, though. No, it had kept her alive to him all those years. Jack crossed his arms. "Easy would be nice for a change of pace."

Kittie unhooked the flask from her belt, offering it to him. He shook his head, and she took a swig. Kittie hadn't drunk like this, not before...everything. Jack figured even a near-sighted knocker could see that alcohol had become her crutch. This was another thing that he knew wouldn't be easy for them. Which was why it would be so *damned nice* if the Confederation didn't have a blasted tantrum over the Gutter.

"Nothing worth fighting for is easy," Kittie mused, though she, too, sounded tired.

The thunder of wings echoed against the canyon walls below.

A sentry pegasus flew into view, the brilliant sunset glinting on the outstretched feathers of the sorrel tobiano mare. She was one of the new pegasi mares who had arrived at Fortitude recently, excited by the prospect of a livelihood. Lured to the rebuilt town by Jefferson's smooth-talking Seledora, much to the delight of the resident stallions.

Things in their world were changing. A smile touched Jack's lips. He leaned over and pressed a kiss to Kittie's forehead, enjoying the scent of smoke that wafted from her hair. "Not gonna be easy, no. But we're gonna make it happen."

They had to. The only other option was the Confederation crushing them, and Jack wouldn't allow that. He pushed those thoughts to the wayside, though, as Kittie leaned against him. She was solid and warm, and Jack almost felt as if he were dreaming as he watched the setting sun paint the walls of the canyon in new, darker hues.

This. This peace, this love, is something to fight for. He smiled.

The outlaw mages will return
in Dreamer.

Acknowledgments

Once again, thanks to so many people for cheering me on as I pounded out this book. Yikes, I've written two entire books now? That's wild.

Big kudos to my beta readers, several of whom asked regularly after reading *Breaker* "when can we read the new book?" I appreciate your enthusiasm! All the gold stars to Jen Abercrombie, Jedidiah Boggs, Samantha Kroese, Sumi Lough, Lindsay Prigge, Elizabeth Reeves, and Jennifer Rupp.

And where would I be without the fun that is NaNoWriMo, and especially my NaNoWriMo team at Harris County Public Library? *Effigest* started in November 2020 and then got a massive overhaul during Camp NaNoWriMo in April 2021, so it's been on a tour of duty with us, and it's awesome to see how the story has grown and changed in that time! (Anyone who saw any November 2020 snippets would have seen a very different story!)

And a tip of the hat to my co-workers at the Katherine Tyra @ Bear Creek Branch of Harris County Public Library. I work with the best people!

I'd also like to thank everyone who reached out to tell me that not only did they enjoy *Breaker,* but that it resonated with them. Blaise is not your typical hero, and I feared that might alienate him, but I'm thrilled to see it had the opposite effect! And even if you didn't reach out to tell me you enjoyed it, but it still resonated with you—*thank you.*

I'd be remiss if I didn't thank my family. My husband, Kirk, who is probably still a little baffled by this author gig of mine. And to my kids, without whom this book would have been finished much sooner. Thanks kids! And thanks to my parents for always believing in me. And I should mention my brother Scott, because you're also great. Cheers!

Soundtrack

BLAISE
This is Me - Keala Settle & *The Greatest Showman* Ensemble
Rise – Valley of Wolves
Something 'Bout Love – David Archuleta
Lions Inside – Valley of Wolves
Life on the Moon – David Cook
Prisoner – Miley Cyrus (feat. Dua Lipa)

MALCOLM/JEFFERSON
Hurricane – Panic! At the Disco
Man On Fire – Oh the Larceny
Sweet Dreams (Are Made of This) – Eurythmics
Declaration – David Cook
Whatever It Takes – Imagine Dragons

JACK
Voodoo Child – Jimi Hendrix
Man on a Mission – Oh the Larceny
Monster – Skillet
You're Going Down – Sick Puppies
Bad – Royal Deluxe

KITTIE
Kings & Queens – Ava Max

I Am the Fire – Halestorm
Hold My Heart – Lindsey Stirling (feat. ZZ Ward)
Bring Me to Life – Evanescence

Stay In the Know!

Sign up for my newsletter for sneak peeks, exclusive short stories, and more!

www.amycampbell.info

And if you enjoyed *Effigest*, please take a moment to leave a review on the platform of your choice! Reviews help indie authors like me gain a foothold in the wild world of publishing. It's a small thing that means a lot!

CPSIA information can be obtained
at www.ICGtesting.com
Printed in the USA
LVHW051933021121
702252LV00004B/818

8